Dear Reader,

I'm delighted to welcome you to a very special Harlequin Bestselling Author Collection for 2024! In celebration of Harlequin's seventy-five years in publishing, this collection features fan-favorite stories from some of our readers' most cherished authors. Each book also includes a free full-length story by an exciting writer from one of our current programs.

Our company has grown and changed since its inception seventy-five years ago. Today, Harlequin publishes more than one hundred titles a month in thirty countries and fifteen languages, with stories for a diverse readership across a range of genres and formats, including hardcover, trade paperback, mass-market paperback, ebook and audiobook.

But our commitment to you, our romance reader, remains the same: in every Harlequin romance, a guaranteed happily-ever-after!

Thank you for coming on this journey with us. And happy reading as we embark on the next seventy-five years of bringing joy to readers around the world!

Dianne Moggy

Vice-President, Editorial

Harlequin

With her roots firmly planted in the South, #1 *New York Times* bestselling author **Sherryl Woods** has written many of her more than one hundred books in that distinctive setting. Her Chesapeake Shores books have become a highly rated series success on Hallmark Channel and her Sweet Magnolias books have recently been released as a much-anticipated Netflix series. Sherryl divides her time between her childhood summer home overlooking the Potomac River in Colonial Beach, Virginia, and Florida's east coast.

Jo Ann Brown has published over one hundred titles under a variety of pen names. A former military officer, she enjoys taking pictures and traveling. She has taught creative writing for more than twenty years and is always excited when one of her students sells a project. She has been married for more than forty years and has three children and two rambunctious cats. She lives in Amish Country in southeastern Pennsylvania. She enjoys hearing from her readers. Visit her at joannbrownbooks.com.

SHERRYL WOODS

A DARING VOW

HARLEQUIN
BESTSELLING
AUTHOR
COLLECTION

**HARLEQUIN®
BESTSELLING
AUTHOR
COLLECTION**

Recycling programs
for this product may
not exist in your area.

ISBN-13: 978-1-335-00882-4

A Daring Vow
First published in 1993. This edition published in 2024.
Copyright © 1993 by Sherryl Woods

An Amish Match
First published in 2016. This edition published in 2024.
Copyright © 2016 by Jo Ann Ferguson

For questions and comments about the quality of this book, please contact us at CustomerService@Harlequin.com.

® is a trademark of Harlequin Enterprises ULC.

Harlequin Enterprises ULC
22 Adelaide St. West, 41st Floor
Toronto, Ontario M5H 4E3, Canada
www.Harlequin.com

Printed in U.S.A.

CONTENTS

A DARING VOW

Sherryl Woods

Prologue

With all the uncertainties in his life—and there were a bundle of them—one thing was absolutely, positively clear to Taylor Matthews. He did not want to handle the estate of Ella Louise Lane. Not under any circumstances. In the first place, the woman was nuttier than a pecan pie. No medical examination had labeled her as such, but there were some things everyone in Port William, South Carolina, just accepted. Ella Louise's eccentricity was one of them.

In the second and far more bothersome place, her primary heir was likely to be her daughter. As Taylor recalled all too explicitly, Zelda Lane was sexier than Julia Roberts and more trouble than half a dozen bank robbers. He wasn't sure which side of her nature worried him more.

Unfortunately, Ella Louise had made up her mind she wanted Taylor for the job. She paced in front of him now wearing a bright orange sweater that clashed dramatically with her red hair, a faded pair of blue jeans that bagged on her too thin body and some kind of feathery, pink high-heeled slippers from another era. Mules, wasn't that what they called them? How could she even stand up on the things? he wondered nervously as she teetered dangerously, then sank onto the sofa. He breathed a sigh of relief.

"Have you got that?" she demanded. He blinked and stared at her.

"Got what?" he asked, still too bemused by her command invitation and unwanted memories of Zelda to pay much attention to the details of a will he had no intention of drawing up.

The only reason he was in this house at all was out of some misguided sense of duty. He knew deep in his gut that he'd bungled things with Zelda and he owed her for it. But not this much. Uh-uh. Definitely not enough to get within five hundred miles of her again. His days of risk-taking had ended. He had a nice, quiet, ordinary life now, and that was the way he wanted things to stay. There was nothing quiet or ordinary about Zelda.

Ella Louise scowled at him, while tapping her foot impatiently. "I declare, Taylor, for a bright young attorney, you don't have a lick of concentration. Sometimes I wonder what my daughter ever saw in you."

She studied him critically, then shook her head in bafflement. Taylor winced at the assessment that had obviously found him wanting. He felt an odd need to defend himself, to prove his desirability by listing the attractive, intelligent, socially acceptable women who'd tried to seduce him since the death of his wife. Fortunately he was able to keep his mouth clamped firmly shut.

Obviously the reference to Zelda and their long-dead relationship was making him a little crazy, stirring him in a way it had no business doing. With that in mind he tried one more time to make Ella Louise see sense. He figured he was wasting his time, given the fact that he was dealing with a woman who'd made a shrine out of her collection of F. Scott Fitzgerald novels, while the rest of the house practically collapsed around her. Still he had to try.

"I really think you should hire another lawyer," he said. "I'll be glad to call over to Charleston and have a friend of mine stop by to see you."

"And how long will that take?" Ella Louise demanded. "Days? A week or two? I don't have time. I want this done and done now."

He regarded her even more nervously, studying the pale complexion and the feverish look in her eyes that he'd attributed to too many glasses of her favorite bourbon on an empty stomach. Was she suffering from some fatal illness, after all?

"Ella Louise," he inquired worriedly, "are you all right? Should I call the doctor?"

"So he can tell me I'm dying?" she said with an unladylike snort. "Don't need to hear him say it. I just need to get this one piece of business taken care of, so I can finally rest. Now can we get down to business or are you going to waste more of my time arguing?"

"You know Zelda and I didn't part on the best of terms," he protested in what had to be the biggest understatement since the local paper had described his political downfall as being the result of a slight mistake in judgment.

"I know," she agreed with such great serenity that Taylor was sure she couldn't possibly remember the details as vividly as he did. She must have forgotten all about the way Zelda had poked holes in every one of his brand new Mustang's tires the night he'd broken up with her. Then she'd painted an unwarranted comment about his parentage on the town's water tower.

How she'd gotten up there was beyond him, but she'd always had a knack for managing the impossible.

Since he'd known deep down that he was the one at fault, he'd been the one who'd climbed that damned tower to remove the graffiti before his daddy went to the sheriff to demand Zelda's arrest. A part of him, a part that remained untamed despite his father's best efforts, had admired her audacity. He doubted she'd changed. The Zelda he remembered was capable of carrying a grudge on into the next century.

Given all that, he found Ella Louise's enigmatic expression disturbing. "How can you ask that she deal with me at a time when she'd be grieving?" He shook his head. "No, Ella Louise, this is a bad idea. I'll get someone else here this afternoon." He could call in a favor at his old law firm. They wouldn't want to come, but they'd respond to the plea of a desperate man. He figured that was a role he wouldn't have a bit of trouble playing convincingly.

"I want you," she said stubbornly, then began a fit of coughing that had her whole body shaking.

Panicked by the increasingly obvious signs of some unnamed illness, Taylor finally agreed to take down her last wishes and put them into a legal will.

"But I won't be the executor," he said flatly. "You'll have to think of someone else. There's no point in upsetting Zelda any more than necessary at such a time.

What about Mabel or Elsie? She always got along with them, didn't she?"

"I'll think about it," she agreed.

Too quickly, it seemed to him, but he was willing to grasp at straws. "Meantime," she said blithely, "just put your name in there, and we'll discuss it when you bring the papers back for me to sign."

Taylor saw the stubborn set to her chin and remembered it all too well from countless quarrels with Zelda. With a sigh of resignation, he stopped arguing and took notes. It troubled him more than he could say, however, that that serene, enigmatic look was back in Ella Louise's eyes when he left. That night his own mother gave him a lecture on generosity of spirit, forgiveness and Christian charity. He wasn't exactly sure which parts of her eloquent speech were applicable to Ella Louise's situation, but he finally threw in the towel. Besides, as nutty as Ella Louise was, she'd probably have half a dozen executors named before she finally died. Come to think of it, she was probably stubborn enough to outlive them all.

The next day, after an endless night filled with memories of all the times he'd defied his parents and sneaked out to that old tumble-down house during high school and college, he pulled to a stop in the front yard. He could still recall as if it had been only yesterday the way Zelda had looked as she'd run down that dirt path from the front door, eyes sparkling with devilment, cheeks flushed with excitement, those long, long legs as bare as pure temptation. She'd had more spirit, more wild passion than any woman he'd ever known. The memory alone was enough to cause his body to grow hard with desire.

Let that be a warning, he thought ruefully as he tried

to think of some way to extricate himself from the dangerous situation that Ella Louise's signature on that damned will would just about guarantee. It was a time bomb, just ticking away, setting him up for disaster.

He tapped on the screen door and peered into the dim interior. When Ella Louise didn't respond, he walked around the outside of the house looking for her, climbing over rusting wheelbarrows and haphazardly stacked piles of firewood. Filled with a sudden sense of impending doom, he returned to the front door, called out one last time, then crept inside.

He spotted her right off. Ella Louise was sitting in a rocker, her head slumped forward. Taylor knew without setting one foot closer that she was dead, that she'd finished up her earthly business with him the previous afternoon and died quietly in her sleep.

So, he thought with wry amusement, she'd gotten her wish, after all. Even without her signature, he knew he could make the will stick in court unless somebody wanted to raise a humdinger of a stink. Just as he'd feared, he was doomed to handling the settlement of Ella Louise's estate.

Which meant seeing Zelda again. God help him.

Chapter 1

So, Zelda Lane thought as she slowly hung up the phone, her mother had finally gone and gotten her wish. She'd fallen asleep in her antique rocking chair and never awakened, according to the neighbor who'd just called.

As she tried to absorb the news, Zelda was torn between the predictable emptiness and a fierce anger that accompanied any loss. There was even an unwelcome touch of guilt mixed in. Her eyes stung but remained dry through a sheer act of will. She would not cry. She wouldn't even mourn. How could she shed so much as a tear over the death of a woman who'd been determined to kill herself as far back as Zelda could remember?

"Damn you, Mama," she whispered with a catch in her voice. "Damn you!"

Her boss regarded her with alarm. "Zelda, are you all right?" Kate Newton asked, coming around from behind her desk to squeeze Zelda's suddenly trembling hand.

Zelda glanced up, feeling dazed, and caught the expression of genuine concern in Kate's eyes. "It's Mama," she said flatly. "She died sometime during the night. She was at home, all alone, just the way she wanted it to happen."

Ready, sympathetic tears immediately sprang into Kate's eyes. "Oh, sweetie, I'm so sorry." Then as if it weren't the middle of an incredibly busy day, she said, "Come on. We'll shut down for the afternoon, and I'll help you pack."

"Pack?" Zelda said blankly, clutching her steno pad more tightly. "For what?"

"I'm sure you'll want to be on the first flight back east. Don't you worry about a thing. I'll call the airlines and take care of the reservations."

Zelda shook her head. "No." Her voice held steady with no sign of the turmoil she was feeling inside. She pretended not to see the look of puzzlement in Kate's eyes as she stubbornly opened her pad to a clean page. "You were about to dictate a letter when I got that call."

Dismay spread across Kate's face. Zelda stared her down. After a moment's hesitation, Kate swallowed whatever lecture she'd been about to begin and finished dictating. But before Zelda could escape to the outer office, Kate gently removed the pad from her hand, a glint of determination in her eyes. When it came to stubbornness, they were an equal match.

"Zelda, I know you must be in shock, but denying what's happened won't help," she said gently.

"I'm not denying anything," Zelda contradicted. "My mother's dead. She finally got her wish. She's been trying to kill herself with booze and cigarettes ever since I can remember."

A wayward tear escaped despite her stoic determination not to admit how much that hurt. Before Kate could ask more troubling questions, Zelda ran from the office. By the time Kate caught up with her, she was already at her computer typing the letter her boss had just dictated. The keystrokes were automatic, though she had to force herself to concentrate on the shorthand that seemed shakier and less precise than usual. Kate finally sighed and gently closed the door between their offices in an attempt to give her the privacy she desperately wanted to avoid.

Her keystrokes finally slowed. Memories forced their way in, more powerful than the determination to avoid them. *Oh, Mama,* she thought wearily. *How could you slip away on me like this?* She asked the question, but she already knew the answer. Her mother had slipped away on her and everyone else years ago.

Everybody in Port William, South Carolina, always knew that Zelda Lane's mama was "under the weather" by three o'clock in the afternoon. Except on weekends, that is. Saturdays and Sundays, when Zelda's daddy was home, Ella Louise started drinking earlier and reached her limit well before noon. It was a well-established pattern that never varied, even when Zelda begged her mother not to touch another drink.

After Joseph Lane died at the age of thirty-eight in a boating accident, Ella Louise no longer wasted time sipping mint juleps in the way of old-fashioned, genteel Southern ladies. She switched to bourbon, taking it smooth and neat, from a coffee mug that appropriately enough said Life's A Bitch… And Then You Die.

Though she loved her mother fiercely, Zelda found Ella Louise to be an embarrassment, especially when she wandered into town and caused such a commotion in the local bar that Sheriff Wiley had to drive her home. It had happened so regularly that people finally stopped commenting on it. They just shook their heads and viewed little Zelda with the sympathy they'd bestow on anyone in her sorry plight.

Refusing to allow her embarrassment to show, Zelda had learned at an early age to poke that stubborn chin of hers into the air and thumb her nose at their condescension. She had a temper to match her fiery red hair and one way or another she'd been telling the whole miserable town of Port William to take a hike practically since the day she was born. It was a skill her mama had instilled in her after years of perfecting it herself.

It had been ten years since Zelda had left Port William far behind to make a new home for herself in Los Angeles. She'd begged her mother to come with her at first, then resigned herself to the fact that Ella Louise would never leave the town where she'd been raised. She'd been determined to die in that decrepit house where she'd lived her whole pitiful life. She'd been a martyr to the bitter end, as far as Zelda could see.

"My life's over, honey. You grab what you can," she'd said more than once.

And so, with only minimal reluctance, Zelda had. She'd put her wild days behind her and settled down, content in the knowledge that no one in Los Angeles knew a thing about her background. She'd fooled her friends into thinking she was just any other normal woman with hopes and dreams and the determination to attain them. None of them realized exactly how driven she was to escape her past.

Now it seemed that past was about to catch up with her. Though she couldn't avoid Kate's worried looks,

Zelda did manage to get through an entire week without having to answer any more questions about her mother or about Port William. Furious with herself for the sign of weakness, she shed her tears late at night. In those dark, lonely hours, she tried desperately not to regret the fact that she hadn't been back home once in all the years since she'd left. She couldn't see much point in going now, when the only person in the entire town she'd ever loved was gone. Already buried, in fact, thanks to the instructions she'd given.

A fleeting image of Taylor Matthews crossed her mind and then was banished. Strong, gentle, wicked Taylor, she thought with a reluctant sigh. Okay, maybe there was one other person in Port William that she had loved, but those glorious days and wild nights were best forgotten. Taylor certainly hadn't been able to put them behind him fast enough, she recalled with a bitterness that time had done nothing to mellow.

The phone rang and as if her thoughts alone had conjured him up, she heard Taylor's voice. She recognized it at once, though it was deeper now, even sexier, which somehow infuriated her. She couldn't quite decide, though, whether it was him she was mad at or herself for responding to that husky and no doubt unintended sensuality.

"Yes," she said coolly, when she could finally catch her breath.

He cleared his throat. "Zelda, I'm real sorry about your mother."

"Thank you," she said stiffly, surprised that he would bother making a condolence call.

"Look, I don't know if your mother told you what she had in mind, but I saw her the day before she died."

"Why on earth would you go see Mama?"

"She asked me to come."

"She asked *you* to come," she repeated with undisguised astonishment.

"Yes. Actually, well, the bottom line is that I'm handling the estate."

"You're what?" *Oh, Mama, what the hell have you
gone and done?* Zelda thought with a mounting sense of
desperation. Determined not to let Taylor hear even one
tiny hint of her dismay, she steadied her voice. "Fine,
Taylor. Do whatever Mama wanted."

"It's not quite that simple." He sighed heavily, sounding more put-upon than Beau Matthews ever had when
he'd been lecturing Taylor on his many indiscretions,
most of which he attributed directly to his son's asso-
ciation with Zelda. "Actually, it's damned complicated.
I think you'd better come home so we can discuss it."

"That's not possible," she said without hesitation.
"You're the lawyer, the executor, whatever. You deal
with it."

"Look," he said with a trace of impatience, "there is
nothing I would like better than to close things up and
send you a check, but it's not that easy. There are decisions to be made, and they have to be made by you. You'll
have to come home."

Being told what she had to do, especially by Taylor,
only strengthened her resolve. "No."

"Why, Zelda?" he said, his voice gentling for the first
time. "You afraid to come back here, sugar?"

With a sinking sensation in the pit of her stomach,
she heard the familiar dare in his tone. He'd gotten her
into trees, onto rooftops, into trouble with those taunting dares of his. *Sugar,* hell!

"I'm not afraid of anything, Taylor Matthews," she

snapped, falling into a trap as old as the first day they'd met. She heard his low, satisfied chuckle and bit off a few more choice words that occurred to her. Finally she gave in to the inevitable. "Okay," she said grudgingly. "I'll do what I can."

"Soon, Zelda."

Was he anxious to see her? More likely, just anxious to get it over with. "I'll be there when I get there," she told him with her very last bit of spunk.

She slammed the phone down then because she couldn't tolerate one more smug word, one tiny little hint of I-told-you-so in his voice. Then she sat staring at the phone, dismayed. She was going home. She would see Taylor again. Dear Lord, what had she been thinking of? What had her mother been thinking of to get her into this mess?

The fact that Ella Louise had left an estate tangled in so much red tape that Zelda had no choice but to go back to Port William to straighten it out didn't particularly surprise her. Her mother never had been one for doing things the ordinary way. It was Taylor's involvement that was a kick-in-the-pants shock.

Still stunned, she went in to explain to Kate that she needed time off, after all.

"Of course, you have to go," Kate said at once, her expression clearly relieved that Zelda had finally seen sense. "Take as much time as you need. I'll call in that temp we used on your last vacation. If there's anything I can do for you from here to straighten things out, if you need legal advice, you just have to call."

Zelda fiddled with the back of the chair she'd been clutching for support. "I hate leaving you in the lurch, though. You have that big divorce case coming up next week. Maybe I should put this trip off. It's not as if I can do anything for Mama now. Besides, how much of an estate can there be? Last I checked, she was dirt poor and wouldn't take a dime from me to change that. Maybe I ought to let the state take her pitiful possessions and get on with my life."

Kate's gaze narrowed at the suggestion. Zelda knew her brilliant legal mind was bound to consider such an idea practically sacrilegious.

"Zelda, is there some reason you don't want to go back to South Carolina?"

Zelda couldn't figure out how to explain that she hadn't been able to leave Port William fast enough. She was a different person now, confident, respected… tamed, some might say. She didn't want to alter Kate's impression of her, but she could see from her boss's determined expression that nothing but the truth would end the cross-examination. As a whole slew of opposing attorneys knew, Kate was a master of the technique.

"You know how you see those shows about slow, backwater towns and you think they're just old-fashioned stereotypes?" Zelda said eventually. "Well, Port William is the prototype. The people there didn't know exactly what to make of Mama, and they certainly didn't know what to make of me. She named me after F. Scott Fitzgerald's loony wife, for goodness' sake. All the townspeople knew about Fitzgerald was what they'd figured out from reading *The Great Gatsby*. It didn't leave a great impression in their narrow little minds."

"Surely they didn't blame you for being named for some dead author's crazy wife?"

"Blame me?" Zelda replied thoughtfully. "I don't suppose so. They just figured I was destined to follow the same path into a mental institution or else live out my days like Mama in some drunken stupor. And that was before I moved to Los Angeles. Now they'll probably want to hold an exorcism to rid me of the devil."

Kate, born and raised in trend-setting, accepting L.A., looked skeptical. "It can't be that bad."

Zelda didn't argue, but she knew in her heart that she'd actually given the town the benefit of the doubt. The sheriff was probably painting up a cell just for her return. Folks in Port William had never entirely understood that the things she'd done had been the high-spirited hijinks of a teenager trying desperately to live up to the failed dreams of a sad and lost mother. If she could have splashed in public fountains at midnight, as her namesake reportedly had, she would have done it. Port William, however, had been short on fountains. It was probably just as well. She'd gotten into enough mischief as it was.

She'd been easy prey for a boy such as Taylor, who'd had his own demons to sort through and had known just how to tease her into accompanying him. Foolishly, she'd thought that their daring exploits would bond them together forever, but she couldn't have been more wrong. In the end, Taylor had proved himself to be every bit a Matthews—disgustingly stuffy, terrifyingly ambitious and thoroughly predictable. He had rid himself of the wild girl from the wrong side of the tracks without a backward glance.

She'd hated him for abandoning her, for leaving her lost and alone in a town that could never understand her longing for acceptance. Even more, though, she had hated seeing the passionate man she'd loved since child-hood become another sacrifice to the Matthews tradition. She wondered if he'd turned out to be every bit as stodgy as his father, or if some spark of that individuality and spunk he'd shown with her had remained.

No use speculating, she thought. She'd find out soon enough. To her deep regret, her pulse bucked a little just at the prospect.

She was going to see Taylor Matthews again. God help her.

Chapter 2

Port William looked exactly as Zelda had remembered it, exactly as it had looked for the past century, probably. Pine trees littered the ground with their long, slippery needles. With the exception of one or two sadly neglected plantation houses on the outskirts of town and the big, brick Matthews place on top of a hill overlooking the river, most of the community consisted of small clapboard houses. Almost without exception, each had a wide front porch, a rocking chair or swing from which to observe the passing of time, and a row of azalea bushes turning brown as the chill air of autumn belligerently pushed its way south. The lazy Waccamaw River wound its way toward the sea, providing a few picturesque settings in the lowland locale that was an otherwise quaint painting that time had faded.

As she drove in from Charleston, her speed slowing with every mile, Zelda made note of the few obvious changes, starting with the familiar welcome sign that announced that the town of Port William, founded in 1756, now boasted a population of 1,027. It had grown.

Beyond that, the only real concession to the nineties that she could see was a strip mall about two miles from the center of town. It consisted of a national discount store, a modern grocery store and a video rental store. On the outside, at least, everything else looked almost the same, except for a new coat of paint here and there and some visible updating of equipment.

Based on the number of pickups jammed along the strip of asphalt in front, Harlan's Feed and Grain was still the gathering place for men, a handful of tobacco growers and the usually out-of-work textile mill employees. The fancy riding mowers displayed on the back side of the parking lot, however, suggested Harlan had updated his stock to more high-tech, high-priced wonders. She couldn't imagine who was buying them.

Vera Mae's Salon de Beauty had new curtains hanging on the windows, but through the open doorway Zelda could see the same old red-vinyl chairs inside. She wondered if Vera Mae was still doing her famous beehive hairdos and cementing them in place with spray.

Next door, Sarah Lynn's Diner was packed with the lunch crowd. Zelda was willing to bet Monday was still the day Sarah Lynn baked her famous lemon meringue pie. She doubted the plump, matronly woman, who'd looked after Zelda like one of her own, had gone trendy and put key lime pie on the menu in its place. The locals would shun such innovation, dismissing it as putting on airs.

Zelda ignored the fact that her mouth was watering at the thought of that lemon meringue pie. She wasn't up to announcing her presence in town quite yet, much less handling Sarah Lynn's sympathy. Instead she drove her rental car straight on to the house in which she'd grown up.

When she pulled onto the tiny patch of lawn, she turned off the engine and sat staring at the old frame house, which was badly in need of paint. It was no better or worse than most of the houses around it, but Zelda had always resented the way her parents had let it go to seed. When she was fifteen, she'd earned enough money to buy paint and had given it a coat of white herself, slapping it on with zeal, if not neatness. From the looks of it, that was the last coat of paint it had received.

Not quite ready to go inside, she rolled down the car window and drew in a lungful of the fresh, pine-scented air. Memories crowded in like so many teenagers trying to be first in line for concert tickets. A few of those memories were even good, like the time she and Jimmy Martin had sat on the creaky front porch swing holding hands while Mama played Grandpa's old Glenn Miller records inside. And there was the time Taylor Matthews had pelted her bedroom window with stones in the middle of the night and dared her to go skinny-dipping in the river with him. Naturally, she hadn't been able to resist.

Taylor Matthews, she thought with yet another sigh. He figured in too many memories of her past. To her disgust, ever since his call, she hadn't been able to get him out of her mind. Once they'd been drawn together as inevitably as any two star-crossed lovers in history. In the end, though, it had all turned to ashes.

Damn his father's political ambitions! she thought with as much vehemence now as she had then. If it hadn't been for Beau Matthews's obsessive drive to see his boy in the state capitol—or the White House, for that matter—she could have claimed Taylor's heart publicly. Everyone in town saw that he was sweet on her, anyway.

But once Taylor had passed adolescence and started listening to his father, he'd begun hating himself for those wicked, wayward feelings he couldn't control. She had seen it in his eyes and slowly withdrew into a protective shell, determined that he would never see how his change in attitude was quietly killing her. She'd had one lapse, the night he'd finally broken up with her, and to this day she regretted letting him know how much his defection had mattered.

She couldn't help wondering now if he'd finally found some suitable, boring woman to stand by his side and satisfy his daddy's standards. In all the years she'd been away from Port William, she had never asked about Taylor and her mother had never volunteered a word. It was just as well. Zelda hated being wrong, and she'd never in her life been more wrong than she had been about Taylor. He might have been sexy as sin and he might have exhibited exactly the kind of dangerous, wild streak that appealed to her in his teens, but he'd grown up into a stuffy, judgmental man—just like her own daddy, who'd trampled on Ella Louise's spirit until she was nothing more than a shadowy presence.

That, she thought, snapping herself back to the present, was a whole other kettle of fish. And one she didn't intend to explore, not today, not ever if she could help it.

The Port William grapevine was apparently still in fine working order. Within minutes of her arrival, Zelda was surrounded by a group of neighbors, all wearing black and all bearing covered dishes. She'd be eating macaroni and cheese, green bean casseroles and Jell-O salads for a month.

"Why on earth did Mama ask Taylor to handle her estate?" Zelda asked the three women in order to cut off their insincere murmurs of sympathy. Not one of them had said a kind word about her mother when she was alive. Still, Zelda credited them with having more insight into her mama's final days than she did. "Did she explain that to any of you?"

"Well, he is a lawyer, honey," Mabel Smith reminded her.

Zelda caught Mabel trying to keep her disapproving gaze off of Zelda's colorful outfit, a thrift-shop ensemble of gauzy, floating materials that bore her own unmistakable flair for the dramatic. No doubt Mabel considered it totally unsuitable for mourning. Zelda knew, however, that her mother would have loved it. In fact, she could probably find some floppy picture hat to match hidden away in the back of her mother's closet.

"Taylor's the only lawyer in town these days, come to think of it," Betty Sue Conner chimed in.

"What happened to Will Rutledge?" Zelda asked, recalling the sweet old man whose office had always reeked of pipe smoke.

"Dead."

"John Tatum?" She tried to keep the note of desperation out of her voice.

Surely she could hire someone else to represent her to deal with Taylor. "Moved to Charleston, five, maybe six years ago," Mabel said.

"Honey, I thought you and Taylor were friends once upon a time. More than that, in fact," Elsie Whittingham said. "Why I can recall plain as day the time that old man

Highsmith found the two of you up in his hayloft. What a ruckus that caused!"

Betty Sue grinned. "Almost gave Beau Matthews a heart attack. He thought sure you'd end up pregnant and ruin all his big plans for Taylor." Her expression suddenly sobered. "Funny how things turn out, isn't it?"

"Betty Sue," Mabel said in a low voice clearly meant to shush her.

Zelda let the warning go by, too lost in memories to question either one of them about it. Why wouldn't those memories—good and bad—wither and die the way they should? Ten years should have been enough time to rob them of any impact at all. Obviously she didn't have a lick of willpower.

She tried harder to put them aside, but she couldn't seem to help recalling in explicit detail the way she'd felt being held in Taylor's arms up in that hayloft, or the surge of adrenaline she'd felt scrambling down and running away when they'd been caught. Their laughter had echoed on the night air, along with old man Highsmith's shouts and the sound of a shotgun being fired into the sky as a warning. She'd never run so fast in her life, clinging to Taylor's hand all the way, knowing that whatever happened they were in it together.

Despite the danger—or perhaps because of it—it had been one of the happiest moments of her life. This wasn't the first time it had come back to haunt her. No man had ever made her feel as exciting and alive as she had that night. The comparisons, whether she liked admitting it or not, were what had kept her single.

But she was a different woman now, and Taylor most assuredly was a different man. That was what she had to keep reminding herself as she tried to block those old feelings.

Before she could satisfactorily push the memory aside, however, the screen door squeaked and the man in question stood before her, bathed in the last rays of fading sunlight. Leave it to Taylor to make an unforgettable entrance. A TV evangelist couldn't have asked for a more dramatic backdrop.

Taylor stood where he was, hands shoved in his pockets, and nodded. "Zelda."

Since one word was all he seemed able to manage, Zelda matched him. "Taylor."

The three fluttering female guests suddenly thought of a dozen excuses for why they had to rush home. During their whirlwind departure, Zelda tried to gather her composure. She figured the best she could hope for was the restraint to keep from throwing herself right smack into Taylor's muscular arms. Why the devil couldn't the man have gone all soft? Maybe even bald? Instead, he was as lean and handsome as ever.

She couldn't seem to stop herself from drinking in the sight of him, from the fancy suit that couldn't hide his football-broad shoulders to the untamed curl in his jet black hair, from the combative angle of his jaw to the spark of defiance in his clear gray eyes. That spark was a dead giveaway that Taylor hadn't changed, after all. He was already just daring her to do something outrageous, something he could no doubt condemn her for afterward. This time, though, she wouldn't give him the satisfaction. She'd outgrown the need to defy the world at every turn. She would be pleasant, calm, mature... even if it killed her.

She rose to her full height, an impressive five foot

nine, and said in her most gracious but distant tone, "May I offer you a cup of tea?"

Taylor blinked, then looked startled by the sight of her mother's treasured silver teapot sitting on the scarred coffee table amid a collection of mismatched but elegant china cups. From the thunderstruck expression on his face, it was clear he hadn't expected her to know the first thing about the social amenities. Zelda could have told him that no female could grow up in the South without learning a thing or two about social graces, whether they ever practiced them or not. Maybe he'd just figured to find her drinking the last of her mama's bourbon.

"I suppose," he said finally.

To her amusement he sounded as if he didn't quite trust her ability to brew a drinkable pot of tea. Or perhaps he wasn't sure even after all this time that she wouldn't lace it with arsenic. Admittedly, the thought did hold a certain appeal.

"I'll taste mine first, if that'll put your mind at ease," she said wryly, causing him to scowl as an embarrassed flush crept up his neck.

When they each had a cup and she'd taken a healthy swallow, she deliberately cast a defiant look in his direction. He regarded her warily. For a man who'd once displayed a remarkably silver-tongued charm, he seemed at a loss for words. She wasn't inclined to help him out. She had enough to do just to keep her cup from rattling in its saucer and betraying her nerves.

"I'm sorry about your mother," he said eventually.

He'd said it before on the phone. She hadn't believed it then, either. Still, she nodded politely, thinking that he had a lot more to feel sorry about. Though Zelda doubted that she'd hear an apology for any of his past transgressions, she waited just the same.

During the gap in the conversation, she filled the time by checking out the status of his ring finger, mad at herself for caring, and trying not to be too obvious about it. No wedding band, she saw with some astonishment. And Taylor was definitely the type who'd want a ring to show the world that he was a family man and therefore suitably settled down and capable of handling the responsibilities of public office. The discovery kept her speechless. It also triggered an alarm, warning her to keep her guard up. A married Taylor would have been beyond reach. An unmarried Taylor spelled danger in capital letters.

Taylor finally broke the silence. "I'm glad you could come home."

"You insisted," she reminded him.

"True. As I explained on the phone, I'm afraid your mother's will is somewhat unorthodox," he said as if that were no less than anyone might have expected of Ella Louise. A nervous smile tugged at his lips, then disappeared under her disapproving gaze.

Because that hesitant smile reminded her of the boy who'd stolen her heart, it played havoc with Zelda's insides. It wasn't a reaction she was wild about. To keep things businesslike and on track, she said hurriedly, "What's so strange about it?"

Taylor leaned forward, his elbows propped on his knees. That posture could make a woman believe she had his full attention, that she was the most important thing in his universe. She wondered how many women, besides her, it had fooled.

"On the surface," he said, "the will seems pretty

straightforward. You're her only heir. This house belongs to you now, along with some cash, some nice shares of several blue chips she'd bought years ago and, of course, all of her personal possessions."

Though it was considerably more than Zelda had expected, the details didn't sound complicated to her. She regarded him in confusion. "What's so odd about that?"

"Nothing," he admitted. "However, there is a condition."

Zelda's pulse skipped a beat. "Which is?" she asked with an increasingly familiar sense of dread. What crazy notion had Ella Louise gotten into her head in those final months? She stared nervously at Taylor and waited.

He met her gaze and a flicker of some long-forgotten emotion rose in his eyes. He cleared his throat, tugged at his already loosened tie, blinked and looked away. Finally he said, "She wants you to live in the house for one year."

Zelda could feel the panic building inside. She glanced around the dreary room with its tattered wallpaper of fading cabbage roses, dusty drapes and uncomfortable furniture, and felt as if she'd just been sentenced to prison. Why on earth would her mother ask such a thing? Even though she hadn't had the gumption to act on it, Zelda knew that Ella Louise had longed all her life to be away from here.

"And if I don't?"

"It all goes to establish a scholarship for a writer, the F. Scott Fitzgerald Memorial Scholarship, to be exact. You'll get nothing except her collection of books. They are first editions, by the way."

Zelda held back a desire to moan. It wasn't that she wanted the property, the handful of stocks or the paltry amount of cash. Kate paid her well and she was happy in Los Angeles without any of that. But this place, this hated place, was her mama's only legacy. How could she walk away from that as if it didn't matter? How could she ignore her mama's last wish, no matter how bizarre, no matter how it might turn her life upside down?

"There is no way around this crazy stipulation?"

"None. I drew it up myself. It's airtight."

Taylor sounded almost regretful about that, she noted, wondering if he hoped she'd try to break the will, anyway. Maybe Kate could find a loophole, she thought with a flash of hope. She dismissed the idea almost as readily as it had come to her. She couldn't even consider such an action unless she understood what had been in her mother's mind when she drew up the document.

"How long ago did she make out this will?" she asked.

"The day she called me to the house, the day before she died."

"So recently?" she said in amazement. "Was there any question...? Could she have been confused?"

"You know how Ella Louise was," he said dryly. "But I'd have to say her mind was clear as a bell. She knew exactly what she wanted. Knowing how you'd feel about it, I even tried to argue with her about naming me executor, but she was determined. She wouldn't hear of asking someone else to do it."

"Why was it so important to her that I come home? Did she tell you that?"

Apparently he heard the dismay in her voice. For the first time since he'd walked into the house, Taylor regarded her with real sympathy. "She said that deep down you were two of a kind, that eventually you'd figure it out."

"Cryptic to the end," Zelda said, because she absolutely refused to say what she was really thinking, that despite Taylor's impression otherwise, her mother had finally lost her always fragile grip on reality like one of those pathetic, dreamy Southern heroines Tennessee Williams wrote about so well.

His mission completed, Taylor rose with an obvious expression of relief. "What will you do?"

Zelda sighed. "I don't know," she said honestly. "I just don't know."

"Is there... Are you involved with someone in Los Angeles? Do you need to get back?"

She couldn't tell from looking at him how he might feel about it if there was a man waiting for her. Pride made her want to invent the hottest romance on record. But even as the words of the lie formed on her lips, she was already shaking her head.

"A career?" he asked. "You've been out there a long time now. It must seem like home."

"It does. I have friends. I have a wonderful job. I'd hate to leave it," she admitted, but she knew that Kate would probably grant her a leave of absence to do whatever she had to do. In the past few months, since her own marriage, Kate had placed a whole new emphasis on the meaning of family.

Zelda looked directly at Taylor, into eyes that had once gazed on her with so much love and tenderness. Were any of those old emotions left at all? Did she even want there to be? Because she'd once respected his opinion, once believed he knew her even better than she had known herself, she asked, "What do you think I should do? Should I fight this? Should I give everything up? Or should I stay here and make the best of it?"

She wasn't sure what she hoped to hear him say in response to that—that he'd missed her, that he wanted her back in Port William for his own selfish reasons. Naturally, though, those were not the words that crossed his lips.

"I can't advise you on something this personal. You have to do what you think is best, Zelda," he said as if he'd rehearsed it a dozen times.

To her irritation, he'd refused to look her in the eye when he'd said it. "That's right," she snapped, suddenly furious at his careful, noncommittal response. "It wouldn't do for you to have an opinion now, would it? Maybe I should just call Beau and ask him." She glared at Taylor, saw the immediate, angry glint in his eyes that told her she'd gone too far. "Oh, never mind. When do I have to decide?"

"There's no rush, but the sooner we get things rolling, the better, if you decide you want to sell."

She couldn't miss the hopeful note in his voice. She knew in that instant that Taylor Matthews wanted her as far away from Port William as it was humanly possible for her to get.

Perversely, that was all it took to make her want to stay.

Chapter 3

Word spread faster than a brushfire that Zelda Lane was back in town. There was some subdued whooping and rejoicing over coffee at Sarah Lynn's the morning after her arrival, mostly from men who recalled her daredevil nature, flaming red hair and statuesque proportions. Some of them were the same men Taylor had once warned rather emphatically to steer clear of her.

Now he shook his head just listening to them. A part of him wished he could say what he was thinking and feeling so easily. Hell, he didn't even know exactly what he was feeling. Guilt was probably part of it, guilt over treating her so shabbily. Anger that he'd let her get away?

No, damn it. Anger would imply caring, and he refused to admit how much he'd cared and how foolishly he'd tossed it all aside. Besides, emotions were costly. He'd learned that the hard way. Emotions were something he hadn't allowed himself for a very long time.

He found himself wondering how Zelda would react to all the attention. For a woman who claimed to want her presence to go unnoticed, she certainly hadn't done much to assure it. That red convertible she'd rented stuck out like a sore thumb among the standard gray sedans and pickups of most of Port William's residents. Yet he couldn't help thinking it was typically Zelda, flashy, sexy as the dickens and definitely inappropriate for a woman in mourning. The general consensus around him seemed to be that Zelda probably hadn't changed one whit.

Taylor had to agree. The woman he'd seen the day before had been dressed with no regard to fashion sense or propriety. There might have been yards and yards of that orange and yellow fabric, but it had draped and clung in a way that had tantalized. Her earthy sensuality had simmered just below the surface, even as she sedately offered him some of that tepid tea. There'd been a defiant spark in those turquoise eyes of hers that offered up a ready challenge. And yet he'd sensed that under it all the vulnerability that had once touched his heart was still there. He'd also known that she would have denied it vehemently.

As he recalled his gut-level reaction to just being in the same room with her again, he caught the speculative glances cast in his direction. The conversation around him swirled on, with Zelda very much at the center of it. He felt as if battery acid were pitching in his stomach. Maybe it was no more than the caffeine he'd consumed during a long and restless night, but he doubted it. Chances were he could blame it all on seeing Zelda again.

He'd hoped—no, he'd prayed—that he'd be immune to her, that he'd walk into that house, take one look at her and wonder how she'd ever been able to tie him in knots. Instead his pulse had reacted as if she'd been buck naked and pleading for his touch, when all she'd done was stand there prim and proper and offer him tea. It just proved that time and common sense were no match for wayward hormones.

Oh, well, he'd done his duty, he consoled himself. There was no need for him to be in the same room with her again, at least not for longer than it took to sign a document or two. Despite the uncertainty she'd expressed, he'd been able to tell from her panicked expression and the desperate look she'd cast around that awful house that she would hightail it back to her exciting life in Los Angeles the first chance she got. Temptation would depart with her.

At that prospect, he uttered a heartfelt sigh of relief and finished his coffee. Before he could set down the cup, Sarah Lynn bustled over with a fresh pot.

"More, hon?"

Taylor shook his head. "I've got to get to the office."

Sarah Lynn didn't take the hint. She didn't even know the meaning of the phrase. She slid into the seat opposite him. "Not before you tell me all about Zelda," she said, clearly in the mood for a long chat. "I heard you were out at her house first thing."

"Because I'm handling her mother's will," he pointed out, not liking the way she seemed to have transformed his purely professional visit into something personal. If it hadn't been for that damned will, he wouldn't have been within a hundred miles of the Lane house, at least not with Zelda in it. Sarah Lynn ought to know that about as well as anyone. She'd been there for Zelda, when the girl had been spitting mad and hurt because

Taylor'd walked out on her. She'd given him her two cents on the subject, listened to his pitiful explanation, then somehow managed to stay loyal to both of them.

"Don't try to turn my stopping by on her first day home into anything else," he warned.

Sarah Lynn looked unconvinced. Still, she kept her opinion of his defensiveness to herself. "Whatever," she said blandly. "How's she look?"

Before he could muster a disinterested reply, a knowing, delighted grin spread across Sarah Lynn's round face. "Never mind, I can see by the look in your eyes that she must be as gorgeous as ever. She still gets to you, huh?" she said, rubbing it in.

"You two were hotter than a bowl of five-star chili once upon a time. It's damn near impossible to put out that kind of a flame. I oughta know. I've never forgotten that gorgeous Texan who swooped through town and swept me off my feet forty years ago. Talk about fireworks! You and Zelda used to get that exact same look in your eyes when you'd spot each other and thought no one else was looking."

Taylor scowled at her but tried to keep his irritation out of his voice. It wouldn't do to overreact. It would just set more tongues wagging. "Sarah Lynn, honey," he teased, "has anyone ever told you you have an overly active imagination?"

"No one whose opinion I trust," she smart-mouthed back. "Why don't you bring her on by for lunch?"

At her assumption that he and Zelda would pick up right where they'd left off, his fragile hold on his patience snapped. "If Zelda wants to eat here, she knows the way," he reminded her irritably as he slid from the booth. "Frankly, I'm not all that sure she'll be around long enough."

Sarah Lynn chuckled, obviously putting her own interpretation on his sour attitude. "Bye-bye, hon. You have a good one, you hear."

Taylor doubted any day that had started out with one of Sarah Lynn's inquisitions about her silly, romantic imaginings could possibly turn out to be good. The walk down the block to the old clapboard house that served as both his home and his office was short enough to be uneventful, but also too short to improve his mood.

Inside the office, the normally effusive Darlene Maitland greeted him with a subdued expression. Darlene was twenty-two, recently married and could type with fervor, if not accuracy. She was the only person in town who'd applied for the job of secretary when he'd posted a notice on the bulletin board at Sarah Lynn's. Since she was known for her bubbling enthusiasm—she'd been head cheerleader every year in high school—Taylor had a feeling her downcast look did not bode well for the rest of his morning.

"Guess what?" she said, following him into his office and plunking a handful of pink message slips onto his desk.

"What?" he said, in no mood to play guessing games.

"I'm pregnant!"

He regarded her as if she'd just announced that a bomb had arrived in the morning mail. Obviously he could not voice his real reaction to the news. "Congratulations!" he said with what he hoped was enough sincerity to cover his dismay.

If Darlene sensed his lack of enthusiasm, she didn't show it. "Thanks," she said, practically bursting with excitement now that the news was out. "Tommy Ray and I weren't counting on this, but it'll be okay." She shook her head, her hand resting protectively on her still-flat stomach. "A baby! Can you imagine?"

"It's something, all right."

She regarded him more somberly. "It means I'm going to have to quit, though."

There it was, the bombshell he'd been waiting for. The pregnancy, with its prospects of morning sickness and time off for shopping and lunchtime showers couldn't possibly have been enough. Oh, no. Darlene had to go and quit, too. It just about clinched the day's status as one of the worst in his life.

"Quit? Why on earth would you want to do that?" he demanded, unable to keep the cranky note from his voice. What had happened to all those women who wanted to have careers and motherhood? Taylor wondered miserably. "When's the baby duc, anyway?"

"Not for another six months, but Tommy Ray figures I ought to go ahead and quit now so we can work on building a nursery and getting it all fixed up. I won't leave you in the lurch or anything. I figured you ought to be able to find somebody to replace me in two weeks. I could start looking around for you right away, if you want me to."

Taylor didn't have a lot of hope that two weeks was enough time since it had taken him three months to find Darlene, but he gave her his blessing. If anyone could track down a replacement, it would be Darlene. She had the instincts of a bloodhound. He'd turned her loose a couple of times to track down information that might otherwise have required a private eye. She'd had it so fast, he'd been awed.

"You find me a couple of good candidates," he told her, trying to muster a smile. "I'll do the final interview."

"You bet. Just leave it to me. By the way, Caitlin's school called. The headmistress wants to talk to you."

"Did she say what it's about?" he asked. Given the way the day was going, his seven-year-old had probably burned the place down.

"Nope. Just that it was important. The number's right here." She handed him the message slip on the top of the pile. "Want me to place the call?"

Taylor shook his head. "I can do it."

A few minutes later he had Josephine Lawrence Patterson on the line. Every time he talked to her, he couldn't help imagining her whacking his knuckles with a ruler.

"Mr. Matthews, I'm worried about Caitlin," she announced in that direct fashion he'd always admired until now. Now it set off alarm bells.

"Is she sick?"

"Homesick is more like it. Perhaps you could pick her up this weekend for a visit?"

If there was a hint of censure in Ms. Patterson's tone, Taylor couldn't identify it. Still, he was filled with guilt. He'd had to go to Charleston the previous weekend and had canceled Caitlin's regular visit home. He hadn't allowed himself to hear any disappointment in her voice. In fact, he'd convinced himself she'd sounded happy about staying with her friends. Apparently, though, his daughter was almost as adept as he was at hiding her real feelings. It wasn't a trait he was particularly proud about handing down.

"Please tell her I'll pick her up on Friday afternoon."

"Isn't that something you should tell her yourself?" she said, and this time the mild rebuke was clear.

"Of course. I'll call later today, when classes are out. Thank you, Ms. Patterson. It means a lot to me to know how well you look out for Caitlin."

"She's a lovely child, Mr. Matthews. I wish…well, I wish your circumstances were different."

"So do I, Ms. Patterson," he said. "So do I."

For some reason, as he spoke, an image of Zelda immediately came to mind. He did his damnedest to banish it before it could land him in a heap of misery.

Less than a week later, just when Taylor had almost managed to block Darlene's imminent departure from his mind, she showed up with the astonishing news that she'd found the ideal person to be her replacement, someone with seven years of legal secretary experience, plus paralegal training.

"In Port William?" Taylor said, regarding her skeptically.

"Yeah. Isn't that great? She just moved here. Perfect timing, huh? It's like an omen or something."

Omen was not the word that popped into Taylor's mind. A slow, steady pounding throbbed in his head as he guessed exactly who Darlene had discovered. Unless someone had had visitors he'd heard nothing about, only one person had returned to Port William in recent weeks. He'd been clinging desperately to the idea that her return was not permanent enough to require employment. Apparently the gods were dead set on making his life hell.

"Darlene, tell me you are not talking about Zelda Lane."

If she heard the panicked note in his voice, she didn't let on. "Why, of course, I am," she said blithely. "I'd for-

gotten you know her because of the will and all. She'll
be terrific, don't you think?"

The only thing terrific Taylor could think of was the
fact that Darlene was too young to recall his prior relationship with Zelda. At least she'd created this awkward
situation innocently. Perhaps it wasn't too late to steer
her toward looking for some other candidate for the job.

"You haven't said anything to her, have you?" he inquired, though admittedly without much hope. Darlene
was not known for her reticence.

"You mean about the job? Sure. I told her all about
it, about what a great boss you are."

"Did you happen to mention my name?"

Darlene regarded him blankly. "I didn't need to.
You're the only lawyer in town. Everyone knows that."

"But she might not, especially if she just moved here."
It was his only hope, that Zelda would back out of the
interview the minute she found out who she'd be working for. The prospect of having her here, in this office,
not more than two dozen steps from his bedroom, made
his pulse kick.

"Oh, she knows," Darlene announced blithely. "In
fact, she's sitting out front right now, waiting for the interview I scheduled." She studied him worriedly. "Boss,
you look kinda funny. Did I do something wrong? I
mean, I could tell her you're busy or something."

Wrong, he thought, trying not to panic at the understatement. Bringing Zelda into this office wasn't wrong.
It was flat-out guaranteed emotional suicide.

Zelda wasn't sure what had possessed her to agree to
an interview with Taylor. Not that Darlene hadn't been
persuasive. That girl could sell pinecones to someone

living in the forest. She'd swooped down on Zelda with so much enthusiasm that Zelda had almost forgotten exactly who it was Darlene wanted her to work for. To her astonishment, she'd found herself nodding and agreeing to show up this morning, even though she hadn't even decided whether or not to stay in Port William. She'd even used Harlan's brand new machine to fax Kate for a letter of recommendation. She'd told herself she was just going through the motions, that it was a way to get under Taylor's skin. She couldn't think of anyone more deserving of a little discomfort.

Now here she was in Taylor's reception area, wearing one of her best business suits in a turquoise fabric that matched her eyes, and wondering if she'd gone and lost her mind. What had gotten into her?

Perhaps it was that same quirky streak that always encouraged her to do the unexpected. Perhaps it was a desire to see the look on Taylor's face when she walked into his office. Perhaps, if she was prepared to admit the truth, it was a deep-seated desire to show him and everyone else in this town that she was an intelligent, responsible woman and not the flake they all remembered.

Not that she needed to prove anything to anyone at this late date, she told herself staunchly. She knew who she was. Wasn't that all that really mattered?

She was just about satisfied with that mature, rational explanation, when Darlene announced that Taylor was ready to see her. Her heart thumped unsteadily as she walked into his sedate, mahogany-paneled office, an office she could have described down to the last detail in advance thanks to all the times he'd daydreamed aloud to her about how it would look one day. The genuine surge of pleasure she felt at the expression of absolute bewilderment on Taylor's face told her that all that stuff about maturity was so much hogwash. She liked seeing Taylor shaken up. Even more, she supposed, she liked knowing she could be the one to do it.

As soon as the door closed behind Darlene, Taylor started shaking his head.

"Zelda, I can't imagine what you're doing here. You know this isn't a good idea."

Thoroughly enjoying herself now that she'd admitted to herself why she'd come, she regarded him innocently. "Why is that?" she inquired sweetly.

"It just isn't. There's too much…" His voice trailed off.

"Chemistry?" she suggested, to fill the conversational void.

Taylor glared at her. "No, damn it."

"History?"

He rubbed his temples. "Zelda, it's just a bad idea. I can't make it any plainer than that."

"You don't think I'm qualified?" she asked. She pushed the recommendation from Kate across the desk. "I think my letter of reference speaks for itself."

He glanced at the letterhead, obviously prepared to dismiss it. She could tell the precise instant when the name registered. Thanks to some highly publicized celebrity cases, Kate Newton had a national reputation as a crackerjack divorce lawyer. His eyes widened as he read every glowing word Kate had written. He cleared his throat.

"Well, your former boss certainly speaks quite highly of your work," he admitted.

Zelda tried not to gloat. "Yes," she said briskly. "Now, then, if we're agreed that I'm more than qualified for the job, what exactly is the problem?"

Taylor was too much the lawyer to say anything that might later be used against him in a discrimination suit. Zelda regarded him smugly while he struggled to find a suitable answer that wouldn't fuel her desire for revenge for his walking out on her. He choked back every response that apparently came to mind, then finally settled for saying, "I thought you were going back to Los Angeles."

She had to admit she enjoyed the little hint of desperation in his voice. "I never said that," she corrected.

"Then you've decided to fulfill the terms of the will?"

"Let's just say that knowing I'd have a job would make me more inclined to stick around. So, what's it going to be, Taylor? Do I have the job or not?"

He regarded her intently. "Zelda, are you sure you want to do this?"

"You mean, stay in Port William?"

"No. I mean, do you seriously want to work for me?"

It was the closest he'd come to conceding that she might have cause not to want to be in the same room with him. She leveled a perfectly bland look straight at him. "It's a job, Taylor. It happens to be one I'm trained for. Beyond that, I don't think there are any other considerations."

Her defiant gaze dared him to contradict her. Finally he sighed. "I suppose we could give it a try."

Zelda nodded. "Shall we say, one month?"

"One month would be fine." He seemed to stumble over the response.

Zelda caught the distress he tried valiantly to hide and grinned. "I'll see you bright and early Monday morning, then. I can't tell you how much I'm looking forward to it."

Taylor looked as if he'd rather eat dirt.

Chapter 4

Unfortunately, Zelda didn't realize until she was walking back home that her perverse desire to rattle Taylor had overcome her own instincts for self-preservation. If she'd managed to open Taylor's eyes to another side of her personality thanks to Kate's glowing recommendation, then he had taught her something, as well. All Taylor Matthews had to do to make her pulse flutter was breathe. That was it. His mere existence in a room set her heart racing.

There was no reasoning with a reaction like that. Without half trying, Taylor made her want to do all those wicked, outrageous things that had so appalled the strait-laced people of Port William a decade ago, the very things that had sent Taylor himself scurrying out of her life.

And she had just agreed to go to work for the man! She'd probably be chasing *him* around his desk by the end of the first week.

Since such clear evidence that her daredevil streak was far from dead appalled her, she stopped by Sarah Lynn's for something calorie-laden to combat outright depression. A hot-fudge sundae ought to do it. The more decadent, the better.

Though it was early for the lunch crowd, at least half a dozen people were lingering over coffee and gossip. Since all conversation stopped the minute she walked in, Zelda had a hunch she was the current topic. It was hardly the first time, but it made her uncomfortable just the same. She suddenly longed for L.A., where the only people who knew her name were the ones she told.

Though most of the faces at the counter were familiar, she merely waved a greeting. She pointedly avoided making the sort of eye contact that would invite anyone to join her. As she headed for the nearest empty booth, Sarah Lynn bustled out from the kitchen and embraced her. She smelled of cinnamon and apples. It must be apple crisp day, served hot and topped by melting vanilla ice cream, Zelda recalled as she returned Sarah Lynn's hug.

That hug and the genuine warmth behind it brought the salty sting of tears to Zelda's eyes for the first time since she'd gotten home. Just being in this place, with the scent of fresh-baked pies in the air and the Formica and chrome polished to a spotless gleam, was enough to carry her back in time. She had more happy memories here than she did of that house a few blocks away.

"Zelda, honey, I've been wondering just when you were going to come to see me," Sarah Lynn said in a tone that gently scolded her for the delay. "Now sit right down here and tell me all about Hollywood. Have you met any stars out there? Why, I'll bet you know Kevin Costner."

She sighed dreamily at the prospect, a reaction that seemed somewhat unexpected from a woman edging toward sixty and built as solidly as one of those mowers over at Harlan's. Zelda knew, though, that Sarah Lynn's practical, down-to-earth nature hid a romantic streak almost as wide as her own mama's had been.

Laughing at the evidence of it, Zelda shook her head. "Sorry to disappoint you, but I've never met him. I did arrive at a restaurant one night right after he'd left with carry-out. Does that count?"

"Not for much," Sarah Lynn said with a laugh. "Well, never you mind. What can I get you, hon?"

"A hot-fudge sundae," Zelda said at once. "The biggest one you can make."

Sarah Lynn didn't remind her that it was before noon. She'd never been one to criticize her customers' dietary whims. Given her cholesterol-laden menu, it would have been decidedly bad for business. "Extra whipped cream, the way you always liked it?" she said immediately.

The one thing Zelda had always known about small-town living was that people never forgot anything— good or bad. In this case, it genuinely made her feel as if she'd come home. "Of course."

When Sarah Lynn brought the sundae with its mound of freshly whipped cream and sprinkle of nuts, she settled down opposite Zelda. Her expression turned sober.

"I don't have much time before this place gets busier than rush hour at a train station, but tell me how you're doing. I want the truth, too, not one of those polite evasions you use with acquaintances. You getting along okay out at the house? I know you must miss your mama."

Zelda paused with a spoonful of ice cream halfway to

her mouth and said softly, "Yes, I do. I don't think I really accepted that she was gone until I came back here."

"They buried her next to your daddy, just like you asked. I planted some mums. I thought she'd like that. You been out to the cemetery?"

Zelda shook her head. "I couldn't. Not yet."

"Well, never mind. You'll go when you're ready."

"Did people talk because I didn't make it back for the funeral?"

"Honey, people in this town always talk. Ain't no point in worrying about it. Besides, we all handle things the best way we can."

Zelda sighed, grateful that this woman to whom she'd once been so close wasn't making any judgments. She regarded Sarah Lynn with genuine fondness. "You were one of the few people in this town who really understood what she was like, you know. You never judged her. Or me. I always appreciated that."

"Maybe because I knew what it was like to have dreams go awry." She reached over and patted Zelda's hand. "Whatever her idiosyncrasies, she loved you, honey. I know that as surely as I know the sun comes up in the morning."

Zelda had known that, too, but it didn't hurt to be reminded, especially now when her mother's final act seemed to contradict the fact. Maybe Sarah Lynn was the one who could explain Ella Louise's whim.

"Do you know why she wanted me to come back here and stay, then?" she asked, unable to keep a trace of bitterness out of her voice. "How could she insist on that when she knew how much I hated it, when she knew I had a new life in Los Angeles?"

Sarah Lynn didn't show the slightest hint of surprise

at Zelda's question. Obviously news of the will's terms had reached her. Either that or Ella Louise had discussed them with her. Apparently not the latter, Zelda realized with regret as Sarah Lynn shook her head.

"She never said a thing about her will or about wanting you back here, at least not straight out. She did worry about you being all the way out in California, though. We talked about it more than once."

The response only added to Zelda's confusion. "She never gave me a clue that she was worried. She never was the kind of mother to issue warnings about every little thing. Besides, it's no more dangerous in L.A. than anyplace else these days."

"Hon, I don't think it was crime that worried her."

Before Zelda could ask her what she meant by her cryptic remark, the diner's door opened and a half dozen customers flocked in. Sarah Lynn patted her hand once again. "Let's get together real soon. You need anything in the meantime, you just give me a holler."

Since there seemed to be no point in trying to pursue the conversation now when Sarah Lynn was distracted, Zelda just squeezed her hand. "Thanks. It's good to see you."

Sarah Lynn winked at her. "And don't you let Taylor work you too hard." Zelda stared after her in astonishment. It seemed some things in Port William never changed. She and Taylor were still making news.

That afternoon Zelda put on a pair of shorts and an old shirt she'd found hanging on the back of a hook in the bathroom. She knotted the shirttails at her waist, then settled down on the front porch with a glass of iced tea. The sun filtered through the trees in a way that made the yard seem prettier than it was. She barely noticed it. She figured it was time she had a serious talk with herself.

It appeared she'd decided to stay in Port William, despite whatever misgivings she might have had only a few short hours ago. Her conversation with Sarah Lynn had only confirmed that her mother had wanted her back here for some very specific reason. She had to stay long enough to figure out what that was, or at least to satisfy herself that it had been no more than a flighty whim.

The decision to stay made, that left her to wrestle with the equally troubling matter of Taylor Matthews. She reminded herself that nothing was likely to start up with Taylor again unless she allowed it. She told herself that pride alone ought to keep her from forgiving him too quickly for the way he'd treated her. And then she conceded dryly that Taylor hadn't exactly looked as if he was interested in spending eight hours a day in an office with her, much less pursuing anything more personal.

The last thought fueled enough anger that she left the porch and grabbed up all the old hooked rugs in the house and took them out to the clothesline in back. Then she proceeded to beat the daylights out of them. Clouds of dust swirled around her and left her sneezing. She backed up in search of fresh air and bumped straight into something solid. She knew from the way the goose bumps instantaneously rose all over her that the something was Taylor. His low chuckle confirmed it and sent sparks scampering straight down her spine.

"Taking out your frustrations on the carpet?" he inquired in a lazy drawl that was friendlier than just about anything else he'd said to her since her return.

"Just cleaning," she said. She kept her tone curt so

he wouldn't guess how that drawl of his affected her. "What are you doing here?"

"I've been thinking about something ever since you left my office this morning."

"Oh?" She glanced up and looked into troubled gray eyes that immediately cut away from hers. "What would that be?"

He started to say something, then stopped. Finally, after some internal struggle she couldn't begin to fathom, he said, "We never discussed salary. I can't afford to pay what you were making in Los Angeles."

Zelda could tell from his uneasy expression that her pay was not what had brought him out here. "You trying to wriggle out of our deal?"

"No, but this arrangement's going to be difficult enough without any misunderstandings. I just wanted to be up-front with you about a potential problem."

"That would be a pleasant change." The sarcasm crept out before she could stop it.

Looking guilty, he shoved his hands in his pockets. "Damn it, Zelda, you're not making this any easier."

She regarded him evenly. "Is there some reason why I should?"

He groaned. "Okay, I can see you're still angry. I suppose you have every right to be."

"Suppose?" she echoed incredulously. Ten years' worth of rage exploded. Caution flew out the window. She poked a finger in his chest. His rock-solid chest. She tried not to let that distract her from her fury.

"You suppose? Taylor Matthews, I was in love with you," she blurted out to her regret. Once she'd said that, there didn't seem to be much point in holding back. "You led me to believe you felt the same way. Then the minute your daddy suggested I might be a liability to the long-range political ambitions of the Matthews family, you dumped me with no more concern than you would have felt swatting a fly. I'd say that gives me cause to be angry."

He leveled a gaze at her that almost took her breath away. It seemed he was looking straight into her soul. "It's been a long time now," he reminded her.

His apparent conviction that time should have healed her wounds just riled her up all over again.

"Being told you're not good enough isn't all that easy to forget," she informed him. "I thought you were the one person in town I could count on, the one person who didn't give a damn about my mama's eccentricities, the one person who cared about *me,* no matter what. Instead, you bailed out on me when my reputation got a little inconvenient, a reputation, I might add, that you had contributed considerably to creating."

"It wasn't your reputation… I mean, not exactly," he began unconvincingly, then held up his hands. "Never mind. I can see coming by here was a bad idea. I'll see you on Monday."

Watching Taylor turn around and start to walk away in the middle of a fight infuriated Zelda almost more than any words he could have spoken. He hadn't taken half a dozen steps when she instinctively flew after him, leaping on him from behind. Her arms looped around his neck and her knees dug into his sides as if she'd jumped astride a runaway horse.

"What the hell…?" he muttered just as they fell to the ground in a tangle. The air whooshed out of him as he landed with an ungraceful thud. Zelda's own fall was cushioned, but she was beyond caring if she broke every bone in both their bodies.

"Damn you, Taylor Matthews, don't you dare walk away from me like that again," she shouted, pummeling his back with her fists.

He was absolutely still beneath the onslaught. In fact, he took it for a full minute, allowing her to vent her fury. Then, before she could catch her breath, he flipped her over as if she were no more trouble than a gnat and pinned her to the ground. She felt an almost forgotten surge of excitement race through her as she saw the angry sparks in his eyes. This was the man she'd adored, the man filled with passion, the man who tilted at windmills, the man who'd lavished more tenderness on her than both her parents combined.

"Come on, Taylor, fight with me," she taunted. "Used to be we argued half the night away, then spent the rest of it making up."

She could feel the heat rising in his body, even as his stormy expression gave way to something far more dangerous. Suddenly, just as she realized exactly what she'd set loose, his fingers were cupping her head and his mouth was on hers—hot, urgent, demanding. Years of pent-up hunger were in the kiss that shocked then thrilled with its deepening intensity. There was no tenderness on his part, no hint of gentle longing, just a raw, primitive need. Deep inside Zelda, a matching need exploded, even as it set off warning bells that clanged so loudly only an idiot would have ignored them. "Taylor," she murmured, too softly, too ineffectively. Her body, crushed beneath his, seemed to have a will of its own. Even as her mind screamed that she needed to get away, her hips arched to fit more intimately with his, seeking the source of the heat that had raged between them as quickly as a brushfire.

It had always been this way with them. Always.

And it never solved anything, a voice inside her warned.

This time Zelda listened. She shoved hard against Taylor's chest, tumbling him off her. He looked at her and groaned, his expression torn between guilt and a desire he couldn't do a thing to hide.

"I will not allow this to happen," he muttered under his breath, as if a sheer act of will was all that was required to shatter an unbreakable bond.

She glared at him. "What, Taylor? What is it you won't allow?"

"This," he said, waving his hand to encompass the two of them, the ground, their rumpled clothes.

"You were the one who kissed me," she reminded him.

"I'm not denying that," he snapped, scrambling back to his feet and brushing the grass off his suit. "It was a foolish mistake, okay? It won't happen again."

Zelda watched him flee, then murmured with an odd sense of exhilaration, "Bet it will."

"Taylor, what's this I hear about Zelda Lane being back?" Beau Matthews asked that night over dinner.

Taylor almost choked on a mouthful of black-eyed peas. Given the events of that very afternoon, he viewed Zelda as an even more dangerous topic than usual. He glanced toward his mother, appealing to her to switch the direction of the conversation. Unfortunately she didn't take the hint.

"I saw her myself," Geraldine Matthews said. "She

was sitting in the diner before lunchtime, talking to Sarah Lynn. She looked even lovelier than I recalled."

"There is nothing lovely about that girl," Beau said. "She's trouble. Always has been. That mother of hers was a drunk. If you ask me, Zelda's bound to turn out just like her."

The comment made Taylor see red. "Dad, you don't know a thing in the world about what Zelda's been doing the past ten years," he retorted, defending her now as he should have done long ago. Guilt for his past silence gnawed at him, even as he tried belatedly to make his father see reason. "People change. She's had a responsible job with a very important lawyer out in California."

Beau's head snapped up. "Now how would you know a thing like that, unless you'd seen her? You haven't seen her, have you?"

"As a matter of fact, I asked Taylor to see to Ella Louise's will," his mother chimed in, shooting a warning glance at him. "Naturally, he's had to see Zelda."

"Now why would you go and do a damn fool thing like that?" Beau demanded, his anger now directed at the pair of them. "You know the last thing Taylor needs is to get mixed up with that girl again."

Taylor stood up slowly and glowered at his father. "Dad, I'm past the age where you can control who I do or don't see. Maybe if I hadn't been such a damned idiot ten years ago and hadn't listened to you, my life would have turned out differently."

Ignoring his father's stunned expression, he leaned down and kissed his mother's cheek. "Thank you for dinner. I think I'd best be going before Dad and I wind up saying things we're likely to regret."

"I don't believe in regrets, son," his father shouted after him.

"I know," Taylor said softly. "More's the pity."

As he drove back toward town, he was thankful he'd managed to keep quiet about hiring Zelda to work in his office. Of course it was only a matter of time before the news reached Beau. Well, that was just something he'd have to deal with when the time came. He'd had his reasons for hiring her...though damned if he could think of one of them at the moment.

He sighed heavily. How different things might have been if he'd listened to his heart all those years ago instead of paying attention to his father's misguided if well-intentioned demands!

He'd played things by the book, though. He'd finished law school, married a girl from the best sorority on campus, one with all the right bloodlines—a descendant of the original South Carolina settlers, no less. They'd bought a fancy house in Charleston. He'd joined the most prestigious law firm in town, thanks to Maribeth's family influence. Caitlin had been born almost nine months to the day after the wedding, right on time, with a minimum of fuss.

Within a year Taylor had been positioned to run for public office. Beau had been ecstatic. His golden boy was exactly where he wanted him, on schedule and destined for greatness.

At the time it hadn't seemed to matter much to Taylor that he was miserable. There was little time for introspection, anyway. Maybe if he'd stopped long enough to take a good long look at his life and his marriage, things wouldn't have turned out the way they had.

Without realizing what he was doing, he found himself instinctively driving by Zelda's house. Those five minutes this afternoon when he'd disregarded every warning and kissed the woman senseless had been the first time he'd felt alive in more years than he could recall.

But it wouldn't work between them, not after all the lessons he'd learned. Zelda was high-spirited and impetuous, a combination that had very nearly destroyed him once. He wouldn't risk that kind of anguish again.

Chapter 5

Zelda marched into Taylor's office on Monday morning with her shoulders squared and her head held high. She was determined that Taylor would never detect even the tiniest hint of the nervousness she felt. She wore another power suit just to make a statement—black this time. There was nothing more professional than basic black.

Admittedly, though, her uneasiness had nothing to do with the job. She knew after working for Kate that she could handle the workload of a small-town lawyer with one hand tied behind her. It was the memory of that unexpected, searing kiss that had her jumpy as a June bug.

Fortunately the first person she saw when she walked into Taylor's office was Darlene, not her new boss.

"Hey, there," Darlene said, beaming. "You're right on time. Today should be a light day. Mr. Matthews had to take Caitlin back to school. Then he planned to go on over to Charleston to file some motions in a case he's handling over there."

Zelda stopped in her tracks. "Caitlin?" she questioned, her pulse hammering.

"His daughter," Darlene said, totally unaware that she'd just dropped a bombshell of atomic proportions. "Haven't you met her yet? She's the cutest little thing. She'll be eight pretty soon. Looks just like her daddy. She's in boarding school, has been ever since…" She paused and bit her lip. "Well, maybe that's something you ought to hear about from Mr. Matthews. He wouldn't want me gossiping about his personal life."

Of all the times for Darlene to decide to hold her tongue, Zelda thought in frustration. She didn't dare probe too deeply for fear the talkative Darlene would later mention her interest to Taylor.

"All lawyers rely on their secretaries' discretion," she said diplomatically. "I'm sure he must appreciate yours. Of course, if I'm going to be working here, it would help to know if I should expect his wife and daughter to be popping in, and whether he minds being disturbed."

To Zelda's regret, Darlene grinned mischievously. Obviously she was quicker than Zelda had given her credit for being.

"Oh, Mr. Matthews will fill you in on all that kind of thing, I'm sure," she said. She regarded Zelda speculatively. "You know I was talking to my mother about you. She remembers you from when you lived here before."

"Oh, really?"

"Her name's Jeannie Wilson. She'd already had my older sister, that's Danielle, by then. Anyway, she said you and Taylor—I mean, Mr. Matthews—well, that you had something real special going."

"We were friends," Zelda said a little too emphatically.

Darlene regarded her disbelievingly. "Sounded to me like it was a whole lot more than that."

"Well, you know how rumors are."

"How come you didn't mention any of that when I asked you if you wanted to apply for my job? I mean, I knew you knew him because of his doing your mama's will and all, but I'd never guessed about the rest."

"It hardly seemed relevant," Zelda said.

"Yeah, I suppose not. My mother said you split up and then you left for California."

"That's about it," Zelda agreed, knowing that the capsulized version didn't begin to cover all the heartache involved. "Darlene, don't you think we ought to get to work?"

Darlene blinked at the pointed suggestion. "Oh, yeah, sure. I guess we should. Mr. Matthews told me to explain which cases he's working on, where we keep things, that sort of stuff. Mondays are usually pretty busy because he sits in that house all weekend long with his dictating machine. I spend the whole day typing."

"Perhaps I should do that today," Zelda suggested. "I ought to get used to it while you're still around to explain how he likes his letters and notes done."

"Why, sure," Darlene replied, looking pleased at being considered an expert on her boss's ways. Suddenly her complexion turned chalk-white. "Whoops! 'Scuse me," she exclaimed, and raced for the bathroom.

While Darlene dealt with her morning sickness, Zelda moved into position behind the computer terminal. Judging from the instruction books piled up, the office clearly had the most up-to-date programs. As soon as Darlene returned, she pointed out the codes, all of which were exactly like the standard ones Zelda was used to.

"I think I'm all set," she said finally.

"Then I'll just try to catch up on some of this filing," Darlene said. "Mr. Matthews pulls files and leaves 'em scattered all around when he's done, especially on weekends. Then he yells like crazy because he can't find what he's looking for."

Sounded just like Taylor, Zelda thought wryly. When push came to shove, he apparently never could take the blame for his mistakes. She certainly knew that first-hand.

By midafternoon she had caught up on the typing and she and Darlene had finished the filing. The filing had taken longer than usual because Darlene kept throwing up. Worried by the expectant mother's pallor, Zelda sent her home.

Left alone, she sat quietly for a minute trying to absorb the fact that she was actually working in Taylor's office. Her gaze was drawn toward the wall that separated the work space from his home.

She hadn't heard a sound from next door all morning. Did that mean there was no wife, after all? Was that what Darlene had refrained from telling her, that Taylor and his wife were divorced? Or was it something more? She tried to imagine what might have made Taylor send a seven-year-old off to boarding school. Surely it wasn't just that he didn't like the role of single parent? He had always talked about how much he wanted kids, lots of them, since he'd been an only child.

When she tired of coming up with questions for which she could think of no answers, she picked up the morning's work and took it into Taylor's office. As she stacked the letters for his signature and the file notes for him to look over, she spotted the silver-framed photograph of a child in a swing. She glanced around, but could find no companion picture of the girl's mother. She couldn't resist picking up the photo of Caitlin to study it more closely, even though it was a poignant reminder that she had once hoped to share a family with Taylor.

With her fingers trembling more than they should, she touched the glass. The lovely, pint-size angel appeared to be about six or seven, which meant the picture had to be fairly recent. Her face was flushed, her black curls in disarray, but it was the devilish sparkle in her eyes that enchanted Zelda. How many times had she seen that exact same gleam in Taylor's eyes right before he'd led them both into some mischief?

"Oh, I'll bet you're a handful," she murmured, somehow pleased by the thought despite the pang of longing deep in her heart.

She had just replaced the photo on his desk when she sensed Taylor's presence. Thanks to the thick carpeting, she hadn't heard a sound. A guilty heat crept into her cheeks as she looked into eyes the exact color of storm clouds.

"Hi," she said, offering a tentative smile that wasn't returned. "I was just putting the work we did this morning on your desk."

His gaze went from the photo to her and back again, proving that he'd arrived before she'd put it down. The angles in his face looked harsher than ever. Whatever he was thinking, though, he kept to himself.

"Where's Darlene?" he asked finally.

"We were all caught up, so I suggested she go on home. She had a rough morning."

For the first time he actually looked directly at her in a way that wasn't condemning. "Rough how?" he asked.

She was pleased by the genuine concern in his voice. It proved he wasn't as heartless as he sometimes liked to pretend. "Morning sickness," she told him. "It's come on with a vengeance. I hope you don't mind that I let her go."

He shook his head and eased past her to sit behind the desk. "Of course not. Everything quiet around here?"

"Harlan wants to stop by when it's convenient to talk about filing suit against one of his suppliers. I scheduled him for ten tomorrow morning. He told me a little about the case, and I looked up some of the case law for you. The notes are on top of that stack to your left."

If he was startled or pleased by her initiative, he didn't display it by so much as the flicker of an eyelash. "Fine. Anything else?"

Oddly disgruntled by his failure to react, she shook her head. "I'll be at my desk if you need me."

At the door, she hesitated. "Taylor?" He glanced up.

"How do I handle it if your wife calls or drops by when you're busy? Should I interrupt you?"

The haunted expression that washed over his face stunned her. "That's not something you'll have to worry about," he said, his curt tone so cold it could have chilled wine. "Now, if you'll excuse me, I have work to do."

The abrupt dismissal stung. Back in the outer office, Zelda wondered if these first few minutes were an indication of the way things were going to be from now on. Taylor hadn't done anything she could rightfully complain about. He had been thoroughly professional, even if somewhat distant, right up until she'd mentioned his wife.

What on earth had gone wrong in that marriage? Whatever it was, Taylor was still clearly distraught by it. Zelda felt her heart wrench as she thought of Caitlin. What effect would such obvious anguish have on that beautiful, lively little child of his?

It was none of her business, she reminded herself sharply. None. She was just passing through Taylor's life again.

As the door to his office closed, Taylor shoved his trembling fingers through his hair and muttered a curse. Why the hell had he taken his anger at Maribeth and events that had happened a lifetime ago out on Zelda? He'd seen the unmistakable flash of hurt in her eyes, the proud tilt of her chin. Damn it, she wasn't just being nosy. As a new secretary, she'd made a perfectly natural inquiry. She couldn't possibly know the story of his disastrous marriage and its tragic outcome. Beau Matthews had seen to it that the worst of it never reached the media. It was one of the rare times that Taylor had been grateful for his father's power and influence. What little gossip that had made the rounds was bad enough. Sooner or later he'd have to tell Zelda at least that much of it or someone else in town was bound to do it first. Heaven knew how they would embellish it, but he doubted he'd come out the hero.

In the meantime, though, he had to find some way to coexist with Zelda for the next month without letting her very presence rattle him. Walking in here today, seeing her at his desk, had brought on a flood of old daydreams.

Once they'd talked for hours on end about how much he wanted to have an office that was attached to his home, so his family—Zelda and all of their adorable, redheaded little children—would be close by.

Well, that hadn't happened, he reminded himself fiercely. He hadn't married Zelda. His wife, well, he didn't even want to think about Maribeth. And his beautiful, precious daughter was away at boarding school so he wouldn't have to cope with raw memories that hurt too much. It shouldn't have been this way, but nobody ever said life came with guarantees.

Suddenly he recalled the very first time he'd been truly aware that the redheaded daredevil who was two classes behind him in school was something more than a pint-size pest. He'd thought of her as little else than a girl who was always anxious to follow his lead, who always looked at him with the kind of adoration he hadn't deserved, but which had made him feel ten feet tall. He'd been a rebellious kid. Zelda had been a more than willing co-conspirator.

He'd been a sophomore in high school when that had changed. Zelda had still been in junior high. In age difference it hadn't been much. In terms of pretended sophistication, it had been light-years.

Even so, like a bolt from the blue, he'd noticed the endlessly long legs, the already curvaceous figure, the hair that gleamed like fire in the sun. His pal, his best friend, had grown up on him.

Unfortunately, he wasn't the only one aware of the changes. When he'd first recognized that he was thinking of her differently, Zelda had been cornered outside Sarah Lynn's by a half dozen taunting boys, whose tasteless comments were fueled more by rampaging hormones than cruelty.

Driven by some primitive instinct, Taylor had been about to rush to her rescue when he'd noticed the sparks in her eyes and recognized that the fourteen-year-old wasn't intimidated. She was furious. He knew better than to get on the wrong side of Zelda's temper, but her assailants obviously didn't. Bobby Daniels had missed the signs completely and made one taunting comment too many. Zelda's knee had caught him strategically and a left hook bloodied his nose. The stunned, open-mouthed boys had scattered, taking the moaning Bobby with them. Even Taylor had been awed.

"You throw a mean punch," Taylor recalled telling her, falling a little bit in love with her at that moment. He'd known then that she was destined to be a woman who'd be a spirited match for any man. As young as he'd been, he'd wanted desperately to be that man. "How'd you learn to fight?"

"Practice," she'd retorted with an expression he couldn't fathom.

Then she'd sashayed into Sarah Lynn's and ordered a hamburger, fries and a hot-fudge sundae as if punching out a bully had only whetted her appetite. She hadn't even blinked when an irate Patty Sue Daniels had stormed in a few minutes later to threaten Zelda with jail for decking her precious son.

"Go ahead," she'd said, calm as you please. "But you won't like hearing the filth that was coming out of his mouth testified to in court."

"Who'd believe you?" Patty Sue had retorted derisively. "Everybody in town knows your mama's a mental case and that you're just like her."

Zelda had turned pale at that, every drop of color washing out of her skin. Her hands had clenched into fists once more. She'd slid off her stool at the counter, her intentions clear to anyone who knew her as well as Taylor did. Before she could deck Patty Sue, Taylor had interceded, even though he figured the obnoxious woman deserved whatever she got.

"I heard him, too," he'd said, stepping between them. "Think the judge and jury will believe me? Let me see now, what were his exact words?" In a low voice he'd repeated Bobby's remarks word for word, avoiding Zelda's gaze the whole time.

Patty Sue had turned red as a beet while listening to the crude remarks. "I ought to tan your hide, young man. Or maybe I ought to have a word with your daddy. Nobody talks that way to a lady."

"Exactly," he'd said. "But I'm not the one you ought to be explaining that to."

Patty Sue had left in a huff. Considering how gingerly Bobby had inched into his seat in class the next morning, apparently his mother had taken Taylor's advice to heart. Even after all these years, the memory made him chuckle. He doubted if the town's newly elected mayor—*Robert* Daniels—would recall the incident so fondly.

That defiant spark in Zelda that had first fascinated him had been very much in evidence on Friday when he'd made the foolish mistake of stopping by her house. She was still a hellion, all right. And she could still pack a wallop. He had the bruises on his back to prove it.

And, no matter how much he might hate it, he was still fascinated. This time, though, he'd die before he'd do a damned thing about it. He sighed and wondered exactly how many times he'd need to remind himself of that over the coming weeks.

After that first awkward day, Zelda told herself things had to improve. Instead, each day turned into torment. They were both so polite it made her want to scream. She wasn't sure what she'd expected, but it wasn't this cool civility. Taylor was a good lawyer, smart and instinctive, and more than willing to listen to her suggestions. He was even lavish with his praise, though most often it came in the form of notes jotted on the corner of papers she'd written for him. The ideal boss.

Unfortunately, Zelda had wanted her old friend back, if not her old lover.

She made it through the first week and then the second. By the third she was ready to admit that this had been the third worst mistake of her life. The first had been falling in love with Taylor all those years ago. The second had been not getting over him.

She ought to quit. She sat at the computer, glaring at his office, and tried to convince herself to walk out and go back to Los Angeles where life was far less complicated.

"You are not a quitter," she snapped finally. "You are not."

Suddenly she realized she was not alone. She looked up from her computer and caught Taylor watching her with something akin to longing on his face. It was the first tangible sign she'd had that he didn't outright loathe her for putting them both into this awkward situation.

"Is everything okay?" she asked, her voice far too breathless to suit her. Obviously she was reading too much into that unguarded expression she'd just witnessed, an expression that had vanished faster than a wisp of smoke.

"I suppose I was just wondering why I never realized you were so…" He fumbled for a word.

"Smart? Responsible?" Zelda supplied with an automatic edge of sarcasm. Then her innate good humor crept in. Her tone lighter, she taunted, "It's hard to pick up on things like that when you're skinny-dipping at one in the morning or sneaking into Sarah Lynn's to make ice-cream sundaes in the dark."

Taylor's gaze softened. His chuckle crept in and, like a touch of spring air, it warmed her heart.

"It's a good thing Sarah Lynn has a forgiving nature, or we'd have served time for that one," he said.

"It was still the best hot-fudge sundae I ever had," she replied, unable to keep the wistful note from her voice.

A smile tilted the corners of his mouth, then disappeared in a beat. "Yeah, me, too."

While Zelda stared after him with her heart thudding, he quietly closed the door to his office. Now what, she wondered, was that all about?

Chapter 6

That fleeting moment under Taylor's speculative gaze was the last straw. He'd looked so lost, so lonely in that one instant when his expression hadn't been guarded. Why? What had happened to him over the past ten years to rob him of the zest for living they had once shared?

Darlene had already whetted Zelda's curiosity about what had gone on in Taylor's life while she'd been in Los Angeles. No one so far had satisfied that curiosity, and she had never tolerated secrets very well. Maybe that's why she'd taken the paralegal courses, so she could be in a profession that allowed her to probe behind the facade most people displayed to the public and get at the truth of their lives.

Her one attempt to get Taylor to say anything about his marriage had failed miserably. Obviously if she was going to learn a thing, someone else would have to be the one to tell her. She sorted through the possibilities and picked Elsie Whittingham.

Elsie was lonely. She liked to talk. She had once provided an after-school refuge for Zelda. And she knew more about what went on in Port William than any other ten people combined, with the possible exception of Sarah Lynn. Zelda didn't dare ask her old friend. Sarah Lynn might care about Zelda as if she were her own daughter, but she was also loyal to Taylor. Zelda didn't want to test that loyalty.

That night on her way home from work, she stopped by Elsie's for a glass of lemonade and some of her homemade gingersnaps. It wasn't the first time she'd dropped in unannounced, acting on an old habit from childhood. But this evening was the first time she'd shown any interest in lingering beyond a few polite minutes. Elsie beamed as Zelda settled in a chair in front of the fireplace and sipped on her second glass of lemonade.

"First fire of the season," Elsie said. "There's a real bite in the air tonight."

"Feels good," Zelda said, referring as much to the chill outside as to the blazing warmth of the fire. She was enjoying the real changing of the seasons again.

"I sure am glad to have you stop by now and again," Elsie added. "You remember how you used to do this when you were a girl? I recall it like it was yesterday. You always did love my gingersnaps. You and Taylor both. I must have baked twice a week just to keep you two satisfied."

"That was Taylor. He could eat a dozen for every two I got." She sighed. "Mama never baked," she added wistfully. "Never cooked if she could help it. I used to pray that just once I'd come home from school and be able to sniff the scent of warm cookies fresh from the oven. Instead, all I ever smelled was bourbon."

As soon as the words were out, Zelda regretted them. Keeping silent about her mother's drinking had once been habit. "Sorry. I shouldn't have said that."

"And why not, I'd like to know?" Elsie said indignantly. "It wasn't right."

Zelda suddenly felt the need to defend her mother… again. "Mama did the best she could," she said sharply, trying to make up for her indiscreet remark just moments before. "There were times when she was just fine, when she'd tell me stories or read to me from those books of hers. Sometimes she'd take down her big old atlas and point to places far away and talk about what it would be like to travel there. I knew more about geography by the time I was in grade school than some kids do when they graduate from college."

Elsie pursed her lips. "It was your father I always felt sorry for. Poor Joseph had no wife looking after his needs the way she should."

Zelda felt as if an old wound had been stripped open. "That's not true," she said in a low voice. "It was his fault. You don't know what he was like."

"He was a fine, Christian man," Elsie insisted, looking shocked that Zelda would dare to suggest otherwise.

"He was selfish, rigid and judgmental. Why the hell do you think my mother drank in the first place?" she said furiously. "Because nothing she ever did was good enough to satisfy him. Not one blessed thing."

Stunned by her outburst, Zelda snapped her mouth shut before she revealed far more than she'd ever intended to say about the horror of living in that house with Joseph Lane. He punished not with spankings, not even with yelling, but with his cold silence. Just the memory of it made her freeze up inside.

She set her unfinished glass of lemonade down carefully. "I think I'd best be going."

Elsie regarded her worriedly. "There's no need for you to run off. Let's talk about something more pleasant. You shouldn't go getting yourself all upset over things that can't be changed. I'm sorry we got into it. All that was a long time ago. Tell me how things are going now that you're back. Are you settling in okay over there? Is there anything you need?"

Zelda drew in a deep breath and finally sat back. "I'm fine," she said. "Sooner or later I'm going to need to do something about the sorry state of the house, but for now I'm making do."

Zelda saw the speculative look in Elsie's eyes. She could guess what was really on the woman's mind and since it would head the conversation in the direction she wanted, she just waited for curiosity to get the better of Elsie.

"You and Taylor getting along okay?" she asked eventually.

"He's a good boss," Zelda said.

Elsie rolled her eyes at the bland remark. "I wasn't referring to his dictating skills."

"We see each other at the office. That's it." She hesitated, then added in what she hoped was a casual tone, "But I was wondering something."

"Oh?"

"Did Taylor come straight back to Port William after law school?" Judging from Elsie's expression, she wasn't fooled by Zelda's casual air.

"No, indeed," she said. "He went into practice over in Charleston, just like he always talked about doing."

"Then how did he end up back here?"

Elsie hesitated, then shook her head. "I can't say I know the whole story. Besides, that's something you'd best be asking him," she said.

It was a surprising display of discretion for a woman who loved to gossip. First Darlene, now Elsie. It appeared to Zelda if she stuck around Port William long enough this time, the whole blasted town would reform.

"I can't ask my boss something like that," she said piously. "It's too personal."

Elsie winked. "I know. If you were just asking because he's your boss, I'd tell you what I do know. But you're looking for more than the bare facts, and that's something you ought to hear from him."

"Why does everybody act so mysterious about this?" she snapped impatiently. "It's not like I'm some scandal-monger from a tabloid. Taylor and I were close once."

"A lot of water's gone under the bridge since then, for both of you. Seems to me if you expect to be close again, you'd best open up those lines of communication."

Zelda scowled at her, then grinned at the common sense suggestion. Whatever else her flaws might be, Elsie Whittingham had always had good solid advice for a lonely girl who hadn't always trusted her own mother's slurred words of wisdom. "Okay, okay, you've made your point."

"Can I offer one more word of advice?"

"You're asking?" she said incredulously. "Would a *no* stop you?"

Elsie chuckled. "Not likely. Don't go stirring things up unless you've got a good reason for doing it. Taylor's had a rough time of it. He doesn't need someone else to come along and hurt him."

"What makes you think I could do anything to hurt Taylor?"

"Because, honey, you always could, and some things just flat-out never change."

All night long Elsie's warning seemed to reverberate in Zelda's head. Was it possible that Taylor did hold some deeply buried feelings for her, even after all this time? It would explain that unguarded expression she'd caught on his face, the hunger in that kiss.

If so, then, what right did she have stirring things up? Was she still hoping for revenge? Or were there feelings of her own, feelings that went beyond resentment, that she hadn't yet grappled with, that maybe she didn't want to face at all? Common sense told her to proceed with caution.

Of course, according to legend in Port William, anyway, common sense wasn't something Zelda Lane had ever given a hang about. Since she'd already been tarred with that particular brush, she couldn't see much reason to prove them wrong now.

The next day when Zelda placed a stack of letters on Taylor's desk, instead of beating a rapid retreat, she lingered. Seeing the tense set of his shoulders, she longed to stand behind him and massage away the ache. Given his overall attitude toward her, though, he'd probably charge her with assault. Maybe even attempted murder, if her fingers happened to skim his neck.

"I was surprised to find you living in Port William after all this time," she confessed in what she hoped was a casual tone.

He barely glanced at her. "Why? It's home."

Though his response was hardly an invitation for an intimate tête-à-tête, she sat down, anyway. "But you were always so determined to live in Charleston or Columbia, and run for office."

He straightened and regarded her evenly. "I did live in Charleston, and I did run."

"You did?" she said, unable to hide her astonishment. If Taylor had run for office, why wasn't he in the capital now? He wasn't the kind of man who would even enter a race, unless he'd been virtually assured of winning. "What happened?" she asked finally, since he didn't seem inclined to enlighten her on his own.

A dark look crossed his face. He drummed his fingers on his desk, then shoved them through his hair. The nervous ritual was familiar, but in the past she'd only seen him act that way around Beau, when he'd been struggling not to tell him off. She was absolutely certain now that he intended to toss her out without replying.

Instead, he merely glared at her impatiently, then bent back over his work. A wise woman would have taken the hint. Zelda, however, wasn't about to let it rest, now that she'd finally opened up the subject.

"Taylor?"

He looked up, scowling. "Damn it, I don't have time for this. I hired you to work, not to cross-examine me."

"I can't do the best possible job, if I don't really know the person for whom I'm working."

"You've known me for the better part of the past thirty years," he reminded her.

She shook her head. "I knew you ten years ago. You've changed, Taylor. You used to be just as big a risk-taker as me, maybe even more daring. Now you've settled for boring. I can't help but wonder why."

He tossed his pen aside. "Zelda, what's this really all about? I seriously doubt whether you're worried about how stodgy I've become. Besides, you're here on a temporary basis, right? Maybe for one more week. Less than a year, if you decide to fulfill the terms of your mother's will. I don't see much need to confess all my deep, dark secrets to you."

"Who better to talk to than an old friend who's leaving town?" she shot right back, angered by his assumption that she wouldn't last one instant beyond the year necessary to satisfy the terms of the will. "I'll take your secrets with me."

"How reassuring. I'll keep that in mind if I ever feel the need to make a confession."

Zelda groaned and barely resisted the urge to shake him. Or kiss him until he looked as bemused as he had at her house a few weeks back. "Why can't you stop being so evasive and just answer me? Is the truth so terrible? Maybe you could just start by telling me about Caitlin. In the past three weeks, you've never once mentioned her name."

A faint spark of warmth lit his eyes. "Seems to me you already know about her," he said dryly as he glanced pointedly at the framed picture on his desk.

"I know she exists," she corrected, refusing to be baited. "I don't know anything about her or about her mother."

"Frankly, I can't believe no one's filled you in," he muttered. His gaze narrowed suspiciously. "Or is that why you're asking, just so you can gloat?"

"Gloat about what? No one's told me a damn thing.

In fact, everyone's so tight-lipped, you'd think I was asking about national security. If you don't want to talk about your marriage, then tell me about the election."

"Look it up in the local paper. There were plenty of stories at the time."

"I've worked for a highly publicized attorney in L.A. I know how the media can distort things. I'm asking for your version," she said with exaggerated patience.

Taylor uttered a sigh of resignation. "Damn it, you always were persistent," he grumbled.

She grinned, relaxing slightly. Victory was just within her grasp. She could sense it. She just had to reel him in. "Glad to know I haven't lost the knack for it. I'm still waiting for an answer, by the way."

"I lost, okay?" he said, then added with undisguised bitterness, "That ought to make you happy."

The words were curt, but it was the bleak expression in his eyes that distressed her. Taylor rarely showed signs of his vulnerabilities. Whatever had happened had hurt him deeply. With anyone else that might have dissuaded her from pursuing the topic, but she sensed that Taylor needed to talk. He wouldn't, unless she badgered him into it. So she kept at him, but her tone softened.

"Why would that make me happy?" she asked, genuinely puzzled by the comment. "I always wanted what was best for you. Remember when we used to talk about how we would redecorate the White House one day? I believed in that dream, Taylor. Even when I knew I wouldn't be the woman there with you, I still wanted you to get there someday."

"Sure," he said disbelievingly. "Once upon a time, maybe you felt that way, but I suspect I haven't exactly been in your prayers in recent years."

"Maybe, maybe not, but I do know how much being elected to public office meant to you and your family. In fact," she added dryly, "who would understand that better than I would? I paid a high enough price, so you could fulfill Beau's ambition."

"It was my ambition, Zelda, not just my father's, but you're right. It sure as hell did ruin things between us. The blame for that's as much mine as my father's."

Once again filled with regret, Zelda sighed. "It didn't have to ruin things for us, Taylor. I think that's what made me angriest. You bought into your father's assumption that I'd be a liability." She shook off the memories. It was too late now to change what had happened back then. "Look, all I'm saying is that I know how disappointed you must have been, but that still doesn't explain why you're here in Port William again. Losing a campaign wouldn't send you running back home."

He regarded her intently for the space of a heartbeat and then he sighed deeply. "No," he said quietly, "but losing my wife did."

Zelda felt as if the wind had been knocked out of her. "Losing your wife," she echoed in dismay. "How? Surely she didn't divorce you just because you lost an election."

"No. She died," he said bluntly.

The succinct reply explained a lot…and nothing at all. This time, though, Taylor's dark, forbidding gaze kept Zelda from pressing for more answers. But it didn't keep her from wondering.

After she'd left his office, Taylor felt all of the old pain and anguish wash over him. The wound, which had been healing nicely at long last, had been ripped open with just one sympathetic look from Zelda. He didn't want her sympathy. He didn't even want anyone to know how much pain he was in. He just wanted to be allowed to exist in peace. He wanted a life with no expectations and no bitter disappointments. No highs. No lows. With a woman like Zelda, there'd always be plenty of both. He shuddered at the thought.

Clearly, though, Zelda didn't intend to let him get off that easily. Just behind her sympathetic expression, he'd seen the familiar stubborn determination to probe until she knew everything. He'd remembered too late how persistent she could be and how perceptive. She'd guessed, when no one else ever had, how much he'd resented Beau's control of his life, even when they'd shared the same goals.

It was obvious, too, that Zelda blamed his father for everything that they'd lost. Someday he would have to correct that impression. In the end, it had been his mother who'd persuaded him to see reason, who'd gently pointed out how much more suitable a woman like Maribeth would be when he eventually ran for office. No one regretted the success of her persuasion more than his mother did today. He wondered if perhaps that was why she'd been so insistent that he help Ella Louise with her will, a gesture to make amends for a wrong done to Ella Louise's daughter.

Or maybe even a gesture meant to give him a second chance at happiness. What a laugh that was! He'd botched his life up royally and, bottom line, he had no one to blame but himself. He hadn't been an impressionable kid when he'd cut Zelda out of his life. He'd made choices, bad ones, and he was going to spend the rest of his miserable life paying for them. Wasn't that what penance was all about?

Taylor sighed as he struggled to face the fact that it was only a matter of time before Zelda heard the whole story about his marriage. He knew he should be the one to tell her, but the words just hadn't come. It had been easier to talk about the election. Losing a political race was one thing. Failure was another.

He admitted to himself that pride had kept him quiet. That and the fact that they both knew her presence here was only temporary. There was no point in sharing secrets, in allowing a touch of intimacy that could delude either of them that things could ever be the same between them. His decision to keep silent had been a good one, he told himself repeatedly.

If that were true, though, why was that gnawing turmoil in his stomach worse than ever? And why did he sense that he'd missed an ideal opportunity to strengthen a bond that never should have been broken in the first place?

He still hadn't answered those questions by Friday afternoon. At three that day, as he'd sworn to Ms. Patterson that he would do religiously once a month, he drove to the small private boarding school where he'd sent Caitlin. Ignoring his parents' objections, he'd told himself that he was no match for a precocious seven-year-old who needed rigid discipline. Except for those lonely hours in the evening, when he desperately missed the sound of Caitlin's laughter, he almost believed it.

He stood outside the gates and watched her come down the walkway in her blue and gray uniform, her wild black curls tamed into braids, her pace sedate. Something inside him wrenched at the sight, but he didn't dare admit to himself that he'd preferred the exuberant child who'd flung herself into his arms with sticky kisses only a year before.

"Hello, Daddy," she said in a soft, emotionless voice. Her eyes, the same gray as his own, were shadowed in a way no child's should be.

"Hey, puddin'. How's my best girl?" He tugged on a braid and a familiar, impish grin flitted too briefly across her face. "How's school?"

"It's okay. I got an A in math. My teacher says I have a very orderly mind."

Taylor winced. How could he ever have thought that such praise would delight him? It sounded so dull, so predictable. It sounded like something to be said once all the life had been squeezed out of a person, not words to be used to describe a seven-year-old.

Had seeing Zelda again reminded him of what it had been like to be a child? Before they'd met, he'd been every bit as studious and diligent as his daughter was now. Zelda had breathed the spirit back into him. What terrors they had been! For the first time in a very long time, he found himself smiling at the memories.

Caitlin regarded him curiously. "What's so funny, Daddy?"

The surprise written all over her face reminded him of how seldom he smiled these days. "I was just thinking back to a long time ago."

"About Mom?"

He felt as if the blood drained out of his face. "No," he said, trying to keep the edge out of his voice. "No, I wasn't thinking about your mother."

Caitlin's expression, which for one brief instant had been that of a happy, exuberant kid again, shut down immediately at his terse response.

Taylor cursed himself for his insensitivity. He'd vowed that he would never do anything to destroy the love Caitlin had felt for her mother, no matter how much he blamed Maribeth for ruining their lives. Obviously he was going to have to guard his words more closely.

During the drive back to Port William, he tried to put that spark back into her eyes with silly teasing, but Caitlin was too sensitive to his moods to respond. She was silent all the way, lost in thoughts. Looking at her sitting stiff and silent beside him came very close to breaking his heart.

Chapter 7

Zelda stood at the front window of the office long past six o'clock, watching for Taylor. Dusk settled in right along with anxiety over his likely reaction to her presence on his return. Still, she couldn't make herself go. She switched on the outside lights illuminating the driveway and waited.

Though he hadn't said a word about his destination, she knew from what Darlene had told her that he was probably going to pick up his daughter. Even knowing that he would be furious to find her still around, she had dragged out her work until it seemed silly not to stay just a little longer. She needed to see for herself the child she might have shared with Taylor if only things had been different, needed to try to understand the currently unfathomable dynamics of their father-daughter relationship.

She knew what she was doing was foolish, that it

would be emotionally costly. Still, she stood there, gazing down the street, wondering how she dared to get involved. Once she'd left Port William, would she be able to bear thinking of that little girl going through life without a mother and banished by a father for reasons Zelda couldn't begin to comprehend? Wouldn't it be better not to know what Taylor's child was like, how much she needed to be loved?

Too late for caution now, she thought. Her heart began to hammer with anticipation as Taylor's car turned the corner. As he pulled into the driveway, her breath seemed to catch in her throat. Finally the car door opened and Caitlin emerged.

Instantly Zelda felt the tug on her heart, the sting of tears in her eyes. She wasn't sure what she'd expected, but it certainly wasn't this placid, too thin child who walked so sedately at her father's side instead of skipping ahead. She carried an expensive overnight bag rather than some outrageously colorful tote like the ones most youngsters preferred. So little, yet pretending to be so grown-up. Zelda's heart ached for her.

Picking up her own purse and firming her resolve, Zelda swiftly left the office, locking the door behind her. She met the pair on the walk, defiantly ignoring Taylor's forbidding expression. She hunkered down in front of Caitlin and held out her hand.

"Hi, I'm Zelda. I'm your dad's new secretary. I've been looking forward to meeting you."

Caitlin placed one delicate hand in Zelda's. "Hello," she said, her tone very proper, very reserved. "I'm pleased to meet you, too."

She glanced up at her father for approval. Then with

an obvious flash of childish curiosity, she asked, "What kind of name is Zelda?"

"A troublesome one," Zelda admitted with a self-conscious laugh. "My mother happened to love a particular author and since she couldn't name me after him, she named me after his wife. When I was your age, I really hated my name. Now I don't mind it so much."

"You probably just got used to it," Caitlin said, displaying a wisdom beyond her years. Zelda couldn't help wondering how often the child had been told that she would get used to something eventually, just to be patient. "Maybe I did get used to it," Zelda agreed. "Or maybe it was that someone used to say my name with so much love in his voice that it suddenly seemed very special." She could feel Taylor's gaze burning into her, but she refused to look at him.

"Your boyfriend?" Caitlin asked, obviously every bit as fascinated as she might have been by some gloriously romantic fairy tale.

Zelda glanced up at Taylor, then back at his daughter. "Yes. He was, back then."

"Did you marry him?" Caitlin inquired ingenuously.

Before Zelda could respond, Caitlin confided, "I'm going to marry a prince someday and live in a castle."

Zelda nodded seriously. "Now that seems like a very good goal to me," she replied approvingly. "Have you picked out the castle?"

Caitlin giggled. "No. I've never even seen one, but daddy promised to take me to…" She looked at her father. "What's that place you said you'd take me?"

"Europe," Taylor said, his lips twitching with amusement. "It's across the Atlantic Ocean. Remember, I showed you once on the globe."

"He showed me pictures of castles in a book, too," Caitlin confided to Zelda. "I think I liked the one at Disney World best."

Taylor laughed aloud at that. Something inside Zelda twisted free at the sound. How long had it been since she'd heard his laughter?

"Sweetheart, that wasn't Disney World," he said, his hand caressing his daughter's head. "That was Neuschwanstein in Germany. It was built by King Ludwig."

Caitlin wasn't impressed by the historical information. "Well, it looked like the one at Disney World. I see it all the time on TV." She inched a little closer to Zelda. "Maybe you'd like to stay for dinner and I could show you the castles, too. Do you know any princes?"

Zelda heard the hopeful note in her voice, but she also caught the dismayed expression on Taylor's face. Discretion called for polite excuses.

"Maybe another time," she promised. "Your dad probably already has other plans for tonight. I'm sure he wants to hear all about what you're doing at school. And I can be thinking about whether I've ever crossed paths with any princes."

"But I'm not home very much," Caitlin said wistfully, casting an appealing look up at her father. "It would by okay, wouldn't it, Daddy? Please."

Zelda saw Taylor's resolve wavering and knew that there was very little he would deny his daughter, no matter how hard he'd tried to distance himself from her by putting her out of sight in that boarding school. "If Zelda has the time, of course, she can stay," he conceded with undisguised reluctance.

Caitlin obviously wasn't aware of the subtle nuances

between the adults. Her eyes lit up. "See. I told you it would be okay. You can stay, can't you?"

Zelda regarded Taylor intently. He gave a faint, albeit unhappy, nod. "I would love to stay," she told Caitlin, and meant it. She had been instantaneously charmed by this pint-size version of Taylor. A maternal instinct, long ago forced into dormancy, rebelliously reappeared.

As if she sensed that she'd found an ally, the child immediately tucked her hand into Zelda's and led her inside. "Maybe you can teach me to cook," she said. "Daddy's not very good."

"I know," Zelda said, casting a sly look at the indignant Taylor, who was scowling with feigned ferocity at his traitorous daughter. "Once he tried to make me a hamburger and burned it to a crisp."

What she neglected to say was that he'd been so busy kissing her, he hadn't given the hamburgers a second thought. It was clear from the heat that rose in Taylor's eyes that he remembered the incident every bit as clearly as she did, that he, too, recalled how her skin had heated beneath his touch, how her mouth had opened so readily beneath his. Now his gaze lingered on her face as if they could recapture the sweetness and passion of that moment without so much as a touch. Awareness shimmered through her, followed all too quickly by desire.

But even as her body hummed with longing, Taylor visibly composed himself. Through some supreme act of will that Zelda wished she could emulate, he replaced intensity with determined amusement.

"Perhaps if I hadn't been so distracted that night," he taunted, bringing a flush to Zelda's face as he ushered them into the kitchen. With one lasting knowing look cast in Zelda's direction, he grinned and said, "Now, sit down, you two, and let me prove how you've both mis-judged me."

"Misjudged, hell," Zelda murmured, thinking that she'd had Taylor pegged almost as far back as she could remember. Too bad he didn't seem to know her at all. He'd pasted a label on her years ago and hadn't both-ered to note that it was outdated.

"Daddy, maybe you should let Zelda cook," Caitlin insisted, regarding him worriedly as he stripped off his jacket and rolled up his sleeves.

Giving his daughter yet another indignant look, he tugged open the refrigerator and pulled a casserole from inside. With a deliberately dramatic flourish, he turned on the oven and popped the dish in. "See," he said tri-umphantly. "All done."

Hands on tiny hips, Caitlin made a face at her father. "Grandma made it, didn't she?" she guessed, then added with childish derision, "That's not cooking."

He winked at her. "Maybe not, but at least we know it'll be edible. Now, scoot, and put your things away. Let me talk to Zelda for a few minutes and catch up on what happened at the office after I left to pick you up."

Caitlin bounced off her chair and ran to the door. Then she hesitated and shot a worried look at Zelda. "You won't go, will you?"

"And miss this casserole your father has so expertly warmed up? Not a chance."

When Caitlin had gone, Zelda turned to Taylor. "I'm sorry she put you on the spot."

"Are you really?" he inquired skeptically. "We both know you'd probably finished your work a good hour before Caitlin and I got home."

She chafed under his knowing look. "Are you accusing me of engineering this meeting?"

"Yep."

She took heart from the fact that he didn't appear as angry as he might have been. "Okay, so what if I did?"

"Look, it has nothing to do with you personally, or even you and me," he insisted when she raised a skeptical brow. "Caitlin lost one person who was very important to her. I won't have her form an attachment to someone else who's only going to disappear from her life."

Zelda's indignation flared, then vanished in the space of a heartbeat. How could she argue with a warning that only stemmed from Taylor's obvious love and concern for his daughter? "I'll be careful, Taylor. I promise."

He sighed and shook his head. "Careful?" he echoed. "I didn't think the word was in your vocabulary."

It was something Beau Matthews might have said, Zelda thought as her temper began to flare. She'd spent the past three weeks practically standing on her head to prove to Taylor that she was no longer some impetuous, irresponsible kid. Obviously she hadn't made a dent in that thick skull of his.

Fueled by irritation and a sudden streak of pure mischief, she turned slowly and began moving toward him. Her pace was lazy, but relentless. He backed up a step, apparently warned by something he read in her expression that she was on the warpath and had no intention of playing fair.

"Zelda?"

"Don't worry, Taylor," she soothed. "This will be painless."

Alarm rose in his eyes. "What are you up to?"

"No good," she said cheerfully. "Isn't that what you usually expect from me?"

He backed into the counter. Zelda kept coming until her body was pressed against his, toe to toe, thigh to thigh, hips to...well, there was no doubt at all about what impact she was having on him. So, he wasn't nearly as immune as he pretended to be. Unfortunately, she thought as a shudder swept through her, neither was she. This game of hers could have dangerous consequences. Even knowing that, she wasn't about to stop.

Looking him straight in the eye, she braced her hands on his chest. She began to fiddle with the buttons on his shirt until the first four were undone and she could slide her fingers into the mat of crisp hairs on his chest. His skin blazed beneath her slow, tantalizing touch. She could feel the sudden racing of his heart, heard the sharp intake of breath as she provocatively skimmed a fingernail across one taut masculine nipple.

"Zelda, what the hell do you think you're doing?" he demanded in a choked whisper.

She noticed with a measure of satisfaction that for all of his protests, he wasn't trying very hard to escape. "If you don't know, then you've obviously been out of circulation for far too long."

He brushed at her hands, but the gesture lacked conviction. She simply laced her fingers together behind his neck and touched her lips to his feverish cheek, liking the way the rough stubble felt against her own softer skin. There was no mistaking the shudder that swept through him or the desire that darkened his eyes. She pressed a kiss on the opposite cheek, then another on his furrowed brow. Then, when his breath was coming in ragged gasps, she began the same slow, deliberately provocative pattern all over again.

"Zelda? Why are you doing this?"

"Just living up to expectations," she replied innocently as she skimmed a finger across his mouth, tracing the outline of his lips.

"Expectations?" he echoed weakly.

"Sure. I'm still wicked, untamed Zelda Lane, right? Daughter of the town's most eccentric lady." She emphasized her words with a slow, deep kiss that left them both trembling. She nodded in satisfaction. This was working out rather nicely. She was enjoying herself. So was Taylor, if his dazed expression was anything to judge by. Just to make sure he didn't get to thinking too hard about what was happening, she kissed him again, molding her mouth to his, teasing his lips with her tongue until the whole world tilted.

When she could finally manage to speak again, she added nonchalantly, "Might as well enjoy myself, right?"

As bemused as he was, as badly as his traitorous body ached for her, Taylor couldn't ignore the sad, wistful note in her voice. There was a lot of hurt behind that jaunty comment, a hurt he didn't begin to understand, but which touched him deeply just the same.

It also made him feel like a heel for allowing her to go on this way, *for enjoying it, damn it!* He admitted the latter to himself only after some deep and troublesome soul-searching. He was tempted, all right, tempted to play this scene straight through to the end.

Only the knowledge that they would both hate themselves in the morning—and Caitlin's inconvenient presence in another part of the house—kept him from giving in to the wild sensations Zelda's determined touches were arousing in him. He put his hands on her waist and lifted her away, putting a much needed inch or two of space between them. No more, he noticed ruefully. He could still feel the heat radiating from her, still catch a whiff of some subtle, exotic fragrance.

Ignoring the rebellious glint in her eyes, he smoothed her hair back from her face with one hand. He caressed the pale shadows under her eyes, traced the outline of her kiss-swollen lips with his thumb.

"I'm sorry," he said finally.

She regarded him with obvious bewilderment. "Sorry? For what?"

"Because you've been trying so hard for weeks now to prove what a changed woman you are, and I obviously haven't been paying attention. That's what this seduction ritual is all about, isn't it?"

She regarded him with feigned astonishment. "Well, hallelujah! I'm so glad something finally got through that incredibly thick skull of yours. What was it? The kiss? That certainly couldn't have been it. You were definitely afraid I was about to have my wicked way with you."

"Was not," he said, unable to resist being drawn into the argument. The desire to laugh with sheer exhilaration shimmered just beneath the surface. Terrified of giving in to it, of succumbing to Zelda's seductive ways, he choked back his amusement.

"Were, too," she taunted right back. "I dare you to kiss me back."

Mustering every bit of self-restraint he could, he gave her an impersonal peck on the cheek. A quick, hit-and-run kind of kiss. A meaningless kiss. So meaningless he almost couldn't stop himself.

"Be careful what you ask for, you wicked little she-devil. You could get it," he warned.

Zelda sighed so heavily it almost broke his heart. "Not me, Taylor," she said in a way that expressed resigned acceptance rather than self-pity. "For some of us, nothing comes easy. They tell me it builds character."

For Taylor, who'd learned all about struggling only after years of feeling blessed, the lesson had done just that. He was a stronger man today than he had been when he'd allowed his father to drive Zelda out of his life. Strong enough to say no to temptation. He couldn't help thinking, though, that it was too bad that the lesson had come too late for the two of them.

"Be grateful you learned how to fight back at such an early age," he told her. "You had more character at fourteen than I did ten years ago when I let you go. I think maybe you've always known exactly who you are and what you wanted out of life. I'm just finding out about myself. I'm not so sure I like what I'm discovering."

He turned away and busied himself getting the silverware for the table. Zelda's hesitant hand on his shoulder sent a wave of pure longing washing through him, a longing for something as real and normal as a wife and home, nights like this with their teasing intimacy.

He glanced back at her and saw that she was regarding him quizzically. Because he didn't want her fussing over him or asking a lot of unanswerable questions, he met that inquisitive gaze with a defiant look.

"Don't go making anything out of that," he warned.

His sharp tone didn't seem to faze her, however. Her gaze never wavered. "Don't be too hard on yourself, Taylor," she scolded. "Remember, you're still the man

I fell in love with. Anyone who could capture Zelda Lane's hard heart couldn't be all bad, now could they?"

He was prevented from answering by Caitlin's noisy arrival. It was just as well, he told himself. He'd had no idea what to say, what Zelda had expected him to say. Just as he was trying to puzzle out the answer to that, he heard Caitlin's dismayed yelp, followed almost immediately by Zelda's unrestrained hoot of laughter.

Glancing their way, he groaned at the sight that greeted him. "Daddy," Caitlin scolded, "you burned dinner again."

Zelda winked at him. "Habit, I guess."

Chapter 8

Taylor grabbed a pot holder and snatched the smoldering casserole from the oven. "It's just a little crisp around the edges," he informed them, fanning aside the smoke.

Zelda peered over his shoulder, the exotic scent of her perfume counterpointed by the aroma of burned noodles. "Crisp?" she repeated. "Quite an understatement, I'd say."

"It's still edible," Taylor insisted.

"I don't want any," his traitorous daughter insisted. "It's yucky."

Taylor refused to meet Zelda's gaze. Given how the dish had wound up in its charred state, he could just imagine the sparks of tolerant I-told-you-so amusement lighting her eyes.

"Okay, I'll put a frozen pizza in for you," he told Caitlin. "Zelda, how about you? Pizza or some of this delicious casserole."

Caitlin regarded their guest expectantly.

"Your mother didn't know I'd be here when she sent this over, right?" Zelda inquired.

His gaze narrowed suspiciously. "Right," he agreed. "So, what's your point?"

"Then I suppose I could risk the casserole," she said thoughtfully. "Surely a little charcoal won't poison me, and I wouldn't want to do anything to undermine your masculine pride."

He shot her a wry look. "Very funny. My ego doesn't need any mercy stroking by you."

That devilish glint immediately rose in her eyes. "Oh, really?" she said softly.

He cast a warning look in Caitlin's direction. His daughter, however, seemed oblivious to the innuendos. She'd climbed on a chair, removed a pizza from the freezer and already had it on a baking sheet. It was all too obvious that it was a routine they'd been through before. Taylor avoided looking at Zelda as he took the pizza from Caitlin, put it in the oven and turned up the heat.

"I'll watch it, Daddy," she informed him.

Zelda shot her a conspiratorial grin. "I think that's probably a very good idea, Caitlin. Your father seems to be easily distracted tonight."

Taylor couldn't think of a single response he could utter with his impressionable daughter in the room. It didn't prevent him from regarding Zelda in a way that promised very sweet revenge for her sassy tongue. He hadn't looked forward to anything so much in ages, a fact that scared the daylights out of him.

Zelda spent Saturday having another long talk with herself. It was getting to be a disconcerting habit. Pretty soon she'd be surrounded by cats and acting like a slightly dotty old spinster.

Still, she had things to work out. After Friday night she knew that she was treading on dangerous turf. Coming back to Port William had stirred up old longings.

She picked up one of her mother's favorite books, *This Side of Paradise,* and clung to it, rubbing her fingers over the worn cover. "Oh, Mama, what should I do?" she murmured.

She was beginning to get an inkling that this turmoil was part of her mother's plan. Maybe Ella Louise had recognized that too many things had been left unresolved when Zelda fled to Los Angeles with her heart in tatters. Maybe she'd known, as Zelda hadn't until the night before, that she'd never be able to get on with her life in L.A. or in Port William until she'd dealt once and for all with the permanent ache Taylor Matthews had left inside her.

But a whole year? She'd barely been home a month and already things were more complicated, instead of less. Another eleven months and she probably wouldn't have a strand of hair left in her head with the way Taylor's impossible ways made her want to tear it out.

Okay, this wasn't something she could blame entirely on Taylor. These were her emotions. Stupid, wasted emotions, as near as she could tell. Just because he'd kissed her as though he'd meant it didn't prove he was about to get tangled up in something more lasting.

Go or stay? Stay or go? The choice tormented her for the rest of Saturday and all through the endless night.

On Sunday morning, with the memory of the challenge in Taylor's eyes on Friday still very much on her mind and Saturday's uncertainty even fresher, Zelda went to church. Sheer instinct had her up and dressed in a subdued silk dress before she considered the ramifications of showing up in a place where she was bound to run into Taylor's parents. Besides, it had been so long since she'd been inside a church, she ought to be praying that the rafters wouldn't collapse.

The minister, if it was still Jesse Hall, would probably offer up a few prayers of his own at the sight of her. He'd once had to call the volunteer fire department to drag her and Taylor down from the steeple. Not satisfied to ring the bell by pulling the rope, they'd climbed all the way up to give it a push or two at close range. The memory of Beau's horrified expression as he'd watched their undignified descent to the ground brought out a smile.

As she strolled across the lawn in front of the Port William Methodist Church, she glanced up at the steeple and felt an old familiar urge to do something outrageous. Maturity kept her feet planted firmly on the ground. Or so she told herself.

She nodded politely at half a dozen acquaintances. She couldn't help noticing the wary looks some of the women cast first at her and then at their husbands. Wanda Sue Oglethorpe actually latched possessively onto her husband's elbow and spun him around as if she feared that a simple nod in Zelda's direction might turn the man into a pillar of salt. Given Denny Oglethorpe's preference for bib overalls, flannel shirts and chewing tobacco, Zelda could have reassured Wanda Sue that she was welcome to him, if only the woman had asked.

Trying hard not to let the general lack of welcome bother her, Zelda made it as far as the door of the church before she heard her name called with anything resembling enthusiasm. She turned around just in time to see Caitlin running toward her, her face alight with pleasure.

"Well, good morning," she said, forcing herself not to look beyond the child for the father she was sure couldn't be far away. "Don't you look pretty?"

"Thank you," Caitlin said primly. "My grandmother bought this dress for me."

That didn't especially surprise Zelda. The gray wool dress with its simple white collar was precisely the choice she would have expected from Geraldine Matthews. Expensive and tasteful, it had about as much personality as oatmeal.

"I like yours better," Caitlin confided. "I wish I had a dress that color. What's it called?"

"Teal," Zelda said. "That's a shade of blue."

"Like your eyes, sort of." She spotted her father and ran to grab his hand and drag him over. "Look, Daddy, isn't Zelda's dress beautiful? It's called teal. Do you think I could have one that color?"

To Zelda's amusement, Taylor looked thoroughly bewildered. A typical male, she surmised.

"You have an entire closet full of clothes," he said finally. "Surely you already have something blue."

Caitlin regarded him impatiently. "Not blue, Daddy. Teal."

"We could find some material and make you one," Zelda offered. "If your father wouldn't mind."

"Please, Daddy," Caitlin implored. "I could wear it to my birthday party."

A sudden, indulgent twinkle lit his eyes. "Are you having a birthday party?" he teased.

"Next month. Remember? You promised. Grandmother said she'd bake a cake. And you said I could bring some of my friends from school home for the whole weekend."

"Is that next month? I could have sworn your birthday wasn't for ages yet."

A grin broke across Caitlin's too solemn face. "You're teasing me, aren't you? You remembered."

Taylor smiled. "Yes, I remembered. How could I possibly forget such an important occasion? As for a new dress, I suppose I could take you shopping for one." He looked as if he'd rather spend a month in jail.

"I'd really enjoy making one for her," Zelda offered again, not entirely certain why she was so hell-bent on insinuating herself into Taylor's life. Perhaps it was the forlorn, lost look she saw so often in Caitlin's eyes. Perhaps it was merely her own need to experience what family life with Taylor might have been like, even if it was only for a few hours of pure make-believe.

"It wouldn't be any trouble," she insisted when she saw him wavering. "I could pick her up one afternoon to go look for material, then drive her back to school. My mother's sewing machine still works. I used it just the other day to make some curtains for the bedroom."

"Please," Caitlin said again. Wide gray eyes regarded her father with wistfulness.

In the end, Taylor was clearly no match for his daughter's appeal. He smiled. "I suppose it would be all right. I'll speak to the headmistress when I take Caitlin back tomorrow. Then you'll be able to make the arrangements with her whenever it's convenient for you to drive over."

Caitlin flung herself into her father's arms. "Thank you. Thank you. Thank you." She grinned at Zelda. "It'll be so much fun. Maybe we can even go for ice cream after."

"Oh, I think ice cream would be an absolute necessity after a long afternoon of shopping."

Just then Caitlin caught sight of her grandparents and went running to tell them her news. Zelda's breath caught in her throat as she saw Geraldine Matthews shoot a questioning look in her direction. Beau Matthews looked thunderstruck. An instant later he was striding in their direction, his expression stormy.

Zelda stood her ground. Taylor didn't budge from where he stood next to her. The air around them seemed to crackle with sudden tension.

"Good morning, Father," he said.

"Damn it all," Beau thundered, glowering at Zelda.

Before he could launch into an embarrassing tirade, Taylor interceded. "You're standing on the church steps, Father, with all the neighbors listening to every word. Don't you think a little discretion is called for?" he said mildly.

A dull red flush crept up Beau's neck as he bit back whatever he'd been about to say. "We don't need the likes of you back in this town," he said in a low growl meant only for Zelda's ears.

"Dad! That kind of talk is uncalled for," Taylor said, his own tone furious. In a deliberate gesture of defiance, he put his hand protectively on Zelda's waist. He glanced down at her, his gaze filled with compassion. "I think we should be going inside now."

Zelda fought to blink back the sudden onset of tears. Damn it, the last thing she wanted was this man's pity. "Taylor, you don't need to do this."

"Yes," he said flatly, squaring his shoulders defiantly. "I do." He looked toward his mother, who'd remained a discreet distance away to prevent his daughter from overhearing whatever his father was likely to blurt out. "Caitlin, let's go inside now."

She scampered immediately to his side and tucked one hand into his, the other into Zelda's. Zelda felt her heart lurch at the unexpected display of solidarity. Together, ignoring Beau's furious oath and his wife's attempt to placate him, they walked inside and made their way to a pew at the front of the church.

It wasn't much of a triumph. Zelda knew that sooner or later she'd pay a price for it. An angered Beau Matthews was always a formidable enemy. Worse, she knew that by the end of the day word that Taylor had chosen her over his family would be all over Port William. The news would be dissected with almost the same surgical precision as the chicken at most Sunday dinners. Sides would be chosen. Bets would be placed. And once again, the romance of Zelda Lane and Taylor Matthews would be the hottest topic in town.

It was late Monday afternoon before Zelda had a chance to discuss with Taylor privately what had happened at church and its likely aftermath. Even then she hesitated to bring it up. She didn't want him denying as meaningless something that had meant so much to her. That stance made up in some small way for his failure to stick by her years ago.

She stood in the doorway to his office, watching as he bent over his law books, exhaustion evident in the weary set of his shoulders. She longed to have the right to massage away the tension, just to have the right to touch him at all in a way that wasn't sexual. Sometimes, if she allowed herself to think about it, it cut right through to her soul that he would tolerate an intimate caress, but refused any pretense of real caring. It reminded her all too clearly that he still thought of her as a woman whose morals were no better than they had to be.

And yet he had stood up to his father in public the day before, she thought with a faint stirring of hope. She had to know why he had been willing to risk all the speculation and potential embarrassment.

"Taylor?" she said finally.

He glanced up at her, his expression wary. "Yes?"

"Do you have a minute?"

"I'm right in the middle of researching the precedent on this case."

"I'll help you do that," she volunteered. "It won't take long."

"That's not your job," he protested.

"Maybe it's not exactly what you hired me to do, but I'm qualified as a paralegal. You might as well take advantage of all of my skills."

An unexpected spark of mischief danced in his eyes and made her heart flip over.

"All of them?" he taunted.

"You know what I meant." She drew in a deep breath. "Taylor, there's something I need to ask you."

As if he sensed that she was about to bring up a subject he didn't want to hear, he nodded with obvious reluctance. "Go ahead. Ask."

"Why did you do what you did yesterday? Why did you defend me to your father?"

"It was nothing."

"It was, and you know it. So did everyone else on the church lawn. I need to know why."

"Because I refuse to allow him to humiliate you like that. You've done nothing to deserve it."

"I hadn't done anything to deserve it ten years ago, either," she reminded him.

He sighed and rubbed his eyes. "I know that. But ten years ago, I wasn't very wise or very brave. I was single-minded and ambitious, and I thought my family knew what was best." He leveled his gaze on her. "I regret that more than I can ever tell you."

There was no mistaking the genuine anguish in his voice, the regret in his eyes, the absolute sincerity in his voice. It might have been the first genuinely honest thing he'd said to her in years.

"Maybe it's time to put the past behind us," she told him, her voice little more than a whisper. Now, just maybe they could move on. She realized that as hard as she'd been fighting it, that was what she wanted more than anything else in the world.

He nodded at her suggestion. "It's probably way past time to do that," he agreed.

Her heart leapt, then crashed as she saw the expression in his eyes. Suddenly she recognized the *but* she should have heard in his voice. He struggled with it, then clearly lost the internal debate.

"But, Zelda…" He hesitated again.

"What?" she demanded impatiently. Whatever his reservations were, she wanted him to spell them out. She couldn't fight something that remained unspoken.

"I need to be honest with you."

A sense of dread welled up inside her. Those were the kind of words always spoken before bad news, before rejection. He'd said the exact same words ten years before, though his voice had been shaking then, had lacked the conviction she'd just heard. Unable to encourage him to continue, after all, she simply waited, wishing there was more of a hint of turmoil in his eyes.

"I wouldn't want you thinking that meant we have a future," he said finally. "Or even a present."

An icy knot formed in the middle of Zelda's chest at his flat, unequivocal tone. In the end, the apology had been his way of closing a door, not opening one.

"No, of course not," she said around the lump in her throat.

And then, because she didn't think she could bear it another minute, she fled.

An hour later she was cursing herself for not telling him that she wasn't looking for anything from him, for not salvaging some tiny shred of pride by laughing in his face.

"Who needs you, Taylor Matthews?" That was what she should have said. "Who wants you?"

The problem, unfortunately, was that the answer to both questions seemed to be that she did. Ten years of separation and festering anger had not done a damn thing to dim the needing or the wanting. If she were very wise, if she had an ounce of pride left, she would walk in tomorrow morning and hand in her notice. The month's trial was ending, anyway. She could claim she missed Los Angeles more than she'd expected, that the estate meant nothing to her, and that a writer's scholarship in her mother's memory would be for the best. She could do that. She should.

But she knew in her heart that she wouldn't. She was going to stay in Port William and play this damnable charade out to the end. No matter how it turned out. No matter how much it hurt. Because this time she would not take the coward's way out and run. She would stay and fight for the man she loved as she should have ten years before.

Chapter 9

Zelda was slapping a fresh coat of paint on the outside of the house when she heard the muffled laughter behind her. Whirling around, she saw Sarah Lynn, her face alight with barely concealed mirth.

"Interesting color," she observed. "You trying to make a statement or what?"

Zelda regarded her indignantly. "There is nothing wrong with raspberry."

"For fruit, maybe even kitchen curtains, but a whole house? Can't say I've ever seen one that exact shade."

Zelda stepped back and studied the house intently. It was bright, somewhere between the color of cotton candy and actual ripe berries. With white trim, it ought to look downright cheerful. "I like it," she said staunchly.

"I take it, then, that you aren't planning to sell it, after all."

Zelda's gaze narrowed. Going or staying wasn't something she was prepared to commit to aloud. "Why would you say that?"

"Because you'd be painting it a nice subdued white if you hoped to find a buyer."

Zelda grimaced at Sarah Lynn's perceptiveness. "Okay, I'm painting it raspberry because I like raspberry," she conceded cautiously. "It's a happy color."

"And it'll drive Beau Matthews crazy every time he has to ride past this place."

Zelda grinned unrepentantly. "That, too."

"Has Taylor seen it?"

"No. I don't expect him to be dropping by anytime soon, not after what happened the last time he was here. In fact, I doubt he'd come into the office if he could help it."

Sarah Lynn settled into a rocking chair with an expectant look on her face. "Sounds fascinating."

"Don't look at me like that," Zelda chided. "I don't kiss and tell."

Sarah Lynn nodded as if she'd revealed every detail of a torrid love scene. "That would explain his behavior on the church lawn Sunday morning."

"You weren't even there."

"Didn't need to be. I had three phone calls by noon. The accounts were generally the same. Beau expressed his disapproval of your presence in Port William and Taylor told him off. Then, with his daddy about ready to explode, Taylor and Caitlin defied him and went inside with you. Accurate?"

"Close enough."

Sarah Lynn nodded in satisfaction. "I knew that boy'd wake up one of these days. Has he asked you to stay here permanently, yet?"

"Hardly. Offhand, I'd say this little display was nothing more than a belated rebellion on Taylor's part. I don't think it had much to do with me."

"Honey, it had everything to do with you. It's been eating away at Taylor for ten years the way he mistreated you back then, whether he wants to admit it or not. He still loves you. Always did. Always will."

Zelda shrugged. "I wish I could believe that, but I don't think so. I think he considers Sunday's act the ultimate apology. My guess is that he'd be perfectly happy if I skedaddled out of town so he wouldn't have to take another stance like that."

"I'm not sure who you're selling short here, yourself or Taylor. You're a woman any man would be proud to marry. And Taylor might have been a little misguided once upon a time, but he's a decent, honorable man, to say nothing of being a certified hunk who's aged like vintage wine."

"I'm not selling either of us short. I've developed a fair amount of self-confidence over the past ten years. And nobody ever knew Taylor's attributes better than I. They've kept me awake more nights than I care to admit to."

"Then what are you worrying about? It's just a matter of time before you all work things out. Some things in life are just meant to go together. Ham and eggs. Coffee and cream. You and Taylor."

Zelda regarded her wryly. "Do you know how many people no longer eat ham *and* eggs? Do you know how many take their coffee black? I think you've overestimated the certainties in life."

"Give it time, hon."

Zelda shook her head. "No. He flat-out told me not to

read anything into what he did. What's past is past. We have no present and no future. He was adamant about that," she said, turning away so Sarah Lynn wouldn't see the tears that automatically sprang up as she repeated Taylor's words. She rubbed at her eyes with the backs of her paint-spattered fists, probably leaving streaks of raspberry down her face so she looked like a sad-faced clown.

Sarah Lynn uttered an unladylike sniff of derision. "Sounds an awful lot like a fool who's protesting too much. Did you believe him?"

"He wants me to," Zelda said firmly.

"Did you believe him?" Sarah Lynn repeated.

Zelda scowled at her. "I'm painting this damned house, aren't I?"

Sarah Lynn nodded in satisfaction. "Good. Just remember that sometimes a woman knows what's good for a man a lot sooner than he recognizes it. With Taylor, there's a whole lot of history to overcome."

"He says that's behind us."

"I'm not talking about your history with him, hon. Hell, one of these days he'll see that you were the best thing that ever happened to him. It's his marriage he has to get beyond. No one around here knows all the details, but Maribeth's death left Taylor with a lot of pain and bitterness. He's not over it yet."

"I'm not sure I want to get into a competition with the ghost of the undying love of his life."

"I don't think that's something you need to worry yourself about. To my knowledge, you're the first and only woman ever to get a rise out of him, including that so-called society woman he married. Taylor's a calendar-worthy hunk. A lot of women have tried to comfort him

or straight-out seduce him, before, during and after his
marriage. Since his wife's death, none have succeeded,
so far as I know. He's always polite, but disinterested.
He needs you, hon, needs you to put some joy back into
his life. Maybe even more than you need him."

With that enigmatic declaration, Sarah Lynn hefted
herself out of the rocker and headed for home. After she
was gone, Zelda tried desperately to convince herself
that Sarah Lynn was right, that staying in Port William
and fighting for Taylor wasn't going to be the costliest
mistake of her life.

Whether it was or it wasn't didn't seem to matter in
the end. She might not have admitted it to Sarah Lynn,
but she was staying for as long as it took and that was
that.

Taylor studied the calendar on his desk and tried not
to count backward to the first day Zelda had come to
work for him. He didn't need to finish to know that she'd
been there one month. Four weeks. All she'd committed to. It wouldn't surprise him to discover that she'd
flown back to Los Angeles over the weekend. No one
in Port William, least of all him, had exactly made her
feel welcome. In fact, it would take a tough hide to withstand the insults his father alone had uttered.

One thing that Taylor knew, though few others did,
was that Zelda's very attractive hide barely protected
her vulnerabilities. She might have a smart mouth and
daring ways, but underneath it all she still bore all the
hurts of a kid who'd only wanted to fit in and somehow never had.

But if Ella Louise's eccentricities had caused her
pain, they had also given her strength. No one would

ever see Zelda Lane looking defeated; no one would ever guess how difficult things had been for her.

Except Taylor. And he had only made things worse. Damn, a man could hate himself for a mistake like that.

He glanced at his watch, then at the door. It was five before eight. Zelda was always at her desk on the dot of eight o'clock. Other people in Port William might be lax about opening and closing their offices, but she was always prompt. He watched the sweep of his second hand as it went around once, then twice, then a third time. To his deep regret, his heart seemed to thud with anxiety. What if she had gone? How would he feel about that?

The quiet opening and closing of the outside door kept him from having to be honest with himself. Even so, he couldn't deny the relief that washed over him as he heard her call out.

"Taylor, are you here already?" She poked her head into his office, obviously startled to find him behind his desk rather than at Sarah Lynn's where he could usually be found until eight-thirty, sometimes nine.

"Thought I'd get an early start today," he said. "I wasn't sure you'd be in."

"Why wouldn't I be?" she inquired.

"The month is up," he reminded her, "and we didn't discuss how you felt about staying on."

She grinned in a way that made his blood pump harder. It was a smug, savvy look that told him she knew things that he didn't, like maybe the feelings he hadn't wanted to admit to. She'd had that same look on her face the night they'd made love for the first time, within minutes of his firm vow that he would not, under any circumstances, touch her. She had a way of testing a man's resolve.

"Taylor, you're not shy about expressing your likes and dislikes," she said. "I figured if you weren't satisfied with my work, you'd have fired me before now, deal or no deal. As for me, if I'd intended to quit, I'd have told you."

"So you're staying on?" he said, trying not to sound too concerned about the answer.

"Looks that way," she said cheerfully. "Any problem with that?"

There was a daring glint in her eyes that worried him, but he wasn't about to question her motives. She was staying and, for the moment, God help him, that was enough.

"There is one thing I ought to warn you about, though," he said. "My father's coming by this morning. He insisted on meeting here, rather than out at the house."

He considered suggesting she might want to take the morning to go over to Caitlin's school, maybe take his daughter on that shopping spree, but something in her instantly forbidding expression told him he ought to keep that idea to himself.

"Should I send him straight in when he arrives?" she inquired in a crisp, all-business tone she'd probably acquired working for that fancy divorce lawyer in L.A.

Since she obviously considered herself equal to the task of sending his father anywhere, Taylor decided not to question how she intended to pull that off. "That would be fine."

"Will you need me to take notes?"

Taylor almost grinned at the thought of his father's reaction to having Zelda sit in on their private discussion. He decided not to press his luck. "I think I can handle it."

"You're the boss."

She said it so agreeably, Taylor couldn't quite figure out why he thought the tables in the office had been deftly turned and that Zelda Lane was definitely the one in charge.

The same thought struck him again later—along with astonishment and admiration—as he heard her cheerfully greet his father as if he were any other client dropping by for an appointment.

"Taylor's waiting for you," she said. "Go right on in and I'll bring along a cup of coffee. How would you like it? Black? Cream and sugar?"

Taylor's anxiety rose when he couldn't hear his father's reply. Had he had a heart attack at discovering that Zelda was working for his son? Surely he'd heard about that, though Taylor had skirted any mention of it himself. Perhaps he was busy strangling her, Taylor thought, and strode across his office, prepared to intercede.

He discovered his father staring at Zelda with openmouthed astonishment. He couldn't really blame him. She did look like a different woman in that trim, navy blue power suit with its expensive gold trim. She'd even taken time in the past half hour to twist her auburn hair into some sort of severe style he'd never seen her wear before.

Taylor took an immediate dislike to the prim style. He had an almost irresistible urge to yank out every one of the pins holding it until it tumbled free again into the sexy style he preferred. As for the suits, he was getting sick of those, as well. He liked her better in bright colors and slinky fabrics, material that clung and molded and tempted.

Still, he couldn't help admiring her for trying to create a professional image that even her most judgmental critic couldn't quarrel with. Unfortunately, Beau didn't seem too receptive to the changes.

"Dad?" Taylor said softly.

His father pivoted slowly in his direction. "Have you gone and lost your mind, son?" He didn't bother to lower his voice when he said it.

Taylor saw Zelda's hands clench, even though her expression remained unwaveringly calm. Anger and resentment cut into him at his father's deliberate rudeness.

"Why is this woman here?" his father demanded.

"She works for me, and I'm damned lucky to have her," Taylor said coldly, moving a protective step closer to the woman in question. "Now, did you want to discuss some business with me, or did you drop in to try and tell me how to run my office? If so, you can leave now."

Apparently his father heard the finality in his tone, because his shoulders sagged in defeat. "I'll never understand you, boy," he said wearily. "You'd think you'd have learned something after that lunatic wife of yours all but ruined you and your chances at being elected anything but dogcatcher in this state."

At the harsh mention of Maribeth, a cold fury washed through Taylor. "Dad, that's enough! I think maybe we'd better get together some other time. Better yet, maybe you ought to take your legal affairs over to a lawyer in Charleston. I'm sure you can find one there who'd meet your high moral standards. I'm sick to death of trying."

With the bitter words still hanging heavily in the air, Taylor whirled and went back into his office, slamming the door behind him. A moment later the outer door slammed shut, practically shaking the whole structure. Then, as he'd expected, Zelda was in the doorway.

"What was that all about?" she asked quietly.

"That was something that's been building up for a lifetime. I'm sorry you had to witness it."

"You hurt him, you know."

He regarded her wryly. "That's a twist, you feeling sorry for my father."

She shrugged. "Surprised the hell out of me, too. But the look in his eyes… Taylor, whatever he's done, it's only because he wanted what was best for you."

"You know how that road to hell got paved."

"With good intentions. Look, I've always been an easy target for Beau's frustration and, believe me, I haven't liked it, but I never doubted his love for you. Some people just don't recognize that sometimes loving means letting go, letting a person make his own mistakes."

Taylor shook his head impatiently. "Zelda, you're only the tip of the iceberg. My father's always wanted to control my life. He handpicked Maribeth for me. Now he blames me because the marriage didn't turn out the way he wanted it to. It wasn't my fault. It wasn't his fault. Hell, it probably wasn't even Maribeth's fault."

"What happened?"

"She died. I told you that."

"Taylor, I can see that there's more to it than that. Your father said the marriage ruined you and your chances at public office. Whatever happened, it's eating away at you."

"I don't see any point in talking about it," he insisted stubbornly. "It won't change anything."

Zelda stepped closer and propped herself on the edge of his desk so that their knees were touching. "Taylor."

She said it with such quiet insistence that he was forced to meet her gaze or admit that he was a cow-

ard. He refused to do that. He looked into those clear
turquoise eyes of hers and saw the need to understand,
the compassion that was available just for the asking.

"What happened?" she prodded.

The question hovered in the air, daring him to respond. Drawn by a force he couldn't ignore, Taylor
slowly stood and reached for her. It was an instinctive,
needy action, and he suspected he was going to be furious with himself a few minutes from now. He told
himself he didn't need the compassion or the under-
standing, but he wouldn't deny the need for Zelda. It
had always been a part of him, like the unruly curl of
his hair or the beating of his heart.

As he pulled her into the circle of his embrace, one
hand moved instinctively to her hair, seeking the pins
and withdrawing them one by one. As they dropped
to the floor, curls tumbled loose to skim her shoulders
and flow like silk over his fingers. Some mysterious,
seductive scent was released, as well, surrounding them.

"Your hair's so soft," he told her, his voice a husky
whisper. "Don't ever pin it up like that again."

"I wanted to look professional for your father."

"Not necessary." He heard the catch in her breath as
he skimmed her cheek with his fingers, reveled in the
quick little flutter of her pulse. "You could ditch the
prim little suits, too."

A flash of mischief sparked in her eyes. "Now?"
she said, reaching immediately for the top button of
her jacket.

A groan sprang loose from deep inside him. He'd
forgotten just how quick she was to respond to any sort
of dare. Or maybe he hadn't.

"Dear heaven, no," he protested a little too vehemently,

though a part of him prayed she wouldn't listen. She had always been able to tempt him beyond reason, to make his breath lodge in his throat and his pulse race even as he tried his very best to cling to sanity. She was doing it again.

"Just one button," she taunted, sliding one gold circle through its confining hole. The sedate fabric separated an indiscreet inch, just enough to tantalize, just enough to make his heart hammer with anticipation.

"Zelda." It was an undeniable moan, not the sort of warning anyone would have taken seriously, least of all a woman like Zelda.

Instead of reaching for another of her own buttons, though, she began to dabble with his. Eyes sparkling with devilment stayed locked with his. She slipped her fingers inside his shirt, her nails skimming his chest in a gesture he could see was meant to be deliberately provocative. His whole body ached with the effort of trying to hide his response. Some things, however, couldn't be hidden and Zelda knew, she *knew,* that it wouldn't take much and he would be lost. They'd be making love on top of his desk, on the floor of his office, maybe both, before they were done. He wondered a little breathlessly if she'd dare, if he had the will left to stop her.

"Zelda, anyone could walk in at any second," he protested.

She grinned unrepentantly. "Exciting, isn't it?"

As a matter of fact, it was, but he could see that admitting to that would not slow things down. The woman was a danger junkie. She was already fiddling with his belt buckle, an action that made his blood pump harder and faster than a new strike in a Texas oil field.

Finally, reluctantly, with one ragged, indrawn breath,

he reclaimed sanity the way an honorable, upright pillar of the community was supposed to. This wasn't the
time or the place. Nor was his hurting and their desire
any reason to break a long-standing vow to keep his life
on a steady, uneventful course. He'd had all the passion,
all the unexpectedness, he could stand for one lifetime.
Zelda promised more of both.

"I—I have a meeting," he said, struggling with the lie.

"Where?" she inquired with blatant disbelief. She
kept his calendar up to the minute with his appointments and he never, ever, slipped one in without telling her about it. It was an ingrained, orderly habit, and
he knew she knew it.

"Somewhere, anywhere," he muttered anyway, dis-
engaging himself from the embrace and grabbing his
jacket.

He practically bolted for the door, not daring to look
back. Someday he'd have to explain, but not now. Now,
if he stayed, explanations would be the last thing on
his mind. In fact, he doubted if either of them would
be doing any thinking at all. What they were feeling
could keep them occupied—pleasantly, dangerously
occupied—for days.

And it would be more wrong now than it had ever
been.

Chapter 10

Well, that was certainly fascinating, Zelda thought as she absentmindedly rebuttoned her jacket and straightened her skirt. For Taylor to lose control in the office, his feelings had to run a lot deeper than he was willing to admit. If it had been nothing more than lust, he probably would have fired her on the spot just to avoid further temptation.

The fact that he didn't return to the office for the rest of the day didn't particularly surprise her. He always had been one for sorting things out in private. If he considered succumbing to his emotions a weakness, then he'd go to any extreme to avoid having her witness another lapse. Witness? No. Instigate was more like it. She wondered how long he'd manage to stay away and bet herself it would be hours, rather than days.

The challenge of seeing to it that he lapsed quite a bit made her smile. In fact, it cheered her up so much that she bought another can of raspberry paint for the living room walls that she'd stripped of that dreary cabbage rose wallpaper over the weekend.

She had the stereo on full blast and was paint spattered from head to toe, when she sensed that she was no longer alone. In Los Angeles that awareness would have had her tumbling from atop the ladder in a panic. Now she merely glanced over her shoulder and grinned at her expected visitor.

"Hi, Taylor."

Mouth gaping, he was staring not at her, but the walls. "What the hell kind of color is this?"

"Raspberry. Isn't it wonderful?"

"That's not the word I would have chosen."

"Let me guess. Bright? Flamboyant?"

"How about blinding?"

"Wait until I get the new curtains up and re-cover the sofa. With a little white woodwork, it'll be warm and cozy."

"Warm and cozy?" he echoed skeptically. "Couldn't you have picked some subtle, muted shade that's a little easier on the eyes?"

"White, I suppose?"

"White, cream, gray."

She grinned at him. "Boring. By the way, I don't suppose you happened to notice that the outside is the same color."

"No kidding!"

"Nope. Sarah Lynn's reaction was a lot like yours. If this keeps up, I wouldn't be surprised to have the mayor institute a new ordinance restricting the exterior paint on all houses to white after this."

"Not altogether a bad idea," Taylor said with feeling.

"Look, have you had dinner? I was thinking maybe we ought to sit down and discuss what happened at work today."

"You mean your father's visit?" she said, being deliberately obtuse.

He scowled at her. "No. I think that pretty well spoke for itself. I meant what happened after that."

"When I tried to seduce you?"

For an instant Taylor looked unnerved, then he laughed. "Ah, Zelda, you never did bother pulling punches, did you?"

She shrugged from her perch on the ladder. It gave her a sense of security sitting above him. Maybe she should insist on holding all conversations with her at this vantage point. "Never saw much point to hedging, especially not with you. You could always read my mind, anyway."

"Maybe then. Not now."

She gave him a slow, lingering perusal, head to toe and back again. "Oh, really?"

He gave a rueful, tolerant shake of his head. "Okay, I know what you're thinking when you do that, but I don't know why."

She didn't take his bewilderment seriously. He knew. He just didn't want to admit it. "The usual reasons, I suppose," she said evasively.

"Which are?"

"Okay, let me spell it out for you. You're sexy. I want your body," she retorted lightly. Then, because he once again looked so thoroughly disconcerted by her directness, her expression sobered. "Some things never change, Taylor." She regarded him evenly. "Do they?"

His gaze locked with hers. For an instant the question appeared to have left him tongue-tied.

"No," he admitted finally and with great reluctance. "I guess they never do."

The admission hovered between them. Awareness hummed through the air. It took every last ounce of willpower Zelda possessed not to launch herself into his arms. But she was wise enough for once to see that Taylor was still struggling with some inner turmoil. She had to give him time to wrestle with it on his own.

At least through dinner.

"You still interested in dinner?" she said eventually. "I fixed some beef stew earlier. I'll share, if you'll help me paint."

"I'm wearing a suit," he said, as if that wasn't already obvious.

The gray pinstripes were quietly tasteful and becoming. That didn't stop her from wanting to strip him down to basics.

"You don't have to be," she taunted for the second time that day.

Taylor shook his head. "You never give up, do you?"

She nodded in agreement. "Not while there's breath in my body."

To her astonishment, Taylor shucked his jacket and shirt, an act that lacked the finesse of a Vegas stripper, but practically had her panting for more. Unfortunately, though, he stopped there.

"You'll ruin those pants," she warned, an undeniably hopeful note in her voice.

"It's an old suit," he retorted, shooting her a knowing look that made her blood heat. "Now give me a brush and let's get this finished. I'm starved."

Zelda was hungry, too, but beef stew was the last thing that appealed to her appetite. Why did it have to be this complex man with a will of iron who tantalized her? she wondered in dismay. There were successful, handsome, intelligent men in Los Angeles. Her boss's new stepfather, who adored meddling, was more than willing to play matchmaker. But no, she had to come back to a town she hated and a man she had every reason to despise to rediscover this jittery, head-over-heels feeling again. Sometimes fate was a damned nuisance.

"Do you think we could turn the stereo down a little?" Taylor asked eventually. "They can probably hear it in the next county."

She regarded him with a defiant tilt to her chin. "So what?"

Taylor opened his mouth, then clamped it shut again, apparently recognizing a challenge no matter how it was phrased. Whatever argument had been on the tip of his tongue, he kept to himself. Zelda winked at him. "That's more like it," she told him approvingly.

Taylor's expression underwent a slow transformation from indignation to something far more dangerous. He gestured to her, a provocative come-hither wave of his fingers. "Come down off that ladder."

Zelda was no slouch when it came to recognizing a dare, either. She shook her head, just to see how far Taylor was willing to go. "Uh-uh," she said piously. "I've got work to do. So do you."

"Now who's being stuffy, Ms. Lane? Remember this song?"

Zelda hadn't really been paying that much attention to which albums were blaring from the stereo. She just liked all that cheerful noise, that throbbing rhythm. Now she listened more closely and recognized a song that she and Taylor had once claimed as their own. It wasn't slow. It wasn't subtle. In fact, the provocative rhythm was as daring as their love had once been.

"Come on, sugar," he taunted with that lazy drawl that snaked along her spine like pure desire. "Let's see if you've still got those moves."

A deliberate challenge could only be resisted for so long. With her gaze locked with Taylor's, Zelda descended from the ladder. He reached for her hand the instant her feet hit the floor and spun her around. His hips swayed seductively. Hers matched the music's beat. His shoulders counterpointed the rhythm. Relaxing into the music, hers mimicked his. The moves were graceful and as natural as if they'd been practicing them every day of their lives. They circled the room, intent on capturing the music's boldly provocative essence.

Zelda could feel the rhythm deep inside her, its tug almost sexual, especially with Taylor's appreciative gaze lingering on the rise and fall of her breasts, the sensual movements of her hips. Without even touching, they turned the dance into something intimate, four minutes of pure heat that teased the senses and invited acts far more exciting.

When the song ended, they faced each other, breathless, exhilarated, and wanting the one thing neither of them dared. Zelda knew that it would take no more than one gesture—a hand extended, a single step—and they would be making love, turning that subtle, smoldering heat into a blazing fire from which there would be no turning back.

"We're playing with fire," Taylor said softly, as if he'd read her mind.

"Is there some reason we shouldn't?" she asked, her own voice husky with unspoken needs.

Taylor sighed. "I can think of dozens."

"Name one."

"I have a daughter."

"Who's not in this room."

"I have nothing to offer. I can't make you pretty promises. It would be just like before. We'd have this *fling,* get our emotions all tangled up, and then I'd end up hurting you."

"Are you so sure of that?" she said, defeated by his apparent certainty.

Taylor nodded, his eyes bleak. "It's what I do best," he said, reaching for his shirt and jacket.

He didn't stop to pull either of them on, just brushed a kiss across Zelda's forehead and walked out, leaving her alone again. And filled with yearning.

Not even that bright pink paint was a match for the depression that settled over her.

"Zelda, it's Caitlin. Remember?"

Zelda recognized not only the name, but the loneliness and wistful cry for attention in the child's tone. "Hi, sweetheart," she said, shifting the phone to her other ear so she could write down a message. "Did you want to talk to your father? He's out of the office right now."

"I wanted to talk to you," Caitlin said. "Did you forget we were going to go shopping?"

Zelda hadn't forgotten, but she had been putting it off. With everything between her and Taylor growing more awkward day by day thanks to the undeniable and powerful reawakening of their hormones, she hadn't wanted to complicate things even further by getting too close to his daughter.

"I've been so busy the last couple of weeks, I haven't been able to get a single minute free. I'm sorry."

"Oh." Caitlin's voice sank dispiritedly. "I guess if you're too busy, I could call Grandmother."

Of all the things Caitlin might have said, she'd managed to pick the one guaranteed to get Zelda's attention. "No," she said hurriedly, imagining another one of those proper little outfits. "A promise is a promise. Tomorrow's Saturday. Would that be a good day?"

"Are you sure there's still time to make a dress before next weekend? That's when my party is."

"That will be plenty of time. I'll call your headmistress as soon as we hang up and make the arrangements for tomorrow. I'll pick you up at nine so we'll have the whole day."

"You don't need to call," Caitlin said. "She's right here. She let me use her phone."

Zelda grinned. "Put her on, then. I'll see you in the morning."

After the arrangements were finalized and Zelda had hung up, she sat back and mentally congratulated Caitlin. Even at seven, she was a kid who knew exactly what she wanted and how to go about getting it. Maybe there was a lesson or two she could learn from the pint-size strategist.

At eight the next morning she grabbed her keys and headed for the door. Before she could reach it, someone knocked. Force of habit made her peek through the curtains to see who it was. Taylor stood on the porch wearing jeans, a blue oxford-cloth shirt open at the throat, and a khaki jacket. Trying to hide her astonishment, she opened the door.

"Good morning. What brings you by?"

"A command performance," he muttered dryly. "Caitlin was afraid you wouldn't find her school."

"I see. Did you explain to her about maps and directions?"

"In detail. Then she cried," he said. "I really hate it when she cries. Unfortunately, she knows it." He regarded Zelda helplessly. "Is that a genetic thing with females? Do you all just know automatically how to get your way with men?"

Zelda laughed at his genuine bewilderment. "Taylor, if that were true, I'd have landed you long ago." She hesitated thoughtfully. "Of course, I haven't considered tears."

"Don't," he pleaded. "Are you ready?"

"Oh, I'm ready," she said, reminding herself to buy Caitlin the fanciest material she could find, along with a double hot-fudge sundae. She owed her a lot more than that just for this first lesson alone.

Mostly hidden in a grove of ancient oaks, Caitlin's school sat high atop a hill overlooking a wide sweep of lawn that ended at the river's edge. Only a discreet sign at the front gate identified it as being a school rather than someone's home. Spanish moss hung from the live oaks that lined the winding driveway.

When they reached the circular drive in front of the main entrance Zelda had a clearer view of the school itself. Constructed of gray fieldstone, the building's additions looked as if they'd been haphazardly tacked on to make room for an ever-increasing student population. To Zelda it seemed reminiscent of pictures she'd seen of some British country school.

As if she'd been watching from the windows, Caitlin ran out to greet them. Before either her father or Zelda could step out of the car, Caitlin had flung herself into the back seat.

"Hi, Daddy. I missed you," she said, hugging him around the neck from behind.

"Apparently so," he said dryly. "I thought you and Zelda had planned to make this a girls' outing."

"It'll be more fun with you, though," Caitlin said. "Won't it, Zelda?"

Zelda glanced over her shoulder and winked. "Definitely more fun."

"Besides, Zelda doesn't know where the best malls are," Caitlin rationalized.

"And you do?" Taylor said.

"No, Daddy, that's why we need you."

"Oh. I thought I was just along to carry the shopping bags."

"That, too," Zelda said. "It's always good to have a big, strong man along to do the heavy labor, right, Caitlin?"

"Right."

He glanced up into the rearview mirror and regarded his daughter with mock ferocity. "You used to be such a sweet little girl."

"I'm still sweet, but I'm not a little girl," Caitlin replied indignantly. "I'm almost eight. And I want a grown-up dress, not some baby thing with ruffles. Okay?"

"I'll leave that in Zelda's capable hands," he said. He glanced over and studied the vintage dress she'd chosen to wear for the outing. "On the other hand, perhaps I should have let you crawl around in your grandmother's attic. She has lots of trunks up there filled with old dresses just like the one Zelda is wearing."

Caitlin scrambled up until she could peer over the back of the seat. "I think Zelda's dress is beautiful."

"Thank you. Your father obviously has a very traditional sense of fashion. Naturally for an occasion as important as your birthday, we want something original, something with a little flair."

"Something that will give my mother palpitations?" he suggested dryly.

Zelda grinned at him. "If at all possible."

He groaned. "How did I know that?"

In the end they compromised over a pattern for a dress that was both elegant and simple. Caitlin regarded the style with disdain until Zelda led her to the bolts of fabric and found the perfect shade of teal blue velvet. Caitlin touched it carefully, her eyes growing round.

"Oh, my," she whispered. "It's so soft. It's the same color as those ducks we saw last winter, isn't it, Daddy?"

"Exactly the same color." Taylor's expression turned gentle. "You will look beautiful in it," he promised. His gaze caught Zelda's. "So would you."

"Oh, yes," Caitlin said at once. "Make one for you just like mine."

A charming image of mother-daughter outfits flashed briefly in Zelda's mind, then she shook her head. She had no right. "I don't need a new dress. Besides, this material is outrageously expensive."

"My treat," Taylor said. "A thank-you gift for making Caitlin so happy."

Zelda fingered the material longingly. It was truly magnificent. "Maybe just enough for a skirt," she agreed finally, already envisioning the slender lines of it with a daring slit up the back.

When the purchase had been made, Caitlin led them to the mall's food court. "Ice cream," she announced.

"A balanced lunch, then ice cream," Taylor countered.

Zelda rolled her eyes. "Come on. This is a rare treat. There are no rules."

Taylor looked as if he weren't quite sure what to do without a set of dietary guidelines. He glanced around at the various options.

"Okay," he said finally, "you two go for broke. I think I'll have a grilled chicken sandwich."

Zelda planted herself in front of him. "Do you really want a grilled chicken sandwich or is that the only healthy thing you could identify?"

"Healthy habit," he admitted.

"Okay, now, close your eyes," she insisted. "Let all those decadent food choices flow through your mind. Think of this as a day at a carnival or a celebration. What would you really, really like if you couldn't hear your mother or your doctor whispering in your ear?"

He closed his eyes, apparently taking the game she'd suggested seriously. "Nachos," he confessed slowly. "A big plate of chips, covered with cheese and refried beans and sour cream and salsa."

"That's it," Zelda told him approvingly. "Now you sit right over there and I will bring that to you."

Taylor laughed. "You really don't need to wait on me. I can get it myself."

"But you won't. You'll have an attack of conscience halfway over there and come back with that grilled chicken sandwich. Worse, you'll find someplace that makes a salad and has diet dressing."

"You know me too well," he said, still laughing, looking more carefree than he had since the day she came back into town. "Maybe you're good for me, after all."

The surprising admission, made thoughtfully and with some obvious reluctance, was still enough to make Zelda's heart sing.

Minutes later she and Caitlin returned with trays

laden with nachos, pizza and ice cream. Taylor groaned. "We'll all wind up with clogged arteries."

"Not from one day's indulgence," Zelda insisted. "Now don't spoil this. Just enjoy."

His gaze met hers as she bit into the cheesy pizza. With her tongue she tried to catch a strand of errant mozzarella. His eyes deliberately followed every movement, locking onto her tongue in a way that made her pulse buck and made her forget all about food. Her imagination kicked in. She could have been eating sawdust.

Suddenly all she could think about was the rough texture of Taylor's skin, the salty taste of it against her tongue, the way it heated beneath her touch. When he brushed a finger across her lips to wipe away a dab of tomato sauce, she swallowed hard. When he slowly, deliberately, licked the sauce from his finger, she felt the tug of pure longing all the way to her toes. Dear heaven, it was like making love in public.

Dazed, she glanced around guiltily, her gaze finally settling on Caitlin, who was clearly so absorbed with her huge sundae that she was oblivious to whatever was going on between her father and Zelda. When she finally dared another look at Taylor, he, too, seemed innocently unaware of the havoc he had wreaked with her senses. He was busily piling a chip high with cheese and salsa.

Finally, just as he was about to put it into his mouth, he grinned at her. "Nothing like a little spice to liven things up, huh?"

Zelda figured if Taylor Matthews brought much more spice into her life without following through, she'd be limp as a dishrag.

Chapter 11

As the day wore on and Caitlin grew tired and cranky from too much excitement, Taylor watched in wonder as Zelda easily teased a smile back onto her face. From the instant they had met, it had been evident that the two were soulmates. He envied them that easy camaraderie.

In most ways Zelda's easy rapport with his daughter delighted him. That didn't stop him from worrying about what would happen when Zelda left Port William. He determinedly pushed the worry aside because by the end of their shopping expedition, Taylor saw a glimmer of the exuberant, lively child he'd dropped off at boarding school for the first time back in September. He would be eternally grateful that his child's natural liveliness had been restored.

Another thought kept sneaking in as he watched the pair of them, one he couldn't readily dismiss. He wondered if he'd misjudged Zelda all these years. She seemed to know instinctively all the things about parenting that bemused him. She was gentle and patient. She listened. Caitlin was visibly blossoming under all the attention. How could someone who lived selfishly and thoroughly in the moment without a thought for anything beyond that be so attuned to a child's needs? Unless, of course, there was more substance there than he'd been giving her credit for. Of course, it wouldn't be the first time in his life he'd been blind to the truth.

Whatever that truth was in this instance, he was pleased for Caitlin. He couldn't—he wouldn't—take this friendship away from her unnecessarily. She'd already lost too much in her young life.

But just how was he supposed to protect himself from the warmth that spread through him just being around the two of them? Zelda's teasing always included him. Her eyes sparkled like rare gems whenever she looked his way. And her laughter, which she shared unstintingly, eased an ache deep inside him.

As they left the mall, he found himself instinctively reaching for her hand, folding it in his own, marveling at how right it felt, even as the reaction scared the daylights out of him. He had vowed never again to be taken in by a woman's wiles, yet here he was, mesmerized. He had vowed always to let his head overrule his emotions, yet here he was, lost to sensation.

They drove back to Graystone School with the exhausted Caitlin wedged between them. Her head drooped, then came to rest on Zelda's shoulder. He watched a little enviously as she smoothed his daughter's hair from her cheeks, her fingers caressing the soft skin with evident wonder written on her face.

As if she sensed his gaze on her, she glanced over at him.

"You're so lucky, Taylor," she whispered with an unmistakable catch in her voice. Tears shimmered in her eyes. "It must be so wonderful to watch a child grow, to nurture her and know that a part of you will live on in her."

"I suppose," he said, wishing that he could feel the joy as readily as he could the fear. Though he couldn't say it aloud, certainly not with Caitlin nearby and merely drowsing, he was terrified to think that it was not just his genes in his daughter, but Maribeth's. What if her careless nature was what Caitlin had inherited? What if his daughter lived too short a life because she, too, thrived on danger?

And what, he finally asked himself, what if Zelda was ultimately destroyed because of the same addiction to reckless acts? He wasn't sure he could bear another such loss. Wasn't that the bottom line that explained his holding back when he wanted nothing more than to have her back in his bed and in his life?

Zelda regarded him intently, as if she could sense his unspoken reservations without possibly being able to guess the cause. "Taylor?" she said questioningly.

He shook his head, mustering a faint grin. "Don't mind me. Sometimes I get so caught up in what-ifs, I forget to live in the here and now."

"I don't understand."

"There's no reason you should," he said. To avoid further explanation, he directed his full attention to the road ahead. When they arrived at Graystone, he carried Caitlin inside, hoping that by the time he got back to the car, Zelda would have forgotten all about his enigmatic remarks.

Naturally, though, she hadn't. The minute he got behind the wheel, she regarded him evenly. "Suppose you tell me whatever it was you were trying so hard not to say a few minutes ago."

"I don't know what you mean."

"Damn it, Taylor, ever since I got back to town you and everybody else have been hinting that there's some deep, dark secret about your marriage. Now I get the feeling that it has something to do with your daughter, maybe even explains why you've shipped her off to boarding school when a kid her age needs to be at home where she's loved."

A protective anger, already simmering just below the surface, boiled over. "Don't you dare criticize the way I've chosen to raise my daughter," he snapped, wondering if she realized she was starting an argument he'd already had a dozen times with his parents and himself. "You don't know anything about it."

"I know that she's lost and lonely. I know that she adores you and that she doesn't understand why you don't love her."

He simply stared at her, shocked and angered by the unfair accusation. "How can you say I don't love her?" he retorted in a low, amazingly even voice. A deadly calm stole over him, the calm that preceded a storm, he knew from experience.

Zelda laid a hand on his arm. "I'm not saying it. I'm saying it's what Caitlin thinks."

The explanation did nothing to soothe his desire to lash out. "You've seen her twice. What makes you think you know anything at all about what she thinks?"

"Because when I look into her eyes, I see myself at that age," she said, her voice suddenly flat and emotionless, her eyes haunted. "I see the same questions, the same longing, the same hurt. I know what it's like to have one parent you want more than anything to please, a parent who'll never think you're good enough. I know what it's like to have another parent who loves you, but who is distant and withdrawn, a laughingstock."

She lifted her gaze to his. A lone tear spilled down her cheek and something inside him wrenched at the sight.

"It hurts, Taylor," she whispered. "Even now, years later, just thinking about the loneliness in that house makes my heart ache. Caitlin deserves better than that."

His anger disintegrated at once. With fingers that trembled, he brushed away the tear. "Oh, sugar, that was a long time ago. You survived. You turned out just fine."

"Did I? Then why did I run away? Why did I spend ten years hiding out in Los Angeles, where I wouldn't have to deal with any of the pain? Why couldn't I even come back for my own mother's funeral?"

"You're here now. I think she knew you'd come."

"Eventually," she replied bitterly. "She saw to that."

"Maybe because she always knew how badly you needed to come home and find peace."

Zelda's gaze shot to his and the hopeful glint in her eyes nearly staggered him.

"Do you think that was why she wrote the will the way she did?" she demanded. "Do you think she understood me better than I realized?"

"You're here, aren't you? Are you at peace with the memories?"

Zelda seemed to consider the question thoughtfully,

before slowly nodding. "Yes," she said finally, a smile breaking through. "You know, I really am. Sometime in the past weeks I've accepted the fact that my father was who he was. My mother and I could have turned cartwheels and it wouldn't have changed anything. I'm sad for her, sad that he destroyed her life, but I don't hate him for it anymore. And I won't allow him to continue affecting my choices from beyond the grave."

"So coming back hasn't been all bad, has it?" he said.

An impish gleam suddenly sparked in her eyes, putting Taylor immediately on alert.

"Definitely not all bad. Of course," she said slyly, "I think she had another motive in mind all along, too."

Taylor responded to that spark of mischief. "Oh, and what was that?"

She opened her mouth to reply, then shook her head. "Nope. I think I'll keep that one to myself, at least until I see how it turns out." Her gaze narrowed. "You've managed to get me off track, Taylor Matthews, but now it's your turn. Just what is it about having Caitlin at home that worries you so?"

"I can't spend enough time with her," he evaded.

"She's in school all day. Your office is part of the house, so it won't be like she's coming home to an empty place. If that's really a problem, you could afford to hire a housekeeper."

"She needs discipline."

The statement was greeted with obvious puzzlement. "She's the most well-behaved child I know."

Taylor lost patience. "Look, it's just not a good idea, okay. Drop it."

His sharp tone silenced her for the rest of the ride back

A Daring Vow

to Port William. But Taylor knew Zelda well enough by now to realize that the discussion was far from over.

The following Saturday Zelda was halfway out on a branch of an oak tree, with Caitlin scrambling along just ahead of her, when she heard Taylor's cry of panic. Or was it outrage? She couldn't quite tell from her perch high above the ground. A glance down into stormy gray eyes solved it. He was furious.

"What's wrong?" she called down.

"Have you lost your mind?" he muttered indignantly, hovering beneath them as if he were just waiting for one of them to drop into his arms.

Zelda had a feeling if she were the one crashing down, he just might let her go. "Come on up," she suggested. "You used to be able to beat me to the top."

"I was younger then and didn't have a lick of sense." He groaned. "Caitlin, honey, come on down."

Caitlin's chin rose mutinously. "No. You can see everywhere from up here. Zelda says you did this all the time when you were my age."

"I was a boy. Boys climbed trees. Little girls…"

"Zelda climbed, too."

"That doesn't make it right," he snapped.

Zelda could see that the adventure she'd promised Caitlin wasn't working out quite the way they'd planned it. If she didn't get her safely out of this tree this instant, Taylor was going to ruin her birthday by confining her to her room.

"We'll be right down," she promised. "Just let me show her where you carved our initials in the trunk."

"Carved our initials?" Taylor repeated weakly. "Zelda, how do you even know this is the same tree?"

"I wouldn't forget something like that," she retorted indignantly. She reached up and felt along the bark until she came to the ragged heart. She grinned triumphantly. "See, they're right here."

"I want to see," Caitlin insisted, inching past Zelda. She pulled herself upright and lovingly traced the initials inside the heart. "How old were you when you did this, Daddy?"

"Older than you. Now get down from there. And be careful."

"Oh, Daddy," Caitlin muttered with obvious disgust. With an obviously inherited agility and intrepid spirit, she scampered down.

"Into the house," Taylor ordered. "We'll discuss this in a minute."

Undaunted, Caitlin grinned up at Zelda. "See you."

"See you," Zelda echoed.

"Come on down," Taylor said when his daughter was out of sight. "Face the music."

Zelda shook her head and leaned back against the tree trunk. "I don't think so. The view from up here is terrific."

A smile tugged at Taylor's lips, ruining his scowl. "It's not bad from down here," he taunted, gazing up toward her bottom. "Zelda, you just scared ten years off of my life."

"Why?" she asked, genuinely confused.

"I don't think Caitlin's ever been up in a tree before."

"Then it was past time she tried it."

"She could have fallen and broken her neck."

"And she could break a leg going down the stairs at school," Zelda replied reasonably.

"Not if she's careful."

"Have you ever seen an eight-year-old be careful on the stairs or anywhere else? Taylor, you can't protect her from everything."

"But I can keep the odds in her favor."

"By keeping her out of trees?"

"Yes, damn it. I won't have her taking risks. Now will you please get down from there? I'm getting a crick in my neck trying to talk to you."

"Then come on up."

"Zelda!"

"You want to talk, I'm available, but I'm not budging."

"You are the most stubborn—" he grumbled as he grabbed onto the tree's lowest branch and hauled himself up "—most impossible woman it has ever been my misfortune to know."

"But who else could get you to climb a tree?" she countered.

"Not many would even want me to."

"Boring, the whole lot of them."

"There's a lot to be said for boring," he told her, his tone far more serious than the teasing conversation warranted.

"Not much that I can think of," she retorted, watching his face closely in an attempt to judge his reaction.

"Zelda, people get killed taking risks," he said, his tone angry.

"Some of them do," she said slowly, beginning to get an idea of what was behind all the changes she'd seen in him since her return. Her voice dropped a level. "Was Maribeth one of them?"

His expression bleak, he avoided her gaze. "Yes," he admitted eventually. "She drove like a maniac, all the time, even when she was drunk. Which," he added, "was more often than not."

"So she died taking a stupid, unnecessary risk," Zelda whispered, reaching for Taylor's hand. "You can't blame yourself for that. And you can't assume that the rest of us will be so careless."

"But you are. You always have been. And Caitlin is showing all the signs of being the same way."

Zelda felt as if she'd been punched in the stomach. "That's why you sent her away, isn't it? That's why you're so worried about her being disciplined?"

He nodded. "I couldn't bear it if anything happened to her."

Zelda raised his hand to her lips and kissed his knuckles, knuckles scarred by a dozen childish misadventures, most of them involving her. She understood him now, understood the anguish that guided him. What she didn't know, couldn't even begin to fathom, was how to prove to him that life never, ever, came with guarantees, no matter how careful a person was to follow all the rules.

Zelda had had no idea that ten eight-year-old girls could make so much noise. Otherwise she might not have encouraged Taylor to give them the run of the house.

"How much mischief can they possibly get into?" she'd said only minutes before every single door upstairs had slammed shut in succession. The crashes had been interspersed with the thundering of little patent-leather-shoed feet.

"What are they doing?" Taylor inquired, regarding her as if any disasters were all her fault.

"Playing, most likely."

"Playing what? War?"

That would have been Zelda's guess, but she wasn't about to admit it. "Wine?" she suggested. "It'll relax you."

Taylor shook his head. "Something tells me I need to be fully alert for whatever's about to come our way."

"Think of it this way. Caitlin is having a birthday party she'll never forget."

"That makes two of us," he muttered with heartfelt conviction.

"There, there," she consoled. "Let's get the cake and ice cream ready. At least that will get them down here where we can keep an eye on them."

"Good idea. I'll scoop. You carry. When it's on the table, yell upstairs and then stand back out of the way."

Not twenty minutes later, ten girls were sitting demurely at the dining room table. Zelda tried not to notice that the sleeve of one child's dress was ripped, or that another's hair bow was slipping dangerously. She even managed to ignore the fact that half of them were no longer wearing shoes or socks. It was more difficult to pretend not to see that all of them had on more eye makeup than a Hollywood Boulevard hooker. Taylor stared at them, clearly dazed.

He latched onto her arm and dragged her into the kitchen. "What am I supposed to tell their parents?"

"Some of them are staying here. We'll have time to clean them up. As for the rest, leave any telling to them. They'll be so busy talking about what a wonderful time they had, maybe their parents won't even notice the rest."

Taylor regarded her skeptically. "I think you're being overly optimistic." As if to provide backup for his claim, the front door opened and Geraldine and Beau Matthews swept in. Zelda's heart sank. There was no chance *they* wouldn't notice that things had gotten just ever-so-slightly out of control.

Ignoring Zelda, they headed straight for the dining room and practically skidded to a horrified stop.

"Grandma," Caitlin squealed, bouncing down from her chair and running to throw her arms around her grandmother's waist. To Geraldine Matthews's credit, she managed to cover her dismay at the prospect of having pink blusher and peach lipstick smeared down the front of her dress.

"Hi, darling. Happy birthday! Are you having a good time?"

Caitlin looked up, displaying mascaraed lashes and a significant amount of Zelda's blue eye shadow. "The best time I've ever had. Thanks for the cake. I ate three roses. We've got ice cream, too."

"Strawberry and chocolate, I'll bet," her grandmother said.

It was an easy guess, given the streaks down the front of Caitlin's beautiful velvet dress.

"Do you and Granddaddy want some?" Caitlin asked.

"Maybe later. You can save us a piece. We just wanted to stop by with your present."

Caitlin looked from one to the other with obvious puzzlement. Zelda shared her confusion. Neither grandparent was carrying a thing.

"Outside," Beau said, as if he'd just then recovered the power of speech and was afraid to waste words.

Caitlin's eyes widened. "You got me a pony, didn't you?" she said, bouncing excitedly. "I thought you forgot."

"We'd never forget our promises to you, pumpkin,"

Beau said, shooting a warning look in Taylor's direction. "The filly's a beauty, if I do say so myself."

As Caitlin ran outside with her grandparents, her friends raced after them, leaving cake and melting ice cream behind. Zelda kept her eyes on Taylor. There was no mistaking the anguish written on his face, or the barely controlled fury.

"You didn't want her to have a pony, did you?"

"No, and they knew that. We discussed it again just last week."

"But she's so happy," Zelda pointed out.

"Well, of course, she is," he retorted impatiently. "What little girl wouldn't be ecstatic to have her own horse? That's not the issue."

"What is?"

"She's not old enough to ride. She could get hurt. And they knew exactly how strongly I felt about that," he said, striding toward the door.

His intentions were all too clear. Zelda stepped into his path. "Please," she said. "Don't spoil this for her. Or for them, for that matter. They just did it to please her, not to defy you."

"I'm not so sure about that," he said dryly. "What am I supposed to do? Go against everything I feel as a concerned parent just to keep the peace?"

"For this one day," she said. "Let Caitlin be thrilled. There will be time enough tomorrow to set all the rules and regulations you want to about when she can ride and how much supervision she has to have."

"What about just taking the damned horse back?"

"Is that really what you want to do? Or do you just want to make sure that she acts responsibly?"

He finally sighed heavily. "I just want to keep my child safe."

Zelda wound her arms around his waist and kissed the deep furrow in his brow. "There's more than one way to do that, Taylor. Caution is not the same as denial."

He went absolutely still as he pondered what she'd said. Zelda could feel his heartbeat, steady and sure.

"Has anyone ever told you that you're a very wise woman?" he said finally.

"Not in this town."

A hint of amusement sparked in his eyes, along with something else. "I can think of some other activities to which that caution-denial adage might apply."

Zelda's pulse skipped a beat. "And what might those be?"

"Stick around after we get rid of these little hellions and I just might show you."

Chapter 12

An entire night with four little girls in the house and Zelda down the hall in the guest room tested Taylor's willpower, to say nothing of his hearing and his patience.

"They never slept," he grumbled to Zelda over coffee at 7:00 a.m. "Not for one single minute."

"How do you know that?" she asked, yawning herself, but trying to hide it from him.

Suddenly he realized this was the first time he and Zelda had spent an entire night under the same roof. That set off a whole new round of fascinating speculation.

He decided he liked sitting across a breakfast table from her when she was still a little mussed, her face free of makeup, her clothes tugged on haphazardly—jeans and a T-shirt and not much else as near as he could tell. Her feet, propped on another chair, were bare, her toenails painted a shocking red.

With a sense of resignation, he realized that all he could think about anymore was stripping away the clothes, taking her back to bed and making love to her all morning long. Slow, leisurely love-making. His body responded just thinking about it.

"Taylor!"

He blinked. "Sorry. What?"

"I asked how you knew the girls were up all night."

"Because they kept me awake."

She sipped her coffee and regarded him skeptically over the rim of the cup. "*They* kept you awake," she repeated, casting a knowing look at him.

"Well, of course," he grumbled, refusing to admit that it was Zelda's presence—so near, yet so unattainable—that had kept him tossing and turning. His vehement comment didn't seem to fool her, though. Amusement was dancing in her eyes.

"Don't mess with me," he warned.

"I wouldn't dream of it," she said innocently. "Not while there are children in the house."

"That is not what I meant."

"Oh?" she said with that smug expression back on her face.

"I suppose you slept all night."

"Like a baby."

"Humph!"

"Of course, it did occur to me once or twice that I would have been getting a lot less sleep if I'd been a couple of rooms down the hall."

A satisfied smile spread across his face. "So, the truth comes out at last."

"Yeah, those kids sounded as if they were having a wonderful time."

Taylor groaned. "Very funny."

"What's on the agenda for today?"

"I don't suppose I could convince them all we should take naps until, say, midafternoon?"

"Not likely. My guess is that they're all going to want to go over to your parents' house so they can ride Daisy. I'm surprised Caitlin didn't beg to take the horse upstairs with her last night, just so she could remind herself she was real."

"Actually she tried for keeping her in the backyard. I said no." Taylor drained the rest of the coffee and wished desperately that he had some aspirin nearby. Just thinking about that horse made his blood run cold and his head pound.

"But you will take her out there today," Zelda prodded.

"Not a chance in hell," he said flatly. "And first thing tomorrow I am going to have a talk with my father. If he wants to keep the horse, that's up to him, but I won't have Caitlin over there risking her neck."

"Now, Taylor," she said quietly, "you can't disappoint Caitlin and her friends."

"Why is that? Who's in charge around here, anyway?"

"You are," she said dutifully.

He could tell at once she didn't mean it.

"And I know you love Caitlin and only want what's best for her, just as your father always wanted what was best for you."

"Low blow," he muttered, glaring at her.

She watched him expectantly, just waiting to see if she'd scored a direct hit, no doubt. She had.

"Maybe it would be okay if we went over so they could feed the horse," he conceded finally.

"Maybe ride her around the paddock with you leading the horse?" she suggested.

He threw up his hands in a gesture of resignation. "Okay, okay. Damn it, you're worse than Caitlin."

She shook her head. "I'm just trying to save you from all those tears."

He regarded her malevolently. "Right. I'm going to take a shower."

"Good. A nice, cold, reviving one, I hope. You'll definitely need all your wits about you to get through the rest of the day."

"You know, you could be replaced," he muttered as he left the kitchen.

"I dare you to try," she called after him, her tone too blasted cheerful.

"Don't tempt me," he shot back, determined, just this once, to have the last word.

The horse seemed awfully big. Though Beau assured him the filly was gentle as a lamb, Taylor was absolutely certain there was a mean glint in the animal's eyes. He glared over at Zelda for talking him into this peacemaking trip out to his parents' house.

It was too late now to back out, though. With Zelda instructing them, four little girls were holding out their hands, palms flat, a chunk of carrot in the center. Taylor was certain the horse was going to chomp down on more than the carrot at any second. He observed with his heart in his throat.

"Can we ride her?" Caitlin said, approaching him, her expression pleading. "Please, Daddy?"

"Well, of course you can, sweet pea," Beau said before

Taylor could open his mouth. "Why else would I buy you a horse, if I didn't intend to teach you to ride?"

Taylor gritted his teeth. "Once around the paddock," he said reluctantly. "Granddaddy will walk you."

"All of us?" Caitlin asked.

"You can take turns," Taylor agreed.

Zelda, who'd kept her distance from his father and mostly from Taylor, walked over to stand beside him as his father boosted Caitlin into the saddle. The intrepid child never even glanced down at the ground. He supposed her total lack of fear should please him, but it did just the opposite. It was just more evidence that Caitlin was going to have to be watched like a hawk if she was going to grow up in one piece.

"Relax," Zelda whispered, sliding her hand along his spine until it came to rest at the small of his back, right at the edge of his belt.

If she'd meant to distract him, he had to admit she was doing a pretty decent job of it. Even with his gaze riveted on his daughter, his body was completely aware of the woman at his side.

"You're pressing your luck, sugar," he warned lightly, his gaze never wavering from Caitlin who'd reached the far side of the paddock. She looked over and waved at him, her expression filled with excitement. Taylor managed a tight smile and an unenthusiastic wave.

Zelda's hand crept even lower, though her own gaze was directed toward Caitlin, as well. She was finally relinquishing Daisy to one of her friends. He breathed a sigh of relief, even though he knew the morning was long from over.

"One more inch and you are going to be in a heap of trouble," he advised, suddenly feeling more cheerful.

"What kind of trouble?" she inquired in a tone that was all innocent curiosity. Her expression was pure mischief.

Taylor began to wonder if he was going to get more cooperation than he'd bargained for, after all. How would he cope with a willing Zelda, especially when he wasn't so sure any longer that his intentions, like hers, were only to tease?

"Why don't we go for a stroll and I'll show you?" he suggested anyway, seizing her hand and pulling her in the direction of the old barn that hadn't been used as far back as Taylor could remember. Now, in honor of Caitlin's horse, it had a new coat of paint and, with any luck, a freshly stocked hayloft.

Suddenly Zelda looked just a trifle uncertain, just as he'd anticipated she would. He was almost disappointed. He couldn't resist taunting her a little more. He was playing with fire and he knew it, but it suddenly seemed like an impossible-to-resist game.

"What's the matter?" he inquired. "You're not turning cautious on me, are you?"

She shot a worried look in Beau's direction. "Your parents..."

"My mother's still at church. My father has four little girls to walk around that paddock, several more times if that glint of determination in Caitlin's eyes is any indication."

"I thought you were worried about that."

He shrugged. "You told me everything would be just fine. I've decided to believe you."

Zelda's gaze narrowed suspiciously. "Taylor, what are you up to?"

"Me? You're the one with the roving hands."

"True, but I was just...you know..."

"Trying to distract me?"

"Exactly."

"It worked," he said softly. His gaze lingered on her lips, then slowly drifted down. "It worked very, very well, in fact. Now, come along. You were once rather fond of haylofts, as I recall."

"I was eighteen at the time," she reminded him dryly. "And we got caught."

He winked at her. "And that was the best part, wasn't it?"

She seemed to struggle a bit with her conscience over that one. "Well, yes," she admitted finally.

"Then what's the problem?"

"Old man Highsmith used that shotgun to warn us. Beau'd probably aim it straight at my backside."

"So you're scared," he taunted.

"Not scared," she denied. "Just prudent."

"A fine distinction."

"But an important one." She glanced up at him. "Of course, if you were willing to make it worth my while…"

Taylor's mouth gaped. "You want me to pay you?"

"Not exactly. I want you to take me riding."

"Riding?"

"On Caitlin's horse."

"I'd have to get it away from her first."

"Last I looked, the kids were all heading to the pool. By the way, have I mentioned that I think an indoor pool is totally decadent?"

"No, you hadn't mentioned that," Taylor said, still bemused by her unexpected determination to go horseback riding. She seemed to have developed the obsession rather suddenly. Obviously she was better at this game of bait-and-switch than he was.

"How come you never told me about it before? You don't suppose we could sneak in here some night and go skinny-dipping in that pool?"

He regarded her incredulously as laughter bubbled up. "And you think making it in the barn would be risky? Skinny-dipping in my parents' pool would be suicide. That's why I never told you about it."

She winked at him. "Sounds like fun, though, doesn't it?"

Taylor would not admit that it did, not if he was held down and tortured. Okay, so it wouldn't be the first time they'd done it, but they'd been kids then. Respected attorneys did not sneak around skinny-dipping anywhere, much less where they were almost guaranteed of getting caught. An image of Zelda, all slick with water and bare from head to toe, slammed into his head. That image tested his resolve something fierce.

"I think where we both belong this morning is church, confessing like crazy," he muttered.

"Taylor, we are not Catholic," Zelda reminded him. "And so far, I'd like to point out, we haven't committed any sins. Not lately, anyway."

"That's what you think," he retorted. "Let's go ride the damned horse before I agree to do something really insane." He wasn't sure, but he thought he saw Zelda smirk just a little as he turned away. It was all he could do to keep from laughing with sheer exhilaration. She had managed to turn the tables on him once again.

They found the new filly still in the paddock, carefully brushed, her tack removed and placed nearby.

"That's exactly what I was talking about," Zelda said. "Your father has already given them a lesson in responsibility. If they want to ride, then they also have to care for the horse."

"You've made your point," he commented dryly. "Don't beat it to death."

"Yes, boss."

"You only say that when you're trying to irritate me."

"Works, too, doesn't it?"

Chuckling despite himself, Taylor saddled the horse and swung himself up into the saddle. Zelda stepped on a fence rail, then mounted behind him.

"Once around the paddock?" he suggested.

"You have to be kidding. Down to the river."

Her arms circled his waist and she leaned against his back. The soft press of her breasts almost gave him a heart attack. "Comfortable?" he inquired dryly.

"Very."

He set off at a sedate pace. After a few minutes, even with Zelda nestled provocatively against him, he began to relax and enjoy the cool, sunny morning. He filled his lungs with pine-scented air and realized how much he'd missed spending time out-doors. He hadn't even been on a golf course in months, and this part of South Carolina was filled with championship-caliber greens.

"Taylor?"

"Mmm."

"I feel like I'm taking a pony ride at a carnival," she said with an unmistakable sniff of derision.

"Meaning, I suppose, that you'd like to go a little faster."

"If you wouldn't mind. I want to feel the wind rushing through my hair."

"You're wearing one of my old baseball caps," he pointed out.

She punched him playfully in the ribs. "Do you have to take everything so literally?"

"I'm a lawyer. That's what we do."

"Just for today, couldn't you be a wild adventurer? Maybe even a cowboy chasing a cattle rustler?"

"Sugar, I have an active imagination, but I doubt it stretches that far. You create the scenario. I'll pick up the pace."

He nudged the horse into a trot, then a gallop. He had to admit it was more exhilarating.

"Better," Zelda shouted, her voice almost lost in the wind.

Taylor suddenly realized that he felt more alive than he had in years. He was probably going to be sore as the dickens tomorrow and he had a long day in court, but it was worth it to hear Zelda's laughter, to feel this rush of pure adrenaline.

They crested the top of a hill, and the river lay spread below them, its banks blanketed with colorful leaves and pine needles. The setting was peaceful and serene and private.

Taylor was all too aware that Zelda's hands were no longer on his waist, but had drifted to rest on his thighs. His muscles tightened in response. His pulse quickened. He felt as if he'd been aroused for days, as if the need to make love to Zelda had finally overcome every ounce of logic, every reservation. All that verbal teasing had obviously planted some very dangerous notions in his head. And elsewhere.

"Stop," Zelda pleaded now, her voice faintly breathless. Her touch grew bolder, more daring, inflaming his need for her. Caution was looking less and less attractive.

"Not a good idea," Taylor said dutifully, though he did

slow the horse to a leisurely pace and tried not to gasp as deft fingers slid over him.

"Actually, it was your idea," she reminded him. "First, last night. Then just a few minutes ago back at the barn."

"Timing is everything. The kids were still there last night. I figured we were safe. You turned me down at the barn, just like I knew you would."

"I've changed my mind," she said, her breath fanning his neck.

Suddenly he felt the touch of her tongue and almost bolted from the saddle. "Zelda, you're not playing fair."

"Nope," she agreed, scattering little kisses over whatever bare flesh she could get to.

Taylor went absolutely still and tried to will himself not to respond. He wanted her so badly right this second he was afraid he'd explode. Wanting her so desperately sent doubts ricocheting through him. He'd vowed never to want anything or anyone this much again.

It would be one thing for them to share a quick roll in the hay, literally or figuratively. It would be quite another to make love, to linger and savor, to touch with joyous abandon, to open up his heart. He was more afraid of that than he ever had been of anything, and that was exactly what would happen if he and Zelda left this horse and allowed their instincts to take over. He would lose control. He would risk yet another loss, more anguish.

He shifted slightly in the saddle and gazed back at her, saw the bright anticipation shining in her eyes, the undeniable yearning that matched his own. Slowly he shook his head. "I can't."

"Can't, or won't?"

"It doesn't really matter, does it? It's too big a risk."

He saw the light in her eyes dim, the proud jut of her chin. "I won't pressure you again," she said stoically.

Her refusal to argue surprised him, maybe even disappointed him. But he could hardly blame her. How many rejections could she be expected to tolerate and still bounce back?

"I think we'd better be getting back," she said, while he struggled with cold honor versus hot need.

Honor, which suddenly tasted an awful lot like fear, won. He turned Daisy around and headed home, aching in more ways than one.

"Zelda?" he said eventually.

"What?" she said impatiently.

"I'm sorry."

She shrugged. "It was a calculated risk. I lost."

No, Taylor thought to himself. He was the one who had lost. He had lost her for the second time in his life. Pain cut through him like a knife.

He urged Daisy into a trot. Then suddenly, to his astonishment, he felt Zelda knee the horse, sending the filly into an all-out gallop. His hands tightened instinctively on the reins, exactly the wrong thing to do. Terrified and confused, the horse bolted on a dangerous course through the woods.

When she raced head-on for a low branch, Taylor saw it in time and ducked, shouting a warning at Zelda in the same instant. Too late! He heard the sickening *thwack* of the limb hitting her, felt her arms slacken around his waist, and then she was sliding. He tried to cling to her, but realized it was no use. Turning as best he could in the saddle, he hooked an arm around her waist, freed his feet from the stirrups and tumbled to the ground, trying desperately to protect Zelda as they landed.

The fall sent a sharp pain shooting down his leg. His butt was likely to be black and blue, but it was Zelda who concerned him. Her eyes were closed. A huge lump was already forming on her forehead. He pressed his finger to the pulse in her neck and was somewhat reassured when he found it strong and steady.

He stroked her forehead, avoiding that nasty lump. "Come on, sugar, wake up," he murmured. With his heart hammering with anxiety, he touched his lips to hers, then gave a rueful smile. Did he think he was Prince Charming and this was Sleeping Beauty, for God's sakes? The woman could be suffering from a concussion.

"Come on, sugar," he murmured again. Again, because he couldn't resist, he kissed her cheeks, then her lips, light, tender kisses meant to tease her back to consciousness.

Suddenly her eyelids fluttered.

"That's it," he encouraged. "Wake up."

A vague smile drifted across her face. "Thought you weren't going to do this," she said groggily.

"Do what?"

"Make love to me."

"I'm not," he said, but with far less certainty than he had only minutes before.

She sighed. "Too bad."

"Yeah," he said ruefully. "Too bad."

More confident now that she was basically okay, he lifted her into his arms and carried her back to the house. Taylor saw his father glance outside, catch sight of them, and come racing out of the house.

"What the devil's that fool woman gone and done now?"

"That horse you bought spooked," Taylor snapped back furiously. "Zelda slammed into a tree branch. I knew something like this would happen. Don't just stand there. Call the damned doctor."

Ignoring his father's stunned expression, Taylor strode inside and took Zelda straight upstairs to his old room and settled her under the covers. An instant later his mother hurried in.

"I've brought some cool water and towels. Let me just put one on her forehead. It might help with the swelling."

"I'll do it," Taylor said, brushing aside the assistance. Zelda was his responsibility. The accident could have been prevented if only he hadn't given in and taken her on that ride in the first place. Once again he'd failed to protect someone in his life.

He dipped the towel in the water, wrung it out, then pressed it gently to Zelda's forehead. "Where's the doctor?" he demanded.

His mother squeezed his shoulder reassuringly. "Sweetheart, it's only been a couple of minutes."

Minutes? It felt like an eternity. "Why isn't she awake? She was for an instant."

"Seems to me that's a good sign."

He settled on the edge of the bed next to Zelda and held tightly to her hand. Memories of those last hours in Maribeth's hospital room crowded in, filling him with panic.

"I can't lose her," he whispered, barely aware that he'd spoken aloud until he saw the look of shock, then something akin to resignation in his mother's eyes.

"You've always loved her, haven't you?" she said softly.

Taylor couldn't deal with all the ragged, raw emotions tumbling through him. Nor could he make the admission his mother was demanding. He turned back to Zelda, his hand against her cheek.

And then he prayed.

Chapter 13

Zelda felt like Sleeping Beauty, coming to in a strange place with a handsome man hovering over her. Taylor didn't look intrigued, though. He looked worried.

"What's wrong?" she whispered, wondering why her head hurt like the very devil.

"You had a run-in with a tree limb. You lost."

She touched her forehead and winced. "I lost, all right. Let me guess. A concussion."

"You seem familiar with the symptoms. Why do I suspect this isn't the first one you've had?"

"Did you forget the night we fell off Miriam Winston's roof trying to play Santa and his reindeer for her kids?"

Taylor thought back and recalled the incident all too vividly. A well-intentioned good deed gone awry. But Miriam's kids had been thrilled, she'd told them, just as the doctor came to haul them off to a hospital, where their irate parents had shouted blame back and forth.

"I remember," he told her.

"So how bad is it this time?"

"Mild, according to the doctor, but he wants you in the hospital overnight for observation."

"Where am I now?"

"In my old bedroom."

She looked around, instantly fascinated by the mementos scattered around. She managed a wobbly grin. "In your bed at last," she murmured. "Too bad I can't do anything about it."

"Yeah, too bad."

"Your parents must be thrilled. Why don't we take the doctor up on his offer and get on over to the hospital?"

"You're not budging. I told him we'd watch you all night."

"Don't you have to take Caitlin and her friends back to school?" she asked, not liking the idea of being left alone here with Beau and Geraldine Matthews, who were no doubt furious to find themselves saddled with her.

"Dad's taking the other girls back now. Caitlin refused to go. She insisted on staying right here until she sees for herself that you're okay. Threw a hellacious tantrum." He shook his head. "I can't imagine how she got to be so stubborn."

Zelda grinned. "Right."

Just then the door creaked open. Caitlin peeked around it, her face scrunched up with worry.

"Hi, sweetheart," Zelda called reassuringly. "You can come in."

Relief spread across the child's face. "You're okay?"

"My head feels as if its been used as a bowling ball, but other than that I'm just fine."

Geraldine Matthews came in on Caitlin's heels. "Sorry," she apologized. "She was determined to see for herself that you're doing better."

Zelda looked at Caitlin. "Shouldn't you have gone back to school with your friends?"

"I can go in the morning. Granddaddy said he'd take me then, unless you need me to look after you."

Taylor shook his head. "Oh, I think the rest of us can manage to look after Zelda. You don't want to miss classes, do you?"

"You have to go to work," Caitlin said stubbornly. "I could read to her. We could even play games. I know lots of good ones, like Monopoly and Scrabble and Hearts."

"Who taught you those games?" Taylor countered.

"Hey, you two," Zelda interrupted. "It won't be necessary for anyone to look after me. I'll be at work tomorrow, too."

"That's what you think," Taylor retorted.

"It really would be best to take it easy for another day," Taylor's mother said. "You're more than welcome to stay here. I'd enjoy the company."

Zelda was stunned by the unexpected sincerity of the offer. "I really don't think…"

"Please," she said. "It's the least we can do."

Zelda was certain there was an apology in there somewhere, but she wasn't exactly sure what it was for. The least she could do was meet the woman halfway, though how Beau Matthews would feel about all this was troublesome at best. In the end, though, it was just more rational to stay put. She had the feeling that if she budged one inch from this bed, she wasn't going to be happy with the consequences.

"If you're sure it's no bother," she said finally.

"Absolutely none," Mrs. Matthews reassured her. "Now, come along, Caitlin. Help me fix dinner. Let Zelda get some rest."

"What about Daddy?" Caitlin responded defiantly. "He's staying."

"Oh, I doubt we could get him out of there with a blast of dynamite," she retorted, to Zelda's astonishment.

When they had gone, Zelda regarded Taylor intently. "Did I miss something here?"

He shook his head, apparently equally bemused by his mother's behavior. "Maybe she's afraid of being sued," he suggested dryly. "You were on their horse when you knocked yourself out."

"She doesn't look afraid. She looks like a woman who's made up her mind about something."

"You know as much as I do," he said, staring at the now closed bedroom door with a decidedly worried expression on his face.

"Taylor?"

"Yes."

"I think I like being here in the same bed you slept in as a boy."

His lips twitched. "Do you really?"

She reached up and touched his cheek, enjoying the masculine feel of the faint stubble against her skin. "I'd like it even better if you were in here with me."

"I'm right here," he pointed out.

"That's not the same as *in* here."

He scowled at her. "You swore you were going to stop saying things like that."

"What can I tell you?" she said innocently. "That whack on the head must have addled my brain."

Suddenly his arms were under her shoulders and she found herself curled against his chest. She could feel the steady thumping of his heart. His heat seemed to envelop her and make her feel safe.

"You scared the hell out of me," he admitted eventually, his voice ragged. "You were so still out there."

"Given my reputation for nonstop energy, that would have been startling," she teased.

"It's not a joke. You could have been killed. Whatever possessed you to dig your heels into the horse's flanks?"

Zelda thought back to the precise instant when she'd acted so foolishly. "I was angry," she admitted. "I acted without thinking."

Taylor sighed. "See, that's exactly the kind of thing that terrifies me. What if you'd been killed?"

"I wasn't."

"But you might have been," he said angrily, giving her shoulders a shake. "Blast it all, aren't you ever going to learn to think first?"

She knew he was right, but she hated saying so aloud. It would only give him ammunition to use against her later, when he called things off between them one more time. "Sometimes it's as important to take risks as it is to play it safe. It's called living."

"No," he corrected softly, his expression defeated. "Sometimes it's called dying."

With that, he walked out and left her feeling miserable and more alone than ever.

Taylor wondered how many close calls one man could be expected to endure. For once, he wasn't even thinking of dangerous risks, either. He was thinking about sex. He was thinking about it too damned much, it seemed to him. One of these days, he was going to throw caution to the wind and show Zelda just how desperately he wanted her. Surely he deserved that much before he let her go again.

The trick, of course, would be letting her go once he'd known the joy of holding her in his arms, of rediscovering the satin texture of her skin, of losing himself to the scent of her, of burying himself deep inside her. He groaned.

Damn! He was aroused again. He had to stop thinking about such things. He had to concentrate on something else. Maybe a football game. All that violence and competitiveness ought to release a little pent-up sexual tension.

It didn't. Five hours later, he was bleary-eyed, exhausted, and wanted Zelda just as badly as he had before. He went upstairs and slipped into his old room. She was slung across his bed from one corner to the other, the covers kicked aside. His mother's demure little cotton nightgown might have made anyone else look almost virginal. It made Zelda look desirable.

In his current state of perpetual lust, sackcloth would have made Zelda look desirable.

A pale shaft of moonlight streamed in the window and made her skin shimmer like candlelight on silk. He closed his eyes as if that could stop the wave of pure longing that swept through him.

He'd be okay, he told himself firmly. He'd escape before he did anything foolish, if only she didn't stir sensuously, if only she didn't awaken.

She did both. She came awake slowly, sensuously, her gaze instantly locking with his in a way that made his pulse hammer. She stretched, pulling the fabric of that innocent gown taut across her breasts, hiking it above her knees and drawing his attention from the relative safety of bare calves to the pure temptation of that shadowy mound between her thighs. A faint, satisfied smile curved her lips and still he thought he might escape.

Then she lifted her arms, deliberately inviting him, tempting him.

One mortal man could withstand only so much, he thought with a groan as he walked slowly to the door and locked it. His return was even slower, drawing out the anticipation, trying not to acknowledge how one lone woman could scramble his wits.

"This is a bad idea," he murmured, even as he lowered himself onto the bed.

"No," she said, boldly lifting the gown over her head. "This is right. It's always been right."

She was beautiful. That was his one last completely rational thought. Then all that mattered was the way she felt beneath his caress, the way she responded when his lips closed over a nipple and drew it into his mouth, the way her hips seemed to seek his. She was all fire and passion in bed as she was in life, taunting him, inflaming him, luring him.

"Sweet," he murmured as he tasted her skin.

"Taylor, I need you now," she insisted. "Now."

"Not yet," he taunted her. "You don't get your way in everything. We're going to take this at a nice, slow, leisurely pace. It's taken us ten years to get here. I'm not about to rush it."

She bucked beneath him, her skin already damp with perspiration. "Couldn't we try for slow and leisurely next time?" she whispered, lifting his shirt and raking her fingers along his belly. His belt buckle provided only a temporary slowdown in her determined assault. When it was undone, she moved on to the zipper of his jeans. The slow rasp as she pulled it down was pure torment.

"If you keep that up, we'll have to," he said, his whole body aching with the effort of maintaining control.

"You have on too many clothes."

"Self-defense."

She slid down, latched onto the cuffs of his jeans and tugged. Taylor was impressed by her determination. He allowed her to shuck them off, then moaned as she scattered little kisses all the way back up his legs. His breath snagged in his throat as her mouth skimmed over him, her pace fast, her intent clear.

When she reached his mouth, he ended the game, claiming her with a kiss that started out hard and punishing and gentled into something sweet and tender and heart-stoppingly familiar. He recognized then that this moment had been inevitable, that no matter what came after, they had been destined to be in each other's arms again.

And he wanted to savor it, to do all the sensual, exciting things he'd been imagining—remembering—for months, maybe even years. But that wouldn't happen, if they didn't slow down. This fire inside him would blaze out of control. She deserved better than that.

He tempered the kiss, then rolled onto his back. Unfortunately, she came with him. In less than a heartbeat, she was astride him, her face radiant with satisfaction, her red hair cascading to her shoulders in a tangle of curls.

"I see patience is not one of your virtues," he said, his voice coming in a ragged gasp as she settled over him. His arousal strained against his cotton briefs, which were scanty protection against her tempting heat. His whole body throbbed with need. Her gaze locked with his, she wriggled against him in a slow, provocative rhythm, and Taylor was lost.

He somehow managed to scramble out of his briefs with her willing assistance and then she was poised above him again. With careful deliberation, she settled herself over him, taking him deep inside until he was surrounded by that tight, moist, velvet heat. Tears shimmered on her lashes.

"Zelda? Is something wrong?"

"I'm sorry, but I couldn't… I couldn't let you change your mind again," she told him.

"I wouldn't have, not this time. It's too late for that. I think maybe it was too late the first time I ever saw you."

She rode him then, as she had ridden that horse—with wild abandon, unaware of the dangers, lost to everything except pure sensation. As time disappeared and need consumed him, Taylor thought for one fleeting instant that he had discovered something new and magical. Then he realized it was as old as time. It was the freedom to enjoy all that life had to offer, to love with everything in him.

He also knew, as their bodies stilled and passion ebbed, that it couldn't last. It never did.

Floating on a cloud of pure sensation, Zelda thought that nothing could ever be this perfect again. She had known the precise instant when Taylor had given himself up to the emotions, had seen the exultant expression on his face and gloried in it.

But just as she felt the sweetness of triumph, she realized he was slipping away from her and he was doing it intentionally. Though Taylor's arms remained tight around her, she sensed that something indefinable had shifted.

"What is it?" she asked, smoothing that untamable lock of hair from his forehead.

"Nothing."

"Don't tell me nothing. I know you, Taylor Matthews." She recalled what Sarah Lynn had told her. "According to some, I even know you better than you know yourself."

"Meaning?"

"Meaning that you love me, always have, always will." She said it with utter confidence, hiding the doubts that his stiff, unyielding demeanor stirred in her.

To his credit, he didn't deny it. That made it that much worse when he said, "It doesn't matter."

Zelda slowly extricated herself from his embrace, exchanging heated comfort for cold loneliness. "What do you mean, it doesn't matter? It's the only thing that matters."

"You asked me about my marriage."

"That was weeks ago. I've figured out most of it by now."

"I don't want you relying on conjecture. I want you to hear all of it, from me."

Bringing Maribeth into this bed was the last thing Zelda wanted, but she could hardly stop him from answering questions she herself had plagued him with.

"After you were gone, after I'd driven you off, I was in a lousy mood for months," he began. "I didn't want to hear from my parents that I'd made the right decision. I missed you so badly, I think I went a little crazy. When Maribeth was paraded before me as the perfect candidate for the wife of a man destined for politics, I didn't much care. She was sweet and lovely and more than willing, though why she'd take on a man who was still hung up on another woman is beyond me."

"She knew about me?"

"I told her every chance I got. Maybe I was just trying to scare her off. Anyway, after the wedding, I tried my damnedest to make it work, but you were there between us, and she knew it. She began to drink. And when she drank she did things, totally reckless, out-of-character things."

"Why?"

"I wondered that, but because I was so damned afraid that I already knew the answer, I didn't ask the question, not until it was too late, anyway." He regarded Zelda bleakly. "Do you want to hear what she admitted eventually? She told me that she knew she was a disappointment to me. She said she wanted to be more like you so that I would love her as much as I loved you."

"Oh, dear Lord," Zelda whispered, trying to imagine the kind of desperation and pain behind such an admission. "Oh, Taylor, how terrible for her. And for you."

"Me? Don't pity me. I got exactly what I deserved, enough guilt to last a lifetime and then some. I've seen firsthand what recklessness and love can lead a person to do. So if you want to stick around for more sex, if you want to stay on at the office, I'm not strong enough to deny myself the pleasure of that, but as for love, as for commitment, I can't do it."

He looked her straight in the eye, and Zelda felt all the hope drain right out of her.

"I won't do it," he emphasized, just in case she hadn't gotten the message. "I won't get tangled up with all that recklessness again. I know how it ends up."

Foolishly Zelda had thought of tonight as a turning point, linking passion and respect in a way that could endure for a lifetime. She still believed with all her heart that it could, but not if Taylor kept clinging to the past and refused to see the possibilities.

That meant she was going to have to fight with everything left in her. At least now she had some idea what she was up against.

Chapter 14

"Would you say that one more time?" Zelda said very slowly.

Taylor hardened himself against the hurt in her eyes. He couldn't allow himself to forget for one single instant that appearances could be deceiving. He'd learned that from Maribeth, too late to save their marriage, too late to save her life.

It was true that for weeks now Zelda had been acting more responsibly than he'd remembered. He'd never had a better assistant, in fact. She was organized and efficient, intelligent and clever when it came to helping him with cases. But then, just yesterday on that damned horse she'd lost her temper and done something exceptionally foolish. He couldn't trust her not to do that kind of thing again. And again.

Worse, he seemed to be the one who brought out her impetuous nature. He always had. Hell, at one time he'd been even more of a danger junkie than she was, but he'd learned. Now no one could accuse him of being anything but steady and dependable. He shook off the word *boring* when it popped into his head. *Responsible.*

"I was just trying to explain why it will never work between us," he said carefully. "I know what you're like, Zelda. There's a reckless streak inside you that nothing will ever tame."

"A reckless streak," she repeated as if she'd never heard the phrase before. Fire sparked in her eyes. "Maybe I just call it living, Taylor. Maybe I see it as grabbing life and hanging on for all it's worth. Maybe I don't want to cruise through my years on this earth in neutral, letting things pass me by."

She glared at him. "And that includes love."

Love. The word resounded in his head, promising so much. He knew all too well, though, what sins could be committed in the name of love, what tragedies could occur.

"This isn't about love," he said quietly, hoping the denial would silence his own doubts, maybe make him feel more at peace with the choice he was making. He knew in his gut, though, that it was a lousy choice, no better this time than it had been before. He clung to it stubbornly just the same.

"Yes, it is about love. And if you tell me to go this time, it will be for good," she threatened in a low tone that revealed more fury with each word. "I won't waste one single minute mourning you again. I won't waste one single ounce of energy thinking about what we could have had together. You will no longer exist for me. Have you got that, Taylor Matthews?"

A great empty space opened up inside him. He could

already feel the void her going would create in his life and he wondered if anything ever again would hurt so much. He fought the urge to drag her back into his arms. With every last ounce of sanity he had left, he made himself regard her calmly, emotionlessly.

"I've got it," he said softly. "It doesn't change anything."

He watched as the passionate spirit seemed to drain right out of her, and he hated himself for causing it. Still, that defiant chin of hers lifted a notch. A brief flash of anger darkened her eyes to the shade of a turbulent sea. Zelda would be okay. She had a survivalist's instincts. He wondered if he would do nearly as well.

Something cold and lonely settled over him as he watched her slide from his bed, her shoulders stiff with pride. She dragged a sheet with her and wrapped it around herself like a protective cloak.

Without glancing in his direction, she said, "I'll be out of your way in a minute."

"Zelda…" His voice trailed off as uncertainty swept through him.

She paused, but didn't turn around. As he watched her waiting for him to say whatever it was he'd begun, he thought he knew what it must be like in hell. He owed her better than this, but too many things had happened. He didn't have anything better left in him, just regrets.

"Nothing," he said finally. "I was just going to say there's no need to rush. My parents expect you to be here in the morning."

She trembled then as if a draft had chilled her, but he knew better. Her spine went ramrod straight as she walked into the bathroom and quietly closed the door.

Feeling more bereft than he ever had in his life, Taylor cursed softly and climbed from the bed where only hours ago he'd rediscovered magic, the same bed where he'd spent his entire adolescence dreaming of what it would be like to possess Zelda the way he had tonight. As he pulled on a pair of jeans and an old sweatshirt, he tried to reassure himself that he'd had no choice, but the words seemed hollow.

In the kitchen he made a pot of coffee and waited. The slow, methodical click of the clock over the sink marked the agony of waiting. He heard the shower stop, then, after a while, the opening of the bathroom door. All the while his imagination taunted him with images of Zelda's skin, soft and flushed from the steam, smelling of something sweetly exotic.

When she finally came into the room, his heart wrenched at the bleak expression on her face. She'd tugged her hair back into a ponytail and pulled his baseball cap on again. She looked about seventeen, until he sought her gaze and saw the weariness and pain of someone much older.

"I'm going to stop by the office when I leave here, to pick up my things," she said.

"Just like that?" he said without thinking. "Sorry. Of course."

"Will you be coming in tomorrow?"

He shook his head. "I have a meeting in Charleston. I won't be back until late tomorrow."

"Then I'll see if Darlene can work."

A thoughtful gesture under the circumstances, he admitted. *Responsible.*

There was that word again. "Thank you."

He sat there, just staring at her, as if he had to absorb

everything about her in the next few seconds, enough to last a lifetime. She looked unhappy and uneasy.

"I need to borrow your car to get home," she said finally.

He shook his head. "You're in no condition to drive. I'll get my keys and take you home."

"I'd rather you wouldn't. Just lend me the car. I can drive myself."

Irrationally annoyed by her desire to leave alone, he snapped, "I said I'd drive you. I'll be out in a minute."

He went upstairs and snatched his keys off the dresser, then paused long enough to write a note to his parents explaining that Zelda had felt she'd be more comfortable in her own home.

Outside, he found her already sitting in the car, scrunched against the passenger door as if she couldn't quite bear to be so much as a single inch closer. He opened his mouth to say something, anything, to end the silence, but words wouldn't come.

In front of her house, she stilled his move to get out with a single gesture. "I'll be fine."

He bit back an argument. "Call me if you need anything."

"I won't." She regarded him coolly. "Well, then, I guess this is goodbye."

"Zelda, I'm sorry it didn't work out." He struggled with the apology, knowing it wasn't enough, angry with himself for putting them both through this anguish for a second time.

A rueful smile tugged at her lips. "I'm sorry you didn't even give it a chance."

And then, before he could think of a single thing to say to that, she was out of the car, down the walk and inside with the door firmly closed behind her. Only then did Taylor know with absolute certainty that she had taken his heart with her.

"The man is an idiot," Zelda declared emphatically as she threw her personal belongings into a box that had once held computer paper. It was amazing how much a person could accumulate in a few short weeks. Makeup, hair brushes, a toothbrush, a letter opener that could serve as a dandy murder weapon, she noted as she tossed it into the box. Then, of course, there was her broken heart. Not many people got to walk away from a job with one of those.

"Damn him!"

She tried to tell herself that she'd given it her best shot this time. It sure as hell wasn't her fault that things had fallen apart. It was Taylor and his stubborn decision to bury himself right along with that miserable wife of his. That's what he was doing, of course, paying penance for who-knew-what crimes he thought he'd committed. His declaration earlier had absolutely nothing to do with her and everything to do with the bushel of guilt he was hauling around.

All of which might be true, Zelda conceded, but where did that get her? On a fast jet back to L.A., that's where. Will or no will, she was going. First thing in the morning, if at all possible. She'd been wasting time with this futile attempt to recapture the past.

She was already reaching for the phone to make a reservation, when it rang. She hesitated. Who would be calling Taylor at the office at this ungodly hour? She'd waited until the end of the day, when Darlene would be gone, before stopping by to pick up her things. She'd made sure that Taylor's car was nowhere around before using her key to let herself in. It was nearly seven o'clock now, too late for the usual business calls. Obviously this was someone who knew Taylor's workaholic habits, she decided.

Constitutionally unable to ignore a ringing phone, especially one as persistent as this, Zelda finally picked it up.

"Taylor Matthews's office."

"This is Ms. Patterson at Graystone School," the cultured voice that Zelda readily recognized said. "Is Mr. Matthews there by any chance? I've already tried him at home."

Zelda's pulse kicked into overdrive. "No, he's gone to Charleston. Is Caitlin okay? Is there anything I can do?"

"She's not feeling well. Her grandfather just brought her back this morning and she became ill around lunchtime. It's nothing to be alarmed about, I'm sure, but she is running a high fever. Our doctor here has taken a look at her and thinks it's just a touch of the flu. We could keep her in the infirmary, of course, but I thought she might be more comfortable at home."

"I'll be there in an hour," Zelda said without hesitation. She had no idea how Taylor would feel about her going after Caitlin under the circumstances, but right this instant she didn't give a damn.

"Actually, Mr. Matthews really should be the one to come."

"He's not available."

"Caitlin's grandparents, then."

"Really, there's no need to bother them. I'll leave a message for Mr. Matthews with his service, but you and I both know he would want his daughter back here as quickly as possible. I can come right away. That way she'll be home when he gets back."

Ms. Patterson continued to hesitate. If they weren't wasting precious time, Zelda might have admired her for the caution.

"Well, he did give permission for you to pick her up once before," she said finally. "I suppose it would be all right."

"I will take full responsibility for the decision," Zelda reassured her.

She drove with the accelerator pressed all the way to the floor and made it to Graystone in less than an hour. Ms. Patterson was waiting for her in the foyer. "Come with me. Caitlin's in the infirmary. I've told her you were on the way."

At the doorway to the large, sterile room with its gleaming medical equipment and row of beds, Zelda paused and drew in a deep breath. Caitlin was the only child in the room and she was huddled under the covers, her complexion almost as white as the sheets except for the feverish, too bright splashes of color on her cheeks. A momentary panic raced through Zelda. What if she botched this? She'd never nursed a sick child before.

Caitlin's whispery voice cut through her chaotic thoughts. "Zelda, I hurt," she cried miserably. "I want to go home."

Zelda reached her side in an instant and brushed a lock of hair from her forehead. Her skin was burning up, she realized with alarm. Still, she somehow managed to keep her voice even and reassuring. "I know you do, sweetheart. Let's bundle you up and take you home to your own bed. I'll bet you'll feel lots better as soon as you're there."

"I've packed her bag for her," Ms. Patterson said. "It's in the foyer. Just give her lots of fluids, and I'm sure she'll be just fine. If her temperature goes up any more, give the doctor a call. I've put his number in her suitcase."

Zelda nodded. "Then I guess we're all set," she said cheerfully. She scooped Caitlin up into her arms, prepared to struggle with the unaccustomed weight. Instead, she was startled by how light and fragile she felt.

Once she had Caitlin settled on the back seat of the car with a blanket wrapped securely around her, Zelda slid behind the wheel. "You okay back there?"

"I'm hot," Caitlin said, squirming restlessly.

"Don't toss the blanket off, sweetheart. You'll get chilled and then you'll only feel worse."

Aware of the precious cargo she was carrying, Zelda drove far more cautiously on the way home. It seemed to take forever. By the time she pulled into Taylor's driveway, her shoulders were stiff with tension. The thought of going back into that house, of seeing Taylor again after what had happened only hours before made her almost physically ill, but she managed to steel herself against the memory. Right now, Caitlin was the only thing that mattered.

She carried the listless child to her room and tucked her beneath the covers. Downstairs she found a pitcher of fresh orange juice. She filled another with cool water and took both containers upstairs. She grabbed a washcloth from the bathroom.

"Here you go, sweetheart," she said. "I've brought you some juice."

Caitlin shook her head. "I don't want any."

"How about some water, then? You need to drink something."

"No. Where's Daddy?"

"He'll be home in a little while. He had to go to Charleston earlier. He'll be back as soon as he gets the message that you're here. Why don't we take your temperature and see if that fever's down at all?"

It was a hundred and three. Zelda nearly panicked. What was normal? Ninety-eight point six? Wasn't anything over a hundred dangerous? Why the hell couldn't she remember? Forcing herself to remain calm, she went into the hallway and used the portable phone to call the doctor.

"No need for alarm," he reassured her in a voice that had clearly soothed hundreds of overwrought mothers. "Children tend to get very high temperatures, much higher than adults. Still, I wouldn't want to see this climbing any more. Keep her on fluids. Sponge her off with cool water. Give me the number there, and I'll check back with you in a couple of hours. If anything changes significantly before that, don't hesitate to call me. I'll drive on over, if need be."

Zelda tried to imagine a doctor in Los Angeles being quite so responsive and couldn't. In her experience most of them were overworked, impatient and in serious need of training in bedside manners.

"Thank you," she said. "This is all a little new to me. I'm just filling in until her father gets back."

"And you're terrified something will go wrong on your watch," he said. "Well, we'll just have to see that doesn't happen. Now, you go on back to your patient. I'm here if you need me."

Eventually, to Zelda's relief, Caitlin's temperature

seemed to stabilize, no better, but no worse, either. She'd fallen asleep and had managed to kick off all the covers. Zelda replaced them, then sank down in a chair beside the bed and watched her sleep, alert to every hitch in her breathing, every soft sigh, every restless shifting of her body.

Where the devil was Taylor? she wondered again and again as the hours dragged on. Caitlin kept rousing, asking for her daddy, then drifting back into a restless sleep. Zelda talked to the doctor twice more, reassured by his calm demeanor and Caitlin's unchanged condition.

"Oh, baby," she murmured as her cool fingers caressed a burning cheek. She picked up the damp washcloth and sponged Caitlin's forehead. She opened her eyes slowly as if even that much movement hurt.

"How're you feeling?" Zelda asked.

"I'm hot."

"I know, sweetheart. The cool water should bring your fever down soon."

"Can I sit in your lap in the rocker?"

"Absolutely," she said, gathering her up and settling into the rocking chair. Caitlin snuggled closer. "Better?"

"Uh-huh."

"Good." She rocked slowly, holding this child of the man she loved more than life itself. Longing spread through her, followed by the sharp anguish of knowing that she would never share Caitlin or other children with Taylor. These moments, however fleeting, would be all she'd have.

Taylor had never in his entire life had more of a desire to get rip-roaring drunk. Naturally, he didn't. He'd ordered a double bourbon straight up and swirled it around in the glass for the past hour. The bartender had probably never seen anyone nurse a drink the way Taylor was.

"Something wrong with the drink?" he asked finally.

"No."

Worry etched a frown on the man's expressive face. "You trying to kick a habit?"

Taylor's laughter was mirthless. "Something like that, but not what you think."

"Ah, woman trouble," the bartender guessed. He took Taylor's untouched drink and replaced it with a cup of coffee. "Want to talk about it?"

"There's nothing to talk about," Taylor said. "She's gone. I sent her away. That's that."

"Having a change of heart?"

"No. Absolutely not," Taylor said adamantly.

A disbelieving grin spread across the bartender's face. "Hey, I was just asking."

"Sorry."

"Maybe you ought to think about changing your mind, though. In my experience, when a woman has a man all tied up in knots, the only way to get her out of his system is to play it through to the end."

"Didn't work."

"Then you didn't get to the end, did you?"

Taylor appreciated the amateur analysis, but in his opinion the guy couldn't have been further off the mark. His relationship with Zelda was definitely at the end of the road. He drained the last of the coffee and tossed a couple of bills onto the bar. The bartender shoved them back.

"The coffee and the pep talk are on me this time."

"I can't let you do that."

"Sure you can. Just come in sometime and let me know how it turns out."

"Yeah, right. I'll invite you to the wedding," he said dryly.

He drove to an inn in the heart of old Charleston and checked in. He couldn't see one single reason to go back to Port William tonight. With any luck Zelda would be gone by morning and temptation would be out of his life once and for all. The prospect didn't bring him much satisfaction.

He flipped on the TV, took a shower and settled down to read the depositions he'd picked up earlier in the day. The words blurred on the page, and his concentration was shot. The background noise from the television irritated him. He finally switched it off.

Wide awake and determined not to think about Zelda and that soft, vulnerable look in her eyes, he decided he'd call his service one last time.

"Mr. Matthews, thank goodness," Wilma said. "You need to get yourself one of them beepers."

"Why, when I have you?"

"It's your girl, sir."

His heartbeat seemed to skid to a stop. "Caitlin?"

"Yes, sir. Your secretary…"

Secretary? He didn't have one anymore. "Darlene?"

"No, the new one. Miss Zelda. She called earlier this evening and said Caitlin was taken sick at school."

A sense of unreality spread through him. Dread had his pulse hammering. "I'll leave right away. Could you call over there and tell them I'm leaving Charleston now?"

"She's not at the school. Miss Zelda went and picked her up. She's at home. Checked on her myself not more than an hour ago. Her fever hasn't broken yet, but the doctor told Miss Zelda not to worry. Kids spike these fevers all the time. I have four young ones of my own. Every one of them scared the bejesus out of me a time or two. Don't you go driving too fast to get home, you hear?"

"Thanks, Wilma."

It took Taylor less than ten minutes to dress, pack up his briefcase and get on the road. For the first time in his life, he wished he had a car phone so he could call and see for himself that Caitlin was not seriously ill. He hadn't wanted to waste a single second making that call before leaving the hotel.

She's with Zelda, he reminded himself. Whatever his doubts about Zelda and about their own future, he knew she would die herself before she allowed anything to happen to his daughter. Given everything else he knew about her, he wasn't sure why he felt so strongly about this, but he believed it with all his heart.

Chapter 15

It was after midnight when Taylor finally pulled into the driveway at home. Every light in the house seemed to be burning. Why? What had gone wrong? He took off for the front door at a dead run, not certain what he expected to find inside. Doctors? Paramedics? His parents? All foolish thoughts given the lack of a single vehicle in front of the house other than his own and Zelda's bright red convertible.

He opened the door quietly, then listened. There wasn't so much as a faint sound of stirring anywhere. Encouraged by that, he took a quick survey of the downstairs rooms, his mouth dropping open at the mess in the kitchen. Apparently Zelda had tried to fix something to tempt Caitlin's appetite. Judging from the chaos, it had taken several attempts.

Frozen juice cans littered the sink. Eggshells, a tin

of cinnamon and an empty milk carton hinted at an attempt to make custard, which he could have told her was a waste of time. Two pieces of burned toast remained in the toaster as if she'd just taken one look at them and given up that idea. A smile tugged at his mouth. He had to give her high marks for determination, anyway.

He flipped off the kitchen light, dismissing the mess until morning, then climbed the stairs. Up here, the bathroom and hall lights were on, though only a faint glow showed from Caitlin's room. Her night-light. She wouldn't sleep without it. Had she told Zelda or had Zelda guessed?

He walked quietly down the hall and stepped into the dimly lit room, his glance going straight to the bed. It was empty.

Then he looked at the rocking chair, one Maribeth had bought when Caitlin was a baby and which Caitlin had climbed in herself from the first day she could reach it, content to rock for hours. What he saw now brought a lump to his throat. Emotions he hadn't wanted to feel, had thought he could dismiss, crowded in as he studied the two people who were most precious to him in all the world. One of them, his daughter, he had a right to love, a duty to protect. The other was a woman he had to force himself to sacrifice, for all their sakes.

Zelda was sound asleep. Exhaustion had left faint shadows under her eyes. The bump on her forehead had turned an interesting combination of purple and yellow. Though Zelda had to have been in pain herself, Caitlin was cradled protectively in her arms, wrapped in a blanket, the thumb she hadn't sucked in years tucked in her mouth.

He crept into the room and knelt beside them. He

brushed his fingertips across Caitlin's brow and discovered it was cool to the touch. A profound relief spread through him. She was okay. Zelda had seen to it. Even as angry as she must be with him, she had cared for Caitlin. He would be forever in her debt for that.

His daughter stirred. Gray eyes sleepily sought his. "Hi, Daddy. I've been sick."

"So I heard," he whispered, indicating Zelda's sleeping form. "How're you feeling now?"

"I'm all better. Zelda made me custard."

He grinned. "I thought you hated custard."

"That was your custard," she said imperiously. "Zelda's was good."

"I see." He reached out to pick her up. "Let's get you into bed. It's late."

"But I've been sleeping and sleeping."

"It's one in the morning. A little more sleep will do you good."

"What about Zelda?"

Just then Zelda's eyes blinked open. Her gaze met Taylor's then skittered away. Instantly she touched her hand to Caitlin's forehead. The worried expression on her face disappeared.

"The fever's gone," she pronounced with evident relief. "How do you feel, pumpkin?"

Caitlin rolled her eyes at the nickname she barely tolerated from Taylor or his parents. "Better. I told Daddy you make the best custard of anybody. Is there any left?"

"I made enough for an army," Zelda admitted. "The refrigerator is filled with it."

"Can I have more?"

"Now?" Zelda asked incredulously. "It's the middle of the night."

"But I'm hungry. I'll bet Daddy is, too."

"I did miss dinner," Taylor confessed. "How about you?"

"I wasn't especially hungry," Zelda admitted.

"Then that does it. Custard all around," he said, then scowled at his daughter. "Then you, my little one, are going back to sleep."

"Can we eat downstairs?" Caitlin asked, already scrambling out of Zelda's embrace and darting for the door. Her flu or whatever it had been evidently forgotten.

Taylor didn't miss the expression of sadness that suddenly stole over Zelda's face. He knew how it felt to be suddenly bereft. He waited for her at the top of the stairs, then touched her hand. "Thank you. I'll never forget what you did."

"I did it for Caitlin," she said stiffly, still refusing to look directly at him.

He touched her chin, forcing her to meet his gaze. "I know that," he said softly. "I'm grateful just the same. Maybe more than you can possibly imagine."

Seeing the gratitude in Taylor's eyes, the sudden warmth, Zelda felt her spirits slowly begin to lift. It was going to be okay, after all. She was almost sure of it.

Almost.

It was that one tiny shred of uncertainty that made her cautious. Convictions held for as long as Taylor had clung to his about her didn't turn around overnight. She'd learned that lesson just a day or two ago to her bitter dismay. But surely after these tense hours when Caitlin had been left in her care he had seen indisputable evidence of the woman she'd become, not the reckless girl he remembered. Surely that would count for something, she thought, then hated herself for placing her emotions at his mercy.

"Will you read me another story?" Caitlin pleaded just then, interrupting Zelda's thoughts.

Zelda smiled at her. She had agreed to stay on for another day or two until the doctor gave Caitlin permission to return to school.

"Which one do you want?" she asked. She'd been reading *Little House on the Prairie* for hours already. She'd re-read all of *Angelina Ballerina* at least a dozen times, as well.

"The ballerina one," Caitlin said this time. "I asked Daddy if I could have ballet lessons."

"And what did he say?"

"He said when I get well we'd talk about it. Do you think he'll let me? It would mean moving back home."

Zelda was surprised that Taylor hadn't dismissed the idea out of hand. He'd never been willing to bring Caitlin home before. "If your father said he'd consider it, then I'm sure he will."

Caitlin regarded her intently. "He'd need someone to help him, if I came home," she said slyly.

Zelda glanced into guileless gray eyes. "Oh?"

"You could do it. He already likes you. You don't have a little girl of your own at home, so I could be your little girl and then I'd have a mommy and a daddy."

Zelda wiped at the tear that tumbled down her cheek at the ingenuous suggestion. She couldn't even bring herself to look at Caitlin. Suddenly she felt two little arms go around her neck. She heard a faint sniff.

"I'm sorry," Caitlin whispered. "I didn't mean to make you sad."

Zelda hugged her. "Oh, baby, knowing that you'd like me to be your mommy doesn't make me sad. It's the nicest thing anybody's ever said to me."

"Then why are you crying?"

"Oh, just grown-up foolishness."

"Does that mean I can tell Daddy you'll do it?"

Zelda chuckled at Caitlin's persistence. "No, you may not. I think this is one situation you'll have to leave entirely up to your father to handle," she said, regretting more than she could say that she couldn't encourage Caitlin to give the bullheaded man a gentle shove.

To Zelda's astonishment, Taylor did agree to let Caitlin stay at home until after the holidays. Maybe her bout with the flu, as mild as it had been, had awakened him to the fact that she ought to be home where he could look after her. He promised the school he would hire a tutor to see that she kept up with her lessons. Just as he hung up the phone after working out the details with Ms. Patterson, Zelda heard herself volunteering to do it. It was amazing how little relationship there was between her brain and her tongue.

Taylor's startled gaze clashed with hers. "I thought you were leaving."

She shrugged. "I'm in no rush. Christmas is less than a month away. I can always go back to Los Angeles after New Year's."

"If you're going to stick around, you could keep your job with me," he suggested, his gaze fixed on her as if he were trying to gauge her reaction. "That would make more sense."

"I don't think so."

"Afraid to be in the same room with me?" he taunted.

"You're the one who ought to panic at the thought," she said dryly. "You know what everyone says about my temper."

"You're a pushover," he contradicted. "Anyone who can read the same book over and over and over without screaming is an old softie."

"Then let me keep on doing that," she said. "There's no point in hiring a stranger for just a few weeks."

Still, Taylor hesitated. It finally dawned on Zelda why.

"You don't trust me with her, do you?" she said, swallowing hard against the hurt that seemed lodged in her throat.

"Of course I do," he said too quickly.

Zelda regarded him belligerently. "Then prove it."

"This isn't some game of I-dare-you," he chided.

"No," she agreed softly. "It's far more important than any game we've ever played. It's a matter of trust and respect."

"It's a matter of my child's well-being."

"Damn it, Taylor, don't you realize that I would protect your daughter with my life? You know what happened just days ago. It might have turned into something more serious, but it didn't. I watched over her every second. I stayed in constant touch with the doctor."

A sigh shuddered through him. "I know that. Deep in my gut I don't question that at all, but up here…" He tapped his head. "Up here, I keep seeing her mother's car at the bottom of that ravine. But for the grace of God, Caitlin could have been in it with her. And no one loved our daughter more than Maribeth did."

"I am not Maribeth!" Zelda snapped, then threw up her hands in a gesture of surrender. "Why am I

doing this? How many times will I allow you to humiliate me with your unreasonable doubts? I can't prove
something to a man who won't even see what's right in
front of him." She grabbed her coat. "I'm out of here.
Kiss Caitlin for me and tell her I love her and that I'll
miss her."

Shaking with anger, she was all the way through the
front door and on the porch before she felt Taylor's fingers lock around her wrist. Though his expression was
still filled with doubts, he said quietly, "Go upstairs and
tell her you'll be helping with her tutoring for a while."

"Go to hell," she retorted, wrenching free.

"Don't punish Caitlin for my stupidity."

The plea reached her as nothing else might have.
Caitlin wanted so badly to be back at home again. Could
she deny her this chance to live at home like a normal
little girl again? Perhaps by the end of the holidays,
Taylor would see that Caitlin was where she belonged,
at home with him. It could be her gift to the little girl
she'd come to love.

"I'll be here first thing in the morning," she agreed
finally. "After you've left for work."

Taylor's expression hardened, but he nodded. "Fine."

"I'll stay until you get home in the evenings, but not
one second longer. Understood?"

He sighed. "Yes, Zelda. The ground rules are perfectly clear."

She looked into his eyes, hoping to see something
that would make this easier, but all she saw was a man
who had to struggle to trust her. She hated him for that.
More, she hated herself for sticking around for this one
pitiful crumb he'd deigned to toss her. Only Caitlin's
welfare allowed her to live with the decision.

* * *

It might not have been so awful spending her days with Caitlin and avoiding Taylor, if it hadn't been Christmastime. It was a season for joy, a season for families and forgiveness, her very favorite time of year.

It was also a season for the worst loneliness of Zelda's life. She felt cut off from everyone she loved, especially Taylor, and he was close by.

She bought presents for Kate and her other friends in Los Angeles and mailed them off. Suddenly she longed to be back there, to be back in a job where she was respected and trusted, back in a place where she felt a part of things, rather than an outsider, always wanting what she couldn't have. In L.A. anything was possible. She resolved to go back immediately after the first of the year. She would talk to Kate soon and set the wheels in motion for her return.

In the meantime, Caitlin wanted to go Christmas shopping for her father, and Zelda had promised to take her.

"What are you going to get Daddy?" Caitlin asked as they strolled through the mall looking in every decorated window. Carols blared over the loudspeaker system. Santa Claus sat in a winter wonderland display, listening patiently to children's wish lists. Despite their mission, she was having the time of her life. Her depression began to lift.

"I hadn't really thought about it," Zelda said. "We probably won't exchange gifts."

"He's already bought yours," Caitlin confided.

Zelda was startled by the revelation. "Oh?"

"I'm not supposed to tell what it is."

"Then I guess you'd better keep it a secret."

Caitlin looked disappointed by Zelda's refusal to plague her with questions. The truth was, Zelda didn't want to know what impersonal little trinket Taylor might have bought for her. A scarf, probably. Something he'd had Darlene pick out, now that she was working in the office for him again until he could locate another replacement.

"Now, then," Zelda said briskly. "Have you decided what you want to get him?"

"He said he needs a new shirt. A white dress shirt," Caitlin said. She glanced up at Zelda. "I think that sounds awfully dull."

"I agree," Zelda said, suddenly grinning. "Let's choose a shirt with a little pizzazz for him."

Caitlin regarded her uncertainly. "What's *pizzazz?*"

"Trust me."

"He said white."

"What does he know? He's a man." She led Caitlin to the men's department and zeroed in on a table filled with shirts with stripes, colored shirts with white collars and French cuffs. There wasn't a plain white shirt in the lot.

Caitlin immediately reached for one with gray stripes. Zelda would have picked something besides gray, but it definitely had more pizzazz than Taylor's usual selections. She picked one in mauve and gray. Despite her reservations, Caitlin's eyes lit up.

"These are definitely better than white, but I can't afford two."

"You get the gray stripes. I'll get the mauve. Now let's look at ties." She found a couple that were classic in design, but done with more fashionable colors. She draped two choices over the shirts. "What do you think?"

"Beautiful," Caitlin said. "Do you really think Daddy will like them, though?"

"I think he'll hate them…at first. You'll just have to keep telling him how handsome he looks," she said, thinking it was too bad she wouldn't be there on Christmas morning to tell him herself.

Maybe she would even go back to Los Angeles before Christmas, she thought, unable to stop the tiny sigh of regret that eased through her. It might be a miserable, lonely holiday there, but in Port William it was guaranteed to be hell.

Chapter 16

"Kate, I'm coming back," Zelda announced when she reached her boss in Los Angeles early on Christmas Eve morning. "Do I still have a job?"

There was a slight hesitation. "Of course, you have a job," Kate said finally. "But, Zelda, what about the will? What about this man you mentioned, the one you've always loved?"

"None of that matters," she lied. "I'll relinquish everything in my mother's estate. As for any man in my life, I think you'd better call up Brandon Halloran and tell him he can meddle in my love life as much as he pleases."

Kate chuckled. "He'll be delighted to hear that. I think he's been bored since he got me married off. He's been making noises about trying to find someone for Sammy, his granddaughter-in-law's brother. The poor kid is terrified. He's barely twenty. Jason and Dana say that Sammy's threatening to disown them all if Brandon so much as invites one eligible girl to dinner. He'd be forever indebted to you for providing a distraction."

She paused, then asked, "Zelda, do you want to tell me what's really going on back there?"

Zelda sighed at the evident concern. "Nothing that won't be forgotten as soon as I get back to Los Angeles."

"Okay, if you say so, but remember that I'm a good listener."

"I know that. I'll call you when I have my travel details worked out."

"Will you stay there through the holidays at least?"

"No. I'm going to try to get out of here tonight or tomorrow."

"On Christmas Day?" Kate said, sounding horrified. She drew in a breath. "Never mind. If you get back tonight or tomorrow, you'll have Christmas dinner with us. No need to even call first. Just show up about four-thirty. Promise me now."

"I promise," Zelda said, already feeling as if her life was getting back on track. It would be fun to share Christmas dinner with a family, even if it was the wrong family.

When she'd hung up, Zelda walked slowly through the house in which she'd grown up. She wouldn't miss it, wouldn't miss anything about Port William, in fact. She was grateful her mother had forced her to come back. She'd definitely put a few ghosts to rest, not the least of them her love for Taylor. She could finally stop clinging to that as an excuse for avoiding new relationships. Nope, there was nothing left for her here.

Except Sarah Lynn, she thought with a tiny smidgen of regret. Maybe the way the sun filtered through the pine trees early in the morning. And Caitlin. She would really miss Caitlin.

A tear shimmered on her lashes, then rolled down her cheek. Would she ever know the wonder of holding her own child in her arms? Even if she didn't, she would treasure the time she'd had with Taylor's daughter and consider herself blessed for having been part of Caitlin's life even for such a brief interval.

An uncontrollable sob rose in her throat. Damn Taylor for ruining it all! Why hadn't he been able to see that nothing in life mattered a hoot, unless there was someone with whom you could share it? Why hadn't he been able to trust her, to see that she would never, ever do anything to put him or his daughter at risk?

Well, it didn't matter anymore. She was tired of his misjudgments, tired of the way he refused to acknowledge his emotions, just plain tired of being the only one trying to make things work out. She would take her mother's treasured F. Scott Fitzgerald collection, the only thing in the house to which she was legally entitled, and go back to L.A. emotionally free, ready to find someone new and finally make a commitment that would last a lifetime.

She picked up the books and caressed the leather bindings and gold leaf lettering.

"Mama, I'm sorry," she whispered. "I'm sorry I couldn't do what you wanted, but I tried. I know what you wanted for me and I really tried."

Just then Sarah Lynn snatched open the screen door without even bothering to knock. "Hon, I think you'd better come with me."

"What is it? Has something happened to Taylor? Is it Caitlin?" she demanded as an irrational fear sent bile into her throat. Taylor and Caitlin were no longer her concern, she reminded herself sharply. She had to start remembering that. Knowing that didn't stop her blood from pumping faster.

"No, it's nothing like that," Sarah Lynn reassured her.

"What, then? I don't have time for guessing games. I'm trying to pack."

"Pack? To go where?"

"Back to Los Angeles."

"On Christmas Eve?"

"If I can finish this damned packing, yes."

"Well, it's just going to have to wait," Sarah Lynn insisted. "You're coming with me."

"Sarah Lynn, I am not budging from this room until you tell me what's going on."

"Jeez," Sarah Lynn muttered. "I'm not sure which of you has the harder head, you or Taylor."

"Leave Taylor out of this. I don't want to discuss him."

"Oh, really. Then why was he your first concern when I came running in here?"

"Will you just get to the point?"

"The point is that something's happening on the outskirts of town and I think you'd better see for yourself."

Zelda couldn't think of a single thing on the outskirts of town—or in the middle of town, for that matter— that she gave a damn about. Unfortunately she knew that Sarah Lynn matched her and Taylor for sheer bullheadedness. There would be no peace until she'd done what the woman asked. And there was the little matter of her own curiosity.

"Ten minutes," she warned. "I intend to be back here in ten minutes."

"Whatever," Sarah Lynn replied vaguely, dragging her off to her car.

The drive took less than five minutes, giving Zelda plenty of time to turn around and get back home within her limit…if she'd been able to budge once she got a good look at what had Sarah Lynn in such a dither.

"Oh, my God," she whispered softly as she stared up at the Port William water tower. Then she started to laugh, her heart lighter than it had been in months, maybe even years.

Taylor figured he'd gone and lost his mind. Better that, though, than his balance. He was perched precariously several hundred feet above the ground with a can of bright red paint clutched in one hand, a brush in the other.

He looked from the paint to the brush to his narrow perch and wondered how the devil Zelda had managed to splash her rude commentary on his parentage all over the side of this very same tower ten years ago without breaking her neck. For one thing, she must not have looked down. Every time he did, his head swam.

Having established that glancing toward the ground was very bad, he drew in a deep breath, dipped the brush in paint and began the message it had taken him too damned long to get around to sending. He just hoped it wasn't too late.

Red paint dribbled down from the hastily formed *T.* The rest of the letters in his name followed in an equally sloppy, though rather jaunty manner. He paused to admire the effect. Rather bold, if he did say so himself. One thing for certain, no one for miles around could miss it.

The distant sound of a siren told him that one person at least was aware of his highly illegal presence atop the water tower. He figured he had a very few minutes left in which to complete his task.

L, he began, then followed it with *OVES*. There was no time now to admire his handiwork. In the biggest letters he could manage without toppling from the narrow metal catwalk, he spelled out Zelda's name. So, there it was for all the world to see: Taylor Matthews Loves Zelda Lane.

"Taylor Matthews, have you lost your mind?" the sheriff shouted through a bullhorn. "You know you're defacing town property."

"And having the time of my life," Taylor called back, just as he sensed a vibration on the metal stairs up the side of the tower.

He glanced down and saw a familiar red-haired vixen climbing toward him. He tried to catch a good glimpse of her expression, but all he could tell for sure was that her brow was furrowed with concentration. Her knuckles might have been a little bit white as she clung to the railing for dear life.

He sat back, relaxed and waited. He figured no one, not the sheriff, not the mayor, not even his own father, would interfere in whatever drama was about to be played out high above the ground.

Finally Zelda reached the top rung and inched out onto the ledge. "I am too old for this," she murmured, sounding breathless.

Her cheeks were flushed. Wisps of hair curled damply around her face.

Taylor thought she had never looked so beautiful,

so desirable. "Hey," he taunted, "where's your sense of adventure?"

"About five hundred feet below here," she retorted.

The look she cast him was almost shy. And hopeful, he decided. A good sign.

"Did you mean it?" she asked, gesturing toward the brightly painted words above them.

"Sugar, this is not the way to go about keeping a secret. Actually, I had more I wanted to say, but I ran out of room, and I was attracting a crowd."

"The sheriff is beginning to look a little apoplectic down there."

"How's my father taking it? I saw him drive up."

"He was reaching for his shotgun when your mother came along and told him she'd never forgive him if he did one single thing to interfere."

Taylor shuddered. "Thank goodness. He's a great shot."

"He probably would have aimed low," she told him dryly. "So what else were you planning to write up here?"

She'd tried hard to sound casual, but he could hear the uncertainty in her voice, an uncertainty that had never been there until he'd come along to shake her self-confidence. Taylor glanced over at her and waited until she'd turned to face him. He put down the nearly empty paint can and the brush, and took her hand in his.

"I was going to ask if you'd marry me," he said, searching her face for some clue about what her response would be. "I can't promise I'll change overnight, but I know that you're right. I haven't been living these past few years. I've been existing. It's way past time for that to change. I've missed you so much the past few weeks I could hardly bear it."

"I've been right here," she reminded him.

"But not with me."

She studied his expression with evident worry. "Taylor, are you sure? Really sure?"

"Never more so," he said adamantly. "It's time I got a grip on my life and did something to make it better, perfect in fact. Even Caitlin has pointed out that you're the best thing that ever happened to me. I was even thinking I might like a change of scenery, someplace to start over."

He could see the astonishment in her eyes and was glad he still had the capacity to surprise her.

"You'd move?" she said. "Where? Charleston? Columbia?"

Taylor shook his head. "I was thinking about Los Angeles. I know someone who already has some great contacts out there. What do you think?"

Her response was to scramble across the catwalk and fling her arms around his neck. Taylor wasn't sure if she was going to choke him or send the two of them crashing to their deaths. When her mouth slanted over his, he wasn't much sure he cared. It would be a hell of a way to go.

"Is that a yes?" he asked when he could speak again.

A grin spread across her face. "That is a definite, wholehearted yes." Her expression sobered, and she regarded him worriedly. "We don't have to go to L.A., though. We could stay here."

"No. I think two adventurous people such as ourselves belong where there's plenty of action, don't you?"

"Taylor Matthews, wherever you and I are, I promise you there will be plenty of action."

A little tremor of excitement washed through him. "If it weren't broad daylight and if there weren't a hundred people standing down there with their mouths hanging open in anticipation, I'd make you prove that right here and now. Since we can't, let's go down and share the news."

"Judging from the cheering, I think they've guessed," Zelda retorted as Taylor pulled her to her feet. "One last thing."

She took the brush and paint from him and while his heart filled to overflowing, she meticulously added one word to the sign: Ditto.

Yep, Taylor thought as they descended into the waiting arms of friends and the law. Life with Zelda Lane was going to be one grand and glorious adventure.

Her heart filled to overflowing, Zelda sat in Taylor's living room on Christmas morning. She was once again wearing the teal blue velvet skirt she had made from the material he'd given her. Caitlin was wearing her matching dress. Zelda watched with delight as Caitlin tore open her presents, exclaiming excitedly over each and every one, then running to hug whoever'd chosen it.

If Geraldine and Beau Matthews had been stunned to find Zelda here when they'd arrived, they were keeping their opinions to themselves. Beau hadn't mellowed exactly, but he hadn't made one single snide remark. In fact, thanks to Caitlin's exuberance, there hadn't been much time for conversation of any kind.

When she'd opened every last present, Caitlin sat back and announced, "This has been the very best Christmas I've ever had. Now, Daddy, you open your presents."

Taylor ripped off paper with as much enthusiasm as Caitlin had, saving the box from Zelda until last. When he opened Caitlin's gift to him, he hesitated for only a fraction of a second before proclaiming it the nicest shirt he'd ever received.

Then he picked up Zelda's package. Holding her breath, she watched him slowly untie the ribbon, then remove the paper with far more care than he had any of the others. Slowly, as if he was savoring the anticipation, he lifted the lid on the box. "A shirt," he said. "And two ties. They're..."

"Show us, Daddy," Caitlin demanded, shooting a conspiratorial look at Zelda.

Taylor held them up as if he weren't too certain what to make of them.

Zelda winked at him.

"Fancy," Beau declared. "You'll look like a real Hollywood entertainment lawyer in that."

Taylor grinned. "What would you know about Hollywood entertainment lawyers, Dad?"

"I watch *L.A. Law,*" his father retorted. "It's about time you stopped wearing those boring old white shirts."

Zelda, Geraldine Matthews and Taylor all stared at him in amazement. "What?" he said. "I'm too old to know about what's in fashion for men?"

"Of course not, Dad," Taylor said. He gave the shirt one more slightly suspicious look, then said, "Okay, Zelda, your turn."

She picked up the package she knew Caitlin had wrapped. "Now what could this be? It weighs more than a butterfly."

Caitlin came and stood by her knee. "You can't give somebody a butterfly. Hurry up. Open it."

Zelda took her time with the package, to Caitlin's evident exasperation. When she unfolded the tissue paper inside, she found a lovely ceramic frame containing a portrait of Taylor and Caitlin.

"Oh, sweetheart, you couldn't have given me anything I'd have liked more."

Caitlin looked at Taylor. "See, I told you she'd like it."

"Of course I do. Why wouldn't I?"

Taylor regarded her ruefully. "She picked it out a month ago."

"Oh."

Geraldine Matthews handed over a silver-wrapped package then. "We have something for you, too."

Zelda's eyes widened. "You didn't need to get me anything."

"We wanted to give you this." She glanced around at her husband. "Didn't we, Beau?"

He nodded, his expression gruff, but no longer angry at finding her a part of their lives.

When Zelda had unwrapped the package, she found a delicate gold necklace inside with an antique locket. "It was my mother's," Geraldine Matthews told her. "She gave it to me on my wedding day and now I'm passing it on to you."

Zelda felt tears brimming in her eyes. She blinked them back. "Thank you. I'll treasure it."

"We just want you both to be happy. That's all we've always wanted for Taylor."

"Now mine," Taylor said, handing over a small package that looked suspiciously like a jewelry box. "Usually this is something that should be given in private, over candlelight, but I think we've pretty well dispensed with that tradition already."

Caitlin was so excited she reached over to help untie the ribbons. "I helped Daddy pick it out."

"Did you?" Zelda said, almost wishing she could delay opening the box for an eternity so she could treasure the joy she felt right this instant, the sweet shimmer of anticipation.

Unfortunately, Taylor was looking anxious and Caitlin was far too excited to be contained for long. She slowly lifted the lid on the velvet box. Inside was the most gorgeous diamond she had ever seen, surrounded by aquamarines.

"It's like your eyes," Caitlin told her.

"Not nearly so beautiful," Taylor corrected. "Not the way they're shining right now. You're not going to cry on me, are you?"

"I just might," she said.

"Does that mean you're happy?"

"Happier than I have ever been."

"Then you don't want to take back your acceptance of my proposal?"

She slid onto his lap and put her arms around his neck. "Taylor Matthews, you couldn't get rid of me now if you wanted to."

He grinned at her. "Then that makes this good for a lifetime," he said, sliding the ring on her finger.

Zelda glanced at his parents and saw that his mother had slipped her hand into Beau's. Tears were streaming down her cheeks, but she was smiling. Zelda knew then that nothing would interfere with her happiness again. For the first time in her life, she would have a real family.

She looked into Taylor's eyes. "I love you."

"And me?" Caitlin chimed in.

Zelda opened her arms to invite Caitlin into the embrace, as well. "And you, darling."

"Have you picked a date for the wedding?" Mrs. Matthews asked.

"I was thinking New Year's Eve," Taylor said. "How does that suit you?"

"I couldn't think of a better way to start a new year," Zelda agreed.

"Not just a new year," he whispered as his lips claimed hers. "A whole new life."

* * * * *

AN AMISH MATCH

Jo Ann Brown

For Linda Parisi

A dear friend who always makes me smile
just thinking of her

Have not I commanded thee? Be strong and of
a good courage; be not afraid, neither be thou
dismayed: for the Lord thy God is with thee
whithersoever thou goest.
—*Joshua* 1:9

Chapter 1

Paradise Springs
Lancaster County, Pennsylvania

The rainy summer afternoon was as dismal as the hearts of those who had gathered at the cemetery. Most of the mourners were walking back to their buggies, umbrellas over their heads like a parade of black mushrooms. The cemetery with its identical stones set in almost straight lines on the neatly trimmed grass was edged by a worn wooden rail fence. The branches on a single ancient tree on the far side of the cemetery rocked with the wind that lashed rain on the few people remaining by the newly covered grave.

Rebekah Burkholder knew she should leave the Stoltzfus family in private to mourn their loss, but she remained to say a silent prayer over the fresh earth.

Rose Mast Stoltzfus had been her first cousin, and as *kinder* they'd spent hours together every week doing their chores and exploring the fields, hills and creeks near their families' farms. Now Rose, two years younger than Rebekah, was dead from a horrific asthma attack at twenty-four.

The whole Stoltzfus family encircled the grave where a stone would be placed in a few weeks. Taking a step back, Rebekah tightened her hold on both her son's hand and her umbrella that danced in the fickle wind. Sammy, who would be three in a few months, watched everything with two fingers stuck in his mouth. She knew that over the next few days she would be bombarded with questions—as she had been when his *daed* died. She hoped she'd be better prepared to answer this time. At least she could tell him the truth rather than skirt it because she didn't want him ever to know what sort of man his *daed* had been.

"It's time to go, Sammy," she said in little more than a whisper when he didn't move.

"Say bye-bye?" He looked up at her with his large blue eyes that were his sole legacy from her. He had Lloyd's black hair and apple-round cheeks instead of the red curls she kept restrained beneath her *kapp* and the freckles scattered across her nose and cheeks.

"Ja." She bent to hug him, shifting so her expanding belly didn't bump her son. Lloyd hadn't known about his second *kind* because he'd died before she was certain she was pregnant again. "We have said bye-bye."

"Go bye-bye?"

Her indulgent smile felt out of place at the graveside. Yet, as he had throughout his young life, her son gave her courage and a reason to go on.

"Ja."

Standing slowly because her center of balance changed every day, she held out her hand to him again. He put his fingers back in his mouth, glanced once more at the grave, then stepped away from it along with her.

Suddenly the wind yanked on Rebekah's umbrella, turning it inside out. As the rain struck them, Sammy pressed his face against her skirt. She fought to hold on to the umbrella. Even the smallest things scared him; no wonder after what he had seen and witnessed in those horrible final months of his *daed*'s life.

No! She would not think of that time again. She didn't want to remember any of it. Lloyd had died last December, almost five months ago, and he couldn't hurt her or their *kinder* again.

"Mamm," Sammy groaned as he clung to her.

"It's all right," she cooed as she tried to fix her umbrella.

She didn't look at any of the other mourners as she forced her umbrella down to her side where the wind couldn't grab it again. Too many people had told her that she mollycoddled her son, and he needed to leave his babyish ways behind now that he was almost three. They thought she was spoiling him because he had lost his *daed*, but none of those people knew Sammy had experienced more fear and despair in his short life than they had in their far longer ones.

"Here. Let me help," said a deep voice from her left.

She tilted her head to look past the brim of her black bonnet. Her gaze rose and rose until it met Joshua Stoltzfus's earth-brown eyes through the pouring rain. He was almost six feet tall, almost ten inches taller than she was. His dark brown hair was damp beneath his black hat that dripped water off its edge. His beard was plastered to the front of the coat he wore to church Sundays, and soaked patches were even more ebony on the wide shoulders of his coat. He'd gotten drenched while helping to fill in the grave.

"Take this," he said, holding his umbrella over her head. "I'll see if I can repair yours."

"Danki." She held the umbrella higher so it was over his head, as well. She hoped Joshua hadn't seen how she flinched away when he moved his hand toward her. Recoiling away from a man's hand was a habit she couldn't break.

"Mamm!" Sammy cried. "I wet now!"

Before she could pull her son back under the umbrella's protection, Joshua looked to a young girl beside him, "Deborah, can you take Samuel under your umbrella while I fix Rebekah's?"

Deborah, who must have been around nine or ten, had the same dark eyes and hair as Joshua. Her face was red from where she'd rubbed away tears, but she smiled as she took Sammy's hand. *"Komm.* It's dry with me."

He didn't hesitate, surprising Rebekah. He usually waited for permission before he accepted any invitation. Perhaps, at last, he realized he didn't have to ask now that Lloyd was dead.

Joshua turned her umbrella right side out, but half of it hung limply. The ribs must have been broken by the gust.

"Danki," she said. "It's *gut* enough to get me to our buggy."

"Don't be silly." He tucked the ruined umbrella under his left arm and put his hand above hers on the handle of his umbrella.

Again she flinched, and he gave her a puzzled look.

Before she could let go, his fingers slid down to cover hers, holding them to the handle.

"We'll go with you back to your buggy," he said.

She didn't look at him because she didn't want to see his confusion. How could she explain to Lloyd's best friend about her reaction that had become instinctive? "I don't want to intrude on…" She gulped, unable to go on as she glanced at the other members of the Stoltzfus family by the grave.

"It's no intrusion. I told *Mamm* we'd go back to the house to make sure everything was ready for those gathering there."

She suspected he wasn't being completely honest. The *Leit*, the members of their church district, would oversee everything so the family need not worry about any detail of the day. However, she was grateful for his kindness. She'd always admired that about him, especially when she saw him with one of his three *kinder*.

Glancing at the grave, she realized neither of his boys remained. Timothy, who must have been around sixteen, had already left with his younger brother, Levi, who was a year older than Deborah.

"Ready to go?" Joshua asked as he tugged gently on the umbrella handle and her hand.

"Ja." Instantly she changed her mind. "No."

Stepping away, she was surprised when he followed to keep the umbrella over her head. She appreciated staying out of the rain as she walked to Isaiah, her cousin's widower. The young man who couldn't yet be thirty looked as haggard as a man twice his age as he stared at the overturned earth. Some sound must have alerted him, because he turned to see her and his older brother coming toward him.

Rebekah didn't speak as she put her hand on Isaiah's black sleeve. So many things she longed to say, because from everything she had heard the newlyweds had been deeply in love. They would have celebrated their first anniversary in November.

All she could manage to say was, "I'm sorry, Isaiah. Rose will be missed."

"*Danki*, Rebekah." He looked past her to his oldest brother. "Joshua?"

"Rebekah's umbrella broke," Joshua said simply. "I'm walking her to her buggy. We'll see you back at the house."

Isaiah nodded but said nothing more as he turned to look at the grave.

Joshua gripped his brother's shoulder in silent commiseration, then motioned for Rebekah to come with him. As soon as they were out of earshot of the remaining mourners, he said, "It was very kind. What you said to Isaiah."

"I don't know if he really heard me or not. At Lloyd's funeral, people talked to me but I didn't hear much other than a buzz like a swarm of bees."

"I remember feeling that way, too, when my Matilda died." He steered her around a puddle in the grass. "Even though we had warning as she sickened, nothing could ease my heart when she breathed her last."

"She was blessed to have you with her until the end." She once had believed she and Lloyd could have such a love. Would she have been as caring if Lloyd had been ill instead of dying because he'd fallen from the hayloft in a drunken stupor?

No! She wasn't going to think about that awful moment again, a moment when only her faith had kept her from giving in to panic. The certainty that God would hold her up through the horrible days ahead had allowed her to move like a sleepwalker through the following month. Her son and the discovery she was pregnant again had pulled her back into life. Her *kinder* needed her, and she wouldn't let them down any longer. It was important that nobody know the truth about Lloyd, because she didn't want people watching Sammy, looking for signs that he was like his *daed*.

"I know Rose's death must be extra hard for you," Joshua murmured beneath the steady thump of rain on his umbrella, "because it's been barely half a year since you buried Lloyd. My Matilda has been gone for more than four years, and the grief hasn't lessened. I've simply become accustomed to it, but the grief is still new for you."

She didn't answer.

He glanced down at her, his brown eyes shadowed, but his voice filled with compassion. "I know how much I miss Lloyd. He was my best friend from our first day of school. But nothing compares with losing a spouse, especially a *gut* man like Lloyd Burkholder."

"That's true." But, for her, mourning was not sad in the way Joshua described his own.

Lloyd Burkholder had been a *gut* man…when he'd been sober. As he had never been drunk beyond their home, nobody knew about how a *gut* man became a cruel man as alcohol claimed him. The teasing about how she was clumsy, the excuse she gave for the bruises and her broken finger, hurt almost as much as his fist had.

She put her hand over her distended belly. Lloyd would never be able to endanger their second *kind* as he had his first. Now she wouldn't have to worry about doing everything she could to avoid inciting his rage, which he'd, more than once, aimed at their unborn *kind* the last time she was pregnant. Before Sammy was born, she'd been fearful Lloyd's blows might have damaged their *boppli*. God had heard her desperate prayers because Sammy was perfect when he was born, and he was growing quickly and talking nonstop.

Joshua started to say more, then closed his mouth. She understood. Too many sad memories stood between them, but there were *gut* ones, as well. She couldn't deny that. On the days when Lloyd hadn't been drunk, he had often taken her to visit Joshua and Matilda. Those summery Sunday afternoons spent on the porch of Joshua and Matilda's comfortable white house while they'd enjoyed iced tea had been *wunderbaar*. They had ended when Matilda became ill and was diagnosed with brain cancer.

A handful of gray buggies remained by the cemetery's gate. The horses had their heads down as rain pelted them, and Rebekah guessed they were as eager to return to their dry stalls and a *gut* rubdown as Dolly, her black buggy horse, was.

"Mamm!" Sammy's squeal of delight sounded out of place in the cemetery.

She whirled to see him running toward them. Every possible inch of him was wet, and his clothes were covered with mud. Laughter bubbled up from deep inside her. She struggled to keep it from bursting out.

When she felt Joshua shake beside her, she discovered he was trying to restrain his own amusement. She looked quickly away. If their gazes met, even for a second, she might not be able to control her laughter.

"Whoa!" Joshua said, stretching out a long arm to

keep Sammy from throwing himself against Rebekah. "You don't want to get your *mamm* dirty, do you?"

"Dirty?" the toddler asked, puzzled.

Deborah came to a stop right behind Sammy. "I tried to stop him." Her eyes filled with tears again. "But he jumped into the puddle before I could."

Rebekah pulled a cloth out from beneath her cape. She'd pinned it there for an emergency like this. Wiping her son's face, she gave the little girl a consoling smile. "Don't worry. He does this sort of thing a lot. I hope he didn't splash mud on you."

"He missed me." The girl's smile returned. "I learned how to move fast from being around *Aenti* Ruth's *kinder*. I wish I could have been fast enough to keep him from jumping in the puddle in the first place."

"No one is faster than a boy who wants to play in the water." Joshua surprised her by winking at Sammy. "Isn't that right?"

Her son's smile vanished, and he edged closer to Rebekah. He kept her between Joshua and himself. Her yearning to laugh disappeared. Her son didn't trust any man, and he had *gut* reason not to. His *daed*, the man he should have been able to trust most, could change from a jovial man to a brutal beast for no reason a toddler could comprehend.

"Let's get you in the buggy." Joshua's voice was strained, and his dark brown eyes narrowed as he clearly tried to understand why Sammy would shy away from him in such obvious fear.

She wished she could explain, but she didn't want to add to Joshua's grief by telling him the truth about the man her husband truly had been.

"Hold this," he said as he ducked from under the

umbrella. Motioning for his daughter to take Sammy's hand again, he led them around the buggy. Rain struck him, but he paid no attention. He opened the door on the passenger side. "You probably want to put something on the seat to protect the fabric."

"*Danki*, Joshua. That's a *gut* idea." She stretched forward to spread the dirty cloth on the seat. She shouldn't be surprised that he was concerned about the buggy, because he worked repairing and making buggies not far from his home in Paradise Springs. She stepped back while Joshua swung her son up into the carriage. If he noticed how Sammy stiffened, he didn't say anything.

Once Sammy was perched on the seat with his two fingers firmly in his mouth, Joshua drew the passenger side door closed and made sure it was latched so her son couldn't open it and tumble out. He took his daughter's hand before they came back to stand beside her.

Rebekah raised the umbrella to keep the rain off them. When he grasped the handle, she relinquished it to him, proud that she had managed not to shrink away. He smiled tautly, then offered his hand to assist her into the buggy.

"Be careful," he warned as if she were no older than her son. "The step up is slick, and you don't want to end up as muddy as Samuel."

"You're right." She appreciated his attempt to lighten her spirits as much as she did his offer.

Placing her hand on his palm, she bit her lower lip as his broad fingers closed over it. She'd expected his hands to be as chilled as hers, but they weren't. Warmth seeped past the thick wall she'd raised to keep others from discovering what a fool she'd been to marry Lloyd Burkholder.

Quickly she climbed into the buggy. Joshua didn't hold her hand longer than was proper. Yet the gentle heat of his touch remained, a reminder of how much she'd distanced herself from everyone else in their community.

"*Danki*, Joshua." She lowered her eyes, which were oddly almost even with his as she sat on the buggy seat. "I keep saying that, but I'm truly grateful for your help." She smiled at Deborah. "*Danki* to you, too. You made Sammy giggle, and I appreciate that."

"He's fun," she said, waving to him before running to another buggy farther along the fence.

"We'll see you back at *Mamm*'s house," Joshua said as he unlashed the reins and handed them to her.

She didn't say anything one way or the other. She could use her muddy son as an excuse not to spend the afternoon with the other mourners, but she didn't want to be false with Joshua, who had always treated her with respect and goodness. Letting him think she'd be there wasn't right, either. She stayed silent.

"Drive carefully," he added before he took a step back.

Unexpected tears swelled in her eyes, and she closed the door on her side. When they were first married, Lloyd had said that to her whenever she left the farm. He'd stopped before the end of their second month as man and wife. Like so much else about him, she hadn't known why he'd halted, even when he was sober.

It felt *wunderbaar* to hear a man use those commonplace words again.

"Go?" asked her son, cutting through her thoughts.

"*Ja.*" She steered the horse onto the road after looking back to make sure Joshua or someone else wasn't driving past. With the battery operated lights and wind-shield wiper working, she edged the buggy's wheels onto the wet asphalt. She didn't want to chance them getting stuck in the mud along the shoulder. In this weather it would take them almost an hour to reach their farm beyond Bird-in-Hand.

Sammy put his dirty hand on her cape. "That man was mad at me."

"Why do you think so?" she asked, surprised. From what she'd seen, Joshua had been nothing but friendly with her son.

"His eyes were funny. One went down while the other stayed up."

It took her a full minute to realize her son was describing Joshua's wink. Pain pierced her heart, which, no matter how she'd tried, refused to harden completely. Her darling *kind* didn't understand what a wink was because there had been too few cheerful times in his short life.

She had to find a way to change that. No matter what. Her *kinder* were the most important parts of her world, and she would do whatever she must to make sure they had a *gut* life from this day forward.

Joshua walked into the farmhouse's large but cozy kitchen and closed the back door behind him, glad to be inside where the unseasonable humidity didn't make everything stick to him. He'd waved goodbye to the last of the mourners who'd come to the house for a meal after the funeral. Their buggy was already vanishing into the night by the time he reached the house.

He was surprised to see only his younger sister Esther and *Mamm* there. Earlier, their neighbors, Leah

Beiler and her *mamm*, had helped serve food and collected dishes, which they'd piled on the long table in the middle of the simple kitchen. They had insisted on helping because his older sister Ruth was having a difficult pregnancy, and her family had gone home hours ago.

The thought of his pregnant sister brought Rebekah to mind. Even though she was going to have a *boppli*, too, she had no one to help her on the farm Lloyd had left her. He wondered again why she hadn't joined the mourners at his *mamm*'s house. Being alone in the aftermath of a funeral was wrong, especially when she'd suffered such a loss herself.

Take care of her, Lord, he prayed silently. *Her need is great at this time.*

A pulse of guilt rushed through him. Why hadn't he considered that before? Though it was difficult to see her because she brought forth memories of her late husband and Matilda, that was no excuse to turn his back on her.

Tomorrow, he promised himself. Tomorrow he would go to her farm and see exactly what help she needed. The trip would take him a long way from his buggy shop in Paradise Springs, but he'd neglected his obligations to Lloyd's wife too long. Maybe she would explain why she'd pulled away, her face growing pale each time he came near. He couldn't remember her acting like that before Lloyd died.

"Everyone's gone." Joshua hung his black hat on the peg by the door and went to the refrigerator. He poured himself a glass of lemonade. He'd forgotten what dusty work feeding, milking and cleaning up after cows could be.

And hungry work. He picked up a piece of ham from

the plate on the counter. It was the first thing he'd eaten all day, in spite of half the women in the *Leit* insisting he take a bite of this casserole or that cake. They didn't hide the fact they believed a widower with three *kinder* must never eat a *gut* meal.

"*Mamm*, will you please sit and let me clear the table?" Esther frowned and put her hands on the waist of her black dress.

"I want to help." Their *mamm*'s voice was raspy because she'd talked so much in the past few days greeting mourners, consoling her family and Rose's, and talking with friends. She glowered at the cast on her left arm.

The day before Rose died, *Mamm* had slipped on her freshly mopped floor and stumbled against the table. Hard. Both bones in her lower left arm had broken, requiring a trip to the medical clinic in Paradise Springs. She'd come home with a heavy cast from the base of her fingers to above her elbow, as well as a jar of calcium tablets to strengthen her bones.

"I know, but…" Esther squared her shoulders. "*Mamm*, it's taking me exactly twice as long to do a task because I have to keep my eye on you to make sure you *don't* do it."

"There must be something I can do."

Joshua gave his younger sister a sympathetic smile as he poured a second glass of lemonade. *Mamm* wasn't accustomed to sitting, but she needed to rest her broken arm. Balancing the second glass in the crook of one arm, he gently put his hand on *Mamm*'s right shoulder and guided her to the front room that some of the mourners had put back in order before they'd left. The biggest space in the house, it was where church Sunday services were held once a year when it was *Mamm*'s turn to host them. Fortunately that had happened in the spring, because she was in no state now to invite in the whole congregation.

He felt his *mamm* tremble beneath his fingers, so he reached to open the front door. He didn't want to pause in this big room. It held too many sad memories because it was where his *daed* had been waked years ago.

Not wanting to linger, he steered his *mamm* out on the porch. He assisted her to one of the rocking chairs before he sat on the porch swing. It squeaked as it moved beneath him. He'd try to remember to oil it before he headed home in the morning to his place about a mile down the road.

"Is Isaiah asleep already?" he asked. "When I was coming in, I saw the light go out in the room where he used to sleep upstairs."

"I doubt he's asleep, though it would be the best thing for him. You remember how difficult it is to sleep after..." She glanced toward the barn.

His other brothers should be returning to the house soon, but he guessed *Mamm* was thinking of the many times she'd watched *Daed* cross the grass between the barn and the house. Exactly as he'd looked out the window as if Matilda would come in with a basket of laundry or fresh carrots and peas from her garden. Now he struggled to keep up with the wash and the garden had more weeds than vegetables.

Mamm sighed. "What are you going to do, Joshua?"

"Do?"

"You need to find someone to watch Levi and Deborah during the day while you're at the shop."

It was his turn to sigh into his sweaty glass. "I'm not sure. The *kinder* loved spending time with Rose, and it's going to be hard for them to realize she won't be watching them again."

"Those who have gone before us keep an eye on us always." She gave him a tremulous smile. "But as far as the *kinder*, I can—"

He shook his head. "No, you can't have them come here. Not while you've got a broken arm. And don't suggest Esther. She'll be doubly busy taking care of the house while you're healing. The doctor said it would take at least six weeks for your bones to knit, and I can't have the *kinder* at the shop for that long."

Levi and Deborah would want to help. As Esther had said to *Mamm*, such assistance made every job take twice as long as necessary. In addition, he couldn't work beneath a buggy, making a repair or putting it together, and keep an eye on them. Many of the tools at the buggy shop were dangerous if mishandled.

"There is an easy solution, Joshua."

"What?"

"Get yourself a wife."

His eyes were caught by the flash of lightning from beyond the tree line along the creek. The stars were vanishing, one after another, as clouds rose high in the night sky. Thunder was muted by the distance, but it rolled across the hills like buggy wheels on a rough road. A stronger storm than the one that morning would break the humidity and bring in fresher air.

Looking back at his *mamm*, he forced a smile. "Get a wife like that?" He snapped his fingers. "And my problems are solved?"

"Matilda died four years ago." Her voice was gentle, and he guessed the subject was as hard for her to speak about as it was for him to listen to. "Your *kinder* have been without a *mamm*, and you've been without a wife. Don't you want more *kinder* and the company of a woman in your home?"

Again he was saved from having to answer right away by another bolt of lightning cutting through the sky. "Looks like the storm is coming fast."

"Not as fast as you're changing the subject to avoid answering me."

He never could fool *Mamm*, and he usually didn't try. On the other hand, she hadn't been trying to match him with some woman before now.

"All right, *Mamm*. I'll answer your question. When the time is right, I may remarry again. The time hasn't been right, because I haven't found the right woman." He drained his lemonade and set the glass beside him. "From your expression, however, I assume you have someone specific in mind."

"*Ja*. I have been thinking about one special person, and seeing you with Rebekah Burkholder today confirmed it for me. She needs a husband."

"Rebekah?" He couldn't hide his shock as *Mamm* spoke of the woman who had remained on his mind since he'd left the cemetery.

"*Ja*, Rebekah. With a young son and a *boppli* coming soon, she can't handle Lloyd's farm on her own. She needs to marry before she has to sell out and has no place to go." *Mamm* shifted, then winced as she readjusted her broken arm. "You know her well, Joshua. She is the widow of your best friend."

That was true. Lloyd Burkholder had been his best friend. When Joshua had married Matilda, Lloyd had served as one of his *Newehockers*, the two male and two female attendants who sat beside the bride and groom throughout their wedding day. It was an honor to be asked, and Lloyd had been thrilled to accept.

"Rebekah is almost ten years younger than I am, *Mamm*."

"Lloyd was your age."

"And she is barely ten years older than Timothy."

"True. That might have made a difference years ago, but now you are adults with *kinder*. And you need a wife."

"I don't need a wife right now. I need someone to watch the *kinder*." He held up his hand. "And Rebekah lives too far away for me to ask her to do that."

"What about the housework? The laundry? The cooking? Rose did much of those chores for you, and you eat your other meals here. Deborah can do some of the work, but not all of it. With Esther having to do my chores as well as her own around the house and preparations for the end of the school year, she would appreciate having fewer people at the table each night."

"*Mamm*, I doubt that," he replied with a laugh, though he knew his sister worked hard at their local school.

His *mamm* wagged a finger at him. "True, true. Esther would gladly feed anyone who showed up every night." As quickly as she'd smiled, she became serious again. "But it's also true Rebekah Burkholder needs a husband. That poor woman can't manage on her own."

He didn't want to admit his own thoughts had gone in that direction, too, and how guilty he felt that he'd turned his back on her.

His face must have betrayed his thoughts because *Mamm* asked, "Will you at least think of it?"

"*Ja.*"

What else could he say? Rebekah likely had no interest in remarrying so quickly after Lloyd's death, but if she didn't take another husband, she could lose Lloyd's legacy to her and his *kinder*. The idea twisted in Joshua's gut.

It was time for him to decide exactly what he was willing to do to help his best friend's widow.

Chapter 2

Even as Joshua was turning his buggy onto the lane leading to the Burkholders' farm the next morning, he fought his own yearning to turn around and leave at the buggy's top speed. He hadn't slept last night, tossing and turning and seeking God's guidance while the loud thunderstorm had banished the humidity. A cool breeze had rushed into the rooms where his three *kinder* had been lost in their dreams, but he had been awake until dawn trying to decide what he should do.

Or, to be more accurate, to accept what he should do. *God never promised life would be simple.* That thought echoed through his head during breakfast and as he prepared for the day.

Into his mind came the verse from Psalm 118 that he had prayed so many times since his wife died. *This is the day which the Lord hath made; we will rejoice and be glad in it.*

At sunrise on this crisp morning, he'd arranged for the younger two *kinder* to go to the Beilers' house, but he couldn't take advantage of their generosity often. Abram Beiler suffered from Parkinson's disease, and Leah and her *mamm* had to keep an eye on him as he went about his chores. Even though Leah had told Joshua to depend on her help for as long as he needed because Leah's niece Mandy and Deborah were close in age and enjoyed playing together, he must find a more permanent solution.

His next stop had been to drop off Timothy at his buggy shop at the Stoltzfus Family Shops in the village. The other shops as well as the smithy behind the long building were run by his brothers. He asked the sixteen-year-old to wait on any customers who came in and to let them know Joshua would be there by midday. Even a year ago, he could have trusted Timothy to sort out parts or paint sections of wood that were ready to be assembled, but his older son had grown less reliable in recent months. Joshua tried to give him space and privacy to sort out the answers every teenager wrestled with, which was why he hadn't said anything when he'd noticed Timothy had a portable music device and earphones hidden beneath his shirt.

Until he decided to be baptized and join the church, Timothy could have such items, though many members of the *Leit* frowned on their use at any age. Most *kinder* chose to be baptized, though a few like Leah's twin brother turned their backs on the community and left to seek a different life among the *Englischers*.

He stopped the family buggy, which was almost twice the size of the one Rebekah had driven away from the cemetery yesterday. Looking out the front, he appraised the small white house. He hadn't been here since at least three years before Matilda died. Only now did he realize how odd it was that they had seldom visited the Burkholders' house.

The house was in poor shape. Though the yard was neat and flowers had been planted by the front door, paint was chipped on the clapboards and the roof resembled a swaybacked horse. He frowned when he noticed several bricks had fallen off the chimney and tumbled partway down the shingles. Even from where he sat, he could see broken and missing shingles.

What had happened? This damage couldn't have happened in the five months since Lloyd's death. It must have taken years of neglect to bring the house to such a miserable state.

He stroked his beard thoughtfully as he looked at the barn and the outbuildings. They were in a little bit better shape, but not much. One silo was leaning at a precarious angle away from the barn, and a strong wind could topple it. A tree had fallen on a section of the fence. Its branches were bare and the trunk was silvery-gray, which told him it had been lying in the sunshine for several seasons.

Why had Lloyd let his house and buildings deteriorate like this?

Joshua reminded himself he wasn't going to learn any answers sitting in his buggy. After getting out, he lashed the reins around a nearby tree and left his buggy horse Benny to graze on the longer grass at the edge of the driveway. He walked up the sloping yard to the back door. As he looked beyond the barn, he saw two cows in the pasture. Not enough to keep the farm going unless Rebekah was making money in other ways, like selling eggs or vegetables at one of the farmers' markets near the tourist areas.

He knocked on the back door and waited for an answer. The door didn't have a window like his kitchen door, but he could hear soft footsteps coming toward him.

Rebekah opened the door and stared at him, clearly astonished at his unannounced visit in the middle of a workday morning.

He couldn't help staring back. Yesterday her face had been half hidden beneath her bonnet, and he'd somehow pushed out of his mind how beautiful she was. Her deep auburn hair was hidden beneath a scarf she'd tied at her nape. A splotch of soap suds clung to her right cheek and sparkled as brightly as her blue eyes. Her freckles looked as if someone had blown cinnamon across her nose and high cheekbones. There was something ethereal about her when she looked up at him, her eyes wide and her lips parted in surprise. Her hand was protectively on her belly. Damp spots littered the apron she wore over her black dress. He wasn't surprised her feet were bare. *Mamm* and his sisters preferred to go without shoes when cleaning floors.

Then he noticed the gray arcs beneath her eyes and how drawn her face was. Exhaustion. It was the first description that came to mind.

She put her hand to the scarf. "I didn't expect company."

"I know, but it's long past time I paid you and the boy a visit."

For a moment he thought she'd argue, then she edged back and opened the door wider. "Joshua, *komm* in. How is Isaiah?"

"He was still asleep when I went over there this morning." Guilt twinged in him. He'd been so focused on his own problems that he hadn't been praying for his brother's grieving heart. *God, forgive me for being selfish. I need to be there to hold my brother up at this sad time. I know, too well, the emptiness he is feeling today.*

"How's your *mamm*? I have been praying for her to heal quickly."

He stepped into a kitchen that was as neat as the outside of the house was a mess. The tempting scents of freshly made bread and whatever chicken she was cooking on top of the stove for the midday meal teased him to ask her for a sample. When Lloyd and she had come over to his house, she'd always brought cookies or cake, which rivaled the very best he'd ever tasted.

You wouldn't have to eat your own cooking or Deborah's burned meals any longer if Rebekah agrees to marry you, so ask her.

He wished that voice in his head would be quiet. This was tough enough without being nagged by his own thoughts.

Taking off his straw hat and holding it by the brim, Joshua slowly turned it around and around. "*Danki* for asking. *Mamm* is doing as well as can be expected. You know she's not one for sitting around. She's already figuring out what she can do with one hand."

"I'm not surprised." She gave him a kind smile. "Will you sit down? I've got coffee and hot water for tea. Would you like a cup?"

"*Danki*, Rebekah. Tea sounds *gut*," he said as he set his hat on a peg by the door. He pulled out one of the chairs by the well-polished oak table.

"Coming up." She crossed the room to the large propane stove next to the refrigerator that operated on the same fuel.

"Mamm?" came her son's voice from the front room. It was followed by the little boy rushing into the kitchen. He skidded to a halt and gawped at Joshua before running to grab Rebekah's skirt.

She put a loving hand on Sammy's dark curls. "You remember Joshua, right?"

He heard a peculiar tension underlying her question and couldn't keep from recalling how Sammy had been skittish around him at the cemetery. Some *kinder* were shy with adults. He'd need to be patient while he gave the boy a chance to get to know him better.

Joshua smiled at the toddler. It seemed as if only yesterday his sons, Timothy and Levi, were no bigger than little Samuel. How sweet those days had been when his sons had shadowed him and listened to what he could share with them! As soon as Deborah was able to toddle, she'd joined them. They'd had fun together while he'd let them help with small chores around the buggy shop and on the two acres where he kept a cow and some chickens.

But that had ended when Timothy had changed from a *gut* and devoted son to someone Joshua didn't know. He argued about everything when he was talking, which wasn't often because he had days when he was sullen and did little more than grunt in response to anything Joshua or his siblings said.

"Go?" asked Samuel.

Joshua wasn't sure if the boy wanted to leave or wanted Joshua to leave, but Rebekah shook her head and took a cup out of a cupboard. The hinges screamed like a bobcat, and he saw her face flush.

"It needs some oil," he said quietly.

"I keep planning on doing that, but I get busy with other things, and it doesn't get done." She reached for the kettle and looked over her shoulder at him. "You know how it is."

"I know you must be overwhelmed here, but I'm concerned more about the shape of your roof than a squeaky hinge. If Lloyd hadn't been able to maintain the farm on his own, he should have asked for help. We would have come right away."

"I know, but…"

When her eyes shifted, he let his sigh slip silently past his lips. She didn't want to talk about Lloyd, and he shouldn't push the issue. They couldn't change the past. He was well aware of how painful even thinking of his past with Matilda could be.

He thanked her when she set a cup of steeping tea in front of him. She went to the refrigerator, with her son holding her skirt, and came back with a small pitcher of cream. He hadn't expected her to remember he liked it in his tea.

"*Danki*, Rebekah." He gave her the best smile he could. "Now I'm the one saying it over and over."

"You don't need to say it for this." She set a piece of fresh apple pie in front of him. "I appreciate you having some of the pie. Otherwise I will eat most of it myself." She put her hand on her stomach, which strained the front of her dress. "It looks as if I've had enough."

"You are eating for two."

"As much as I've been eating, you'd think I was eating for a whole litter." She made a face as she pressed her hand to her side. "The way this *boppli* kicks, it feels like I'm carrying around a large crowd that is playing an enthusiastic game of volleyball."

He laughed and was rewarded with a brilliant smile from her. When was the last time he'd seen her genuine smile? He was sad to realize it'd been so long he didn't know.

After bringing a small cup of milk to the table, she sat as he took one bite, then another of her delicious pie. Her son climbed onto her lap, and she offered him a drink. He drank but squirmed. Excusing herself, she stood and went into the other room with Samuel on her hip. She came back and sat. She put crayons and paper in front of her son, who began scribbling intently.

"This way he's occupied while we talk," she said.

"Gut." If he'd had any doubts about her love of *kinder*, they were gone now. She was a gentle and caring *mamm*.

"It's nice of you to come to visit, Joshua, but I know you, and you always have a reason for anything you do. Why are you here today?"

He should be thanking God for Rebekah giving him such a perfect opening to say what he'd come to say. Yet words refused to form on his lips. Once he asked her to be his wife, there would be no turning back. He risked ruining their friendship, no matter how she replied. He hated the idea of jeopardizing that.

Samuel pushed a piece of paper toward him with a tentative smile.

"He wants you to have the picture he drew," Rebekah said.

Jacob looked at the crayon lines zigzagging across the page in every direction. "It's very colorful."

The little boy whispered in Rebekah's ear.

She nodded, then said, "He tells me it's a picture of your horse and buggy."

"I see," he replied, though he didn't. The collection of darting lines bore no resemblance he could discern to either Benny or his buggy. "*Gut* job, Samuel."

The *kind* started to smile, then hid his face in Rebekah's shoulder. She murmured something to him and picked up a green crayon. When she handed it to him along with another piece of paper, he began drawing again.

"You never answered my question, Joshua," she said. "Why did you come here today?"

"In part to apologize for not coming sooner. I should have been here to help you during the past few months."

Her smile wavered. "I know I've let the house and buildings go."

He started to ask another question, but when he met her steady gaze and saw how her chin trembled as she tried to hide her dismay, he nodded. "It doesn't take long once wind and rain get through one spot to start wrecking a whole building."

"That's true. I know I eventually will need to sell the farm. I've already had several offers to buy it."

"Amish or *Englisch*?"

"Both, though I wouldn't want to see the acres broken up and a bunch of *Englisch* houses built here."

"Some *Englischers* like to live on a small farm, as we do." He used the last piece of crust to collect the remaining apple filling on the plate. "My neighbors are like that."

"I didn't realize you had *Englisch* neighbors."

"*Ja.*" He picked up his cup of tea. "Their Alexis and my Timothy have played together from the time they could walk."

"Will Alexis babysit for you?"

Joshua shook his head, lowering his untasted tea to the table. "She's involved in many activities at the high school and her part-time job, so she's seldom around. I hear her driving into their yard late every evening."

"Who's going to take care of Levi and Deborah while you're at work?"

God, You guided our conversation to this point. Be with me now if it's Your will for this marriage to go forward.

He took a deep breath, then said, "I'm hoping you'll help me, Rebekah."

"Me? I'd be glad to once school is out, but come fall we live too far away for the *kinder* to walk here after school."

"I was hoping you might consider a move." He chided himself for what sounded like a stupid answer.

"I'd like to live in Paradise Springs, but I can't think of moving until I sell the farm. A lot needs to be repaired before I do, or I'll get next to nothing for it."

"I'd be glad to help."

"In exchange for babysitting?" She shook her head with a sad smile. "It's a *wunderbaar* idea, but it doesn't solve the distance problem."

He looked down at the table and the picture Samuel had drawn. Right now his life felt as jumbled as those lines. He couldn't meet Rebekah's eyes as he asked, "What if distance wasn't a problem?"

"I don't understand."

Talking in circles wasn't getting him anywhere and putting off asking the question any longer was *dumm*. He caught her puzzled gaze and held it, trying to not lose himself in her soft blue eyes. "Rebekah Burkholder, will you marry me?"

* * *

Rebekah choked on her gasp. She'd been puzzled about the reason for Joshua Stoltzfus's visit, but if she'd guessed every minute for the rest of her life, she couldn't have imagined it would be for him to propose.

Her son let out a protest, and she realized she'd tightened her hold around his waist until he couldn't breathe. Loosening her arm, she set Sammy on the floor. She urged him to go and play with his wooden blocks stacked near the arch into the front room.

"He doesn't need to be a part of this conversation." She watched the little boy toddle to the blocks. She needed time to get her features back under control before she answered Joshua's astonishing question.

"I agree," Joshua said in a tense voice.

She clasped her hands in her lap and looked at him. His brown hair glistened in the sunlight coming through the kitchen windows, but his eyes, which were even darker, had become bottomless, shadowed pools. He was even more handsome than he'd been when she'd first met him years ago, because his sharply sculpted nose now fit with his other strong features. His black suspenders drew her eyes to his powerful shoulders and arms, which had been honed by years of building buggies. His broad hands, which now gripped the edge of the table, had been compassionate when they'd touched hers yesterday.

Had he planned to ask her to be his wife even then? Was that why he'd been solicitous of her and Sammy? She was confused because Joshua Stoltzfus didn't seem to have a duplicitous bone in his body. But if he hadn't been thinking about proposing yesterday, why had he today?

The only way to know was to ask. She forced out the words she must. "Why would you propose to me?"

"You need a husband, and I need a wife." His voice was as emotionless as if they spoke about last week's weather. "We've known each other for a very long time, and it's common for Amish widows and widowers to remarry. But even more important, you're Lloyd's widow."

"Why is that more important?"

"Lloyd and I once told each other that if something happened to one of us, we would take care of the other's family."

"It isn't our way to make vows."

"I know, but Lloyd was insistent that I agree to make sure his wife and family were cared for if something happened to him. I saw the *gut* sense and asked if he would do the same for me." He folded his arms on the table. "He was my friend, and I can't imagine anyone I would have trusted more with my family."

Rebekah quickly lowered her eyes from his sincere gaze. He truly believed Lloyd was the man she once had believed he was, too. She couldn't tell him the truth. Not about Lloyd, but she could tell him the truth about how foolish he was to ask her to be his wife.

"There's a big difference between taking care of your friend's family and..." She couldn't even say the word *marry*.

"But I haven't even taken care of you as I promised him."

"We've managed, and we will until I can sell the farm. *Danki* for your concern, Joshua. I appreciate what you are doing, but it's not necessary."

"I disagree. The fact remains I need a wife and you need a husband."

"You need a babysitter and I need a carpenter."

His lips twitched and she wanted to ask what he found amusing about this absurd conversation. Was it a jest he'd devised to make her smile? She pushed aside that thought as quickly as it'd formed. Joshua was a *gut* man. That was what everyone said, and she agreed. He wouldn't play such a prank on her. He must be sincere.

A dozen different emotions spiraled through her. She didn't know what to feel. Flattered that he'd considered her as a prospect to be his wife? Fear she might be as foolish as she had been the last time a man had proposed? Not that she believed Joshua would raise his hand and strike her, but then she hadn't guessed Lloyd would, either. And, to be honest, she never could have envisioned Joshua asking her to marry him.

"Rebekah," he said as his gaze captured hers again. "I know this is sudden, and I know you must think I'm *ab in kopp*—"

"The thought *you're crazy* has crossed my mind. More than once."

He chuckled, the sound soothing because it reminded her of the many other times she'd heard him laugh. He never laughed at another's expense.

"I'm sure it has, but I assure you that I haven't lost my mind." He paused, toyed with his cup, then asked, "Will you give me an answer, Rebekah? Will you marry me?"

"But why? I don't love you." Her cheeks turned to fire as she hurried to add, "That sounded awful. I'm sorry. The truth is you've always been a *gut* friend, Joshua, which is why I feel I can be blunt."

"If we can't speak honestly now, I can't imagine when we could."

"Then I will honestly say I don't understand why you'd ask me to m-m-marry you." She hated how she stumbled over the simple word.

No, it wasn't simple. There was nothing simple about Joshua Stoltzfus appearing at her door to ask her to become his wife. As he'd assured her, he wasn't *ab in kopp*. In fact, Joshua—up until today—had been the sanest man she'd ever met.

"Because we could help each other. Isn't that what a husband and wife are? Helpmeets?" He cleared his throat. "I would rather marry a woman I know and respect as a friend. We've both married once for love, and we've both lost the ones we love. Is it wrong to be more practical this time?"

Every inch of her wanted to shout, *"Ja!"* But his words made sense.

She had married Lloyd because she'd been infatuated with him and the idea of being his wife, so much so that she had convinced herself while they were courting to ignore how rough and demanding he had been with her when she'd caught the odor of beer on his breath. She'd accepted his excuses and his reassurances it wouldn't happen again…even when it had. She'd been blinded by love. How much better would it be to marry with her eyes wide open? No surprises and a husband whom she counted among her friends.

A pulse of excitement rushed up through her. She could escape, at last, from this farm, which had become a prison of pain and grief and second-guessing herself while she spun lies to protect the very person who had hurt her. She'd be a fool not to agree immediately.

Once she would have asked for time to pray about her decision, but she'd stopped reaching out to God when He hadn't delivered her from Lloyd's abuse. She believed in Him, and she trusted God to take care of the great issues of the world. Those kept Him so busy He didn't have time for small problems like hers.

"All right," she said. "I will marry you."

"Really?" He appeared shocked, as if he hadn't thought she'd agree quickly.

"Ja." She didn't add anything more, because there wasn't anything more to say. They would be wed, for better and for worse. And she was sure the worse couldn't be as bad as her marriage to Lloyd.

Chapter 3

Rebekah straightened her son's shirt. Even though Sammy was almost three, she continued to make his shirts with snaps at the bottom like a *boppli*'s gown. They kept his shirt from popping out the back of his pants and flapping behind him.

"It's time to go downstairs," she said to him as she glanced at her *mamm*, who sat on the bed in the room that once had been Rebekah and Lloyd's. "*Grossmammi* can't wait to have you sit with her."

"Sit with *Mamm*." His lower lip stuck out in a pout.

"But I have cookies." Almina Mast smiled at her grandson. She was a tiny woman, and her hair was the same white as her *kapp*. With a kind heart and a generous spirit, she and her husband Uriah had hoped for more *kinder*, but Rebekah had been their only one. The love they had heaped on her was now offered to Sammy.

"Cookies? *Ja, ja!*" He danced about to his tune-less song.

Mamm put a finger to her lips. "Quiet boys get cookies."

Sammy stilled, and Rebekah almost smiled at his antics. If she'd smiled, it would have been the first time since Joshua had asked her to marry three weeks ago. Since then the time had sped past like the landscape outside the window when she rode in an *Englischer's* van last week while they'd gone to Lancaster to get their marriage license. Otherwise she hadn't seen him. She understood he was busy repairing equipment damaged during last year's harvest.

"Blessings on you, Rebekah." *Mamm* kissed her cheek. "May God bless you and bring you even more happiness with your second husband than he did with your first."

Rebekah stiffened. Did *Mamm* know the truth of how Lloyd had treated her? No, *Mamm* simply was wishing her a happy marriage.

A shiver ached along her stiff shoulders. Nobody knew what had happened in the house she'd shared with Lloyd. And she had no idea what life was like in Joshua Stoltzfus's home. His wife had always been cheerful when they'd been together, but so had Rebekah. Joshua showed affection for his wife and his *kinder*...as Lloyd had when he was sober.

She'd chosen the wrong man to marry once. What if she was making the same mistake? How well did she know Joshua Stoltzfus? At least she and Lloyd had courted for a while. She was walking into this marriage blind. Actually she was entering into it with her eyes wide open. She was familiar with the dark side of what Lloyd had called love. His true love had been for beer. She would watch closely and be prepared if Joshua began to drink. She would leave and return to her farm.

When *Mamm* left with Sammy, Rebekah kneaded her hands together. She was getting remarried. If tongues wagged because Lloyd hadn't been dead for a year, she hadn't heard it. She guessed most of the *Leit* here and in Paradise Springs thought she'd been smart to accept the proposal from a man willing to raise her two *kinder* along with his own.

The door opened again, and Leah Beiler and Joshua's sister Esther came in. They were serving as her attendants.

"What a lovely bride!" Leah gushed, and Rebekah wondered if Leah was thinking about when the day would come for her marriage to Joshua's younger brother Ezra. Leah was preparing to become a church member, and that was an important step toward marriage. Even though nothing had been announced and wouldn't be until the engagement was published two weeks before the marriage, it was generally suspected that the couple, who'd been separated for ten years, planned to wed in the fall.

Esther brushed invisible dust off the royal blue sleeve of Rebekah's dress. For this one day, Rebekah would be forgiven for not wearing black as she should for a year of mourning.

"Ja," Esther said as she moved to stand behind Rebekah. "It makes your eyes look an even prettier blue. Let us help you with your apron."

Every bride wore a white apron to match her *kapp* on her wedding day. She shouldn't have worn it again until she was buried with it, but Rebekah was putting it on for a second time today. Pulling it over her head, she slipped her arms through and let the sheer fabric settle on her dress.

"Oh." Esther chuckled. "There may be a problem."

Rebekah looked down and realized her wedding apron was stretched tightly across her belly. Looking over her shoulder at the other two women who were focused on the tabs that closed it with straight pins at the back, she asked, "Are they long enough?"

"I think so." Leah muttered something under her breath, then said, "There. They're pinned."

"Will it hold? It will be humiliating if one of the pins popped when I kneel."

"We'll pray they will stay in place." Esther chuckled. "If one goes flying, it'll make for a memorable wedding service."

Leah laughed, too. "I'm going to make my apron tabs extra long on my aprons from now on."

Rebekah couldn't manage more than a weak smile. "That's a *gut* idea."

The door opened and Joshua's daughter, Deborah, peeked in. "The ministers and the bishop have come in. Are you ready to go down?"

"Ja," Rebekah replied, though she wanted to climb out the window and run as far away as she could. What had she been thinking when she'd told Joshua yes? She was marrying a man whom she didn't love, a man who needed someone to watch his *kinder* and keep his house. She should have stopped this before it started. Now it was too late for second thoughts, but she was having second thoughts and third and fourth ones.

As she followed the others down the stairs to the room where the service was to be held, she tried not to think of the girl she'd been the last time she'd made this journey. It was impossible. She'd been optimistic and naive and in love as she'd walked on air to marry Lloyd Burkholder.

A longing to pray filled her, but she hadn't reached out to God in more than a year. She didn't know how to start now.

As she entered the room where more than two hundred guests stood, her gaze riveted on Joshua who waited among the men on the far side of the room. The sight of him dressed in his very best clothing and flanked by his two sons made the whole of this irrevocably real.

It has to be better than being married to Lloyd, she reminded herself. She and Sammy and her *boppli* wouldn't have to hide in an outbuilding as they had on nights when Lloyd had gone on a drunken rampage. She'd seen Joshua with his late wife, and he'd been an attentive husband. When Lloyd had teased him about doing a woman's work after Joshua brought extra lemonade out to the porch for them to enjoy, Joshua had laughed away his words.

But he doesn't love you. This is little more than a business arrangement.

She hoped none of her thoughts were visible as she affixed a smile in place and went with Leah and Esther to the bench facing the men's. As they sat so the service could begin, Sammy waved to her from where he perched next to *Mamm*. She smiled at him, a sincere smile this time. She was doing this for him. There was no price too high to give him a safe home.

Squaring her shoulders, she prepared herself to speak the words that would tie her life to Joshua Stoltzfus's for the rest of their lives.

* * *

Joshua put a hand on his younger son's shoulder. Levi always had a tough time sitting still, but the boy wiggled more every second as the long service went on. Usually Levi sat with the unmarried men and boys, where his squirming wasn't a problem. Maybe Joshua shouldn't have asked him to be one of his *Newehockers*, but Levi would have been hurt if Timothy had been asked and he hadn't.

He smiled his approval at Levi when the boy stopped shifting around on the bench. He meant to look at Reuben Lapp, their bishop who was preaching about the usual wedding service verses from the seventh chapter of the Book of Corinthians. His gaze went to Rebekah, who sat with her head slightly bowed.

Her red hair seemed to catch fire in the sunshine. A faint smile tipped the corners of her mouth, and he thought of how her eyes sparkled when she laughed. Were they bright with silver sparks now?

He'd almost forgotten how to breathe when he'd seen her walk into the room. This beautiful woman would be his wife. Even though tomorrow she would return to wearing black for the rest of her year of mourning for Lloyd, the rich blue of her dress beneath her white apron banished the darkness of her grief from her face. He felt blessed that she'd agreed to become his wife.

Joshua shook that thought out of his head. He was no lovesick young man who had won the heart of the girl he'd dreamed of marrying. Instead of letting his mind wander away on such thoughts, he should be listening to Reuben.

At the end of the sermon, the bishop said, "As we are gathered here to witness this marriage, it would seem there can't be any objections to it."

Beside Joshua, his oldest mumbled, "As if that would do any *gut*."

Joshua glanced at Timothy. His son hadn't voiced any protests about the marriage plans in the weeks since Joshua had told his *kinder* Rebekah was to be his wife. Why now?

"Let the two who wish to marry come forward," Reuben said, saving Joshua from having to point out that Timothy could have raised his concerns earlier.

Or was his son taking the opportunity to be unpleasant, as he'd often been since he'd turned sixteen? Now was not the time to try to figure that out. Now was the time to do what was right for his *kinder* and Rebekah's while he fulfilled his promise to his best friend.

Joshua stood and watched as Rebekah did the same a bit more slowly. When he held out his hand to her, she took it. Relief rushed through him because he'd been unsure if she would. He should say something to her, but what? *Danki?* That wasn't what a bridegroom said to his future wife as they prepared to exchange vows.

He led her to Reuben, who smiled warmly at them. Joshua released Rebekah's hand and felt strangely alone. Of the more than two hundred people in the room, she was the only one who knew the truth of why they were getting married. He was glad they'd been honest with each other when he'd asked her to marry. Now there would be no misunderstandings between them, and they should be able to have a comfortable life.

Is that what you want? A comfortable life?

His conscience had been nagging him more as their wedding day drew closer. Every way he examined their arrangement, it seemed to be the best choice for them.

As long as you don't add love into the equation, or do you think you don't deserve love?

Ridiculous question. He'd had the love of his life with his first wife. No man should expect to have such a gift a second time.

"Is everything all right?" Reuben asked quietly.

Realizing the battle within him must have altered his expression, Joshua nodded. "Better than all right." He didn't look at Rebekah. If her face showed she was having second thoughts, too, he wasn't sure he could go through with the marriage. No matter how much they needed each other's help.

"Gut." Raising his voice to be heard throughout the room, the bishop asked, "My brother, do you take our sister to be your wife until such hour as when death parts you? Do you believe this is the Lord's will, and your prayers and faith have brought you to each other?"

"Ja."

Reuben looked at Rebekah and asked her the same, and Joshua felt her quiver. Or was he the one shaking? When she replied *ja,* he released the breath he'd been holding.

The bishop led them through their vows, and they promised to be loyal and stand beside each other no matter what challenges they faced. Rebekah's voice became steadier with each response. After Reuben placed her right hand in Joshua's right hand and blessed them, he declared them man and wife.

The simple words struck Joshua as hard as if a half-finished buggy had collapsed on him. Wife. Rebekah Burkholder was his wife. He was no longer a widower. He was a married man with four *kinder* and another on the way. The bonds that connected him to Matilda had been supplanted by the ones he had just made with Rebekah.

But I will love you always, Tildie.

He glanced guiltily at his new wife and saw her own face had grown so pale that her freckles stood out like chocolate chips in a cookie. Was she thinking the same thing about Lloyd?

It might not be an auspicious beginning for their marriage that their first thoughts after saying their vows were focused on the loves they had lost.

Rebekah stifled a yawn as the family buggy slowed to a stop in front of a simple house that was larger than the one she'd shared with Lloyd. The trip from Bird-in-Hand had taken almost a half hour, and Sammy had fallen asleep on her lap. He'd spent the day running around with the other youngsters. She had planned to have him sleep in his own bed tonight until Joshua asked her to return with him to his house. She'd hesitated, because a thunderstorm was brewing to the west. Even when he'd told her, with a wink, that it was his way of getting her away from the cleanup work at the end of their wedding day, she had hesitated. She'd agreed after *Mamm* had reminded her that a *gut* wife heeded her husband's wishes.

Joshua's three *kinder* sat behind them, and when she looked back she saw the two younger ones had fallen asleep, too. Timothy sat with his arms folded over his chest, and he was scowling. That seemed to be his favorite expression.

A flash caught her eye. Through the trees to the left glowed the bright lights she knew came from the house where the *Englischers* lived. She'd always had plain neighbors, and she hadn't thought about how the darkness at day's end would be disturbed by the glare of electric lights.

"The Grangers are *gut* neighbors," Joshua said as if she'd spoken her thoughts aloud. "That's their back porch light. They don't turn it on unless they're going to be out after dark, and they're considerate enough to turn it off when they get home. Brad put up a motion-detector light, but it kept lighting when an animal triggered it. Because it woke us, he went back to a regular light."

"They sound like nice people."

"Very. We have been blessed to have them as neighbors. Our *kinder* played together years ago, but now their older ones are off to college and only Alexis is at home."

"Are we going to sit here yakking all night?" asked Timothy. "It's stifling back here!"

Rebekah stiffened at his disrespectful tone, then she reminded herself they were tired.

Joshua jumped down before coming around to her side. "I'll carry him in." He held out his arms for Sammy.

She placed her precious *kind* in his arms, grateful for Joshua's thoughtfulness. She'd been on her feet too long today, and she'd become accustomed to taking a nap when Sammy did. As she stepped down, she didn't try to stifle her yawn.

"Let's get you inside," he said. "Then I'll take care of the horse."

"I'll put Benny away, *Daed*." Timothy bounced out and climbed onto the front seat after his brother and sister got out.

"*Danki*, but I expect you to come directly into the house when you're done."

"But, *Daed*, my friends—"

"Will see you on Saturday night as they always do."

Muttering something, Timothy drove the buggy toward the barn.

Joshua watched until the vehicle was swallowed by the building's shadow. Rebekah stood beside him, unsure if she should follow Deborah and Levi, who carried the bag she'd brought with a change of clothing for her and Sammy, into the house or remain by the man who was now her husband.

Husband! How long would it take her to get accustomed to the fact that she'd married Joshua? She was now Rebekah Mast Burkholder... Stoltzfus. Even connecting herself to him in her thoughts seemed impossible. She could have called a halt to the wedding plans right up until they'd exchanged vows. Reuben had given her that chance when he'd asked if everything was all right. Joshua had replied swiftly. Had he thought she might jilt him at the last minute?

"I'm sorry," Joshua said, jerking her away from her unsettling thoughts.

"For what?"

"I'd hoped Timothy would want to spend time with his family this one day at least." He looked down at Sammy. "He used to be as sweet as this little one."

Rebekah didn't know what to say. She started to put her hand on his arm to offer silent consolation. After pulling it back before she touched him, she locked her fingers in front of her. The easy camaraderie she'd felt for him was gone. Everything, even ordinary contact between friends, had changed with a few words. Nothing was casual any longer. Any word, any motion, any glance had taken on a deeper meaning.

Feeling as if she'd already disappointed him because she had said nothing, she followed him into the light green kitchen. Joshua turned on the propane floor lamp while Levi lit a kerosene lantern in the center of the table.

Again Rebekah was speechless, but this time with shock. Every flat surface, including the stove and the top of the refrigerator, was covered with stacks of dirty dishes. What looked to be a laundry basket was so full that the clothes had fallen into jumbled heaps around it. She couldn't tell if the clothes were clean or dirty.

"*Daedi* cooked our breakfast," Deborah said in a loud whisper beneath the hiss of the propane.

Joshua had the decency to look embarrassed as he set Sammy on the floor. Her son had woken as they'd stepped inside. "I meant to clean the house before you arrived, Rebekah, but I had a rush job yesterday, and then we had to get over to your house early today and..." He leaned one hand on the table, then yanked it away with a grimace.

Going to the sink beneath a large window, Rebekah dampened a dishrag. She took it to Joshua and as he wiped his hand off said, "You asked me to come back here tonight because you didn't want me to have to straighten up at my house after such a long day. And then you brought me *here* to *this*?" She burst into laughter. Maybe it was fueled by exhaustion and the stress of pretending to be a happy bride. The whole situation was so ludicrous that if she didn't laugh, she'd start weeping.

"I can see where you'd find that confusing," he said as he glanced around the kitchen.

"Confusing?" More laughter erupted from her, and she pressed her hands over her belly. "Is that what you call this chaos?"

Deborah giggled. "*Daedi* always uses twice as many dishes and pans because he starts making one thing and ends up cooking something else entirely."

"It's usually because I don't have one of the ingredients," Joshua said, his lips twitching.

"Or you don't remember the recipe," Levi crowed.

"*Ja*, that's true." Joshua dropped the dishrag on the table and took off his best hat. "I can put a buggy together with my eyes closed—or near to that—but baking a casserole trips me up every time."

Laughter filled the kitchen as everyone joined in.

Picking up the cloth, Rebekah put it on the sink. "I'll face this in the morning."

"A *gut* idea." To his *kinder*, he said, "Off to bed with you."

"Will you come up for our prayers?" Levi asked.

"*Ja*."

Deborah took Sammy's hand. "*Komm* upstairs with me."

"No," Rebekah and Joshua said at the same time.

The little girl halted, clearly wondering what she'd done wrong.

"I'll put him to bed," Rebekah added. "Everything is new to him. Sammy, why don't you give Deborah and Levi hugs?"

The little boy, who was half asleep on his feet, nodded and complied.

"You're my brother now." Deborah's smile brightened her whole face. "When we found out *Daedi* was going to marry you, Rebekah, I was happy. I'm not the *boppli* of the family any longer."

"Sammy will be glad to have a big sister and big brothers." She looked at Levi, who gave her a shy smile. Should she offer to hug the *kinder*, too?

Before she could decide, the back door opened. Timothy came in, bringing a puff of humid air with him.

He glared at them, especially Joshua, before striding through the kitchen. His footsteps resounded on the stairs as he went up.

Rebekah saw Joshua's eyes narrow. Timothy hadn't spoken to her once. At sixteen he didn't need a *mamm*, but perhaps he would come to see her as someone he could trust. Maybe even eventually as a friend.

Subdued, Deborah and Levi went out of the kitchen. Their footfalls were much softer on the stairs.

"I'm sorry," Joshua said into the silence.

She scooped up Sammy and cradled him. "He's a teenager. It's not easy."

"I realize that, but I hope you realize his rudeness isn't aimed at you. It's aimed at me." He rubbed his hand along his jaw, then down his beard. "I don't know how to handle him because I wasn't a rebellious kid myself."

"I wasn't, either."

"Too bad." The twinkle returned to his eyes. "If you'd been, you might be able to give me some hints on dealing with him."

She smiled at his teasing. He'd been someone she'd deemed a friend for years. She must—they must—make sure they didn't lose that friendship as they navigated this strange path they'd promised to walk together.

Joshua pointed at her and put a finger to his lips. She looked down to see Sammy was once more asleep. Joshua motioned for her to come with him.

Rebekah followed him through the living room. It looked as it had the last time she had been there before Matilda died. The same furniture, the same paint, the same sewing machine in a corner. She glanced toward the front door. The same wooden clock that didn't work. With a start she realized that under the piles of dishes and scattered clothing the kitchen was identical to when Matilda had been alive. It was as if time had stopped in this house with Matilda's last breath.

Opening a door on the other side of the stairs, Joshua lit a lamp. The double bed was topped by a wild-goose-chase-patterned quilt done in cheerful shades of red and yellow and blue. He walked past it to a small bed his *kinder* must have used when they were Sammy's age. Another pretty quilt, this one in the sunshine-and-shadow pattern done in blacks and grays and white, was spread across it. Drawing it back along with the sheet beneath it, he stepped aside so she could slip the little boy in without waking him.

She straightened and looked around. The bedroom was large. A tall bureau was set against the wall opposite the room's two windows, and the bare floors shone with years of care. A quartet of pegs held a *kapp*, a dusty black bonnet and a straw hat. She wasn't surprised when Joshua placed his *gut* hat on the empty peg.

This must have been Joshua and Matilda's room. Suddenly the room seemed way too small. Aware of Joshua going to the bureau and opening the drawers, she lowered the dark green shades on the windows. She doubted Sammy would sleep late in the morning. Usually he was up with the sun.

She faced Joshua and saw he had gathered his work clothes. He picked them up from the blanket chest at the foot of the bed. His gaze slowly moved along her, and so many emotions flooded his eyes she wasn't sure if he felt one or all at the same time. Realizing she was wringing her hands, she forced her arms to her sides.

It was the first time they'd been alone as man and wife. They stood in the room he'd shared with his first wife. She didn't trust her voice to speak, even if she had the slightest idea what to say as she looked at the man who was now her husband. The weight on the first word she spoke was enormous. There were a lot of things she wanted to ask about the life they'd be sharing. She didn't know how.

"Gut nacht," he said into the strained silence. "I'll be upstairs. Second door to the left. Don't hesitate to knock if you or Samuel need anything. I know it'll take you a while to get used to living in a new place."

"Danki."

He waited, but she couldn't force her lips to form another word. Finally, with a nod, he began to edge past her. When she jumped back, fearful he was angry with her, he stared at her in astonishment.

"Are you okay?" he asked.

She nodded, though she was as far from okay as she could be. It was beginning again. The ever-present anxiety of saying or doing the wrong thing and being punished by her husband's heavy hand.

"Are you sure?" His eyes searched her face, so she struggled to keep her expression calm as she nodded again.

He started to say something else, then seemed to think better of it. He bid her *gut nacht* again before he went out of the room.

She pressed her hands to her mouth to silence her soft sob as the tears she'd kept dammed for the whole day cascaded down her cheeks. She should be grateful Joshua had given her and Sammy this lovely room. And she was. But she also felt utterly alone and scared.

"What have I done?" she whispered to the silence.

She'd made, she feared, another huge mistake by doing the wrong thing for the right reasons.

Chapter 4

Joshua's first thought when he opened his eyes the next morning was, *Where am I?* The angle of the ceiling was wrong. There was a single window, and the walls were too close to the bed.

Memory rushed through his mind like a tempest, wild and flowing in every direction. Yesterday he'd married Rebekah, his best friend's widow.

Throwing back the covers, he put his feet on the rug by the bed. His beloved Tildie had started making rugs for the bedrooms shortly after they were wed, and she'd replaced each one when it became too worn. As he looked down through the thick twilight before dawn, he saw rough edges on the one under his feet. Sorrow clutched his heart. His sweet wife would never make another rug for the *kinder*.

Rebekah was his wife now. For better or for worse, and for as long as they lived.

He drew in a deep breath, then let it sift past his taut lips. He'd honored Lloyd's request, and he shouldn't have any regrets. He didn't. Just a question.

Where did he and Rebekah go from here?

Unable to answer that, because he was not ready to consider the question too closely, he pushed himself to his feet. He dressed and did his best to shave his upper lip without a mirror. As he pulled his black suspenders over his shoulders, he walked out of the bedroom.

Light trickled from beneath one door on the other side of the hall. He heard heavy footfalls beyond it. Timothy must already have gotten up, which was a surprise because most mornings Joshua had to wake his older son. Not hearing any voices, he guessed Levi was still asleep. Not even the cacophony of a thunderstorm could wake the boy. The other doorway was dark. He considered making sure Deborah was up so she wouldn't be late for school, but decided to let her sleep. It had been late by the time the *kinder* had gone to bed last night.

As he went down the stairs, Joshua heard the rumble of a car engine and the crunch of tires on gravel. His neighbor must be heading into Philadelphia this morning. Brad always left before sunup when he wanted to catch the train into the city, because he had to drive a half hour east to reach the station.

It was the only normal thing today, because as he reached the bottom of the stairs, he smelled the enticing aromas of breakfast cooking. He glanced at the bedroom where he usually slept. The door was closed.

The propane lamp hissed in the kitchen as he walked in to see Rebekah at the stove. She wore a dark bandana over her glistening hair. Beneath her simple black dress and apron, her feet were bare.

"Sit down," she said as if she'd made breakfast for him dozens of times. "Do you want milk in your *kaffi*?"

"No, I drink it black in the morning."

"Are the others awake?"

"Only Timothy." He was astounded how they spoke about such ordinary matters. There was nothing ordinary about Rebekah being in his kitchen before dawn.

"*Gut.* I assumed he'd get up early, too, so I made plenty of eggs and bacon." Turning from the stove, she picked up a plate topped by biscuits. She took a single step toward the table, then halted as her gaze locked with his.

A whirlwind of emotions crisscrossed her face, and he knew he should say something to put her at ease. But what? Her fingers trembled on the plate. Before she could drop it, he reached for it. His knuckle brushed hers so lightly he wouldn't have noticed the contact with anyone else. A heated shiver rippled across his hand and up his arm. He tightened his hold on the plate before *he* let it fall to the floor.

He put the biscuits on the table as she went back to the stove. Searching for something to say, he had no chance before Timothy entered the kitchen. His son walked to the table, his head down, not looking either right or left as he took his seat to the left of Joshua's chair at the head of the table.

Rebekah came back. Setting the coffeepot on a trivet in the center of the table, she hesitated.

"Why don't you sit here?" Joshua asked when he realized she was unsure which chair to use. He pointed to the one separated from his by the high chair he'd brought down from the attic before the wedding yesterday. He'd guessed she would want it for her son, but now discovered it created a no-man's-land between them.

She nodded as she sat. Was that relief he saw on her face? Relief they were no longer alone in the kitchen? Relief the high chair erased any chance their elbows might inadvertently bump while they ate?

He pushed those thoughts aside as he bent his head to signal it was time for the silent grace before they ate. His prayers were more focused on his new marriage than food, and he hoped God wouldn't mind. After all, God knew the truth about why he'd asked Rebekah to be his wife.

As soon as Joshua cleared his throat to end the prayer, Timothy reached for the bowl containing fluffy eggs. He served himself, then passed the bowl to Joshua. That was followed by biscuits and apple butter as well as bacon and sausage.

Each bite he took was more delicious. The biscuits were so light he wondered why they hadn't floated up from the plate while they'd prayed. The *kaffi* had exactly the right bite for breakfast. He could not recall the last time he'd enjoyed a second cup at breakfast, because his own brew resembled sludge.

For the first time in months, Timothy was talkative. He had seconds and then thirds while chattering about a baseball game he'd heard about yesterday at the wedding, a game won by his beloved Phillies. It was as if the younger version of his son had returned, banishing the sulky teen he'd become. Even after they finished their breakfast with another silent prayer, Timothy was smiling as he left to do the barn chores he usually complained should be Levi's now that he worked every day at the buggy shop.

Joshua waited until the back door closed behind his oldest, then said, "Tell me how you did that."

"Did what?" Rebekah asked as she rose and picked up the used plates. After setting them on top of others stacked on the counter, she began running water to begin the massive task of washing the dirty dishes that had gathered since the last time he'd helped Deborah with them.

"Make my oldest act like a human being rather than a grumpy mule," he replied.

"Don't let him—or any of the other *kinder*—hear you say that. He wouldn't appreciate it."

"Or having his sister and brother repeat it."

"And Sammy, too. *Kinder* his age grab on to a word and use it over and over." She smiled as she put soap into the water and reached for a dishrag. Not finding one, she glanced around.

"Second drawer," he said, hoping there was a clean dishcloth. Like the dishes, laundry had piled up, ignored during the past week.

"Danki." She opened the drawer and pulled out a cloth. "I'll get accustomed to where everything is eventually."

He knew she didn't mean to, but her words were like a pail of icy water splashing in his face. A reminder that no matter how much they might pretend, everything had changed.

No, not everything. He still held on to his love for Tildie.

That will never change, he silently promised his late wife.

Never, because he wasn't going to chance putting his heart through such pain ever again.

Everything seemed unfamiliar in the Stoltzfus kitchen, yet familiar at the same time.

Rebekah was cooking breakfast as she did each morning while she waited for the bread dough to rise a second time. She prepared enough for Levi and Deborah. Or she thought she had until she saw Levi could tuck away as much as his older brother. She fried the last two eggs for the boy, who ate them with enthusiasm.

"You cook *gut*! Real *gut*!" Levi said as he took his straw hat off the peg by the back door. With a grin at his sister, he added, "You should learn from her."

"She will," Rebekah replied gently when she saw the dismay on the little girl's face. "After school, Levi, while you are doing your chores, Deborah and I will be preparing your supper."

She was rewarded by a broad smile from Joshua's daughter, who said, "Levi is going to *Onkel* Daniel's shop after school." Deborah picked up the blue plastic lunch box and stepped aside so her brother could take the green one. "I'll be walking home with Mandy Beiler. Mandy lives down the road from *Grossmammi* Stoltzfus. She used to live in Philadelphia, but she lives here now. She is almost the same age I am. We—"

"We need to go." Levi frowned at his sister. "We don't want to arrive after the school bell rings. We won't have time to play baseball if we're late."

Deborah rolled her eyes as if ancient and world-weary. "All he thinks about is baseball."

"Like Timothy," Rebekah said as she wiped Sammy's hands before giving him another half biscuit.

"Timothy thinks about girls, too, especially Alexis next door. He talks to her every chance he can get." Levi put his hand over his mouth and gave a guilty glance toward his sister.

"I'm sure he does," Rebekah said quietly. "They've been friends their whole lives, haven't they?"

"*Ja*, friends." Deborah scowled at her brother. "Saying otherwise is silly. She is *Englisch*."

Levi nodded and opened the door. His smile returned when he added, "At the wedding he was talking to some girls from Bird-in-Hand. I think he really liked—"

"Whom he likes is Timothy's business." Rebekah smiled. "You know we don't talk about such things, so it can be a surprise when a couple is published to marry."

"Like you and *Daedi*?" asked Deborah. "Lots of folks were surprised. I heard them say so."

Nobody more than I, she was tempted to reply, but she made a shooing motion toward the door. The two scholars skipped across the yard to where their scooters were waiting. They hooked their lunch boxes over the handles before pushing them along the driveway toward the road.

She prayed the Lord would keep them safe. There were fewer cars along this road than in Bird-in-Hand, where carloads of tourists visited shops and restaurants.

She remained in the doorway and looked at the gray clouds thickening overhead. She hadn't expected to watch *kinder* leave for school for another couple of years. When Deborah looked over her shoulder and waved, the tension that had kept Rebekah tossing and turning last night diminished.

Help me make this marriage work, Lord, she prayed. *For the* kinder's *sakes. They have known too much sorrow, and it's time for them to be happy as* kinder *should be.*

Seeing Sammy had found the box of crayons she'd packed to bring to Joshua's house, Rebekah turned to the sink. She had to refill the sink with the water heated by solar panels on the roof. When she'd met Joshua's second-youngest brother, Micah, at the wedding, he'd mentioned how he had recently finished the installation.

She hummed a tuneless song as she washed dishes, dried them and put them in the cupboards. Outside, it began to rain steadily. Maybe she should have told the *kinder* to take umbrellas to school.

By the time she had baked the bread as well as a batch of snickerdoodles, it was time for the midday meal. Lloyd always wanted his big meal at noon, but Joshua worked off the farm, so she would prepare their dinner for the evening. She had no idea what Joshua and his *kinder* liked to eat.

Rebekah pushed aside that thought as she put Sammy in the high chair and gave him his sandwich and a glass of milk. Sitting beside him, she ate quickly, then returned to work. She was scooping up an armful of dirty laundry from the floor when she heard Sammy call her.

Turning, she asked over her shoulder, "What is it, *liebling*?"

"Go home?" Thick tears rolled down his full cheeks.

She dropped the clothes to the floor. Sitting, she lifted Sammy out of the high chair and set him beside her. There wasn't enough room on her lap for him any longer. Putting her arm around his shoulders, she nestled him close. Her heart ached to hear his grief.

"I thought we would stay here and see Deborah and Levi when they get home from school," she said and kissed the top of his head.

"When that?"

"After Sammy has his nap."

He wiggled away and got down. "Nap now?"

"Not until you finish your sandwich." As she set him

back in the high chair, she smiled at how eager he was to see Joshua's younger *kinder* again.

In Bird-in-Hand, Sammy had encountered other *kinder* only on church Sundays. Their neighbors didn't have youngsters, and even if they had, Sammy was too young to cross the fields on his own. She'd become accustomed to remaining home in the months before Lloyd's death because he had flown into rages when he didn't know where she was. After his death, she'd had an excuse to stay behind her closed door.

But it hadn't been fair to Sammy.

Guilt clamped around her heart. Now *that* was familiar. Each time Lloyd had lashed out at her, she'd tried to figure out what she'd done to make him strike her again.

She was Joshua Stoltzfus's wife now. Her past was gone, buried with Lloyd.

Repeating it over and over to convince herself, she cleaned Sammy up after his lunch. She took him into the bedroom for his nap, but he was too excited. Each time she settled him on the small bed with his beloved stuffed dog, he was up afterward and sneaking out of the bedroom to explore the house.

Rebekah gave up after a half hour. Skipping his nap one day wouldn't hurt him, and she was curious, too, about the rest of the house. She glanced around the kitchen. The dishes were cleaned and put away, though she suspected she hadn't put them in their proper places. She would check with Deborah so everything was as it should be when Joshua arrived home. The dirty clothes were piled on the floor in the laundry room. In the morning before breakfast, if the rain stopped, she would start the first load. She hadn't mopped the floor. That made no sense when Joshua and the *kinder* would be tracking in water and mud.

There wasn't any reason for her *not* to explore the house.

Sammy grinned and chattered like an excited squirrel as they walked into the large front room where church could be held when it was their turn to host it. She wondered when that would be. Surely no one would expect the newlyweds to hold church at their house right away. Most newlyweds spent the first month of their marriage visiting family and friends nearby and far away. Joshua hadn't mentioned making calls, and she guessed his business wouldn't allow him time away. Just as well, because she didn't want to upset Sammy by uprooting him day after day.

When her son scrambled up the stairs, dragging the stuffed dog with him, she followed slowly, not wanting to slip on the smooth, wooden steps. But there was another reason she hesitated. She hoped Joshua wouldn't care if she went upstairs while he was at the buggy shop. Last night he'd told her to come and get him if she or Sammy needed anything, so her exploring shouldn't make him angry.

She wrapped her arms around herself. She hated how every thought, every action, had to be considered with care. After Lloyd's death, she'd been gloriously free from a husband's expectations. Now she was subjected to them once more. But would Joshua be as heavy-handed as Lloyd had been? She must make sure she never found out.

Lord, is this Your will? If so, guide my steps and my words on a path where we will remain safe.

Rebekah opened the first door on the second floor. A pair of dresses hung from pegs on the wall, along with a white apron Deborah would wear to church. A black bonnet waited beside them. By the window, the bed was covered with a beautiful quilt. The diamond-in-a-square pattern was done in cheerful shades of blue, purple and green. A rag rug beside the bed would keep little feet from the chill of a wintry floor.

The room beside it clearly belonged to Timothy because a man-size pair of shoes were set beneath the window, but a second mattress had been dragged into the room. She realized Levi must have given up his room to Joshua and was sleeping with his brother. She appreciated the boys' kindness, especially when they had no idea how long Levi would be sharing with Timothy.

Sammy ran to the door across the hall. She hurried after him, not wanting him to disturb Joshua's things. Grabbing her son's arm, she remained in the doorway.

Nothing about the room gave her a clue to the man she'd married. It was the same as the other rooms, except the ceiling slanted sharply on either side of a single dormer. Like his *kinder*'s rooms, the bed was neatly made and a rag rug brightened the wooden floor. She hadn't realized how she'd hoped to find something to reassure her that he was truly as gentle as he appeared. If he proved to be a chameleon like Lloyd...

"Cold, *Mammi*?" asked Sammy.

She smiled at him, even as she curbed another shiver. If a *kind* as young as her son could sense her disquiet, she must hide her feelings more deeply. She could not allow Joshua to suspect the secrets of her first marriage. If the truth of Lloyd's weaknesses became known, it could ruin her son's life.

She wouldn't let that happen.

Ever.

Chapter 5

As he drove toward his house, Joshua couldn't recall another day at the buggy shop that had seemed so long. Usually the hours sped past as he kept himself occupied with the work and trying to teach Timothy the skills his son would need to take over the shop after him.

He *had* been busy today, but his thoughts hadn't stayed on the antique carriage he was restoring for Mr. Carpenter, an *Englischer* who lived in a fancy community north of Philadelphia. Too often instead of the red velvet he was using to reupholster the interior of the vehicle that dwarfed his family buggy, Joshua had seen Rebekah's face.

Her uncertainty when she'd stood beside him in front of their bishop to take their wedding vows. Her laughter when they'd come into the messy kitchen. Her glowing eyes filled with questions as he bid her *gut nacht*. Her kind smile for his teenage son this morning.

"Watch out!" Timothy shouted as Levi yelped a wordless warning from behind him.

Joshua yanked on the reins, though the horse had already started to turn away from the oncoming milk truck. The driver gave a friendly wave as the vehicle rumbled past before turning into the lane leading to a neighboring farm.

Lowering his hands to his lap, Joshua took a steadying breath. He couldn't get so lost in his thoughts that he missed what was going on around him. He'd lost Tildie. He couldn't bear the idea of losing his two sons.

Help me focus, Lord, on what is important in my life.

"Want me to drive, *Daed*?" asked Timothy with a grin.

"I'll drive!" Levi wasn't going to be left out, especially after assisting his *onkel* at Daniel's carpentry shop.

"*Danki*, but I think I can manage to get us home from here in one piece." Joshua kept his eyes on the road as he guided the horse onto the driveway. He sent up a prayer of gratitude that he and his two sons hadn't been hurt.

What was wrong with him? He was showing less sense than his teenage son. If Timothy had been driving, Joshua would have reprimanded him for not paying attention. Even after he'd brought the buggy to a stop between the house and the barn, his hands shook. He nodded when Levi offered to help Timothy unhook Benny and get the horse settled for the night.

"Dinner will be on the table soon," he said as he did every evening after work. "So don't dawdle."

"Are you sure your bride will have it ready?" Timothy asked.

He glanced at his grinning teenage son. Tempted to remind his son that Timothy didn't know anything about Rebekah, he refrained. Joshua would have to admit he didn't know much about her, either. He wasn't going to confess that to his *kinder*.

"We'll see, won't we?" Joshua strode toward the kitchen door.

He paused to check the garden. It needed weeding again. He glanced at the chicken coop. The patch he'd put on the roof last month was still in *gut* shape. Reaching up, he gave the clothesline that ran from the back stoop to the barn a gentle tug. The tension remained *gut*, so he didn't need to tighten it yet to keep clean clothes from dragging in the grass.

Joshua sighed. He'd told the boys not to dawdle, and he was doing it himself. *Coward!* When he'd asked Rebekah to wed him, he'd known there would be changes. There had to be, because the marriage was bringing her and a toddler and soon a *boppli* into the family. He'd convinced himself he understood that.

But he hadn't.

Not really.

Knowing he could not loiter in his own yard any longer, he climbed the two steps to the small porch at the back door. He wasn't sure what he'd find, but when he opened the back door, he stared. Every inch of the kitchen shone like a pond in the bright sunlight. Even the stain he'd assumed would never come out of the counter was gone. Dishes were stacked neatly in the cupboards, and each breath he drew in contained the luscious aromas of freshly baked bread as well as the casserole Rebekah was removing from the oven.

The last time the kitchen had smelled so enticing was before Tildie became ill. Supper at his *mamm*'s house was accompanied by great scents, but his own kitchen had been filled with odors of smoke and scorched pans and foods that didn't go together.

His gaze riveted on her. Strands of red hair had escaped her *kapp* and floated around her face like wisps of cloud. Her face glowed with the heat from the oven, and she smiled as she drew in a deep breath of the steam coming from the casserole.

He had never seen her look so beautiful or so at ease. The thought shocked him. He'd always considered her pretty, but he'd never thought about how taut her shoulders usually were. Not just since he'd asked her to marry. Every time he'd seen her.

"Daedi!"

Deborah rushed over and threw her arms around his waist. He embraced her, turning his attention from Rebekah and the kitchen's transformation to his daughter. Her smile was wider than he'd seen in a long time. She must have enjoyed her time with Rebekah and Sammy after school.

A pulse of an unexpected envy tugged at him. He dismissed it, not wanting to examine too closely how he wished he could have shared that time with them.

"Perfect timing," Rebekah said as she carried the casserole of scalloped potatoes to the table. Platters of sliced roast beef were set beside bowls holding corn and green beans. Sliced bread was flanked by butter and apple butter. Chowchow and pickled beets completed the feast. She looked past him, and he realized Timothy and Levi stood behind him when she asked, "Do you boys need to wash up?"

His mouth watered. His sons' expressions were bright with anticipation, and he wondered if his own face looked the same. Even so, he motioned for the boys to go into

the laundry room to wash their hands. They went with
a speed he hadn't seen them show before dinner…ever.

As he went to the kitchen sink, he almost bumped
into Sammy, who was racing to his *mamm*. The *kind*
glanced at him fearfully. He hoped the little boy would
get used to him soon. Maybe in his own young way
Sammy mourned for Lloyd and wasn't ready to replace
his *daed* with another man.

Joshua doubted he could ever be the man Lloyd
Burkholder had been. When people spoke of Lloyd,
they always mentioned his dedication to his neighbors
and his family. More than once, he'd heard someone
say Lloyd always accompanied Rebekah wherever she
went. A truly devoted husband. With his work taking
him to the shop each day, Joshua couldn't be the dot-
ing husband his friend had been. He hoped Rebekah
understood.

As soon as everyone was seated at the table, he sig-
naled for them to bow their heads for silent grace. He
was pleased to see Sammy do so, too. Rebekah had
taught her son well.

He didn't linger over his prayers, which again had
more to do with making his new marriage work and less
to do with the food in front of him. Clearing his throat,
he raised his head. The *kinder* didn't need prompting
to start passing the food along the table.

His worry about what to discuss during the meal
vanished when Levi monopolized the conversation. His
younger son was excited that he'd learned how to use
one of the specialty saws Daniel had for his construction projects. As he described the tool in detail, Rebekah
helped Sammy eat with as little mess as possible. Deborah and Timothy were busy enjoying the meal.

Joshua realized he was, too. He'd been dependent on his own cooking or Deborah's struggling attempts for too long. There had been plenty of meals at his *mamm*'s house, but even she wasn't the cook Rebekah was. Each dish he tried was more flavorful than the one before. Like his sons, he had seconds.

"Don't fill up completely," Rebekah said as she smiled at his daughter. "There's peach pie for dessert."

"You're spoiling us with your *wunderbaar* food," he replied.

She flushed prettily when the boys hurried to add their approval. She deflected it by saying quietly, "God gave each of us a unique talent, and the praise should go to Him."

Deborah jumped up, announcing she would serve dessert. She cut the pie and brought the first plate to the table and set it in front of Joshua with a hopeful smile. "Try it, *Daedi*." Her voice dropped almost to a whisper. "I made it."

"You made the pie, Deborah?" He hoped his disappointment didn't come through in his voice. As *gut* as the rest of the meal had been, he'd been looking forward to sampling Rebekah's peach pie. She'd brought one to the house years ago, and he still recalled how delicious it had been.

Her brothers regarded the pieces their sister handed them with suspicion. As one they glanced at him. Neither reached for a fork, even when Deborah sat again at the table. When dismay lengthened his daughter's face, he couldn't delay any longer.

Picking up his fork, he broke off a corner from the pie. Flakes fell on to the plate. That was a surprise because Deborah's last attempt at making a pie had resulted in a crust as crisp as a cracker. Aware how everyone was watching, he raised the fork to his mouth.

Flavors came to life on his tongue. Peaches, cinnamon and even a hint of nutmeg.

"This is…" He had to search for the best word. Not *surprising* or *astounding* and most especially not *impossible*, though he couldn't believe Deborah had made the flaky crust that was as light as the biscuits at breakfast. When his daughter regarded him with anticipation, he finished, "Beyond *wunderbaar*."

"Danki," his daughter said as she turned toward the other end of the table to watch her brothers dig in now that Joshua had announced the pie was *gut*. "Rebekah taught me a really easy way to make the crust. It's important not to handle it too much. Mix it, roll it out and get it in the pan."

"She did a *gut* job." He broadened his smile as he took another bite.

"It wasn't hard when I have such an eager student," Rebekah replied.

When they finished the meal with a silent prayer, Joshua asked Timothy to help Levi with the dishes while Deborah played with Sammy. Before they could answer, he stood and invited Rebekah to come out on the front porch with him. He wasn't sure who looked the most surprised at his requests.

But one thing he knew for certain. He and Rebekah needed some time to talk and come to terms with the life they had chosen together. He had put off the discussion since he asked her to be his wife.

Rebekah lifted Sammy down from the high chair and told him to show Deborah the pictures he'd colored earlier. As the toddler rushed to the little girl, he shot an uneasy glance in Joshua's direction. His *mamm* looked dismayed, and she bit her lower lip.

Joshua said nothing as he motioned for her to lead the way to the front door. When he reached over her head to hold the screen door, she recoiled sharply. Had he surprised her? She must have known he was right behind her, and she should have guessed he'd hold the door for her.

A grim realization rushed through him. She must be worried that if she lowered the walls between them, even enough to thank him for a common courtesy, he would insist on his rights as her husband. He wanted to reassure her that he understood her anxiety, but anything he could think to say might make the situation even more tense.

If that were even possible.

Scolding herself for showing her reaction to Joshua's hand moving past her face, Rebekah knew she needed to take care. He hadn't been about to slap her, and acting as if he was could betray the secret she kept in the darkest corners of her heart. She hurried to the closer of the two rocking chairs on the front porch. She'd always loved the rockers Joshua and Matilda had received as wedding gifts. Whenever she and Lloyd had visited, she had happily sat in one and watched the traffic on the narrow road in front of the house.

Now...

She pushed aside thoughts of being a trespasser. Upon marrying Joshua, this had become her home. She had to stop considering it another woman's.

"I thought you might appreciate a bit of rest," Joshua said as he leaned against the railing so he could face her. "I never expected you to toil so hard in the kitchen."

"You know how it is. You do one thing and that leads to another and then to another, and before you know it, the whole task is done."

He smiled and something spun with joy within her. He was a handsome man, even more so when he grinned because his dark brown eyes glistened. He was past due for a haircut, and strands fell forward into his eyes. She folded her hands on her lap to keep from reaching up to discover if it was as silken as it looked.

"And I had lots of help," she added so silence didn't fall between them. "Deborah is like a sponge, soaking up everything I tell her."

"Especially about making pie." He patted his stomach. "I may have to take up jogging like the *Englischers* if you keep feeding us such amazing food."

"If you do, I will sew an under-the-chin strap for your hat like I do for Sammy's so it won't bounce off."

He roared a laugh, slapping his hand against the roof pole beside him. She smiled, glad she'd been able to ease the strain on his face…if only for a short time.

When he waved at a buggy driving past, he said, "Daniel is late returning home tonight. I wonder if he is courting someone again."

"Sometimes it takes time to find the right person to marry."

"Oh, that doesn't seem to be his problem." He stared after the buggy until it vanished over a hill. "I hope this time he doesn't get cold feet and put an end to it. He's courted two different girls we thought he might wed. The girls joined the church in anticipation of a proposal, but he hasn't been baptized. They married other men."

"Maybe he isn't ready."

"I was baptized, married and had a *kind* by the time I was his age."

She slowed her rocking to stop. "Each of us is different, Joshua. Daniel will make the right decision when it's God's will for him to do so."

"*Ja*. Daniel is a *gut* man." With a sigh he looked back at her. "I meant to ask you. Daniel was glad to have Levi help him this afternoon. He'd like Levi to come back a day or two each week if you can spare him."

"It would be *gut* for Levi to learn more about what his *onkel* does." She smiled as she began rocking again slowly and watched the lights from a car ripple through the trees along the road. "With only a few years of school left for him, he can learn about a craft he might want to pursue."

"My thoughts exactly, but I don't want him neglecting his chores here. The garden needs—"

"Deborah, Sammy and I will take care of the garden. You don't need to worry about it."

"I wasn't." He paused and looked everywhere but at her. "How did Sammy do today?"

"He spent the day exploring the house. Fortunately I was able to block the cellar door with a chair before he took it into his head to investigate down there."

Again he drew in a deep breath. "I know it may take time, but I wish he felt more comfortable around me."

"It *will* take time."

"I know that, but I wish he wouldn't cringe away in fear. Every time that happens, I feel like a horrible beast."

Was he still talking about Sammy, or was he referring to her reaction by the door? She must not ask.

"Sammy has had a lot of changes in his life over the

past couple of days. He was too wound up today to take a nap, so he's overly tired, too."

"At least he's happy to spend time with Deborah."

"And she with him." She started to add more, but put her hand to the side of her belly when the *boppli* kicked. "Ouch!"

"A strong one?" he asked.

She smiled. "It kicks like a horse. Maybe it's warning me that I won't get much chance to sit once it's born. When I'm busy, it's quiet. As soon as I take a moment's rest, it begins its footrace."

"Do you have names chosen?"

She shook her head, not wanting to hear his next words. The ones everyone said. If it was a boy, surely she would name it for its late *daed*. How could she explain Lloyd was the last name she would select? Without being honest about the man he'd been, she would sound petty and coldhearted.

"Don't let the *kinder* know," he said, startling her with his smile. "You'll be bombarded with more name suggestions than you could use for a dozen litters of kittens. I doubt the names Mittens and Spot would be of much use to you."

She laughed honestly and freely. The sound burst out of a place within her she'd kept silent for so long she'd almost forgotten it existed. Tears teased the corners of her eyes. Not tears of pain or fear but tears of joy.

"That's a nice sound," he said, his smile growing wider. "It gives me hope that we're going to make this marriage work better than either of us can guess right now."

"I hope so."

"And to that end…" He moved to the other rocking chair. When he began to ask about her daily schedule and if she wanted him to pick up the few groceries they'd need from his brother's store or if she preferred to do the shopping herself, his questions showed he had many of the same anxieties she did, along with the determination to overcome them.

She answered each question the best she could. She had some of her own, which he replied to with a smile. More than once he mentioned he was glad she had thought of some matter he hadn't. His words made her feel part of the family, not an outsider who'd come to cook and clean and watch over the youngsters.

By the time they rose to go inside and spend time with the *kinder*, her shoulders felt lighter. She brought Sammy to sit beside her on a bench not far from the stove that would warm the room next winter. With her arm around him, she watched Joshua don a pair of dark-rimmed glasses. She'd had no idea he needed glasses.

Joshua read from Psalm 146, and she was comforted by the words of praise. "Happy is he that hath the God of Jacob for his help, whose hope is in the Lord his God… The Lord preserveth the strangers, He relieveth the fatherless and widow…"

She stroked her son's hair while he fell asleep. Holding him, she listened as Joshua continued. His warm voice rose and fell with the joyous words, and she found her own eyes growing heavy as she let the sound soothe her.

This was the future she'd imagined when she had accepted Lloyd's proposal. Evenings with the family gathered together, savoring the words inspired by God's love. The perfect end to the day as the gas lamp hissed and the last light of the day faded into night. An affir-

mation of faith and love with the people who were in
her heart.

It wasn't perfect. Her marriage to Joshua wasn't a
true one. However, there was no reason they couldn't
work together to make a *gut* and happy home. He had
treated her with kindness, and she prayed she'd seen
the real man and that he had no secret life as Lloyd had.

After Joshua finished reading and the family prayed
together, Rebekah took Sammy into the downstairs bedroom while Joshua and his *kinder* went upstairs. Their
footfalls sounded along with the occasional creaking
board while she settled her son into bed. He roused
enough to ask for Spot, the stuffed dog he slept with
each night. Telling him to stay where he was, she went
into the dark kitchen. She used the flashlight she'd
found in a drawer earlier, but had no luck finding Spot.

Sammy had had the stuffed toy with him when they'd
gone upstairs that afternoon. Maybe he'd left it up there
somewhere. If she hurried she could retrieve it before
the other *kinder* were asleep.

After pausing to tell Sammy she would bring Spot
to him in a few minutes, she went up the stairs far more
slowly than Deborah and Levi had a few minutes ago.
Gas lamps were on in the two bedrooms on the right
side of the hallway. From beyond the first door to the
left, she heard water splashing and guessed someone
was brushing his or her teeth.

She glanced into Deborah's room. It was empty, and
a quick scan told her Sammy's precious toy wasn't there.
Maybe in the room the boys shared...

As she went to look there, a voice came from the
half open door on the other side of the hall. Low, deep

and fraught with pain. She froze when she realized it belonged to Joshua.

She should back away, but she couldn't move. She saw Joshua sitting on the bed with his back to her. His head was bowed, and, at first, she thought he was praying. Then she realized he held something in his hands.

A rag rug that was frayed with wear around the edges.

He held it as if the worn fabric was a treasured lifeline. His gaze was so focused on the rug he was oblivious to everything else, even the fact his door had come ajar.

Go! she told herself, but her legs refused to work.

"Tildie, I hope you understand why I've done what I have," Joshua said. "I know you'd want our *kinder* to have the best care, and Rebekah is already giving them that. You told Lloyd often that he was blessed to have her as his wife. He was, and I am blessed to have her help and to be able to help her. But I miss having you here, Tildie. Nobody will ever take your place. Even if I can't show it any longer in public now that I'm married again, I'll never stop loving you."

The pain in his words matched what twisted through her heart. Her hope Joshua would be open and honest with her was dashed. So easily he spoke of keeping his love for his late wife a secret.

Secrets! They had dominated her first marriage. Now they dashed her hopes for her second one.

She edged away and pressed back against the wall so not even her shadow would betray her presence. Eavesdropping was wrong, especially during such a private conversation.

She walked away as quietly as she had come up the stairs. She knew it would be silly to run away as she longed to. She could fall and hurt herself on the stairs.

When she looked in the bedroom to check on Sammy, she saw him curled up in bed, his toy in his arms. He must have remembered where he'd left it and gotten it on his own. She blinked back abrupt tears. The way Sammy cuddled with his precious Spot reminded her of how Joshua had held the worn rag rug with such love and sadness. A peculiar sensation surged through her.

Envy.

Envy that Joshua's love for his wife had survived even after her death, while Lloyd's had vanished as soon as he had had that first drink after their wedding. She wondered what it would be like to be loved like Joshua loved his Tildie and if she'd ever find out for herself.

Chapter 6

"*Gute mariye!*"

Joshua's *mamm* called out the greeting. Deborah rushed to hug her *grossmammi*. Wiping her hand on a towel, Rebekah smiled at Wanda Stoltzfus. The older woman's casted arm was wrapped in a black sling, but her eyes twinkled as she handed a basket topped with a blue cloth to her granddaughter.

During the two weeks since the wedding, the *kinder* had often visited the house down the road where Wanda lived with her six unmarried sons and younger daughter. Rebekah and Joshua and Sammy had been invited along with the rest of the family to dinner one night last week, but a bad storm had kept them at home. At church services on Sunday, Rebekah had appreciated her mother-in-law introducing her again to people she'd met at the wedding. She hoped she'd match names and faces better when the next church Sunday came around.

The past fourteen days had been a whirlwind. The lives of Joshua's family and her own had fallen into a pattern with meals and work and family time in the evening, but Rebekah avoided spending time on the porch—or anywhere else—alone with her husband. If he'd noticed, he hadn't said anything. Perhaps he was relieved she expected no more from him.

"Wanda, why are you waiting for an invitation?" Rebekah asked, glad a visitor gave her the excuse to think of something other than her peculiar marriage. "Come in, come in."

Putting her arm around her granddaughter, Wanda walked in. Her expression softened when her gaze alighted on Sammy.

"How is our big boy?" she asked.

Sammy clutched Rebekah's skirt. She scooped him up and settled him on her hip. He pressed his face against her shoulder.

Wanda winked at Rebekah before she said, "I hope you don't hide too long, my boy. Chocolate chip cookies are best when they're warm."

He didn't look up, but shifted so he could watch what the others did. The cookies smelled *wunderbaar,* and she guessed he was wavering between his shyness and his yearning for a treat.

"Deborah, will you unpack the basket?" Rebekah asked, earning a wide grin from the little girl. "Wanda, would you like to sit down?"

"*Ja.* This cast feels like it weighs more every day." She sat at the table and grimaced as she readjusted her arm. "I thank God I broke my left arm, though I had no idea how much I did with that hand until I couldn't use it."

"I discovered that when I broke my finger." She fought to keep her smile from wavering as the brutality of her past poked out to darken the day. "I appreciate you coming for a visit."

· "I wanted to give you time to become accustomed to your new home." She looked around. "I'd say you are settling in well and making this a home again."

Deborah piped up, "She's teaching me to make lots of yummy things, *Grossmammi*."

"So I hear from your brothers." She winked at Rebekah. "Maybe I'll even share the recipe for my chocolate chip cookies with her."

"And me?" asked the little girl.

"Of course." She wagged a finger at the *kind*. "As long as you listen to me and don't try to make up your own recipes as you used to."

"*Daed* always did that."

"And how did it turn out?"

When Deborah burst into giggles, Rebekah laughed, too. "Let me heat some water, and we'll have tea. Deborah, would you mind getting the tea down?"

The little girl pulled a chair beside the cupboard and climbed up to take out a box of teabags.

As she turned to put on the kettle, Rebekah almost stumbled. She tightened her hold on Sammy.

"Give him to me," Wanda urged.

She doubted he would go to Wanda. "I don't want him to bump your injured arm."

"He won't."

"He's shy."

"So I see, but, Sammy, I know you want one of my chocolate chip cookies."

Her son astonished her when, after a quick glance

at Wanda, he stretched out his arms to her. Hoping her face didn't reveal her surprise, Rebekah placed him on the older woman's lap. Wanda pointed to the plate on the table beside her.

"I've never met a boy who didn't like chocolate chip cookies." Wanda smiled when Sammy reached past her to take a cookie. "What a *gut* boy you are! Only taking one."

"More?" he asked.

"Why don't you try this one?" the older woman asked. "Tell me if you like *Grossmammi* Wanda's cookies."

"*Grossmammi* Wanda," he repeated as he stared at the cast. "Boo-boo?"

"*Ja*, but it is getting better."

"Give kiss to make better?"

"Aren't you a sweet little boy?" She nodded and tapped her cheek. "Why don't you kiss me right here?"

Rebekah was surprised when Sammy did. After serving tea to her mother-in-law, Rebekah gave the *kinder* glasses of milk. She sat and joined the easy conversation about the end of the school year, two new babies in the district and Deborah's friend Mandy, who seemed to be a favorite of Wanda's, too, because the little girl was often at the house. Nothing strayed too close to the unusual circumstances of Rebekah's marriage. Like her son, Rebekah grew comfortable with the kind older woman.

As soon as he'd finished his first cookie, Sammy had another and downed his milk with a gulp. He nodded when Rebekah asked him if he wanted more, then he looked across the table.

"Debbie!" He pointed with his cookie. "Milk, too?"

"*Ja.*" Deborah grinned. "*Danki*, Sammy."

Rebekah refilled both glasses. "It sounds as if you've got a new name."

"He has trouble saying my whole name. So now we're Sammy and Debbie."

Wanda nodded. "That sounds perfect for a sister and brother."

"I have lots of brothers now." The little girl leaned on the table. "Rebekah, please have a girl."

Though she secretly harbored the same hope, Rebekah replied, "We shall be blessed with the *boppli* God has chosen for us." Even at her darkest times while she had been pregnant with Sammy, she hadn't doubted God was sending her a *boppli* to help ease her heart.

Before anyone could reply, the back door opened, and Joshua walked in. He smiled as he hung his straw hat on the peg by the door.

Her heart quivered, missing a beat when his gaze met hers. A warmth she'd never felt before swirled within her like a welcome breeze on a hot day. His light blue shirt bore the stains from his work at the buggy shop, and more grease was ingrained across his hands, emphasizing his roughened skin. She had always considered him a *gut*-looking man, but as his eyes crinkled with his broadening smile, she could not keep from thinking that he was now her *gut*-looking husband.

But he wasn't. Theirs wasn't a true marriage. It was an arrangement to ensure Sammy and his *kinder* were taken care of. Her head knew that, but not her heart that continued to pound against her breastbone.

"I didn't realize you were here, *Mamm*," Joshua said after greeting them.

"Your sister is cleaning the house, and she made it clear I was in the way." She smiled to take any sting from her words. "She's so worried I'll slip and break something else."

"Because you try to do everything as you did before you broke your arm." He reached across the table and snagged a pair of cookies.

"One," Sammy scolded. "Only one."

Rebekah's heart faltered again, but for a very different reason. Lloyd never tolerated his son telling him what to do. How would Joshua react to being scolded by a toddler? She clenched her hands. If he raised his hand to strike Sammy, she would protect her son.

But Joshua chuckled. "You're right, Sammy. One cookie at a time. But *Grossmammi*'s cookies are *gut*, aren't they?"

Sammy smiled and nodded. When he picked up his glass that was coated with crumbs, he offered it to Joshua.

After taking it, Joshua pretended to drink before saying, "*Danki*, Sammy. Just what I needed."

Her son's smile glowed. Rebekah looked from him to her husband. Was Sammy sensing, as he had with Wanda, that he had nothing to fear from Joshua?

"What are you doing home in the middle of the day?" Wanda asked. "Come to see your pretty new wife?"

"*Ja*, and my pretty daughter." He winked at Deborah, who giggled. "I told Levi I'd stop by on my way back from dropping off a repaired buggy. He's riding in with me so he can help Daniel at his shop."

"How is Daniel doing with him?" his *mamm* asked.

"Well. Having someone to teach has given my little brother a purpose."

"He is a *gut*, hardworking boy, but he's avoiding decisions he should make about joining the church and finding a wife." Wanda sighed. "I shouldn't feel *hochmut* that four of my *kinder* so far have made the decision to be Amish."

"It isn't pride, *Mamm*." Joshua patted her right shoulder carefully. "You want what is best for each of us."

"True." Wanda smiled again. "And it sounds as if Daniel teaching Levi is *gut* for both of them."

"Levi is eager to learn. I wish I could say the same about his brother." He glanced at the two *kinder*. "Deborah, will you take Sammy outside and wash the cookie crumbs off his hands and face?"

"Ja," she replied, though her expression said she'd prefer to stay.

As soon as the *kinder* had closed the door after them, Joshua sighed. "I could use some advice, *Mamm*. Timothy is growing less and less interested in learning about buggies."

Rebekah went to get a dishrag to scrub off the cookie crumbles that would grow as hard as concrete if left on the table. She listened as Joshua and Wanda discussed Timothy's reluctance to do anything at the shop. Not even building wheels, a task he used to look forward to, engaged his attention now.

She should say nothing. Timothy wasn't her son, and, other than being enthusiastic about the food she put on the table, he hadn't said much to her. She seldom saw him other than at breakfast and dinner. He was with Joshua during the day, and he always seemed to be somewhere else once the evening meal was over. He came in for Joshua's nightly reading from the Bible or *Martyrs Mirror*, but vanished again after their prayers.

"I don't know what else I can tell you," Wanda said with a sigh. "You've tried everything I would have."

"Having every day be one long debate about what I

need him to do is getting old very fast." Joshua ran his fingers through his beard and looked at Rebekah. "Do you have any ideas?"

"Timothy does his share of chores here, doesn't he?" she asked, choosing her words carefully. Joshua might not like what she was about to say, but he'd asked her opinion.

"Ja."

"Without complaint?"

"Usually." His brows lowered with bafflement. "What does that have to do with his attitude at the buggy shop?"

"Maybe Timothy doesn't show any interest in your work because it isn't the work he wants to do."

Joshua stared as if she'd suggested he flap his arms and fly around the yard. "I plan to hand the business over to him when I am ready to retire."

"It's *your* plan. Not his." She met his gaze steadily.

Wanda stood and patted Rebekah's arm. "Now I'm even more glad you're a part of our family. You have put your finger on the crux of the problem." She looked at her son. "Have you asked Timothy if he wants to take over the shop?"

"No." He drew in a deep breath and let it out slowly. "I assumed because he used to be curious about what I was doing that he wanted to learn the work himself."

"He was a *kind*," his *mamm* said with a gentle smile. "As his *daed*, you were what he wanted to be when he grew up. Now he is nearly a man, and he sees the world and himself differently." She made a shooing motion with her fingers. "You need to talk with your son, and it's not going to get easier by putting it off."

"True." Joshua's tone was so dreary his *mamm*

laughed. When he began to chuckle along with her, Rebekah joined in.

She'd forgotten how *wunderbaar* shared laughter could be. She hoped she wouldn't have to forget again.

The rumble of a powerful engine surprised Rebekah. Turning from where she was folding the quilts she had aired, she stared at the bright red car slowing to a stop not far from the house. She grabbed Sammy's hand when he took a step toward it.

"Go! See!" he shouted.

She was about to reply when Timothy ran around the house and toward the car. She hadn't realized he was home yet.

The driver's window rolled down, and Timothy leaned forward to fold his arms on the open sill. She heard him laugh and wondered if it was the first time she'd ever heard him do so.

After dropping the quilt in the laundry basket, she began to cross the yard to where the teen was now squatting so his face was even with whoever was inside the car. She absently pushed loose wisps back under her *kapp*, because she wasn't sure who was behind the wheel.

Deborah skipped down the front porch steps. She'd been beating dust out of rag rugs. She waited for Rebekah and walked with her toward the vehicle.

Rebekah's eyes widened when she realized the driver was an *Englisch* girl, one close to Timothy's age. The girl's black hair was pulled back in a ponytail. Unlike many *Englisch* teenagers, she wasn't wearing layers of makeup. She didn't need any because her lightly tanned cheeks were a healthy pink. She wore a simple and modest black blouse.

"I'm Alexis Granger," said the girl. "Hey, Tim, move back so I can see your new mom." She laughed, and Timothy did, too. Leaning her elbow on the car's open window, she said, "You must be Joshua's new wife."

Startled by the *Englisch* girl's effusiveness, Rebekah smiled. "*Ja*, I am Rebekah." She looked at Sammy who was eyeing the girl and the car with the same interest Timothy was. "And this is my son Samuel."

"A big name for a cute, little boy."

"We call him Sammy."

The pretty brunette chuckled. "Much better. Hi, Sammy."

He gave her a shy grin but didn't say anything.

"He's a real cutie," Alexis said before holding out a stack of envelopes. "These were delivered to our mailbox by mistake, and Mom asked me to drop them off over here on my way to work."

"Where do you work?" Rebekah asked to be polite.

"At one of the diners in Bird-in-Hand where the tourists come to try Amish-style food." She hooked a thumb in Timothy's direction. "*He* thinks I got the job because my boss was impressed my neighbors are plain, but it was because I was willing to work on weekends." She rolled her eyes. "Saving for college, y'know. Anything I can pick up for you while I'm in town?"

"*Danki*, but we're fine."

"Okay. See ya, Tim!" She backed the car out onto the road. Small stones spurted from under the back tires.

Rebekah half turned to protect Sammy. Even though the tiny stones didn't come near them, a dust cloud billowed over them.

The glow that had brightened Timothy's face while Alexis was there faded. Without a word, he walked back to the house. As he did, he tucked his fingers into one side of his suspenders and tugged at them on each step, clearly deep in thought.

"Don't mind him," Deborah said, warning Rebekah she'd stared too long. "He's like that when Alexis stops by."

"She comes often?"

"*Ja*, but not as much as she used to. She's always got something going on at school or at work. Timothy misses having her around. He thinks she's hot."

Shocked, Rebekah began, "Deborah—"

"Will you call me Debbie as Sammy does?" the little girl asked with a grin.

"We'll talk about your name in a minute. You shouldn't make such comments about Alexis. It isn't nice."

The girl frowned. "Timothy said it was a compliment."

"I'm sure he did, but your brother hasn't learned yet that what's inside a person is more important than the outside."

"But *Daedi* said *you're* pretty when he told us he was going to marry you."

Rebekah ignored the delight that sprang through her, but it wasn't easy. "He and I have known each other for years. He didn't marry me for what I look like." She put her hands on her distended belly. "Certainly not now!"

That brought a laugh from the little girl, and Rebekah changed the subject to the chores they had left to do before Joshua and Levi got home.

As Deborah turned to head back to the front porch, she asked, "Will you call me Debbie?"

"As long as your *daed* agrees. He'll want you to have a *gut* reason."

The little girl considered her words for a long minute, then said, "I want to be called Debbie so Sammy feels part of our family."

Unbidden tears filled Rebekah's eyes. What a *wunderbaar* heart Debbie had been blessed with! As she assured Debbie she would speak with Joshua about the nickname after dinner, she had to keep blinking to keep those tears from falling. She hugged the *kind*.

Dearest God, danki *for bringing this little girl into my life.* Sweet Debbie was making Sammy a part of her family, and Rebekah, too. For the first time in longer than she could remember, Rebekah felt the burden she carried on her shoulders every day lift. It was an amazing feeling she wanted to experience again and again. Was it finally possible?

Joshua heard the screen door open after supper, but he kept reading the newspaper's sports section. The last light of the day was beginning to fade, and he wanted to finish the article on the new pitcher who had signed with the Phillies. He'd been following the Philadelphia baseball team since he wasn't much older than Sammy. His sons were baseball fans, too, and he'd expected Timothy or Levi to come out and ask for an update before now.

When a question wasn't fired in his direction, he looked up. His eyes widened when he saw Rebekah standing there.

Alone.

The last time she'd spent any time with him without one of the *kinder* nearby was the first evening when they'd tried to work out aspects of their marriage. How guilty he'd felt afterward! Though he knew his life was now entwined with Rebekah's, his heart belonged to Tildie. He wanted to be a *gut* husband, but how could he when he needed to hold on to his love for the first woman he had exchanged vows with?

My brother, do you take our sister to be your wife until such hour as when death parts you? Do you believe this is the Lord's will, and your prayers and faith have brought you to each other?

The words Reuben had asked him at the wedding ceremony rang through his head. They were identical to the vows he had taken with Tildie. Why hadn't anyone told him how he was supposed to act once death parted him from Tildie? The *Ordnung* outlined many other parts of their lives. Why not that?

Renewed guilt rushed through him when he saw Rebekah regarding him with uncertainty. She must be enduring the same feeling of being lost without Lloyd, though she never gave any sign. Perhaps she was trying to spare him.

"I'm sorry if I've disturbed your reading," she said. "The *kinder* are practicing their parts for the end-of-the-school-year program next week. Sammy is their rapt audience."

He chuckled. "The end-of-the-school-year program is important to them. It's hard to think how few more Levi will be in. At least there will be others with Deborah and Sammy."

"I thought you should know Deborah wants to be called Debbie now."

"Why?"

Her soft blue eyes glistened as she told him how his daughter longed to help Sammy feel more at home with his new family. Were those tears, or was it a trick of the light?

His own voice was a bit rough when he said, "Debor— Debbie has always been thoughtful. I wish I could say the same for her older brother."

"May I talk to you about Timothy?"

He lowered the newspaper to his lap and lifted off his reading glasses. "Has he been giving you trouble?"

"No," she said as she sat in the rocker. "He treats me politely."

"I'm glad to hear that." He didn't add he'd worried his older son would take out his frustrations with his *daed* on Rebekah. He was jolted when he realized that unlike his younger siblings, Timothy had perceived the distance between the newlyweds.

Was it obvious to everyone?

He didn't have a chance to answer the unanswerable because Rebekah said, "But I have noticed something about Timothy that concerns me."

"What?" He silenced his sigh. After trying to motivate his son to do something other than mope around the buggy shop, he didn't want to deal with Timothy again tonight.

Instantly he chided himself. A parent's job didn't end when the workday did. Because he was worried about his failure to reconnect with the boy who once dogged his footsteps was no reason to give up. His son was trying to find his place in the world, as every teenager did.

"Have you noticed," Rebekah asked, drawing his attention back to her, "how Timothy stops whatever he's doing whenever Alexis Granger and her snazzy car goes by?"

"Snazzy?"

"It's a word, right?"

He smiled. "It is, and it's the perfect description for the car. I know Brad wishes he'd gotten a less powerful one. Letting a new driver like Alexis get behind the wheel is like giving Sammy the reins to our family buggy."

"I'm not as worried about the car as I am about Timothy's interest in it…and the girl who drives it."

"They've been friends since they were little more than babies."

"But they aren't babies any longer." She sighed. "I don't want to cause trouble, Joshua, but Timothy lit up like a falling star when she was here, and I noticed him watching her go the whole way up the Grangers' driveway tonight. As soon as supper was over, he was gone."

"Saturday nights are for him to be with his friends."

"I realize that, but Alexis fascinates him. If you want my opinion…"

"I do."

She met his eyes evenly. "He'd like more than a friendship with her."

Joshua folded his glasses and put them on the windowsill by his chair. He did the same with the newspaper as he considered her words. Maybe he had been turning too blind an eye toward his oldest's friendship with the neighbor girl. He didn't want to do anything to cause his son to retreat further from the family. To confront Timothy about the matter could create more problems.

When Rebekah didn't say more, he was grateful. She wasn't going to nag him about his son as his older sister Ruth did. Ruth's *kinder* didn't seem to have a rebellious bone in their bodies, so she couldn't understand what it was like to have a son like Timothy. But he'd think about what Rebekah had said.

"*Danki* for caring enough for my son to be worried about him," he said, reaching out to put his hand on hers.

She moved her fingers so smoothly he wouldn't have noticed if he hadn't seen her flinch away too many times. As she came to her feet, unable to hide that she wanted to put more space between them, she said, "I'm not Timothy's *mamm*, but I care about him."

Do you care about me, too? The question went unasked, and it would remain unasked, because he realized how much he wanted the answer to be *ja* and how much he feared it would be no.

Chapter 7

The yard of the simple, white schoolhouse at the intersection of two country roads was filled with buggies, and more were pulling in as Rebekah climbed the steps after Joshua. She was glad Sammy could manage the steps on his own, because it was more difficult each day to pick him up and carry him. Inside, the schoolroom looked almost identical to the one she had attended. The same textbooks were on the shelves at the back of the room, and the scholars' desks were set in neat rows with the teacher's desk at the front of the blackboard.

An air of anticipation buzzed through the room. The scholars were eager to begin their program as well as their summer break. Younger *kinder* looked around, excited to get a glimpse of where they would be attending school. Parents used the gathering as a chance to catch up on news.

Most of the *mamms* sat at the scholars' desks, but

Rebekah decided to remain at the back with the *daeds* and grandparents and other relatives. She was unsure if her ever-widening belly would fit behind one of the small desks.

The room was filled with sunshine, but its glow wasn't as bright as the smiles on the scholars' faces while they stood near their teacher's desk. On the blackboard behind them, someone—probably Esther Stoltzfus, their teacher—had written in big block letters: HAVE A FUN AND SAFE SUMMER!

Joshua's younger sister looked happy and harried at the same time. Levi and Debbie talked with fondness and respect for their teacher who was also their *aenti*. Now Esther was trying to get each of the scholars in the proper place for the beginning of the program. The youngest ones complied quickly, but the oldest ones, knowing this was their final day of school, seemed unable to stand still or stop talking and giggling.

But Esther treated each *kind* with patience and a smile. When two of the younger scholars went to her and whispered below the buzz of conversation in the room, she nodded. They ran out the side door and toward the outhouses at the back corner of the schoolyard.

After she turned to scan the room, Esther smiled warmly when her eyes met Rebekah's. She went to her desk and pulled out her chair. She rolled it to the back of the room and stopped by Rebekah.

Esther motioned at the chair. "Would you like to sit down?"

"I don't want to take your chair."

"I won't have a chance to sit." Her dimples rearranged the freckles scattered across her cheeks and nose. "Please use it."

"Danki." She wasn't going to turn down the *gut*-hearted offer a second time.

Joshua took the back of the chair from his sister and shifted it closer to the last row of desks. "You should be able to see better from here, Rebekah."

"Danki," she repeated as she sat with a relieved sigh. She settled Sammy on her knees. While the men talked about farming and the weather and the latest news on their favorite baseball teams, she pointed out the posters and hand-drawn pictures tacked on cork strips that hung about a foot below the ceiling. He was delighted with each one and asked when he could come to school with the older *kinder*. With a smile, she assured him it would be soon.

When the two young scholars returned, they took their places. Rebekah smiled when she saw Debbie at the far right in the front row of girls while Levi peered over the head of the scholar in front of him from the other end of the back row.

"Debbie! Levi!" called Sammy as the room became silent.

Everyone laughed, and Rebekah whispered to him that he needed to be quiet so he could hear the songs.

Sammy bounced on Rebekah's knees as the *kinder* began to sing. He clapped along with the adults at the end of each song. The recitations made him squirm with impatience, but each time another song began, he tried to join in with a tuneless, "La, la, la."

Rebekah enjoyed the program and was pleased when Debbie and Levi performed their poems without a single hesitation or mistake. She glanced up to see Joshua smiling. Though pride wasn't considered a *gut* thing among the Amish, she could tell he enjoyed seeing his *kinder* do well after their hard work to memorize each word.

Sammy grew bored during a short play performed by the oldest scholars. Other toddlers were wiggling and looking around, as well. Even a cookie couldn't convince him to sit still.

"Down," he said. When she didn't react, he repeated it more loudly.

Not wanting him to disrupt the program, she let him slide off her knees. She whispered for him to stay by her side.

"Hold hand?" he asked.

She nodded and held out her hand. She was astonished when he took Joshua's fingers. Leaning his head against Joshua's leg, he smiled when her husband tousled his hair without taking his eyes off the program.

Sammy obviously had changed his mind about Joshua. A warm glow filled her. She'd seen signs of the change in recent days, but her son had remained tentative around Joshua in public. For the first time, he wasn't clinging to her.

Her joy disappeared when Sammy suddenly darted past her as the *kinder* began to sing again. She jumped to her feet, but he grasped Debbie's hand and announced, "Sammy sing, too."

Rebekah's face burned as she started toward the *kinder* who were giggling at her son's antics. Her sneaker caught, and a broad hand grasped her shoulder, halting her. Time telescoped into the past to the night Lloyd had kept her from leaving the house by seizing her from behind and shoving her against a wall. Her reaction was instinctive.

Her arm came up to knock her captor's hand away. "No! Don't!" she gasped and whirled away so fast she bumped into a desk and almost tumbled off her feet.

Hands from the people around her steadied her. She

was grateful, but as panic drained away, she saw startled and alarmed expressions on all the faces around her.

No, not *all* the faces. Joshua's was as blank as the wall behind him. He stood with his arm still outstretched. To keep her from falling, she realized. His eyes contained a myriad of emotions. Mixed in with confusion and annoyance was…hurt. A new wife shouldn't shy away from her husband's touch. She had embarrassed him in front of his family and neighbors. If she could explain without risking Sammy's future…

Esther's cheerful voice sounded forced. "Let's start over with our final song of this year's program. Sammy and any of the other younger *kinder* are welcome to join us."

While more little brothers and sisters rushed up to stand beside their siblings, Rebekah groped for her chair. Joshua steadied it as she sat, but she couldn't speak, not even to thank him. She lowered herself to sit and stared straight ahead.

Sammy now stood beside Levi in the back row with the other boys. As the *kinder* enthusiastically sang their friendship song, he looked up at Levi with admiration and tried to sing along, though he didn't know the words.

It was endearing, but she couldn't enjoy it. Adrenaline rushed through her, making her gasp as if she had run a marathon. Her pulse thudded in her ears so loudly she had to strain to hear the *kinder's* voices. She clapped along with everyone else when the song came to an end.

The *kinder* scattered, seeking their parents. Hugs and excited voices filled the schoolroom.

Rebekah pushed herself to her feet again when Levi, Debbie and Sammy eased along an aisle to where she and Joshua waited. She hoped her smile didn't look hideous while she thanked the *kinder* for a *wunderbaar* program. If her voice was strained, the youngsters didn't seem to notice.

However, the adults around her must have. More than one gave her a smile. Not pitying, but sympathetic, especially the women who carried small babies. Their kindness and concern was almost too great a gift to accept.

And, she realized, nobody looked toward Joshua with censure. None of them could imagine him hurting her on purpose. That thought should have been comforting, but who would have guessed Lloyd could be a beast when he drank? She certainly hadn't.

She'd made one mistake. Now she wanted to avert another, but would the mistake be trusting Joshua or not trusting him?

The schoolyard was filled with happy shouts and lighthearted conversation. Everywhere, including where Joshua stood with his family. The noise came from the *kinder*, who were as agitated as if they'd eaten a whole batch of their *grossmammi's* cookies. But he was glad no one paid attention to the fact neither he nor Rebekah said anything as they walked with their *kinder* to the buggy. Everyone was too wound up in happiness to notice his misery.

And Rebekah's?

He wasn't sure what she was thinking or feeling. She hid it behind a strained smile.

What happened? he wanted to shout, though he seldom raised his voice. Nothing could be gained by yelling and things could be lost, but his frustration was reaching the boiling point.

He hesitated as he was about to assist Rebekah into the buggy. Would she pull away as she had in the schoolhouse? Humiliation burned in his gut as he recalled the curious glances aimed in his direction, glances quickly averted.

But stronger than his chagrin was his need to know why she'd acted as she had. Until she'd pulled away from him, he'd thought they were becoming accustomed to each other and had found a compromise that allowed them to make a *gut* and comfortable home for the *kinder*. He had dared to believe, even though theirs was far from a perfect marriage, it had the potential to become a comfortable one.

Now he wasn't sure about anything.

God, help me. Help us! Something is wrong, and I don't know what it is.

Wondering if he really had anything to lose, Joshua offered his hand to Rebekah, and she accepted it as if nothing unusual had happened. As the *kinder*, including Sammy, scrambled into the back, he stepped in, as well. He picked up the reins and slapped them against the horse.

Rebekah remained silent, but he doubted she would have had a chance to speak when the *kinder* chattered like a flock of jays rising from a field. Sammy was eager to learn the words to the final song they had sung, and Debbie was trying to teach him while Levi described every bit of the program as if none of them had been there. They kept interrupting each other to ask him and Rebekah if they'd liked one part of it or another.

He answered automatically. Every inch of him was focused on the woman sitting beside him. Her fingers quivered, and he was tempted to put his own hand over them to remind her, whatever was distressing her, she wasn't alone in facing it. He resisted.

The *kinder* rushed out of the buggy as soon as it stopped beside the house. When Rebekah slid away and got out on her side, he jumped out and called her name. She turned as he unhooked the horse from the buggy.

"Come with me and Benny," Joshua said simply.

"I should…" She met his gaze and then nodded. "All right."

She walked on the other side of the horse as they went to the barn. She waited while he put Benny in a stall and gave him some oats.

He stepped out of the stall. "Rebekah—"

"Joshua—" she said at the same time.

"Go ahead," he urged.

"Danki." She paused so long he wondered if she'd changed her mind about speaking. He realized she'd been composing her thoughts when she said, "I don't know any other way to say this but I'm sorry I embarrassed you at school. I will apologize to Esther the next time I see her."

"Rebekah, if I was embarrassed or not isn't important. What's important is why you said what you did. Tell me the truth. Why did you pull away like you did?"

"Haven't you heard pregnant women often act strangely?" Her smile wobbled, and he guessed she was exerting her flagging strength to keep it in place.

"Ja, but…" He didn't want to accuse her of lying. Not that she was, but she was avoiding the truth. Why? "I was trying to prevent you from falling."

"I know." Her voice had a soft breathlessness that urged him closer, but her face was stiff with the fear he'd seen at school. "I need to be careful I avoid doing anything that might injure my *boppli.*"

Maybe he'd misread her reaction, and her anxiety about the *boppli* had made her words sound wrong. He hadn't always been correct in his assumptions about Tildie's reactions, either.

The thought startled him. Since Tildie's death he hadn't let such memories into his mind. At first he'd felt ungrateful if he recalled anything but the *gut* times they'd shared. Even a jest from his brothers about married life had fallen flat for him. He didn't want to admit, even to himself, his marriage to Tildie had been anything less than perfect.

But that was the past. He had to focus on keeping his current marriage from falling apart before it even had a chance to thrive. He refused to believe it was already too late.

"One of the reasons I asked you to be my wife is to make sure you and your *kinder* are taken care of," he said as he walked with her out of the barn. "I told you that right from the beginning."

"I know you did."

"Do you believe I was being honest?"

When she paused and faced him, he was surprised. He'd expected her to try to keep distance between them. Now they stood a hand's breadth from each other. She tilted her head enough so he could see her face beneath her bonnet's brim. Even as she drew in a breath to speak, he wondered if he could remember how to breathe as he gazed into her beautiful blue eyes.

"I believe you aspire to being as honest as any man can be, Joshua Stoltzfus," she whispered.

"Then believe I don't want you to worry about you and your *kinder*. I take my vows seriously to face every challenge with you, Rebekah. God has brought us together, and I believe His plans are always for *gut*."

"I do, too."

"It pleases me to hear you say that." He admired the scattering of freckles that drew his gaze to the curve of her cheekbones and then to her full lips. His imagination sped faster than a runaway horse as he speculated how her red hair would brush her face and his fingertips if it fell, loose and untamed, down her back. She was his wife, and he'd thought often during the long nights since their wedding of her sitting in their bedroom and brushing out those long strands.

She was his wife, and he was her husband.

He framed her face with his hands before another thought could form. Her skin was soft and warm...and alive. How many times had he reached out in the past few years and found nothing but the chill of an old memory?

Her blue eyes beckoned but he hesitated. A man could lose himself within their depths. Was he ready to take the step from which there would be no turning back? The memory of Tildie and their love remained strong, and Rebekah's loss was still fresh and painful.

But didn't God want them to put others aside and cleave to one another, heart to heart, now that they were wed? The thought shook him. He wanted to live the life God had set out for him, but he hadn't been when he let the past overwhelm the present.

He saw her lips forming his name, but the sound never reached his ears as he bent toward her...toward his wife...his lovely Rebekah...

The squeal of tires on the road jerked him back to reality, and he released her as Timothy strolled up the driveway whistling. His son grinned as he waved at Alexis who tooted the car's horn to him.

Joshua heard the kitchen door shut, and Rebekah was gone. He stood there with his hands empty. He had let his opportunity to hold her slip away. He prayed it wouldn't be his only chance.

Chapter 8

A dozen contrasting emotions flooded Rebekah as the buggy entered the lane leading to the house where she used to live with Lloyd. It had been her home for more than five years, but the site of her greatest nightmare. Sammy had been born there and taken his first steps in the kitchen. It was also the place where Lloyd had first struck her in a drunken rage.

She hadn't expected Joshua to suggest a drive on the Saturday morning a week and a half after the school program. Previously on Saturdays he'd tended to chores in the barn or gone through catalogues to plan for what he needed to order for the buggy shop. Her heart had leaped with excitement because she'd hoped he was going to give her a tour of his shop. She wasn't sure why he hadn't asked her and Sammy to visit, but as each day passed, asking him seemed more difficult.

At first she'd needed to concentrate on getting the

house back into acceptable shape. A stomach bug had made the three younger *kinder* sick and claimed her time and attention last week. As soon as they were well, Timothy had gotten sick. Yesterday was the first day he'd joined them for a meal, and he'd eaten no more than a few bites before he'd excused himself and returned to bed.

Keeping herself busy allowed her not to spend time alone with her husband. He hadn't said anything, but she knew he was curious why she continued to avoid him. If his son hadn't arrived when Joshua had clasped her face in his broad hands, he would have kissed her. What she didn't know was what would have happened if she'd kissed him back. The precarious balance of caring for the *kinder* at the same time she struggled not to care too much for her husband was a seesaw. A single step in the wrong direction could destroy that fragile equilibrium.

Now he had asked for her to go for a drive with him, and she'd accepted because she didn't have a *gut* excuse not to, especially because she liked spending time with him as long as they kept everything casual. She had been astonished when she learned their destination wasn't Joshua's buggy shop but Bird-in-Hand and Lloyd's farm. She'd agreed it was a *gut* idea to check on the house. When Joshua had told her that Timothy would bring the other *kinder* over in the open wagon after they finished their Saturday chores, she was grateful for her husband's thoughtfulness. She couldn't put any of the larger items she wanted to bring back to Paradise Springs in the family buggy, but they would fit easily in the wagon.

While they drove on Newport Road to bypass most

of the busy tourist areas, she'd pointed out various landmarks. Joshua nodded as they passed the butcher's shop and suggested they stop on the way back to Paradise Springs, because his brother's store had a very small meat section with not a lot of items. She'd showed him the white schoolhouse Sammy would have attended and the medical clinic between a florist shop and a store selling quilts and Amish-built furniture.

"They've contacted my brother Jeremiah about selling some of his pieces there," he had said. "He's done well enough at our family's shops, but he's wavering. He likes the work, but not the paperwork that selling directly to customers requires." He looked at the medical clinic. "Shouldn't you be seeing a doctor for regular checkups?"

"I went before the wedding, and the midwife suggested I find another clinic in Paradise Springs. Is there one?"

"Ja," he had replied. "Do you want me to make an appointment for you?"

"That might be a *gut* idea."

He had changed the subject, but now neither she nor Joshua said anything as he brought the buggy to a stop near the kitchen door. He stepped out, and she did the same. She looked around.

Each inch of the house and the barns and the fields held a memory for her, *gut* and oh-so-bad. It was as if those memories were layered one atop another on the scene in front of her. The most recent ones of her and Sammy were the easiest, because they weren't laced with fright.

The farm had been her prison, but it had become a symbol for her freedom from fear since Lloyd's death. It still was, she realized in amazement. The farm was her sanctuary if she needed it. She didn't know if she would, but she wasn't going to be unprepared ever again.

Joshua crossed his arms over his light blue shirt. "What do you think?"

"About what?" She wasn't going to share the true course of her thoughts.

"The appearance of the farm. From what I can see, most of the buildings don't need much more than a coat or two of paint to make them look *gut*."

"I agree, except the roof on the field equipment barn is sagging. It should be shored up."

He gave her a warm smile. "True, and I know just the man for the job."

"Your brother Daniel?"

"*Ja*. He has repaired buildings in worse condition. I asked him to meet us here, so he can see what needs to be done. We want the buildings to look their best, so someone will offer a *gut* amount of money for the farm."

"Money for the farm?" she repeated, shocked at how easily he spoke of selling the farm. *Her farm!*

"*Ja*. Once it is fixed up, I thought we'd hold an auction for the land and buildings, as well as for anything else you want to sell—furniture, household goods and any farm equipment. Several neighbors have stopped by the buggy shop in the past couple of weeks to ask me when I plan to put it on the auction block, so the bidding should go well."

He was going to sell her farm. Just like that. Lloyd had insisted on making the big decisions, too, and she'd learned not to gainsay him. Why had she thought Joshua might be different?

Or maybe he wasn't the same as Lloyd. After all, Joshua had invited her to the farm to consider what needed to be done in order to sell it. He hadn't sold it without allowing her to see her home one more time.

The thought gave her the courage to say, "Joshua, I don't know if I'm ready to sell the farm yet."

"Why do you want to hold on to it?" He glanced from her to the weatherworn buildings. "If you're thinking you shouldn't sell it because it's Lloyd's legacy to Sammy, you need to consider how much upkeep it's going to need until he's old enough to farm. You could rent out the fields and the house, but buildings require regular upkeep, and it might cost as much or more than what you'd get from the rent. Selling the farm will provide money for Sammy when he's ready to decide what he wants to do as a man."

She knew he was right…about Sammy. But he had no idea about the true reason she couldn't bear to let the farm go. How she'd longed for a refuge when Lloyd had been looking for someone to blame for his ills! Nothing Joshua had done suggested he would be as abusive as her first husband, but she needed a place to go with Sammy if that changed.

Not just Sammy, but the other *kinder* if they needed shelter, too.

Rebekah hoped her shrug appeared nonchalant. "I hadn't thought about what would happen with the farm." That much was the truth. "I need time to think about selling it." Walking to where hostas were growing lush near the porch, she took the time to pray for the right words to persuade Joshua to listen.

From where he hadn't moved, he said, "It'll take time to repair the buildings, especially as Daniel will need to do the work around his other jobs. At this time of the summer we can't ask for others to help." He paused, then asked, "Rebekah?"

She faced him. *"Ja?"*

"You'll have plenty of time to make up your mind. You don't need to decide today." He gave her a cockeyed smile that made something uncurl delightfully in her center.

Something drew her toward him, something that urged her to think of his arms around her. She halted because she'd learned not to trust those feelings after they'd led her to Lloyd.

The rattle of the open wagon came from the end of the lane, and Rebekah saw Timothy driving the other *kinder* toward the house. As they neared, the older ones looked around, their eyes wide with astonishment. She guessed they were comparing their *onkel* Ezra's neat and well-maintained farm to this one.

But her gaze went to her son. She'd protected him from much of what had happened between her and his *daed*, and his young age would wash away other memories. Still, she didn't want this visit to upset him. She realized she didn't have anything to worry about when she heard his giggles as he played in the back of the wagon with Debbie.

Joshua lifted the younger *kinder* out while the boys jumped down. At the same time, he asked Rebekah where the lawnmower was. He sent Levi to get it from the shed. Timothy was given the task of collecting any canned food and other supplies from the kitchen and the cellar, while Debbie volunteered to look for any vegetables in the neglected garden.

"Sammy help?" her son asked.

"Help me," Timothy said, picking him up and hanging him upside down over his shoulder. While Sammy kicked his feet and chortled in delight, he added, "I'll keep a close eye on him in the kitchen, Rebekah. Before I go down to the cellar, I'll take him out to help Debbie."

"Danki." She didn't add how pleased she was Timothy had volunteered to spend time with her son. It would be *gut* for both boys.

If Joshua was surprised by his oldest's actions, he didn't show it as he walked into the backyard. He went to the chicken coop, which she'd kept in excellent shape. It was the only building that had been painted in the past three years.

"Where are the chickens?" he asked as he looked over his shoulder.

"I gave the leftover chickens to my *mamm* so she can have fresh eggs." As she crossed the yard to where he stood, she rubbed her hands together, then stopped when she realized the motion showed her nervousness at being on the farm again. Maybe it wouldn't be the best haven.

But it was her only one.

She shivered and hastily added, "Most of the chickens were used for the wedding."

"I remember." He gave her a wry grin. "Though I don't remember much about what else we ate."

"I don't, either."

He paused and faced her. She took a half step back before she bumped into him. His mouth tightened. She'd given him every reason to believe a commonplace motion like trying not to run into someone had a great significance.

Before she could think of a way to explain, his expression eased again. He took her right hand between his and gazed into her eyes with a gentle honesty that threatened to demolish her resolve to keep her secrets to herself.

"What I do remember vividly," he said in little more than a whisper, "is how when you came down the stairs I forgot everyone else in the room. I remember how you made sure my *kinder* didn't feel left out and how you welcomed them to participate in each tradition. Not many brides would have insisted on the *kinder* sharing our special corner during the wedding meal."

"Sammy was fussy, so I wanted to keep him nearby. How could I have had him there with us and not the others?"

"You don't need to explain, Rebekah. I'm simply saying I know our marriage isn't what either of us planned on, but—"

"It could be worse?"

When he laughed hard, she released a soft breath of relief. His words had become too serious, too sincere, too…everything. She couldn't let herself be swayed by pretty words as she had with Lloyd. Hadn't she learned her lesson? Even if Joshua wasn't like Lloyd, and she prayed every day he wasn't, she couldn't forget how he still loved his late wife.

"I don't want to farm this land or any other, Rebekah." He gave her a lopsided grin. "I know every Amish man is supposed to want to be a farmer, but I don't. God didn't give me the gifts he gave my brother. Ezra seems to know exactly when to plant and when to harvest. He can communicate with his herd of cows like he's one of them. That's why we agreed, rather than having the farm go to Daniel as the youngest son, Ezra should take over after *Daed* died. To be honest, Daniel was relieved, because he likes building things. It worked out well for each of us."

"It did."

He became serious again. "Rebekah, if you hoped I'd farm here, I'm sorry. We probably should have discussed this before our wedding."

As well as so many other things, she wanted to say. But the most important truths must remain unspoken.

"*Danki* for being honest with me," she said. "No, I didn't expect you to take over the farm, especially when it's so far from your home and your shop." She didn't hesitate before she added, "I hope you'll invite me and Sammy to visit the shop one of these days."

His eyes grew wide. "You want to visit the buggy shop? I thought you weren't interested, because you haven't said anything about going there."

"Joshua, you love your work, and as your wife I want to understand what is important to you."

He smiled as broadly as Sammy did when offered a sweet. "Whenever you want to visit, drop in. I'll show you around so you can see how we make and repair buggies. Come as often as you wish."

When she saw how thrilled he was, happiness bubbled up within her from a hidden spring she thought had long ago gone dry. She felt closer to her husband than she ever had.

Had he sensed that, too? She couldn't think why else he would rapidly change the subject back to the condition of the farm buildings.

"Daniel should be here soon," he said. "The project he's been working on isn't far from here. If you see him, will you send him to the main barn? I'll start there."

"All right." She felt as if she'd been dismissed like a *kind* caught eavesdropping on her elders.

As she turned to go to the house, he added, "It's going to take time to get the buildings fixed up. Once everything is in decent shape, we'll talk about the future of the farm. Okay?"

"Ja," she said, though they were postponing the inevitable clash of wills. There must be some way to explain why she needed to keep the farm without revealing the truth about Lloyd.

But how?

Joshua watched as his youngest brother poked at a beam with a nail, and he tried not to sneeze as bits of hay and dust and spiderwebs drifted down onto his upturned face. Daniel was trying to determine if any insects or dry rot had weakened the wood. If the nail slid in easily, it was a bad sign. A board along the side of the barn could easily be replaced, but if one of the beams failed, the whole building could collapse. From where Joshua stood at the foot of the ladder, he couldn't see what his brother was discovering at the top.

"Looks *gut*," Daniel said as he came down the ladder at the same speed he would have walked up the lane.

His younger brother was finally filling out after spending the past five or six years looking like a black-haired scarecrow, disconnected joints sticking out in every direction. His shoulders were no longer too wide, and his feet and hands seemed the right size. The gaze from his bright blue eyes was steady. He and his twin Micah looked identical except for the cleft in Daniel's chin, something Daniel hated and was looking forward to hiding when he grew a beard after he married.

"No dry rot?" Joshua asked.

He shook his head. "In spite of how it looks, the barn was kept up well for many years. Any damage is recent, say the past five years or so, and it's only on the surface."

He dropped the nail into a pocket of his well-worn tool belt. "But if the barn doesn't get some maintenance soon, it'll tumble in on itself."

"I know at least that much about construction, brother *boppli*." Joshua smiled, knowing how the term annoyed Daniel, who had been born more than a half hour after his twin.

"Are you sure your ancient mind can hold so much information?" his brother shot back.

Laughing with Daniel erased the rest of the tension he'd been feeling since he decided to bring Rebekah and the *kinder* to Lloyd's farm. Much of it had eased when she'd told him she would like to visit the buggy shop. Her effort to learn more about his life showed she wanted their marriage to have a chance, too.

His relief at hearing that revealed how uncertain he'd been about her expectations from their marriage. *Maybe you haven't given her a chance before today to tell you that she wanted to visit,* scolded the little voice from his conscience. He couldn't expect her to be candid when he withheld himself from her. At first he hadn't wanted to mention Tildie, because he hadn't wanted Rebekah to think he was comparing her housekeeping and interactions with the *kinder* to how his first wife would have handled them. Again he regretted not taking more time to talk before they spoke their vows. If they'd had more discussions then, the situation might be easier now.

"So how long to fix up the place?" Joshua asked.

"At least a month to do the basics, including the painting. That's assuming I can get *gut* helpers. It's not easy this time of year when everyone's so busy." He rubbed the cleft in his chin and arched his brows. "If the barn burned, everyone would be here even sooner."

"I'm hoping you aren't suggesting burning it down so we can have a barn raising."

Daniel laughed. "I never thought I'd hear my big brother, the volunteer fireman, make such a comment."

"I wanted to make sure *you* didn't." He clapped his brother on the shoulder, then looked around again. "Just a month to repair and paint? That's faster than I'd guessed."

"That's assuming I can get plenty of help. I may be able to get it done even more quickly if you're willing to hire a few of my *Englisch* coworkers."

Now Joshua was surprised. "Why wouldn't I?"

"*Englischers* think we Amish are the most skilled construction workers. I wasn't sure what you thought."

"I think I want this job done quickly and well."

"*Gut.* There are a couple of *Englisch* guys I work with who can run circles around me with a hammer and nails. I can ask them if they'd like some extra work."

He knew his brother was being modest, because Daniel's skills had an excellent reputation. "Sounds like a plan."

"I'm pretty sure one will, because he's been talking about his wife wanting him to take the family on a trip to Florida."

"How much are you planning to charge me?" Joshua asked with mock horror.

"Don't worry. It'll be fair. Let me talk to the guys I have in mind, and I'll get back to you soon. Okay?"

"*Ja.*"

After Daniel left, Joshua wiped his brow with a soiled handkerchief and walked across the freshly mown backyard. He waved to Levi, who was now cutting the front yard. A glance at the garden told him Debbie and Sammy had finished there. The back door was open, so he headed toward it to find out how much longer Rebekah needed at the house.

He jumped back as a large box was carried out of the kitchen. Only when it had passed did he realize his oldest was toting it. He watched, puzzled, as Timothy set it in the wagon beside a pair of ladder-back chairs.

"What's in the box?" Joshua asked.

"Some stuff Rebekah wants to take home with us."

He nodded, even though he was curious what was in the box. Her clothing and the boy's as well as the clothing she'd prepared for the *boppli* were already at his house. He'd brought Sammy's toys and several of her quilts the first week after they were married.

"I hope the rest will fit," his son said.

"Depends on how much else there is," Joshua replied as his mind whirled.

Rebekah hadn't said anything to him about bringing any of her furniture to his house. Tildie had remarked often what a comfortable home it was. Didn't Rebekah have everything she needed?

What if their situations were reversed? There were some items he'd want to bring with him into her house. His buggy supply catalogues, the lamp that was the perfect height when he was reading, his favorite pillow and the quilt *Grossmammi* Stoltzfus had made for him, some of Tildie's rag rugs…and, most important, the family Bible.

"I don't know what else she's planning to bring," Timothy said. "She's in the house. You can ask her while I pack the rest of the canned food."

"I will."

As his son headed toward a bulkhead door and vanished down the stairs to the cellar, Joshua went to the kitchen door. The last time he'd come this way was to ask Rebekah to marry him.

He entered the kitchen. "Do you intend on bringing much more…?" His voice faded as he glanced around in disbelief. The kitchen cabinets looked abandoned because the stove and refrigerator were gone. The table where he'd sat while he discussed marriage with Rebekah had vanished, too. He looked through to the living room. Except for the sewing machine, the other room was empty, too. He frowned. Timothy had brought out only a box and the two chairs. Where was everything else?

He heard footfalls upstairs. He climbed the steps two at a time and followed the sound of muffled voices past a bathroom. Glancing into a room on the other side of the hall, he guessed it'd been a bedroom. It was empty except for a carved blanket chest. The top was open, and a tumbling-blocks quilt in shades of green, black and white was draped over the edge.

He kept going and looked into the other bedroom. Rebekah stood in the middle of it, her hands pressed to her mouth as if trying to hold in a cry. Debbie and Sammy stood on either side of her, for once silent.

Catching his daughter's eyes, Joshua motioned with his head for Debbie to leave. She obeyed, bringing Sammy with her. He smiled at her and patted her shoulder.

"Rebekah's sad," she whispered before she led the little boy down the stairs.

No, he thought as he walked into the room. Rebekah

wasn't sad. She was furious. Every inch of her bristled with anger.

"Where is your furniture?" he asked when she didn't acknowledge him.

"Gone," she said, slowly lowering her hands.

"Gone?" He knew he sounded silly repeating what she'd said, but he was stunned to find another room stripped of everything including the dark green shades. "We need to let the bishop know you've been robbed. He can inform your neighbors and the police."

She put a hand on his arm, halting him. His astonishment that she'd purposely touched him instead of shying away eclipsed his shock with the stripped house.

"There's no need to alert the bishop. The day of our wedding I told my *mamm* to let Lloyd's family know they were welcome to take anything they could use." She drew in a deep breath and gave him a weak smile. "I guess they needed a lot."

"They took all the furniture?"

"Except my sewing machine, a pair of wooden chairs that belonged to my *aenti* and the blanket chest my *grossdawdi* built for me when I was twelve." She struggled to hold back the tears shining in her eyes. "I put the linens they left in the box Timothy's already taken out."

He thought about the box in the wagon. It wasn't very large. "What about your cradle? Where is it?"

"I don't have a cradle. Sammy slept in a drawer for a few months after he was born, and then I devised a pallet for him until he was big enough to sleep in a regular bed."

Joshua frowned. He recalled very clearly Lloyd bragging about the beautiful, handmade cradle he had ordered from a woodworker in Ephrata. His friend apologized for his boasting, saying he was excited to be able to give such a fine gift to his wife. He'd even stopped by to show it off. Joshua remembered it well because it'd been his and Tildie's wedding anniversary, and Joshua had had to push aside his grief to try to share his friend's excitement. Lloyd had said he planned to present it to Rebekah the following week.

But he hadn't. What had happened to the beautiful cradle? Uneasiness was an icy river running through him. For some reason, Lloyd must have needed to sell the cradle before he gave it to Rebekah. Joshua tried to guess what would have been more important to his friend than providing for his wife and *kind*.

Chapter 9

Rebekah drew back on Dolly's reins to slow the buggy as it neared the parking lot where a sign painted with Stoltzfus Family Shops was set prominently to one side. The long, low red clapboard building held the local grocery store, which was owned by her brother-in-law, Amos, as well as the other shops where the brothers worked. The scent of hot metal came from Isaiah's smithy behind the main building, a *gut* sign because Isaiah was again working after taking time off in the wake of his wife's death.

Joshua's brother was moving forward with his life, and she must do the same. The sight of the empty rooms at the house in Bird-in-Hand had been shocking, but also felt like closing the pages of a book. An ending. She was beginning a new story with Joshua's family in Paradise Springs. Everything that had been part of that life was gone, except for the farm. She was grateful she wouldn't have to make a decision about it now.

A few cars and a trio of buggies were parked in front of the grocery store. When she halted her buggy, she heard the clip-clop of several horses. An *Englisch* man came around the end of the building leading four horses. He nodded toward her as he walked toward a horse trailer at the far end of the parking lot.

She watched him load the horses in with the ease of practice. It was amusing to think of horses riding.

"Sit here? No go?" Sammy asked when she didn't move to get out of the buggy.

Rebekah looked at her son, who held a bag of cookies he'd brought from the house. He wanted to see the buggy shop, too. The other *kinder*, who'd been to the shop often, were helping *Grossmammi* Wanda and *Aenti* Esther prepare pots of flowering plants to sell at the end of the farm lane. Passersby stopped and bought them along with the cheeses Joshua's brother Ezra made.

"Let's go." She smiled at his excitement. It was infectious. She was eager to see where Joshua spent so many hours each day.

Still holding the bag, Sammy grabbed her hand as soon as she came around the buggy and swung him down. She winced when the motion she'd done so often sent a streak of pain across her back. A warning, she knew, to be careful. The ache subsided into a dull throbbing that matched her steps across the asphalt parking lot and up onto the concrete sidewalk in front of Joshua's shop.

Stoltzfus Buggy Shop.

The small sign was in one corner of the window beside the door next to another one announcing the shop was open. The hours were listed on the door, but Joshua was willing to come in early or stay late to help a customer.

As she opened the door, a bell chimed overhead and a buzzer echoed beyond an arch at the far end of the large room. It must lead into another space, but a partially closed door kept her from seeing. A half wall was a few paces from the doorway. On the other side were partially built buggies, spare parts and several hulking machines. The only one she recognized was a sewing machine with a table wider and longer than her own. She guessed it was for sewing upholstery for the buggies.

"What are you doing here?"

Rebekah recoiled from the deep voice coming out of a small room to the right, then realized it belonged to Timothy. She hadn't realized before how much he sounded like a grown man. There wasn't any anger on his face, even though his voice had been sharp. Maybe it was as simple as he always sounded annoyed.

"Cookies!" Sammy announced, oblivious to the teenager's tone. Running to the half wall, he held up the bag. "Yummy cookies."

"*Danki*, little man." Timothy gave a gentle tug on Sammy's hair.

Her son smiled as if Timothy was the greatest person in the world. He offered the bag again to the teenager. Timothy took it, unrolled the top and held it out so Sammy could select a cookie.

Biting her lower lip, Rebekah stayed silent. It was such a sweet moment, and she didn't want to do anything to shatter it.

The older boy looked over Sammy's head. "*Danki*, Rebekah."

"The cookies are—"

"No, I mean *danki* for telling *Daed* I don't want to build buggies. We had a long talk about it this morning."

"You did?"

"*Ja*. He suggested I try working a while with each of my *onkels* and see if I want to learn a craft from one of them." He grinned. "So, starting next week, I'll work here half the day and with *Onkel* Jeremiah the other half. If making furniture doesn't interest me, and I'm not sure it will, I can apprentice with a different *onkel*. I think I'll like working at *Onkel* Isaiah's smithy or at the grocery store best."

"What a *gut* idea!"

"It was mine. *Daed* actually listened when I suggested it."

"Your *daed* is always willing to listen to a well-thought-out idea shared with him in a calm tone."

He rolled his eyes, making Sammy giggle. "Okay, Rebekah. I get the message. Lower volume, more thought."

She laughed and patted his shoulder, pleased he allowed it. "Timothy Stoltzfus, that sounds like something a grown man would say."

He started to roll his eyes again, but halted when Joshua came around the door in the arch. "Who's at the door, Timothy?" He wiped his hands on an oily cloth as he walked toward the half wall. A smile brightened his face. "Rebekah, you should have told me you were planning to come this afternoon. I would have cleaned up some of this mess."

"It looks fine," she replied. "We decided you needed some cookies."

"Cookies!" Sammy pointed to the bag Timothy held.

"More like crumbs." Timothy shook the bag so they

could hear the broken cookie pieces in it. "But they taste *gut*, don't they, Sammy?"

"Gut! Gut! Gut!" The toddler danced around in a circle.

Joshua chuckled. "Why don't you take Sammy over to *Onkel* Amos's store, Timothy, and buy each of you something cool to enjoy with your cookie bits? Tell him I'll stop by later to pay for it."

"I've got money." Timothy squared his shoulders, trying to look taller. "Brad Granger paid me for helping him clean out his garage a couple of weeks ago. C'mon, little man. Let's see what *Onkel* Amos has that's yummy."

Sammy gave him his hand and went out the door. He waved back through the glass.

"What a surprise!" Joshua ran his fingers through his beard as he stared after the boys until they walked out of view. "I didn't expect him to spend his hard-earned money. He's been saving up for something, though he hasn't said what."

"Timothy has a *gut* heart," she said.

"Which he hides most of the time."

"All the more reason to be appreciative when he reveals it."

"True." He opened the swinging door in the half wall and motioned for her to come in. "What would you like to see first?"

"Everything!" She laughed as she lifted off her bonnet and put it on a nearby table. Smoothing her hair back toward her *kapp*, she said, "Now I sound like Sammy when he's excited. Can you show me what you're working on?"

He led the way past the machines, identifying each one by what it did. All were powered by air compression. Most were for working with metal when he built buggy wheels or put together the structure for the main part of the buggy. As she'd guessed, the sewing machine was used for making the seat upholstery. Tools hung from pegboard along one long wall. Hammers of every size as well as screwdrivers and wrenches. Those were the tools she recognized. Others she'd never seen before. She wanted to ask what they were used for, but her attention was caught by the fancy vehicle on the other side of the arch.

The grand carriage was parked in front of wide double doors. It was much larger than their family buggy and painted a pristine white. Open, with its top folded down at the back, it had two sets of seats that faced each other behind a raised seat, which had been painted a lustrous black at the front. The curved side wall dipped down toward a single step so someone could enter the carriage. The tufted seats were upholstered in bright red velvet. Large white wheels were topped by a curved piece of metal so no mud or stones from the road could strike the occupants. Narrow rubber tires edged the wheels.

"This is my current project," Joshua said as he placed one hand on the side of the carriage.

"What is it?"

"Mr. Carpenter, the *Englischer* who asked me to restore it, told me it's called a vis-à-vis. It's a French phrase that means the passengers face each other."

"It's really fancy and really fanciful, like something a princess would ride in." She stroked the red velvet. "Does he drive it?"

"Apparently he intends to use it on his daughter's wedding day. He tells me he has two matched bay horses to pull it to the church."

She arched her brows, and he chuckled. After walking to the body of a plain gray buggy, she bent to look inside it. "Are you repairing this, too?"

"No. I'm building it for a family near New Holland. I start with a wood base, then make the frame out of metal. Once it's secure, boards enclose it and the body is painted. Next I need to add wiring for lights and put in the dashboard Jeremiah is making." He glanced at a wall calendar from the bank in Paradise Springs. The squares were filled with notations in a multitude of colored inks. She guessed it was Joshua's schedule for each vehicle he was working on when he added, "He's supposed to have the dash to me soon."

She listened, fascinated, while he described making and fitting the wheels to a vehicle, as well as building the shafts to harness the horse to it. The interior would be completed to the new owner's specifications. He pointed to a list of options tacked on the wall. She was amazed to see almost two dozen items until she realized it was for many different kinds of vehicles. A young man wanted a certain style of seat in his courting buggy, while a family might need an extra bench seat or choose to have a pickup-style bed for moving bulky items.

"I never guessed it took so many different steps to make a buggy," she said when he finished the tour. "They're far more complicated than I'd guessed."

"It's our goal to let our customers think their buggies are simple so they won't need much maintenance to keep them going. That's why I want each buggy we make to be the best we can do."

"That sounds like pride, Joshua Stoltzfus," she teased.

"It does." He patted the unfinished buggy. "But what

if I say I'm glad God gave me the skill to put a *gut* buggy together?"

"Better."

"*Gut*. Let me show you the sewing machine. I think you'll find it interesting."

Rebekah took a single step to follow him, then paused as she pressed her hands to her lower back. The faint throb had erupted into an agonizing ache when she moved.

Did she groan? She wasn't sure, but Joshua rushed to her. He put his arm around her shoulders, urging her to lean on him. Her cheek rested on his chest while he guided her to a chair by the half wall, and she felt the smooth, strong motion of his muscles.

"Are you okay?" His warm breath sifted along her neck, making her *kapp* strings flutter…and her heart, as well.

"*Ja*. I strained my back while lifting Sammy out of the carriage. He's getting bigger, and so am I." She tried to laugh, but halted when another pang ricocheted up her spine. "I won't make that mistake again."

"Take Debbie with you when you're going out with Sammy. She'll be glad to help."

"I know." She glanced up at him. "She's helping your *mamm* and Esther today. She was hoping her friend, Mandy, would come over, too."

"But she would be happy to help you."

"I know. You have raised a very sweet daughter."

Her words touched him, she saw. *Hochmut* wasn't a part of the Amish way, but he knew how blessed he was that his *kinder* had stayed strong after the death of their *mamm*.

With his hand at the center of her back, he steered

her toward the half wall, where she could sit while they waited for Timothy and Sammy to return. It was a simple motion she'd seen him use with the *kinder*, but his light caress sent a powerful quiver along her. Even when he didn't touch her, she was deeply aware of him. To have his fingers brushing her waist threatened to demolish the wall she had built around her heart to keep any man from ever touching it.

When she lowered herself to the chair, he knelt beside her. He took her hand between his much broader ones. Worry etched deep threads in his brow. Before she could halt them, her fingers stroked his forehead to ease those lines. They slipped down his smooth cheek, edging his soft but wiry beard.

His brown eyes, as liquid and warm as melted chocolate, were filled with pleasure at her caress and questions about what she intended it to mean. How could she explain when she didn't know herself?

Drawing her hands away, she clasped them atop her full belly. The motion seemed to free them from the powerful connection between them. Or so she thought until he put his hand over hers, and the *boppli* kicked hard enough that he must have felt it, too. A loving glow filled his eyes exactly like when he looked at his own *kinder*.

"A strong one," he murmured.

"The *boppli* doesn't like to be ignored."

A slow smile curved his lips and sparkled in his eyes. "Maybe it's giving us fair warning to be prepared for when it's born."

She laughed. "I would prefer to think it's getting its antics out of the way so it'll be a *gut boppli*."

"You sound as if you're feeling better." His voice remained low and tender.

"I am. Sitting helps."

"*Gut.* Tomorrow I'll stop at the clinic and make an appointment for you. I'll ask them to see you as soon as possible."

"I told you, Joshua, the back pain was nothing but me being foolish."

He shook his head. "That may be so, but you need to see a midwife. You've been here more than a month, and if I remember right, you should be having appointments with her frequently at this point."

"I should." She resisted stroking his face again. "*Danki*, Joshua. I appreciate your kindness more than words can express."

He opened his mouth to reply, but whatever he intended to say went unspoken because the door opened and the boys rushed in. As Timothy launched into an explanation of how long Sammy had taken to select something to drink and how the little boy had delighted the other customers with his comments, Joshua stood and pretended to admire the sweet cider Sammy had chosen.

She watched and smiled and complimented her son on his choice, but her eyes kept shifting toward Joshua. He was watching her, too. Something huge had changed between them. Something that could not go back to the way it had been.

Joshua greeted his family as he came into the kitchen the next evening. He glanced first at Rebekah, but she was, as she'd assured him at breakfast, recovered from the muscle strain that had sent waves of pain across her face at the buggy shop.

Walking to the stove where Rebekah was adding butter to peas fresh from the garden, he asked, "How are you doing today?"

"Fine." She smiled at him, and his insides bounced like a *kind* on a trampoline.

"I made an appointment for you at the clinic." He held out the card he'd been given.

"Danki." She took the card and slipped it into a pocket in her black apron. "Why don't you sit? Dinner is almost ready."

"And I'm in your way?"

He heard Debbie giggle by the sink as Rebekah nodded. Walking back to the table, he lifted Sammy into the high chair set between his chair and Rebekah's. His gaze slipped to the far end of the table where the chairs Rebekah had brought from Bird-in-Hand awaited guests. It was odd to have the extra chairs by the table, but he knew they would be useful when company came.

He still wasn't accustomed to seeing her sewing machine by the largest window in the living room or having Tildie's blanket chest at the foot of Debbie's bed. Tildie's old sewing machine was stored in the attic, waiting for someone who could use it. He'd planned on giving his daughter the chest when she married, not so soon.

His sons came in freshly washed and making no secret of how hungry they were. Rebekah put the peas and thick, smoky slices of ham in the middle of the table. Debbie filled their glasses from a pitcher of ice water before getting warm biscuits from the oven.

Another feast! Joshua patted his stomach when it growled and everyone laughed. As soon as Rebekah was sitting beside the high chair and Debbie across from her brothers, he bowed his head for grace. He had so much to be thankful for: his family, the food and how God had brought Rebekah into his life. Grateful his prayer was silent because he could speak directly from his heart, he cleared his throat and looked up when Sammy moved impatiently beside him.

The conversation was easy and as plentiful as the food. When Joshua reached for another biscuit, a strange sound erupted from beneath the table. A dull thud. He looked at his glass. The water inside was fluttering.

"What was that?" Debbie asked, her eyes round and wide.

The *kinder* as well as Rebekah looked at him in bafflement. He wished he had an answer, but he didn't.

"Maybe it was an earthquake." Levi nearly bounced off his chair with excitement. "*Aenti* Esther taught us about them last year, and I read a book from the school library about the big ones in California. Maybe we're having one, too."

"Unlikely," Joshua said. "There aren't many earthquakes in Pennsylvania."

"Oh." His son looked disappointed.

"Then what was that sound?" asked Timothy. "Why did the table shake?"

"I don't know."

Rebekah shrugged her shoulders when Joshua glanced at her again. "I don't have any idea, either."

"Whatever it was is over," he said. "Eat up. If—"

A louder thump sounded. The table vibrated hard enough so the silverware bounced. Faces around the table paled.

Joshua looked down. This time, he'd felt whatever it was hitting the floor under his feet. No, not the floor.

Something had struck the cellar's ceiling…right below the kitchen table. Right where the fuel lines came into the house from the propane tank in the backyard.

He jumped to his feet. "Rebekah, take the *kinder* outside. Now!"

"You should come, too." Her face had lost all color. "Timothy, go next door and call 911."

"Let me do a quick check before you make that call." He locked eyes with his oldest. "Be ready to run to the Grangers." He crossed the kitchen in a trio of quick steps.

"Joshua?"

He looked back to see Rebekah picking up Sammy who held a piece of bread in one hand and a slice of ham in the other. "What?"

"Be careful." Her intense gaze seconded her soft words. She'd lost one husband, and she didn't want to lose another.

For a second he was warmed by that thought and considered heading out with the rest of the family, because he didn't want to be separated from a single one of them. It would mean another of the volunteer firemen having to go into the cellar to find out what was happening. He couldn't ask another man to do what he wouldn't.

Throwing open the cellar door while his family hurried out of the kitchen, he instinctively ducked when something exploded not far from the bottom of the steps. He sniffed, but didn't smell any gas. If it wasn't a fuel leak, what was blowing up?

He took one cautious step, then another. Groping along a shelf, he pulled out the flashlight he left there for emergencies. He took another deep breath to assure himself there wasn't a gas leak. Even the small spark created by the switch on the flashlight could set off a huge explosion if the cellar was filled with propane.

The air smelled sweet. No hint of the rotten odor added to propane to alert them to danger.

Even so, he held his breath as he turned on the flashlight. Nothing erupted. He swept the cellar with light. Everything looked as it should. He took a step. When something cracked beneath his boot, he aimed the light at the floor. Shards of glass were scattered across it.

He whirled when he heard footsteps overhead. Who was in the house? He saw Rebekah at the top of the stairs. "What are you doing? I told you to get out."

"Timothy opened some of the cellar windows from the outside, and he didn't smell any gas."

"I don't, either. I don't know what exploded. I—"

He put his arms over his head as a detonation came from his left. Something wet struck him. His skin was sliced by shattered glass.

"Joshua!" Rebekah shouted.

"Daed!" That was Timothy.

"Daedi!" The younger *kinder* yelled at the same time.

Raising his head and lowering his arms, he grimaced as liquid dripped from him. Some of it was blood, he realized when a drop splattered on his boot. Above him on the stairs, Rebekah and the *kinder* wore identical expressions of dismay.

He shook the fluid off him. Or tried to. It was sticky. He sniffed his lacerated forearm. "Root beer."

Glancing at the shelves where the canned food was stacked, he saw four more bottles of root beer. He grabbed them and stuffed them beneath a wooden crate. Just in time because another exploded, making the crate rise an inch from the floor.

"No," he heard Rebekah say. "You can't go down there until you put on shoes."

Within minutes, his sons had joined him and Rebekah in the cellar. Sammy stayed with Debbie at the top of the stairs, because the little boy was too young to help clean up glass. After he reassured them he was fine other than being covered with root beer from head to foot, Joshua asked Timothy to bring water from the spring at the back corner of the cellar. They needed to wash the concrete floor before ants discovered the spilled soda. When another bottle erupted beneath the crate, everyone jumped even though they'd known it could happen.

"I didn't realize there was any root beer left," Joshua said as he swept water and glass toward the center of the floor where Timothy scooped it up and put it in the bag Levi held. "I wonder why it exploded tonight."

"It's my fault, *Daedi*." Levi stared down at his sneakers.

"Your fault? How?"

"I moved the bottles." He looked up quickly, then at his feet again. "Rebekah asked Debbie and me to help sort out what was down here. I found the bottles and hid them behind the canned peaches."

"So you didn't have to share them? Levi, that isn't like you."

Rebekah put a hand on Joshua's arm, startling him. When he turned to her, she shook her head and gave him a gentle smile. He realized her thoughts were on his son, not on him. As he replayed his words in his mind, he knew he had spoken too harshly.

Levi was a *gut* boy, but no boy was perfect. If one

who loved root beer tried to hide a few old bottles to enjoy later by himself, he should be reminded sharing something special was the best way.

"I won't do it again, *Daed.*" Levi was near tears.

He clasped his younger son's shoulder. "I know you won't. Are there any more bottles back there?"

"Let me check." Timothy stepped toward the shelves. "You need to get those cuts looked at, *Daed.*"

"He's right," Rebekah said gently. "Levi can finish cleaning up this mess while I tend to your injuries."

He nodded when he realized this was her way of ensuring his son wouldn't forget the bad decision he had made. Handing the broom to Levi, he said, "I know you will do a *gut* job, son."

The boy sniffed back tears, but said, "I will, *Daed.*"

Joshua walked up the stairs after Rebekah. When she wobbled, he put his hand at her back to steady her. She didn't pull away. His steps were light as he went into the kitchen. Timothy being helpful, Levi admitting to the truth right away…and Rebekah not shrinking from his touch. Maybe they'd reached a turning point and their lives would get better. As he sat at the kitchen table so Rebekah could put salve on the many small cuts on his arms, he prayed that would be so.

Help me find a way to bring happiness into our lives. He hoped the prayer would be answered soon.

Chapter 10

When Levi brought the buggy and Dolly out of the barn, Rebekah smiled. The boy had made every effort to be on his best behavior since the episode with the exploding root beer bottles three nights ago. Even on Sunday during the church service, he hadn't squirmed once or poked the boy beside him.

Now she thanked him for hooking up the horse. He gave her a shy smile before jogging toward the house where Debbie was washing the breakfast dishes and keeping an eye on Sammy.

The road was empty while Rebekah headed toward the village. The sunlight shimmered on the road in front of her, warning the day was going to be a hot one. Usually she looked forward to summer heat, but not while she was pregnant. Every degree higher on the thermometer added to her discomfort.

She went past the Stoltzfus Family Shops sign. The

parking lot was filled as usual with cars and buggies. When the door of Joshua's shop opened and he bounded out, waving his hands, she drew back on the reins in astonishment.

"What's wrong?" she asked.

He didn't answer her question. He asked one of his own. "Where are you bound?"

"To my appointment with the midwife."

He grimaced, then looked down at his grease-stained shirt and trousers. "I forgot your appointment was today. Let's go." He put his foot on the step, then halted because she didn't slide across the seat.

"You don't need to come with me, Joshua. I know you're concerned about getting Mr. Carpenter's carriage done on time."

He shook his head, his most stubborn expression tightening his lips as he dropped back onto the ground. "I need to come with you. You are my wife. We will, God willing, be raising this *kind* together for many years to come." He put his foot on the step again and held out his hands.

She gave him the reins and moved to the left side of the buggy. She was glad her bonnet hid her face, because she wasn't sure what his reaction would be to the tears filling her eyes. She thought of the days since she'd visited the buggy shop and how solicitous he had been, making sure the *kinder* helped in the house and with Sammy so she could rest a short while each afternoon. Each kindness was a *wunderbaar* surprise she treasured, knowing how fleeting such benevolence could be. He'd welcomed her concerns about Timothy and accepted her silent chiding to be more gentle with his son after Levi had stashed the bottles of root beer in the cellar.

Am I being foolish to consider trusting again, God? The question came from the depths of her heart, bursting out of her unbidden. Only now did she recognize how desperately she longed for a real marriage.

As Joshua steered the buggy onto the road, a white van pulled up in front of Amos's store. An elderly man and woman were waiting with their bags of groceries, each of them holding an ice cream cone. The driver parked, jumped out and opened the door to let them in while he put their purchases in the back.

It was a scene Rebekah had witnessed often at the grocery store in Bird-in-Hand, but her breath caught when she noticed how the elderly man helped his wife into the van as if she were as precious and essential to him as his next breath. Every motion spoke of the love they shared, a love that required no words because it was part of them. She felt a pinch of envy as she imagined having a love like that to share.

When Joshua spoke, it unsettled her to realize his thoughts closely mirrored hers. "The Riehls were married before I was born. Even though Amos has offered to deliver groceries to their house, they insist on coming to the store. He suspects the real reason is the soft ice cream machine he put in last year."

"Ice cream *is* a *gut* reason." She smiled, letting her uncomfortable thoughts drain away. "Do you ever make ice cream with the *kinder*?"

"Our ice cream maker broke a few years ago."

"I brought one from the farm."

He flashed her a grin. "I'm surprised Levi hasn't been begging to make ice cream. The boy has a real sweet tooth."

"He's mentioned it several times, but…" She sighed. "There are only so many hours in each day."

"I was wondering, Rebekah, if it is wise for you to be doing so much of the housework."

She looked at him, baffled. Why wouldn't she do the house chores? It was what a wife did. Dismay twisted in her middle. Had she failed to keep the house or make his meals or clean the laundry as well as Matilda had?

"Why?" It seemed the safest question to ask.

"I see how exhausted you are. You cook and clean for four *kinder* as well as you and me. In addition, you work in the garden every day and spend hours making and keeping our clothes in *gut* repair."

"You work as hard at the buggy shop."

"But I'm not going to have a *boppli* soon." He shot her a grin. "What do you say to getting a girl in to help before the *boppli* is born? She could do the heavier chores so you can rest?" His smile broadened. "And have time to supervise making ice cream for Levi."

"That would be *wunderbaar*." Again she had to blink back tears. They seemed to be her constant companion recently. His concern touched her heart, piercing the barriers she'd raised to protect it from being hurt over and over.

"I asked around and Sadie Gingerich may be available." He drew in the reins when they reached the main highway.

Route 30 was always busy. The buggy rocked when eighteen-wheelers roared past, but Dolly acted as if she encountered them every day. The horse stood still until given the command to go. The buggy sped across, and Rebekah grasped the seat with both hands to keep from being rocked off.

When they were driving along a quiet residential street, Joshua added, "Sadie helped my sister Ruth during her last pregnancy, and Ruth was very satisfied. You haven't spent much time with my sister, but I can tell you she's not easy to please."

"Ruth knows what her family needs, and she isn't afraid to voice her opinions."

He smiled. "That's a nice way of saying she's bossy, but she's the oldest, so she's used to looking out for us. If you want, I can contact Sadie's family. They live south of Paradise Springs, closer to Strasburg. If she can't help, she might know someone she can recommend." He glanced across the buggy. "Do you want me to check if she can come?"

"Ja." She couldn't say more. The tears that had filled her eyes were now clogging her throat until she felt as if she'd swallowed a lump of uncooked bread dough.

"Are you sure?"

She realized he'd taken her terse answer as dismay instead of overwhelming relief and gratitude that he cared enough about her to hire Sadie Gingerich to help. Blinking the tears hanging on her lashes, she said, *"Ja,* I'm sure. *Danki,* Joshua."

"I'll see if she can stop by soon. If you like her—and I think you will because she's a nice girl—she can start right away." He tapped her nose. When she stared at him as if he'd lost his mind, he laughed. "Then maybe my pretty wife won't have dark circles under her eyes because she's doing too much and not getting enough sleep."

"Nice way to give your wife a compliment."

"I don't want you to grow prideful." His gaze cut into her as he added, "And that can't be easy for someone as beautiful as you."

She knew she was blushing, but she didn't care. Lloyd had never given her a compliment. Not even when they were courting. She should pay no attention to fancy words. Yet when Joshua said something nice to her, happiness filled her, making her feel as if the sun glowed inside her.

He didn't add more as he slowed the buggy again and hit the toggle that activated the right turn signal. He pulled into an extrawide driveway and stopped by a hitching post. After jumping out, he lashed the reins to it, though Dolly would wait for them to return.

Rebekah was glad when he assisted her out of the buggy. It wasn't easy to see her feet now, especially on the narrow step. Gravel crunched beneath her feet as she walked with him toward the single-story white building that looked as if it had been a home. Dark green shutters edged the windows. A bright wreath with purple and white blossoms hung on the yellow door, and a small plaque to one side announced: Paradise Springs Birthing Clinic.

Joshua reached past her to open the door. It wasn't until she was inside that she realized she hadn't cringed away from his arm when it had edged around her. She was torn between joy and praying that she wasn't making another huge mistake. She wasn't going to think about the dark times. They had shadowed her life for too long. She was going to focus on the here and now. And the *boppli* who would be born soon.

The clinic was as cheerful and bright inside as it was on the exterior. A half dozen plastic chairs in a variety of colors edged each side of the room. Three were occupied, and none of the women were dressed plainly.

They looked up and smiled as she walked past. She returned their smiles and told herself to relax.

After going to the registration desk near a closed door at the far end of the narrow room, Rebekah gave her name to the receptionist who wore large, red-rimmed glasses. The receptionist welcomed her and handed her a clipboard with forms to fill out.

Rebekah sat and concentrated on answering each question. Joshua took the chair beside her.

"Measles?" he asked when she checked a box on the long list of common diseases. "Didn't you have the shot when you were a *kind*?"

"I did, but I caught them anyhow." She chuckled. "The doctor told *Mamm* it sometimes happens that way and that I would have been much sicker if I hadn't had the shot. I couldn't imagine how, because I was pretty sick with them."

Turning the page over, she was glad the portion on health insurance had already been crossed out. That showed the clinic was accustomed to dealing with the Amish, who weren't required to purchase health insurance because their community took care of any medical bills a family couldn't pay on their own.

But how was she going to pay for the *boppli*'s birth? She couldn't expect Joshua to pay the costs. The *boppli* wasn't his. The answer came instantly: she'd have to sell the farm in Bird-in-Hand. Once the farm was gone, her haven would be, too, but what choice did she have?

Finishing the rest of the pages, she started to rise to take the completed forms to the desk.

Joshua stood and held out his hand. "Let me do that. You should sit while you can."

As she thanked him, a woman sitting on her other side

leaned toward her. "You have a very considerate husband," she whispered. "I wish my husband understood like yours does how tough it is to get up and down." She laughed. "My ankles are getting as big as a house."

Taken aback, Rebekah wasn't sure how to reply. She gave the woman a smile, which seemed the perfect answer because the other woman laughed and went back to reading her book.

Joshua sat beside her again. "The receptionist said it shouldn't be long before you're called in."

"Gut." The plastic chair was uncomfortable.

A few minutes later the inner door opened. A tall woman stepped out. Her dark brown hair was swept back beneath a *kapp* that identified her as a Mennonite. The back was pleated and square rather than heart-shaped like Rebekah's. Her plain gown was worn beneath a doctor's white coat, and a stethoscope hung around her neck. She called out Rebekah's name. When Joshua stood, too, the woman asked him to wait, saying he'd be called back in a few minutes.

He nodded and took his seat. He gave Rebekah a bolstering smile as she went to the door and stepped through into a hallway that branched off past two open doors on either side.

"This way, Rebekah," the woman in the white coat said.

In spite of knowing she shouldn't, Rebekah stared at the woman who limped as she walked. A plastic brace ran from below her right knee into her black sneaker. It was held in place atop her black stockings by a wide strip of what looked like Velcro.

She recovered herself and followed the woman into

a room. The midwife's warm smile was so genuine that she was instantly at ease.

"I am Elizabeth Overholt, but everyone calls me Beth Ann," said the woman before she asked Rebekah to get on the scale. She then checked Rebekah's blood pressure. Rebekah was pleased with both, and so was Beth Ann.

"Excellent," Beth Ann said and led her to a room across the hall. She motioned for Rebekah to come in. "Do you need help getting on the table?"

"I think I can manage still."

"Don't be brave. Ask for help when you need it." She kept her hand near Rebekah's elbow until Rebekah was sitting on the examination table. "Okay, I have your file from your midwife in Bird-in-Hand, so let's see what it says."

Looking around the pleasant room while Beth Ann read the file, Rebekah smiled. Childish drawings hung on the wall. She guessed one of them depicted a kitten or maybe a lamb. Something with curly, fuzzy hair. The other was of a *kind* holding a woman's hand. A small house and a huge tree were behind them, and the sun was bright yellow while a rainbow arched over the whole scene.

Booklets she recognized from when she'd been pregnant with Sammy were stacked neatly by the window. Then she had read every word, hungry for information to make sure her *boppli* was born healthy. Not one had contained any advice on how to keep her husband from damaging their *kind*.

She pushed the dreary cloud of memory away. Lloyd was gone, and Joshua hadn't raised his hand to her. Not yet.

Oh, Lord, help me to trust he's not the man Lloyd was. I want to be able to believe he won't hurt me or the kinder.

Beth Ann looked up, and her smile vanished. "Is everything okay, Rebekah?"

"Ja." She forced a laugh that sounded brittle in her ears. "It's impossible to get comfortable at this point."

"Are you having contractions?"

She shook her head, sorry she was causing the midwife worry. But how could she be honest? She could not let Lloyd's sins become a shadow over his son as people watched to see if he had inherited his *daed's* violent outbursts.

As she began to answer Beth Ann's questions, she told herself again, *Think about now.* Maybe if she reminded herself of that enough times, she'd make it a habit and would finally be able to leave the darkness behind her once and for all.

Joshua had been in places, but not many, where he felt less comfortable than in the waiting room with a group of *Englisch* women who looked ready to give birth at any moment. None of the magazines stacked on the tables interested him enough to page through one until he noticed a sports magazine tucked at the bottom of one pile. He drew it out and almost laughed out loud when he saw it was a year old. The cover story was on baseball, so he began to read. He glanced toward the inner door when it opened, but it was a different woman calling out the name of one of the pregnant women.

"Mr. Stoltzfus?"

At his name, he looked up and saw the midwife who wore the brace and who'd come to get Rebekah was holding the door open again.

"Will you come with me?" she asked with a smile that suggested she knew exactly how eager he was to escape the waiting room.

Joshua had a smile of his own when he entered the room where Rebekah sat on a paper-topped examination table, her feet swinging as if she were no older than Sammy. He went to stand beside her.

After the midwife introduced herself, Beth Ann pulled out a low stool and sat. She handed him a sheet of paper. Scanning it, he saw it was a to-do list for when Rebekah's contractions started, including when to call Beth Ann.

"At that point, I will contact the doctor so he'll be there if we need him," the midwife said. "As Rebekah didn't have any complications with her first pregnancy, I don't see any reason to expect any this time. God willing, of course."

He nodded. "We have been praying for God's blessing on this birth."

"Do you have any questions?" Beth Ann asked.

"Not after having been present at the birth of my three *kinder*."

"All right, *Daedi*," she said with a laugh. "You are clearly an expert."

"I know enough to call for you to come."

That Rebekah didn't correct Beth Ann's assumption he was the *boppli*'s *daed* pleased him for a reason he couldn't decipher. He didn't want to. He wanted to enjoy the *gut* news that Rebekah and the *boppli* were doing well.

He assisted Rebekah from the table, thanked the midwife and nodded when she instructed them to make another appointment for two weeks from today. He took the small bag Rebekah held. She told him it contained vitamins. While she made an appointment, he went to get his straw hat and her bonnet from the rack by the door.

Cautiously he put his hand on her elbow to guide her on the steps and across the driveway to the buggy. Again he was relieved when she didn't tug away or flinch.

She was quiet as he started the drive toward home. He guessed she was exhausted. Crossing the highway took more than twice as long this time because the traffic was even heavier. When a tourist pointed a camera at the buggy, he leaned into the shadows so his face wouldn't be visible in the photograph. Most visitors understood the Amish didn't want to have their picture taken, but a few didn't care.

Once they crossed Route 30 and drove out of the village, no more cars zipped past them. He waved to an *Englischer* who was driving a tractor. He recognized the man from the charity mud sale at his *mamm*'s house in the spring. From what he'd heard, the *Englischer* was planning to run an organic vegetable farm. Joshua appreciated the man's determination to practice *gut* husbandry.

After stopping to collect the mail, Joshua drove up the driveway. He glanced at Rebekah when she stirred. Had she fallen asleep? He didn't want to embarrass her by asking.

"*Danki* for taking me to my appointment today," she said.

"You are my wife, and that *boppli* will be growing up in my house." He felt her tense, but her shoulders became softer next to his as he added, "In our house. I'm sorry I didn't say that first."

"You don't have to apologize. That house has been yours for years. You can't expect to change old habits overnight." She flashed him a smile. "I know I haven't been able to change mine, though I'm trying to."

Was she talking about how she flinched from him? If so, he hoped her words meant she was making an effort to accept him being close to her. Because, he realized, he wanted to be close to her. The sound of her laughter, the twinkle in her eyes when she looked as mischievous as Sammy, the gentleness she used with the *kinder*, the ruddy warmth of her hair…each of these and more drew him to her.

He assisted her out of the buggy, teasing her because she was getting almost too wide for the narrow door. He started to suggest that he grill some hamburgers for their supper tonight so she could rest, but halted when he saw Sammy running toward them with Debbie on his heels. The *kinder* were barefoot, and their clothes were spotted with water above the wet hems.

"*Daedi*, come see!" yelled Sammy. "Froggie!"

Joshua couldn't move as Lloyd's son called him *Daedi* again as he tugged on Joshua's hand. This was a complication he hadn't seen coming. What should he do?

He didn't look in Rebekah's direction, fearing he would see pain and grief on her face when her late husband's son called another man *Daedi*. An apology burned on his tongue, but what could he say even if he let the words out? He wouldn't apologize for loving the *kind*, especially when Sammy reminded him of his own boys at that age. Curious and excited over the most mundane things, filled with joy and eager to share his happiness with everyone around him. Even something as commonplace as a frog was a reason for celebrating.

"Daedi!" Sammy's voice tore him away from his musing. "Quick! Froggie jumping."

"We're coming," Joshua said. "Go ahead. We'll be right behind you." As the *kinder* raced toward the stream beyond the barn, he began, "Rebekah…" Again words failed him.

She gave him the same gentle smile he'd seen her offer the *kinder* when they were distressed. It eased the tightness in his gut.

"It's all right, Joshua. He needs a *daed*, and if you're willing to be his, that's *wunderbaar.*"

"Are you sure?"

"Ja. I think you'll be the very best *daed* he could have."

"Now, you mean." He didn't want to be compared to his best friend when Lloyd had no chance to prove he would be a *gut daed* for Sammy.

She nodded, but her gaze edged away. She was hiding something, but what? He was certain if he could answer that question, so many other puzzles would be solved, too.

Chapter 11

The day was beautiful, and that morning before going to the shop, Joshua and Timothy had finished stringing the new clothesline out to the maple tree. Rebekah gazed at the puffy clouds as she hung a wet sheet that flapped against her in the breeze. She saw no sign of a storm, which meant she could do another load of laundry and have it dried and folded before she needed to leave for her scheduled appointment with the midwife. She'd persuaded Joshua that she was fine to go on her own. He relented only when she reminded him how his *Englisch* client would be stopping by tomorrow to collect his fancy carriage, and Joshua wanted to check it from front to back one last time to make sure he hadn't overlooked something.

"Are you Rebekah?" A cheery voice broke into her thoughts.

She looked around the sheet and saw a woman close

to her own age walking toward her. Glancing past her, she didn't see a buggy. Had the woman walked to the house?

The woman's dark brown eyes sparkled in her round face. Rather short, she was what Rebekah's *mamm* might have described as pleasingly plump. Not overweight, but her plain clothes didn't hide that she had softer curves than what the *Englischers* deemed ideal.

"Ja," Rebekah replied. "I'm Rebekah."

"I'm Sadie Gingerich. Your husband asked me to stop by to talk about working for you." Her gaze slipped along Rebekah. "That *boppli* is coming soon, ain't so?"

She laced her fingers over her belly. "No secret about that. Let's go inside and sit while we talk."

"Sounds *gut*," Sadie agreed, but Rebekah quickly discovered that Sadie's idea of a conversation was doing most of the talking herself.

They'd no sooner sat at the kitchen table than Debbie and Sammy came from the living room where they'd been playing a game. Rebekah was pleased to see how quickly Sammy hoisted himself into Sadie's lap while she explained what work she did for a family before and after a *boppli* arrived.

Even though she didn't get a chance to ask many questions, Rebekah decided Sadie would be a great temporary addition to their household. Sadie, though she was unmarried and had no *kinder* of her own, had helped raise her eleven younger siblings. She'd started hiring out after her *daed* died and clearly loved the work she did. Whenever she spoke with Debbie or Sammy, her smile broadened, and she soon had them giggling.

"When can you start?" Rebekah asked.

"I have another week at the Millers' in the village,

but I can begin after that if that works for you." She bounced a delighted Sammy on her leg as if he were riding a horse.

"That would be *wunderbaar*. Oh…" She abruptly realized they didn't have an extra bedroom for Sadie.

When she explained that, Sadie waved aside her concerns. "If Debbie doesn't mind, I'll share with her. I have almost a dozen sisters and brothers. Sharing with one other person will seem like luxury."

"Say *ja*, Rebekah," the little girl pleaded before turning to Sadie. "I've been praying the *boppli* is a girl because I want a sister."

"I'll be your practice sister." Sadie looked at Rebekah. "If that's okay with you."

"It sounds like a *gut* solution." She'd have to explain to Sadie eventually that Joshua had his own room upstairs, but that was a conversation she wanted to delay as long as possible. It wasn't that she was ashamed of the situation. She felt… She wasn't sure what she felt about it. She simply knew she didn't want to discuss it.

They spoke a while longer, then Sadie said she needed to return to the Millers' house. She left on a scooter like the ones the *kinder* rode to school, which explained why Rebekah hadn't heard a buggy approach.

Rebekah couldn't wait to tell Joshua that Sadie Gingerich had agreed to help. That made her smile even more as she went back outside to the clothesline. Lately, the idea of sharing events of the day and telling him funny stories about the *kinder* seemed natural. And she liked that they were becoming more and more a part of each other's lives. Their marriage wasn't a perfect love story, but it was getting better each day.

Once she'd finished hanging the rest of the laundry,

Rebekah picked up the basket and went into the laundry area off the kitchen. She started the washer and dumped in detergent. Of all the conveniences they enjoyed from the solar panels on the roof, having a washer that wasn't run by a gasoline motor was her favorite. She'd despised the raucous noise and the fumes, even with an exhaust pipe stuck out a window, from the washer in Bird-in-Hand.

She went to the pile of light-colored clothes waiting to be washed. The *kinder* brought their dirty clothes to the laundry room, saving her extra trips up and down the stairs. They tried to sort them properly, but she occasionally found a dark sock in with the whites. She picked up each garment and shook it to make sure nothing hid within it.

When she lifted one of Joshua's light blue shirts to put it in the washer, a familiar odor, one she'd hoped never to smell again, swirled through her senses, stripping her happiness away as if it'd never existed. Her nose wrinkled. She knew that odor…and she hated it. The scent of alcohol. She'd smelled it too many times on Lloyd's breath and on his clothes.

Where was it coming from?

She sniffed the shirt. No, not from that. Dropping it into the water filling the tub, she held another piece of clothing to her nose, then another and another, and drew in a deep breath with each one. She identified the musty scent of sweat and the tangy sauce from the casserole she'd made two nights ago. The unmistakable scent of horse and another of the grease Joshua used at the buggy shop. Green and earthy aromas from the knees of the pants Levi had been wearing when he helped her weed the garden and harvest the cabbage and green beans.

But the scent of liquor was gone. Had she actually smelled it? Maybe the combination of laundry detergent and heat in the laundry room had created the odor she dreaded. After all, though she'd watched carefully, she'd never heard Joshua slur his words or seen him unsteady on his feet. He never struck her or the *kinder*.

Was the smell only her imagination? It must have been.

But what if it wasn't?

She leaned forward against the washer and whispered, "Help me, God! Help us all."

The rest of the day passed in a blur. Rebekah couldn't help taking a deep breath every few minutes. The odor of alcohol, if it'd existed at all, had vanished. It was impossible to forget the stab of fear in the laundry room. Even at her appointment with Beth Ann, she'd struggled to focus on the midwife's questions and suggestions. She'd managed little more than a faint smile when Beth Ann had congratulated her on hiring Sadie Gingerich.

The comment reminded her that Joshua was paying the expenses for Lloyd's *kind*. She shied away from the idea of selling the farm. Even after the house had been stripped clean by Lloyd's relatives, there was enough farm machinery to sell to cover the costs of the delivery and Sadie's help. How could she hold on to the farm when Joshua worked so hard to provide for the family?

By the time she returned home, her head was pounding. She must have looked as bad as she felt, because Debbie urged her to rest. She hesitated until the little girl reminded her that Joshua had volunteered to bring home pizza to celebrate finishing the work on the carriage.

Sleep eluded her. The *boppli* seemed to have acquired a love for step dancing, and her thoughts were strident. Each time she tried to divert them by praying or thinking of something else, she was drawn right back into the morass.

Usually she loved having store-bought pizza with its multitude of toppings, but she could barely tolerate the smell. She picked at a single piece while the rest of the family enjoyed the treat and the celebration. Somehow she managed to put on a *gut* front, because neither the *kinder* nor Joshua asked if something was bothering her. In fact, the whole family seemed giddy with happiness.

She wanted to feel that way, too. Was she going to allow a single scent, which might not even have been there, ruin her whole day? Again she prayed for God's help, adding a silent apology for spiraling into the terror that had stalked her during her first marriage.

The feeling of a worthless weight being lifted from her shoulders brought back her smile…and her appetite. Rebekah finished the slice of pizza and then had two more. She smiled when Timothy and Debbie began to tease Levi about a girl he'd been seen talking to several times during the past week while working with *Onkel* Daniel. As he turned the tables and jested with his sister about fleeing from the chicken coop and a particularly mean hen that had chased her halfway to the house, Rebekah joined in with the laughter.

After they finished their treat, Joshua volunteered his and the boys' help to clean up the kitchen. She started to protest, but he insisted. Grateful, she went with the younger *kinder* into the living room and sat next to the sewing basket where her hand mending was piled. No matter how often she worked on it, the stack never seemed to get smaller. She took the topmost item, a pair of Levi's trousers that needed to have the hems lowered...again! The boy was sprouting up faster than the corn in the fields.

It didn't take Joshua and his sons long to redd up the kitchen and join them. The boys sat on the floor, and she assumed Joshua would read to them as he did each evening.

"I have something else for our celebration tonight." He smiled at Rebekah. "A birthday gift."

"Joshua, it's not my birthday," she replied.

"Who said it was for you?"

She stared after him as he walked out the door. Hearing a muffled giggle from Debbie, she saw the little girl had her hands clamped over her mouth. Her eyes twinkled with merriment. Levi wouldn't meet Rebekah's gaze and Timothy, for once, was grinning broadly. Only Sammy, playing with his blocks on the braided rug, seemed oblivious.

What were they up to?

Her answer came when Joshua returned to the living room. He placed a cradle by her chair.

She gasped when she ran her fingers along the cradle's hood. The wood was as smooth as a rose petal, and it had been polished to highlight the grain. Maple, she guessed, because it had been finished to a soft honey shade. Not a single nail head was visible, and she saw dovetail joints at the corners. Her eyes widened when she realized it had been built with pegs. Only an extremely skilled woodworker could have finished the cradle using such old-fashioned techniques.

"What do you think?" Joshua asked, squatting on the other side of the cradle. "As a birthday gift for the *bop-*

pli? Like I said, it isn't for *your* birthday." He chuckled and the *kinder* joined in.

Rebekah was speechless at the magnificent gift and even more so that Joshua had gotten it for her. A warmth built within her, melting the ice clamped on to her heart.

She whispered the only word she could manage, *"Danki."*

"I hope you like it. Jeremiah built it."

"It's beautiful."

"He does *gut* work."

She stared at the cradle and knew that *gut* was a feeble description of the lovely piece. Jeremiah must have spent hours sanding the wood and staining it and polishing it until the grain was gloriously displayed. She couldn't imagine the amount of time it had taken to cut the corners to fit together so smoothly.

"Do you like it?" Debbie asked, inching across the floor to run her fingers along the wood.

Before she could answer, Levi began a story about how Joshua had asked them to keep the secret until the cradle was finished. Even Timothy added to the tale.

Looking at their animated faces, she smiled at her family.

Her family.

Sometime in the past weeks, this house had become home and these *kinder* as much a part of her life as Sammy. And Joshua? She couldn't imagine her days without him being a part of them. His gentle teasing, his solicitude, his joy when Sammy called him *Daedi*.

Because Sammy loved him.

And, she realized with a start, she wanted to let herself fall in love with him, too. Really in love, not this make-believe marriage. She wished they could share a love not overshadowed by fear and uncertainty.

"It's lovely," Rebekah said to Debbie, giving the girl a hug. "*Danki* for letting this be a surprise."

"*Daedi* said you didn't have a cradle for Sammy, and we wanted you to have one for my little sister." She winked as Levi insisted, as Debbie had hoped he would in response to her teasing, that the *boppli* was a boy.

Joshua glanced at his *kinder*, then said, "I'm glad you like it, Rebekah. I was surprised you didn't have one for Sammy." His gaze slid away from hers, and she wondered if he thought she wouldn't want him speaking poorly of Lloyd.

Hoping to ease his abrupt discomfort, she said, "Lloyd told me that he intended to get Sammy a cradle, but then I guess he didn't have the money for it." She ran her fingers over her belly. "This little one won't have to sleep in a drawer. *Danki*, Joshua."

Before she could think about what she was doing and halt herself, she leaned forward and kissed his cheek.

Joshua wasn't sure who was more surprised at Rebekah's kiss, him or her. She pulled back so quickly and turned away to say something to the *kinder* that he couldn't guess what she was thinking.

But he'd heard what she said. Lloyd had promised to get a cradle for their firstborn, but then hadn't given her the extraordinary one he'd purchased. Where had that cradle gone? Joshua knew it was unlikely that he'd ever get an answer. That bothered him less than the grief he'd heard in Rebekah's voice when she spoke of her late husband.

How could he hope to win her heart when it belonged

to the *daed* of her two *kinder*? He hadn't relinquished his love for his late wife. Astonishment ran through him. Tildie! When was the last time he'd thought of her? He was shocked that he couldn't recall.

He went through his normal evening routine, but his gaze kept wandering to Rebekah. She worked on lengthening Levi's church pants until it was time for prayers and for the younger *kinder* to go to bed. Before she took Sammy into the downstairs bedroom, she gave Debbie and Levi each a kiss on the cheek, and his own skin sizzled with the memory of her lips against it.

Soon the footsteps upstairs disappeared as the *kinder* found their beds. Timothy had gone outside without any explanation, but Joshua was used to his son's changing moods. Not that he appreciated them, but he expected them.

When Rebekah returned, she continued her sewing while he perused a new buggy parts catalogue that had come in today's mail. Neither of them spoke as they sat facing each other across the cradle.

"Joshua, it's time," she said suddenly.

He leaped to his feet and stared at her, dropping the catalogue on the floor. "Already? I thought the *boppli* isn't due for a few more weeks. Will you be okay here while I call Beth Ann?"

She put her fingers lightly on his arm. "Joshua, it isn't time for the *boppli*. It's time to talk about selling Lloyd's farm."

Glad that the *kinder* were elsewhere so they hadn't seen him jump to conclusions, he lowered himself into his chair. He didn't wait for his heart to slow from its panicked pace as he asked, "What has changed your mind?"

"I told you I needed time to think over the decision, and I have," she said.

Joshua's teeth clenched so hard his jaw hurt. She was shutting him out again. He glared at the cradle, which had reminded her of the husband she'd chosen with love instead of the one she'd agreed to wed for convenience's sake. He'd never imagined he'd be jealous of a dead man, but he couldn't restrain the horrible emotion.

Lord, help me walk the path You have chosen for me and forget about other men's. You brought Rebekah and her family into my life for a reason. Let me be Your instrument in helping them live as You would wish for them.

"All right," he said, hoping hurt hadn't seeped into his voice. "I'll make the arrangements with Jim Zimmermann to set an auction date. It'll take some time to prepare the auction and advertise it. He'll want the most bidders there possible so you can get plenty of bids for the farm and the equipment."

"It's been this long. A little longer won't make any difference." She didn't look up from her sewing. "I'd rather not go."

"I understand," he said, even though he didn't. Actually, he comprehended why she didn't want to watch the farm as well as her house go on the block. What he didn't understand was why she'd come to the decision to sell now.

"*Gut.* Lloyd asked you to take care of us as you think best. He'd have trusted you to oversee what needs to be done, Joshua."

"Do you trust me, too?"

She finally met his eyes. *"Ja."*

His heart seemed to bounce in his chest, beating

madly as if it hadn't made a sound since Tildie had drawn her last breath and it was finally coming to life again. Rebekah trusted him. As he held her steady gaze, he knew her faith in him wasn't because he'd given her the cradle and a home for her family. He saw something more in her eyes, something that spoke of respect and camaraderie. He didn't dare look for more. How could he ask for her love when he withheld his own heart? The thought of loving any woman other than Tildie seemed a betrayal.

Or was he seeing what he hoped to in Rebekah's gaze?

He would know, one way or the other, with his next words. "I'd like to talk to you about one very important matter."

"I told you. I trust you to handle the farm auction."

He shook his head. "This doesn't have anything to do with the farm. It's about Sammy and the little one."

She curved her hand over her stomach. "What about them?"

"What do you think of me adopting them?"

Her breath came out in a gasp, and she stared at him without speaking. For the second time that evening, he had shocked her into silence.

"Rebekah, I should have phrased that better. I've been thinking about this since Jeremiah dropped off the cradle. He asked if I intended to become the *kinder*'s legal *daed*."

She started to speak, then stuttered into silence again.

"Take all the time you need to consider it and pray about it, Rebekah," he said. "I'm not asking you to take this step because I want you and the *kinder* to forget Lloyd is their true *daed*, but if Jeremiah is asking, others may be, too. I think we should have an answer to give those who ask."

Finally she spoke in a whisper, "*Ja*, we should have an answer." She put the garment she'd been working on back into the mending basket and slowly stood. "I need to pray about this, Joshua."

"I will, too."

She nodded and again started to speak, but said nothing as she walked out of the room.

He heard the bedroom door softly close behind her, shutting him out as she did each night.

With a sigh, he rose. He glanced at the stairs, but how could he sleep after the evening's events? Rebekah had kissed his cheek, albeit as chastely as she did the *kinder*'s. She'd expressed her faith in him. She hadn't turned him down when he spoke of adopting her and Lloyd's *kinder*, even though he'd failed to mention the true reason why he asked. Not his brother's curiosity or anyone else's mattered as much as how much he had come to consider Sammy his own and the *boppli*, as well.

He walked into the kitchen and noticed light flowing across the floor. He looked out the window and saw two figures silhouetted against the faint light from the lantern in the barn. One was Timothy. Joshua frowned when he realized the other person was Alexis Granger. She held the handles of a large tote bag with both hands, and she was talking earnestly. He couldn't hear what they were saying, but their posture suggested they were discussing something important.

What was the *Englisch* girl doing over here at this time of night? Brad had mentioned more than once that he insisted his daughter be home by dark, except on weekend nights when she could be out until midnight with her friends.

He took a step toward the door, then heard a soft voice say, "Don't."

Turning, he discovered Rebekah coming around the kitchen table. "I thought you'd gone to bed," he said.

"Sammy wanted a drink of water, so I came to get it." She looked out the window. "If you confront Timothy in front of his friend, he won't heed anything you say. You have to talk to him as you did about working with his *onkels*. He listened to you then."

"He needs to listen to me now."

"I agree, but he won't hear you if he feels he has to defend himself. Talk to him tomorrow when you can be calm and present a reasonable argument about how he could hurt his friend's reputation if it's discovered he's meeting her after dark in the barn."

"Do you think they—"

"I think they are *gut* people who care about each other, but I don't think she sees him as anyone other than a friend. He might have a different opinion of their relationship. Even so, you've taught him well. Trust him to know the right thing to do."

He glanced once more at the teenagers, then nodded. "How do you know so much about teenagers when Sammy is only a toddler?"

"I don't know. I'm going with what my instincts tell me."

"I hope your instincts are right." He looked out to see Alexis sprinting across the yard in the direction of the Grangers' house. The large bag flapped against her legs on each step.

"So do I." He heard the fervor in her voice. "So do I."

Chapter 12

On the day the farm was to be auctioned, the *kinder* pleaded to attend with Joshua. Rebekah agreed because she had always enjoyed auctions. She warned them that, other than Timothy, none of them must join the crowd that was bidding unless they were with Joshua or one of their *grossmammis*. Buyers would be annoyed if they were distracted by *kinder* running about.

Grossmammi Wanda handed covered dishes to the *kinder* in the family buggy. Now that her cast was off, she seemed to be trying to make up for lost time. Each *kind*, including Sammy, was given a plate or a pot to watch over. Wanda had insisted on bringing food, even though the members of Rebekah's old district would be offering food for sale. It was a fund-raiser for a husband and wife in the district who each needed surgery.

When Joshua stepped up into the buggy, he said to his *mamm*, "We'll see you at the auction later."

"We'll be there as soon as Esther finishes frosting the cupcakes she's making." After offering a wave, Wanda climbed into her own buggy, turned it and drove down the driveway.

"I get tired trying to keep up with her," Joshua said, shaking his head. "She has more energy than a dozen people."

"True." She looked from Wanda's buggy to the one holding her family.

Sammy was giggling and trying to peek into the plastic bowl on his lap. Debbie steadied it and whispered in his ear. That set him to chortling even more. Beside them, Levi was squirming as he always did when he was excited. Timothy sat in the front with his *daed*, trying to wear an expression of world-weary boredom, though she suspected he was as eager to go to the auction as his siblings were.

They were going away for the day, and she'd be alone in the house. Sadie had gone home for the weekend, leaving food for their meals in the refrigerator. Mending waited, as always, but she didn't want to spend the day doing that or trying to work in the garden. Bending over was getting harder every day.

She wanted to spend the day with her family.

Instantly she made up her mind. "Joshua, can you wait a minute while I get my bonnet and shoes?" She smiled. "It may take more than a minute for me to find my feet and get my shoes tied, but not so long that we'll be late for the auction."

"You want to go, too?" Joshua asked.

She understood his surprise. She'd been adamant about not being there. Joshua believed it would make her sad because of memories of Lloyd. In a way, he was right, but her sorrow focused on how her dreams for a life with Lloyd had faded away into a desperate struggle to survive and protect Sammy from his *daed*.

When Joshua had asked her about adopting Sammy and the *boppli*, he hadn't had any idea how difficult it had been not to shout out *ja* immediately. Once the *kinder* had the Stoltzfus name, they could grow up without anyone watching for Lloyd's weaknesses. Best of all, she wouldn't have to disillusion Joshua about his friend. The secret of Lloyd's abuse could truly and completely be buried along with him.

She needed to find the right time to tell him that she wanted him to be the *kinder*'s legal *daed*. A time when they were alone so the *kinder* didn't hear, and a time long enough after he first asked so he wouldn't ask the questions she didn't want to answer.

"Ja," she said. "I've changed my mind. Women do that, you know."

"So I've heard. More than once." He motioned for Timothy to move to the back with his siblings. Joshua walked with her to the house, offering to help her with her shoes, and gave her the tender smile that made her heart do jumping jacks. "I'm glad you're coming with us."

"Me, too." In fact, she couldn't remember the last time she'd been this happy. She held that close to her heart, intending to savor it through the whole day.

The sale was going well. The farm that had been quiet for so long had come alive as if a county fair had set up its midway between the house and the barns. A crowd of nearly a hundred people stood beside the recently painted barn that shone in the bright sunlight. More mingled and chatted among the buggies, wagons and cars parked in the yard and down the farm lane and out on the road. The auctioneer was making the bidders laugh with his antics as he tried to cajole a few more dollars out of them for each item.

Smoke from grills brought by the members of Rebekah's old district was laced with delicious scents of meat, peppers and onions. Rows of baked goods awaited buyers with a sweet tooth. Cans of soda and iced tea were encased in galvanized buckets of quickly melting ice.

Joshua stood to the side and watched the enthusiastic bidding for a plow that looked as if it had hardly been used. The work his brother had done to fix the buildings was going to pay dividends, he was certain, because he'd heard several groups of men discussing the value of the acreage and buildings. Their numbers were higher than his estimates. His work to arrange the machinery to its best advantage was helping each piece sell for more than he'd dared to hope. The *gut* Lord had brought generous hearts to the auction today.

He smiled as his favorite verse filled his head: *This is the day which the Lord hath made; we will rejoice and be glad in it.*

The *gut* Lord had also brought several young Amish men who were eager to set up their own farms. He recognized a few from Paradise Springs and guessed the others were from the surrounding area. Most of them worked at jobs beyond their families' farmsteads, and they longed to return to the life beloved by most plain men: husbanding God's beautiful creation. By day's end, he hoped one of them would be the new owner of Lloyd's farm, because there were a handful of *Englischers* talking about bidding on it, as well, and it was always disappointing when *gut* farmland was subdivided for another neighborhood. But, either way, the farm should sell well.

Lloyd's legacy to his wife and son and unborn *kind*.

Joshua scanned the crowd, which was intent on what the auctioneer was listing as the next lot. Where was Rebekah? He saw Levi and Debbie playing volleyball with others their age. Timothy had worked with other teens to set up a makeshift baseball diamond where abandoned hubcaps, salvaged along the road, served as bases. Home plate was simply an area scratched out in the dirt.

When the house's front door opened, Rebekah emerged with a pitcher of some fruity drink and paper cups. She went with care down the steps, and he held his breath until her feet were securely on the ground. For her to fall now could turn the *boppli* and make the delivery much more difficult and dangerous.

"Now there's a man who's in love with his wife," teased Ezra. His brother nudged him with an elbow and chuckled. "Can't keep his eyes off her."

Joshua didn't want to admit that his younger brother was right. "Don't you have better things to do than lurk around spying on me?"

"Nope." He rested his shoulder against a nearby fence post. "I've been looking for a seeder, but that one went for more than I thought it was worth. *Gut* for Rebekah, not so *gut* for me. That was what I was mainly looking for, so I need to find something to do while *Mamm* enjoys time with our neighbors."

"And Leah Beiler is here." He eyed his brother with a grin. "Are you two going to be the first to publish your marriage this fall?"

"You know better than to ask that." He chuckled.

"And that's a clumsy way of trying to divert me from noticing how you're mooning over your pretty Rebekah."

Joshua changed the subject to the work Daniel had done on the farm. That seemed to distract his brother, or perhaps Ezra was so enthralled with anything to do with agriculture that he was eager to talk about it anytime. Giving his brother half of his attention, Joshua continued to watch Rebekah.

Like his *mamm*, she was unwilling to sit while others worked. She must not overdo when she had to think of her own health and the *boppli*'s.

Ezra's laugh intruded on his thoughts. Slapping him on the arm, his brother said, "Go ahead and moon, big brother. I'll talk to you later *if* you can think of anything other than your wife." He walked away still laughing.

Joshua considered retorting, not wanting to let his brother get the last word, but what could he say? Ezra was right.

He strode across the field in the opposite direction, away from the crowd and the noise. He needed some quiet to think. He paused by the farm pond where the only noise was the chirping birds and the breeze in the reeds along the water.

Why was he trying to deny the truth? Rebekah was always in his thoughts. When he considered staying another hour at the shop to finish work, he imagined her waiting at home with his meal ready and worrying that he hadn't arrived home at his usual time. He remembered how delicate her touch had been and how she'd fretted about causing him more pain when she cleaned his cuts in the wake of the exploding root beer. Even when his *kinder* came to mind, Rebekah was there, smiling, encouraging them, scolding when necessary, loving them with an open and joyous heart.

Exactly as he longed for her to love him.

Exactly as I love her.

That thought sent a deluge through him, washing away the last remnants of his resolve never to fall in love and put his heart in danger again. Whether he turned his back on her love or tried to win it, he couldn't guarantee that he was avoiding heartbreak. But he was if he ignored the truth.

He'd fallen in love with his sweet wife, the woman he'd promised to cherish. Overwhelmed by the gift of love that God had brought twice into his life, he dropped to his knees and bowed his head as he thanked his Heavenly Father.

To that prayer he added, "Give us your blessing, too, Tildie. I know now that if I'd gone first, I would have wanted you to find someone to bring you and the *kinder* love and happiness. Please want the same for me."

A sense of peace settled upon him as he stopped fighting himself. He almost chuckled at the thought. An Amish man was supposed to play no part in any sort of war, but he'd been fighting one within himself…a futile one, because the resolution was what he'd known all along. God came into their lives and hearts through love.

He needed to remember that.

The raised voice echoed oddly through the empty house. Joshua frowned. What was going on? His *mamm* had told him that Rebekah had gone inside to get out of the hot sun. He'd expected to hear the muffled sound of the auctioneer's voice, but he heard shouts.

He strode into the living room. The room silenced, and he looked from Rebekah who was backed into a corner, one arm protectively around Sammy and the other draping her stomach, to two men he recognized as Lloyd's brothers, Aden Ray and Milo. The latter stood too close to her, clearly trying to intimidate her. Both men stepped back and let Rebekah and Sammy rush to his side.

He urged her to take the *kind* and leave, but wasn't surprised when she shook her head. She didn't want to abandon him to deal with the two Burkholders. He took her hand and drew her closer, feeling her fingers tremble against his palm. Beside her, Sammy clung to her skirt.

"What is this?" Joshua asked in the calmest voice he could.

"Family business." Aden Ray glowered. "As Lloyd's brothers, we've got a right to a share of the profits from this farm."

"Rebekah has been generous with you already. She gave your family permission to take whatever you wanted out of the house. You did. However, the equipment and farm belong to Lloyd's son."

"Which means it goes into your pockets. How convenient for you! Marry the widow and collect the fruits of our brother's labors."

"I would have married her myself if I wasn't already married." Milo, Lloyd's older brother, sneered. "She's not bad to look at when she's not blown up like a balloon."

He stared at the man's crude, greedy smile, not dignifying the stupid comment with an answer. Tugging on Rebekah's hand and calling to Sammy, he turned on his heel to walk away.

They walked out the door. As they reached the bottom step on the front porch, his arm was seized, shocking him. He hadn't expected another Amish man to lay a hand on him in anger.

"Rebekah," he said as he drew his arm away from Milo Burkholder, "*Mamm* would like your opinion about which cakes to auction off first." That wasn't true, but he didn't want her to suffer any more of her brothers-in-law's comments. "Why don't you and Sammy find her now so they can be sold while the crowd is still large?"

She backed away, frustration and fear in her eyes that were as wide and dismayed as her son's. But anger, too, because her face had reddened, making her freckles vanish. He was astonished how much he missed them. As strong as she was in facing every challenge, the freckles softened her expressions while reminding him how gentle she was at heart. He gave her a wink, and her lips quivered before she turned and crossed the yard toward the refreshment area.

"*Gut,*" Milo growled. "Now with her gone we can talk man-to-man."

"We don't have anything to talk about. *Englisch* law and our own traditions are clear on this. The widow and her *kinder* inherit her husband's estate. As I said, she has been very generous and offered your family everything in the house."

"It's not enough!"

"I'm sorry you feel that way, but I believe it is."

Aden Ray's hands curled into fists. As his voice rose in anger, his fists did, too. "We don't care what *you* believe! We want our share!"

Joshua couldn't believe that Lloyd's brother would actually try to strike him until the younger man swung at him. Fortunately the blow went wide. Moving out of range, he said, "We can ask our bishops to decide."

"I can make that decision on my own, and we want our share." He jabbed out with his other fist.

Again Joshua jumped away and bumped into someone. A glance over his shoulder shocked him. Timothy and several of his own brothers stood behind him. Nobody spoke, but Aden Ray lowered his fists.

This time when Joshua walked away along with his son and brothers, he wasn't stopped. He heard the Burkholders stamp in the opposite direction. Thanking his brothers, who nodded in response before they returned to the auction, he kept walking with Timothy until he had strode past most of the bidders who were so focused on the sale that, praise God, they hadn't noticed his unexpected encounter with Lloyd's brothers.

"Are you okay, *Daed*?" asked Timothy as soon as they stopped.

"I will be. This policy of always turning the other cheek is easier some days than others."

His son chuckled. "I know."

"Go and enjoy your game." As his son started to leave, Joshua called his name. He walked to Timothy and gave him a quick hug. He knew his son wouldn't allow more than that when his friends were watching. "*Danki*, son."

"Anytime, *Daed*."

"I hope not."

They laughed, and Joshua went to find Rebekah. He didn't intend to let the Burkholders—or anyone else—bully her again.

It was almost, Rebekah thought, like the night of their wedding day. The *kinder* were slumbering in the back of the buggy, including, this time, Timothy, who'd had as much fun as the younger ones at the auction. Their clothes were dotted with mustard and spots of ice cream, and she was astonished none of them had sickened from the amount of food they'd eaten.

Beside her, Joshua watched the road beyond Benny's nose. "I was glad to see the farm stay with an Amish farmer."

She smiled, recalling how one of the young women had been as giddy as a toddler with a new toy when one of the Tice boys was the highest bidder. "I hope the house and farm have many happy times for its new family."

"God willing, it will." He glanced at her as he said, "I didn't expect you'd want to stay for the sale of the farm equipment."

"Why?"

"Tildie and my sisters only watched when the lots were household items. I assumed women weren't interested in manure spreaders and plows." He grinned, his teeth shining in the streetlight they drove under. "You don't have to remind me that not all women are alike. Esther often tells me that."

"No, all women aren't alike, just as all men aren't." She relaxed against the seat and discovered his arm stretched along it. When his fingers curved down around her shoulder, she let him draw her closer.

All men were *not* alike, and she was more grateful for that truth than words could say.

His thoughts must have been the same because he said, "I didn't realize the Burkholders had such tempers."

"They do, and it doesn't take much for them to lose it." She didn't add more.

"I never saw Lloyd lose his temper."

"I know." This was the perfect opening to explain

about what happened when Lloyd did fly into a rage, but she held her tongue.

Fortunately, his family had left. They discovered they couldn't gain sympathy from the crowd after word spread about how they'd stripped the house of almost everything, which was why there were no household goods for sale. She was glad to see them go.

Forgive me, Father, for not being able to forgive them for their avarice. I try to remind myself that they are a gut *lesson about the importance of being generous to others.* She smiled to herself, hoping God would understand her prayer was facetious. She wished the Burkholders could find the peace and happiness within themselves.

It was too nice a night to discuss Lloyd and his troublesome brothers. "Timothy seems very interested in that red-haired Yutzy girl. He was hanging on her every word when he talked to her after the ball game."

"Like *daed*, like son." He chuckled. "We find redheads catch our eyes."

She chuckled, then put her fingers to her lips, not wanting the sound to rouse the *kinder*. She glanced back to see Sammy curled up between Levi and Timothy, who had his arm protectively around the little boy.

"Thank you for a *wunderbaar* day," she whispered. "I can't remember when I've had so much fun."

"How about the time we went for a canoe ride on the pond and ended up tipping the canoe over?"

She held her breath as she did each time he mentioned a memory that contained Tildie and Lloyd. She had to choose her words with care. This time it wasn't so difficult because she had fond memories of that day, too. "Because you were being silly." She smiled. "It was a *gut* thing that we could get the mud out of our best dresses."

"*Ja.* I heard about that for a long time. Lloyd must have, too."

"That was a long time ago," she replied, not wanting to admit that she never would have dared to scold Lloyd. The next time he was drunk, he would have made her regret her words. "Joshua, I've been thinking about your adopting Sammy and the new *boppli* after it's born."

"And?" Anticipation filled his voice. "What's your answer?" He halted her from answering by saying, "Before you tell me, let me say what I should have the night I asked you. Even before your son called me *Daedi* for the first time, he'd found his way into my heart. I love to hear his laughter and watch him try to keep up with the older boys. I've dried his tears when he has fallen and scraped his knee, and I've taught him the best way I know to catch a frog down at the pond. Rebekah, even though he wasn't born as my son, in my heart it feels like he's always been my son."

She stretched to put a finger to his lips as she whispered, "I know. Don't you think I've seen how you two have grown together like two branches grafted onto the same tree?"

"So what's your answer?"

"*Ja,* I would like you to adopt my *kinder.*"

He turned to look at her, his face visible in the light from the lantern on her side of the buggy. But its faint beam wasn't necessary. His smile was so broad and so bright that it seemed to glow with his happiness.

"That is *wunderbaar,*" he said.

"How do we do this? I'm sure there's a lot of paperwork, but I don't know where to start."

"We'll start by asking Beth Ann."

"Why?"

His eyes twinkled like a pair of the stars glistening overhead. "Didn't you know? She has an adopted daughter."

"I didn't realize that." She thought back to the drawings that hung in Beth Ann's examination room. They obviously had been done by a *kind* because the bright colors had been created with crayons. "I'll ask her at my next appointment."

"When's that?"

"On Tuesday. If you have any questions, I'll be glad to ask her."

"I'll ask her myself. At this point, I don't think you should be driving into the village on your own."

She heard an undercurrent of anger lingering beneath his words. It halted her automatic response that she could handle matters on her own. When she thanked him, his arm drew her closer. It would be so easy to imagine them riding in a courting buggy he'd built himself, except Levi was softly snoring in the back. She shut out that sound and leaned her head against Joshua's strong shoulder.

His breath sifted through her bonnet and *kapp* as he said, "We'll keep Sammy's memories of Lloyd alive by telling him about his *daed*."

"We don't need to worry about that now." *Or ever*, she longed to add, but if she did, then she'd have to reveal how little Joshua comprehended of the man he'd called his friend.

"*Danki*, Rebekah, for agreeing. I should have said that before."

"There is no reason to thank me. It is what's for the

best for the *kinder*." She didn't add that it was the best choice for her, as well.

God, am I being selfish? I don't want Sammy to suffer any longer for the sins of his daed. *Sammy deserves to be happy and secure. And so do I.*

That last thought startled her. For so long she had listened to Lloyd telling her how worthless she was. Only her determination to remain strong for her son and her faith that God would never stop loving her as Lloyd had, had kept her from believing his cruel words.

Not tonight. She wasn't going to let the memory of Lloyd intrude tonight when she sat beside Joshua while they followed the moonlight along the otherwise deserted road. The steady clip-clop from the horse provided a rhythmic undertone to the chirps of the peepers. Lightning bugs twinkled like earthbound stars, creating flashes of light in the darkness.

It seemed too soon when they entered their driveway and came to a stop by the dark house. Beyond the trees lights glowed in the Grangers' house, but in the buggy they were enveloped in soft shadows.

"Rebekah?"

At Joshua's whisper, she looked at him. His lips brushed hers, tentative and giving her a chance to pull back. She didn't want to. His lips were warm and tasted of the fudge some of the women had been selling at the auction. Or were his lips always so sweet? She pushed that silly thought from her mind as she put her arms around his shoulders and kissed him back.

He slanted her closer to him, holding her tenderly. He kissed her cheeks, her eyelids, her nose before finding her lips again. Her fingers sifted up through his hair, discovering it was just as soft as she'd imagined. But she'd never imagined how *wunderbaar* his kisses would be while they lit the dark corners of her heart, banishing the fear and the contempt. Joy danced through her and she melted against him.

At the sound of the *kinder* stirring in the back, he lifted his mouth from hers. She curved her fingers along his face, savoring the variety of textures. She had so many things to say, but not when the youngsters were listening.

She couldn't wait until she had a chance to tell Joshua of the state of her heart and how she had come to trust him as she hadn't thought she ever could trust any man again.

Chapter 13

"Do you want us to carry those bags?" asked Debbie when the buggy stopped under the tree at the edge of the yard early the following Friday.

"I'd appreciate that." Rebekah struggled to smile as the little girl handed a bag of groceries to her brother before picking up the other one.

Last night Rebekah had been awakened by a low, steady ache near the base of her spine. Whether she shifted to her side or her back, she hadn't been able to find a comfortable position. Sleeping had been impossible, so around midnight she'd gotten up and worked on mending more of the *kinder*'s clothing. It was something she could do quietly and without much light, because her fingers had guided her stitches around a hem or a patch.

Now she was so exhausted it felt as if she were wading through knee-deep mud with each step. The idea of getting out of the buggy seemed too much. All she wanted to do was crawl into bed and nap away the rest of the day and maybe tomorrow and the day after.

Nonsense! The best way to stay awake was to keep busy. Otherwise she might not be able to sleep again tonight.

And maybe tonight there would be a chance for her and Joshua to talk. Every other evening since the auction, either he or she had been busy. Sammy had started resisting going to bed without her being there until he went to sleep. He was frightened after what he'd witnessed with Lloyd's brothers. She thanked God that her son wouldn't have to have much to do with that family from this point forward.

As she got out of the buggy, she motioned for Levi to follow his sister and Sammy into the house. "Go ahead. I'll take care of Benny and the buggy." She glanced at the clouds building up along the western horizon. "Will you ask Sadie to bring in the laundry? And please ask Debbie to cut up some of the fruit we bought and make us a salad with the berries you picked yesterday."

He nodded. She was grateful for Sadie's help because she was finding it more difficult with each passing week to hang out the wash and take it down. Last time she'd done laundry, three pieces of clothing had fallen on the grass, and she'd had to ask Sammy to collect them. It was impossible to find the basket by her feet.

Her feet? She almost laughed. She hadn't seen them in so long she doubted she'd recognize her own toes any longer.

She unhooked the horse and led Dolly toward the barn. She wasn't sure how bad the storm was going to be, and she knew Dolly didn't like getting wet. She'd put her in a stall until the rain passed. After that Levi could let the mare out into the pasture. The horse had taken a liking to the boy and vice versa.

The air in the barn was heavy. She made sure the horse had plenty of water, and she thought about having a lovely cold glass of lemonade.

She shut the stall door and turned to leave. Sunlight glinted off something on the floor near a discarded horse blanket. She went to check, not wanting one of the horses to pick up a nail in a hoof.

She started to bend to check the shiny object, then laughed. Hadn't she been thinking that bending was impossible? Squatting was almost as difficult without something to assist her to her feet. She considered calling one of the *kinder* to help her, or she could wait until Joshua came home.

Her eyes were caught by the extra wheel leaning against the stall's wall. She could use it to help her. Checking that it would not tumble over when she grasped it, she chuckled.

"Lord, you keep me humble by reminding me that I can't do everything." She chuckled again and put her hand on the wheel. She hunkered and reached for the glistening piece of metal.

Her laughter disappeared as she realized it wasn't a piece of metal, but a metal can. Connected to five other metal cans. A six-pack of beer. A brand that must be popular among *Englischers* because she'd seen large trucks with the beer's name passing through Paradise Springs.

Her stomach heaved, and she feared she was going to throw up. Lloyd had hidden his stash of beer in the barn. Icy shudders thudded along her, battering away the happiness and contentment she had felt seconds ago.

Had Joshua hidden it here so she wouldn't suspect that he drank as Lloyd had? Her stomach twisted again. She'd thought she'd smelled liquor on Joshua's clothing while doing laundry. Since that day she'd convinced herself that she hadn't really smelled it, that it'd been her imagination or one of the lacquers Joshua used at the buggy shop.

Was this all the beer or was there more?

Rebekah shoved the six-pack under the blanket and then pushed herself to her feet. At the best speed she could manage, she went to the house, not even pausing to answer when Sadie called out a greeting. The *kinder* looked up when she came in. She rushed past where Debbie was slicing fruit and the boys were watching with eager anticipation.

"Are you looking for something?" asked Levi.

"Ja," she replied.

"Can we help?" the ever-helpful Debbie asked.

"Watch Sammy. Make sure he eats with a spoon, not his fingers. I'll be right back." She threw open the cellar door. "I need to get…" Her brain refused to work, stuck on the image of that beer in the barn. Shaking herself, she said, "I need to get a couple of bottles of your *gross-mammi's* pickles for supper."

"Let me carry them up for you." Levi stuck out his thin chest. *"Daedi* asked us to help you when Sadie is busy doing something else."

Tears flooded her eyes. She longed to put her arms around these darling *kinder* and hug them so tightly while she kept the evils of the world away from them. To do so would create more questions. Questions she couldn't answer until she had more facts. Accusing their *daed* of being as weak as Lloyd would hurt them as deeply as it had her.

"Danki, but I think I can manage. I'll call if I need help." She hoped her smile didn't look as grotesque as it felt. *"Ja?"*

"*Ja,*" he replied, but she didn't miss the anxious glance he shared with his sister.

Thankful that Sammy was too young to take notice of anything but his sandwich, Rebekah hurried down the stairs before one of the *kinder* could ask another question. She picked up the flashlight from the shelf by the steps and went to the shelves where fresh jars of fruit had been stored in neat precision along with the ones she's brought from Lloyd's farm. A gasp sent a pain through her. The only sanctuary she had from another alcoholic husband was that farm and now it was gone.

Why, God, did You let me discover this *after the farm was sold?* The pain burst out of her in a single, painful blast.

She couldn't blame God for a man's weaknesses. She did, however, blame herself for not seeing any signs that Joshua hid beer as Lloyd had. Even looking back over the past months, she couldn't recall a single clue that would have tipped her off. Other than that Joshua had been Lloyd's best friend, and they'd spent time together fishing and hunting. Had they been drinking together, too?

Spraying light over the shelves, she looked but didn't see anything that wasn't supposed to be there other than a few spiders. She lowered the flashlight, so the beam narrowed to a small circle on the concrete floor. There were other places where beer or a bottle of liquor could be hidden, but she couldn't squeeze past the shelves to reach them. At that thought, she aimed light through the shelves. She saw tools and what looked like cast-off furniture against the stone foundation, but everything was covered with a thick layer of dust. If it had been disturbed recently, she saw no sign.

Looking up at the ceiling, she wondered if there was

a place in the attic where cans or bottles could be hidden. Lloyd had put his beer there once. A cold snap had frozen the beer and shattered the bottles, making a mess that he'd refused to clean up. She recalled the ignominy of washing the floorboards on her hands and knees while pregnant with Sammy. Rather than being grateful, Lloyd had walked out and hadn't come back for almost a week, lamenting how he'd run out of money.

Tears rolled down her cheeks. She wrapped her arms around herself and her unborn *kind.*

God, I thought Joshua was a gut *man. I dared to let him into my heart, believing that You wanted me to share his life. What do I do now?*

There was one more place to check. Lloyd often put his beer in the well house because the water stored in the tank kept it cold.

Her lower back ached more with each step she took up the stairs, but Rebekah didn't slow when she reached the kitchen. Again she was aware of the anxiety on the *kinder'*s faces. She wished she could say something to comfort them, but she wouldn't lie to them.

Sadie was bringing in a basket of laundry and nearly collided with Rebekah. Waving aside the young woman's apology, Rebekah hurried around the side of the house to where the small well house contained the diesel pump and a holding tank for water. The walls were built with slats so fumes wouldn't build up inside.

After going in, she waited for her eyes to adjust. As soon as they did, she saw sunlight glinting off more metal. She leaned against the slatted walls and wrapped her arms around her belly as if she could protect her unborn *kind* from what was right in front of her eyes.

Five six-packs of beer.

She'd never seen such a collection. Lloyd seldom had had more than two or three six-packs on the farm at any one time. Or at least as far as she knew. Why would Joshua want enough beer for a dozen people?

Her eyes widened. What if the beer didn't belong to Joshua? Maybe she was jumping to conclusions about her husband. What if the cans belonged to Timothy? The teenager was so moody, leaping from cheerfulness to sullen scowls in a single breath. Lloyd had been like that, too, especially contentious when his head ached as he suffered yet another hangover.

She looked down at the six-packs. Timothy went out by himself in the family buggy on Saturday nights. How easy it would be for him to retrieve the beer and hide it beneath the backseat so even if his *daed* or another adult stopped to talk to him the beer would go unnoticed. She had no idea how many members were in his running-around gang, but she knew the gatherings often included a mix of Amish and *Englisch* teens.

So whose beer was it?

Rebekah waited impatiently for Joshua and Timothy to get home. As soon as they did, she went out into the shimmering heat to meet them. Her husband waved as he led Benny into the barn because the slow-moving storm seemed ready to pounce on them.

"Timothy," she said as the teenager started across the yard in the direction of the Grangers' house, "I need to talk with you."

"It'll have to wait. I'm already late."

"Late for what?"

He stopped and frowned. It was the expression he usually reserved for his *daed*, but she wouldn't let it halt her from saying what she must.

"Timothy, it'll take only a second."

"It'll have to wait." His voice got louder on each word until she was sure their neighbors could hear. "I'm going out with friends. I told *Daed* last night. He said it was okay for me to go out on a Friday night as long as I get my chores done tomorrow. Why are you grilling me like I'm some sort of criminal?"

Rebekah hardly considered a single question an interrogation, but her voice had been forceful. All she could think of were those cans of beer. She needed to know the truth. She'd heard about boys racing their buggies when they were intoxicated and how they ended up paralyzed or worse.

"Timothy—"

"Leave me alone!" He stamped away.

Joshua came out of the barn and looked in the direction of his son's angry voice. What was distressing Timothy *now*? When he saw his son striding away with Rebekah trying to keep up with him, he was astonished. Timothy had never raised his voice to her before. Not like this.

They stopped and his son jabbed a finger in Rebekah's direction. His gut twisted when he noticed how she didn't flinch away as she did too often when he reached toward her.

Timothy stepped back when Joshua approached. Fury twisted his son's face, and Rebekah's was long with despair.

Joshua didn't get a chance to ask what was wrong because Timothy snapped, "She's your wife. Tell her to stop trying to run my life. She's not my *mamm*, and even if she was I'm sixteen and I don't need her poking her nose into my business." He stormed past Joshua and into the trees that divided the two houses.

Joshua started to call after him but halted when Rebekah said, "Let him go."

"Why? He owes you an apology for speaking like that."

"No, I owe him one."

Her words kept him from giving chase after his son. "Why?"

"I wanted to ask him something, and I pushed too hard. He's right. I'm not his *mamm*."

"But you are my wife. He should respect that."

"He's sixteen, Joshua."

"A *gut* reason for him to know he needs to respect his elders."

Her smile was sad, and she stared at the ground. "And there's the crux of the problem. He doesn't think of me as his elder. Oh, sometimes I'm sure he thinks I'm too old to recall what it's like to be sixteen. At other times, he thinks I'm too young to be his *mamm*. Either way, he doesn't believe I have the right to tell him what to do."

"I'll talk to him." He started to put his arm around her, but she flinched. As she had when she'd first come to live at his house. He watched in disbelief as she widened the distance between them. She hadn't acted like this since the auction. What had changed?

"I don't think it matters," she said with a sigh. "Timothy isn't going to tell me the time of day at this point. Let me see if I can mend fences with him before you get involved. I don't want him to think we're siding together against him."

He nodded reluctantly. His son needed to show Rebekah respect, but trying to talk sense to Timothy when they both were upset might make matters worse in the long run. But didn't Rebekah owe him the truth, too, about why she was again acting as skittish as a doe?

He couldn't ask. Not when her color was a strained gray beneath her summer tan. He urged her to come inside and allow him to get her something cool to drink.

Maybe later she would tell him why she suddenly found his touch abhorrent.

Please, God!

A crash reverberated through the house, and Joshua sat up in bed. Rain splattered on the window, but that hadn't been thunder. It had been louder and much closer.

He leaped out of his bed and banged his head on the slanted ceiling. He rubbed the aching spot but didn't slow as he raised the shade on the window.

At the end of the driveway a car was stopped. Its lights were at an odd angle, one aiming up into the trees and the other on the grass. It couldn't be on the road any longer.

He grabbed his boots and shoved his bare feet into them. He threw open his door. When Debbie peeked sleepily out of her room, he ordered her in a whisper to go back to bed and stay there. He didn't want her to wake her brothers who were heavier sleepers. Even more important, he didn't want her to follow him out to the car in case someone was badly hurt.

His boots clumped on the stairs and he realized he should have laced up their tops to hold them on more tightly. Too late now to worry about waking up Rebekah and Sammy.

"Joshua?" he heard as he reached the bottom step.

Rebekah stood in the bedroom doorway. She wore a sweater over her nightgown. It could not reach across her distended belly, but she tugged at it.

He reached for the door. "There's a car at the end of the drive. Its lights are shining all wrong."

"A crash?"

"That's what I'm going to find out."

By the time he reached the front door, the rain was coming down hard. He grabbed an umbrella from the crock by the door. After throwing the screen door aside, he went out on the porch. He opened the umbrella and handed it to Rebekah, who had, as he'd expected, followed him from the house.

"Stay here," he ordered over a rumble of thunder.

"I'll wake Timothy."

"He may not be home yet."

Even in the darkness, he saw her face grow ashen. Her voice shook as she said, "Then I'll wake Levi. If someone is hurt, he can run to the Beilers' barn and use their phone to call an ambulance." She glanced toward their *Englisch* neighbors' house. Light glowed in the windows. "The Grangers are up. He can go there. It's closer."

He nodded, relieved that she hadn't argued about coming with him. He turned up the collar on his coat before running down the steps. The grass was slick. Flashes of lightning illuminated the sky and blinded him as darkness dropped around him and thunder boomed above him. He almost lost his footing twice on the grass, so he went toward the driveway. The gravel would be easier to run on. He saw someone moving by the bright red car. He increased his speed, but skidded to a stop when he heard a familiar voice shout for him to stop.

Right in front of him, the mailbox was sheared off. He almost had run into the sharp spikes of wood.

And his older son was leaning on the hood of the battered car.

Chapter 14

Someone must have called the police, or maybe a patrol had been driving by, because they were there before Levi could go next door and call 911. One police car soon became two and an ambulance, even though Timothy insisted he wasn't badly hurt.

Rebekah had joined Joshua when the first police car arrived. A short, stocky man who introduced himself as Steven McMurray, the chief of the Paradise Springs Police Department, insisted that Timothy be checked by the EMTs. The man and woman with the ambulance kept the younger *kinder* entertained while they examined Timothy.

Joshua wished the *kinder* had remained in the house, but the rain had eased so he allowed them to watch as Timothy's blood pressure was taken and a cut on his forehead cleaned and bandaged. He was glad when they took the extra gauze and tongue depressors back to the porch to play with them.

Chief McMurray finished talking with the other officers. Joshua heard them say it was *gut* that his son had been wearing a seat belt. Even though the airbag had gone off, Timothy could have been hurt far worse than a lacerated forehead and what would probably become a pair of black eyes.

The chief worked with easy efficiency as the storm ended, leaving hot and humid air in its wake. Joshua recalled how years ago Steven had been a troublemaker along with Johnny Beiler. Now Johnny had died, and Steven was in charge of the Paradise Springs police. The Lord truly did work in mysterious ways.

Another officer handed the chief a slip of paper and spoke quietly to him. Even though he strained his ears, Joshua couldn't hear what the officer was saying.

"Maybe you should go back to the house, Rebekah," he murmured. "You are shivering."

She shook her head. "No, I'm staying."

He recognized her tone and the futility of arguing with it.

Chief McMurray walked over to them. His expression in the flashing lights from the vehicles was grim. "I wanted you to know that we ran the plates, and the car is registered to Brad Granger." He glanced along the road to their neighbor's house, then frowned at Timothy who still sat on the back bumper of the ambulance. "How did you come to have it, son?"

Timothy held an ice pack to his forehead and shrugged. "It's my friend's car, and she wouldn't care if I used it."

"Her father will care when he realizes the front end is smashed up. Taking someone else's car for a joyride with your friends is a felony."

Beside him, Rebekah gasped, knowing as Joshua did that a felony could mean time in jail.

"Who was with you?" asked Chief McMurray.

"I told you before. I was driving by myself."

The chief shook his head and frowned. "I know you teenagers think adults are stupid, but both airbags went off. The passenger side one doesn't go off unless someone is sitting there."

"Maybe it was broken."

"There's no maybe about it being a really bad idea to lie to the police. Someone most likely saw you and this car tonight. If you had someone with you, they probably saw that person, too."

Timothy blanched even paler.

"It's better for you to be honest now than later." Chief McMurray gave Timothy a chance to answer. When he didn't, the police chief looked at Joshua and Rebekah. "You also need to know that we found half a dozen empty beer cans in the car. We'd like to run a Breathalyzer on your son with your permission."

Joshua nodded, unsure if he could speak. Why hadn't Timothy heeded his warnings about the dangers of drinking and driving a buggy? His son was smart, and he should have realized that those hazards were compounded if he was behind the wheel of a car.

Beside him, Rebekah gave a sob. He started to explain the test wouldn't hurt in any way. She turned away. That surprised him. She wasn't usually squeamish.

The police administered the test, and Timothy seemed to shrink before his eyes. The cocky teenager was becoming a frightened *kind*. Every inch of Joshua wanted to comfort him, but his son had demanded the rights of an adult and now he would have to face the consequences of making stupid choices. Even knowing that, Joshua had to swallow his cheer when the test came back negative.

But if his son hadn't drank the beers, who had?

As a tow truck backed up to take the damaged car away, Chief McMurray came to where Joshua and Rebekah stood beside his son. He handed Timothy a piece of paper.

"This is a ticket for driving without a license," the police chief said. "Don't assume it's the only ticket you're going to get. Joshua, as your son is a minor, I'd like to leave him in your custody while we investigate what happened here." He ran his hand backward through his thinning hair, making it stand on end, before he put his hat on again. "I don't like to see any kid sitting in a jail cell, but I won't hesitate to put him there if I find out he took the car without permission. Do you understand?"

"*Ja*, I understand." He looked at his son, but Timothy wouldn't meet his eyes. "What happens now?"

"As he has been put in your custody, you or your wife must be with him every minute. Don't let him out of your sight. If he does something foolish like trying to sneak out, it won't look good for him when he goes before a judge. Judges, especially juvenile court judges, don't take kindly to such things. He's already in a ton of trouble. Making it worse would be foolish."

"We'll do as you ask. Is there anything else we should do?"

The chief smiled swiftly. "Pray. I know you folks are good at that."

Joshua nodded, but didn't say that he'd been praying since he'd looked out the window and seen the car lights shining at odd angles.

"Danki," Rebekah said softly. "Thank you, Chief McMurray."

"You're welcome." The police chief's gaze shifted to Timothy. "I hope you're being honest when you say you had permission to drive the car." He looked back at Joshua. "We're going to be talking to the Grangers next. If they corroborate his story, I'd still like to send one of my officers over to speak with Timothy about the importance of taking driving lessons and getting his license if he intends to drive again."

"And if the Grangers disagree with what Timothy says?" Rebekah clearly was too worried to wait for Joshua to ask the same question.

"You'll have to bring him to the police station where he'll be booked for stealing a car." The chief looked from her to Joshua. "I hope we don't have to do that, but if he's lying…"

"We understand, Chief McMurray." He motioned for Rebekah to return to the house.

He thanked the policemen and the tow truck driver before he led Timothy toward the house. His son was silent. Why wasn't he apologizing and asking to be forgiven? On every step, Joshua's frustration grew.

As soon as they were inside, he ordered the younger *kinder* to their rooms. They stared at him as if they feared he'd lost his mind, because he seldom raised his voice to them.

For some reason that infuriated him more. As Levi and Debbie hurried up the stairs and Sammy grasped a handful of his *mamm's* nightgown, Joshua spun to face his oldest and demanded, "Have you lost your mind?"

"Daed—"

"No!" he snapped. "I'll talk and you'll listen. After

all, you didn't want to talk to the police. You took your friend's car and smashed it into our mailbox. You were driving a car filled with empty beer cans. Where did those come from?" He didn't give his son a chance to answer. "You act as if everyone else is to blame except you. You spin tales nobody would swallow. On one hand you expect to be treated like an adult, but then you make decisions Sammy knows better than to make."

"You don't understand, *Daed*!"

"Then help me understand. Why don't you start with why you had Alexis's car? If you don't want to start there, start with how the beer cans got into the car and who drank the beer. Don't think that I didn't understand what the police were saying. They didn't say you hadn't been drinking. Only that you hadn't drunk enough to be legally intoxicated." When he saw the tears in his son's eyes and saw bruises already forming around the bandage on his forehead, he wanted to relent. He couldn't.

He reached out to grasp his son's shoulder, hoping a physical connection would help Timothy see that Joshua truly wanted to help him. His hand never reached Timothy.

"No!" Rebekah stepped between them, batting his hand away. "Calm down, Joshua, before you do something you'll regret."

"I am not the one who needs to worry about that." He scowled at his oldest and at Rebekah. Didn't she realize what an appalling situation his son was in? Timothy could be arrested.

He took her by the arm and drew her aside. She stared at him, hurt and betrayal in her eyes. When he reached toward her again, she skittered away, wrapping her arms around herself as she had when the Burkholder brothers threatened her. Did she think he was doing *that*? He wasn't angry as much as he was frustrated. With her, with his son, with himself for not being able to handle the rapidly deteriorating situation.

"Rebekah," he said, trying to keep his voice even. "The boy needs to realize the consequences of what he's done. Drinking and driving—"

"I didn't drink and drive!" Timothy shouted.

"Listen to him," she urged.

Looking from one to the other, he said, "Be sensible, Rebekah. Even if he wasn't drinking, he was with kids his own age who were. Kids who think they can make the rules because they know more than anyone else. I know how it goes. They start drinking together occasionally, then more often. A couple of times a week become every day. By that time, they need more and more to get the buzz they're looking for. Who knows where it'll lead?"

"I know." Her voice, though barely more than a whisper, cut through the room like the snap of a whip. More loudly, she ordered, "Don't lecture me about the dangers of alcohol, Joshua Stoltzfus! I know them too well." She held up her right hand and tapped her smallest finger. "I know how it feels when my bones are broken in a drunken rage. I know too well how a fist can shake my teeth loose and how to look through one eye when the other has swollen shut. I know what it's like to pray every night that tonight is the night my husband doesn't turn to alcohol, that tonight isn't the night his fists will harm our unborn *kind*. I know what it's like to keep all of it a secret so the shame that is my life won't ruin my son's."

"Lloyd?" he gasped. "Lloyd struck you?"

"Ja." Tears edged along her lashes, then rained down

her cheeks as she said, "He loved drinking more than he loved me. I learned that when I found out he was selling our wedding gifts to pay for his beer."

"And selling your cradle for it." Joshua wished he could take back those words as soon as he said them because he saw devastating pain flash across her face.

Her voice broke as she whispered, "My cradle? He sold the cradle he promised me for our son in order to buy himself beer?" She pressed her hands over her mouth, but a sob slipped past her fingers. Closing her eyes, she wept.

No one spoke. Even Sammy was silent as he stared at her. How much of what she'd recounted had the little boy witnessed? How much did he remember? No wonder Sammy had shied away from him at first. If the one man he should have been able to trust—his own *daedi*— had treated his *mamm* so viciously, then how could the *kind* trust any man?

How could Rebekah trust any man, either?

He watched Timothy cross the room and embrace Rebekah. She hid her face against his shoulder as sobs swept through her. Over her head, his son's eyes shot daggers at him.

None of them could pierce Joshua's heart as deeply as his own self-recriminations. How could he have failed to see the truth? He'd seen her bruises, but accepted Lloyd's excuses that she was clumsy. She wasn't clumsy. Even pregnant, she was as graceful as the swans on the pond near the shop.

He thought of the many times she'd avoided his hand when it came close to her, though he never would have raised it toward her in anger. She'd begun to trust him enough not to flinch…until today. What had changed today? He needed to ask, but how could he when he had failed her completely?

Where did he start to ask for her forgiveness?

Why didn't Joshua say something? He stood there, staring at her as Rebekah thanked Timothy for the hug. The teenager murmured that he was sorry.

"For what?" she asked. "You didn't even know Lloyd."

"I'm sorry for everything." He shuffled his foot against the rag rug, then looked at his *daed*. "I really am."

Joshua nodded and put his hand on Timothy's shoulder and gave it a squeeze, but his gaze met hers. "All I can say, Rebekah, is that I am sorry, too. I had no idea what was going on."

"I know. Nobody did."

"Why didn't you go to your bishop for help?"

She hung her head and sighed. "I tried. Once. But I didn't tell him the whole story because I knew Lloyd would be furious if he discovered what I'd done. The bishop told me to try to be a better wife. I tried, but I kept making mistakes. Lloyd would yell at me at first and then…" She glanced at Sammy. She'd already said too much in his hearing.

"You did nothing wrong. None of this was your fault."

Tears streamed down her cheeks, and she didn't bother to wipe them away. "I believed that. At the beginning. Then I began to wonder if I'd failed him in some way that caused Lloyd to drink." Her shoulders shook so hard, she wobbled.

He rushed to her side. "Rebekah, you need to sit down."

"Help me?"

"Gladly." He put his arm around her, and she leaned

against him as he guided her to a chair. She wished she could always depend on his steady strength.

As Timothy took Sammy's hand, Joshua knelt beside her and put his fingers lightly over hers, which were protectively pressed to her belly. "Listen to me, Rebekah. I'm going to tell you two things that are true. If you don't believe me, ask God."

"You've never lied to me."

"And I won't. Look deep in your heart, and you'll know what I'm about to say is the truth. First, any choices Lloyd made were *his* choices. Nothing he chose to do or not do is your fault. God gives us free will, even though it must pain Him when we make bad choices." When Timothy shifted uncomfortably behind them, he didn't look at his son. His gaze remained on her. "Second, Rebekah, with our *kinder* here to witness my words, I vow to you that I will never intentionally hurt you in word or deed."

A hint of a smile touched her trembling lips as she spoke the words she had the day he asked her to marry him. "You know it isn't our way to make vows."

"Other than vows of love. Those we proclaim in front of everyone we can gather together. Before our *kinder*, I vow that I love you."

"You love me?"

"Ja, ich liebe dich." The words sounded so much sweeter in *Deitsch*, and her heart soared like a bird on a summer wind.

A loud knock sounded on the back door. Joshua rose as Timothy tensed, fear on his face. Rebekah reached out and took the boy's hand. When he looked at her, she gave him a loving smile. If the police had returned, Timothy wouldn't have to face them alone.

When Joshua opened the door, Brad Granger stood on the other side. He was a balding man, who was wearing a plaid robe over a pair of gray flannel pants. He had on white sneakers but no socks. "May I come in?"

"*Ja.* Of course." Joshua glanced at her, but she had no more idea than he did what to expect from their neighbor.

Brad had every right to be furious if Timothy had taken the car without his permission. Their neighbor entered and called over his shoulder, "C'mon in. Lurking out there won't resolve any of this." His voice was raspy with the emotion he clearly was trying to control.

A slender form edged into the kitchen. Alexis's hair covered most of her face, but when she looked up, Rebekah could see that the girl's eye was deeply bruised, and a purplish black line followed the curve of her left cheekbone. She stared at the young girl whose face looked like reflections Rebekah had seen in her own mirror. Pain lashed her anew as she glanced at Timothy who quickly looked away. No! She didn't want to believe that the young man who had comforted her so gently had struck his friend. *Oh, please, God, don't let it be true!*

"How are you?" Timothy asked, stepping forward. She couldn't miss the concern in his words or his posture.

"It'll look worse before it looks better," Brad said with a sigh. "The EMTs who stopped by warned her that she's going to have two reasons for a headache in the morning. The bruises and a hangover." He looked at his daughter. "Go ahead. This won't get any easier if you put off doing what you should have done in the first place."

Rebekah was surprised when Alexis turned to her. "Tim thinks you found the beer in the barn."

"And the well house," she said, putting her hand on Joshua's arm when he opened his mouth to ask a question. He remained silent as she added, "I did find it. I was afraid it might belong to someone in this family, but it didn't, did it?"

"No. The beer in the barn was mine."

"Alexis—"

She interrupted Timothy with a sad smile. "You don't need to cover for me any longer, Tim. I've told my parents everything. Now I need to be honest with your folks so they know the truth."

He nodded, his shoulders sagging in obvious relief.

"I didn't think it was any big deal," the girl said, then shivered. "That is, until the police came to the house. They told me that Tim might get arrested because he took my car and crashed it. That's when I knew I had to be honest. I can't let Tim pay for my mistakes when he was simply trying to be a good friend." She took a deep breath and squared her shoulders. "I asked Tim to hide the beer so my parents wouldn't find it. I brought it over the other night and he agreed, though I could tell he didn't like the idea of deceiving our parents. Tonight I picked him and the beer up, and we went to a party out by the Conestoga River with some of my friends."

"Where you drank the beer?" Joshua asked.

"Yes. You must have seen the beer cans in the car." She grimaced. "Chief McMurray sure did! But Tim didn't have any beer."

"I don't like it." Timothy shrugged and smiled weakly. "Tastes worse than it smells."

"I did drink some of the beer." Alexis sighed when her *daed* glared at her. "Okay, I drank a lot of the beer. Too much to drive home. Tim suggested I call my folks, but I didn't want them finding out that I'd had so much to drink. I insisted I was okay to drive home. He took my keys and wouldn't let me."

Rebekah patted Timothy's arm and said, "You did listen to your *daed* about drinking and driving."

"Hey, sometimes he's right."

Even Sammy laughed at that, though he couldn't have understood why. When he yawned, Joshua picked him up and cradled him in his arms. Rebekah's heart almost overflowed with joy at the sight of the strong man holding the little boy so gently.

Her attention was pulled back to Alexis, who was saying, "So it's true that Tim drove without a license, but he did it to keep me from driving drunk."

"And you told the police that nobody else was in the car, Timothy, because you didn't want Alexis to get into trouble," Joshua said as if he were thinking aloud. "You shouldn't have lied to the police."

"I was honest with them. I didn't say I was alone, *Daed*. I said I was driving by myself. I was because Alexis was asleep in the passenger seat, so she wasn't helping me."

"Timothy, a half truth is also a half lie."

"I know."

Alexis interjected, "If that deer hadn't jumped in front of us, he would have gotten us home without anyone knowing the truth."

"But God had other ideas," Brad said quietly. "He was tired of Alexis's behavior and brought it out of the shadows." He turned to Timothy. "I'm sorry you were caught up in this mess, son, but thank you for being such a good friend to Alexis."

Timothy took the hand Brad held out to him and shook

it. "I didn't want Alexis to risk getting kicked out of school. She has her heart set on attending the University of Pennsylvania."

Looking to where Joshua had come to stand beside Rebekah, Brad added, "You've raised a fine son, Joshua. I hate to think what might have happened if he hadn't been there tonight."

"Then don't think of it," Joshua said quietly.

Brad turned to Timothy. "The police will still want to talk with you, son, but now to confirm what Alexis has already told them."

"We will cooperate with the police." Joshua gave his son a look that said he would tolerate no more half truths.

"I know you find that uncomfortable, so I'm doubly thankful to you." Brad smiled. "Chief McMurray has assured me, Timothy, that any pending charges against you, other than the driving without a license, will be dropped. Even extenuating circumstances won't wipe out that ticket, but Alexis will be paying the fine for you."

"Danki," he said.

"No, son, thank *you* for making sure my daughter got home alive tonight."

"I'm sorry," Alexis whispered. "I hope we can still be friends, Tim."

"We'll always be friends." He glanced at his *daed.* "Just friends."

Brad and his daughter urged them to sleep well and left. As soon as the door closed, Timothy turned to Joshua.

"I am sorry about the half truths," the boy said. "Even though I thought I had a *gut* reason, I know there's never any *gut* reason to lie. I hope you can forgive me."

"I already have." He handed Sammy to Rebekah.

She took him and almost cried out as a pain cut through her back and around across her stomach. It faded as quickly as it had started, so she carried Sammy in and set him on the sofa. He curled into a ball, never waking.

Turning around, she watched Joshua put his hand on his son's shoulder. "If we expect to be forgiven, we must be forgiving. Now I must ask you to forgive me."

"For what?" Timothy asked.

"I should have given you a chance to explain. I shouldn't have jumped to conclusions."

"You didn't have far to jump. I *was* driving the car, and it's my fault it crashed."

"But it's a *daed*'s job to listen and learn if he expects his *kinder* to do the same. I'll try to do better next time, if you'll forgive me for this mistake."

"I heard a wise man once say that if we expect to be forgiven, we must be forgiving."

Joshua glanced at Rebekah, and she smiled. There were many challenges before them with their *kinder*, but she and Joshua would weather each storm as it came.

Together.

"We have to stop hiding secrets from each other," Joshua said. "Secrets don't have any place among the loving members of a family. They ended up causing us even more pain."

"I know that now, *Daed*."

Joshua looked at her.

"I know it, too." She blinked back tears. "But I couldn't bear the thought of people looking at Sammy and judging everything he does to decide if he's starting to take after his *daed*."

"No one will. They'll see that he is like his *mamm*. Generous and loving. I've said it before, but I need to say it again, because I can't keep it a secret any longer. *Ich liebe dich*."

Happiness welled up in her at his words and his loving gaze. As she reached out to take his hands, she stiffened. Pain scored her again. Harder this time. When she bent, holding her hands over her belly, she heard Joshua and Timothy ask what was wrong.

She had to wait for the pain to diminish before she could gasp, "It's the *boppli*. It's coming."

Joshua kept one arm around her as he ordered, "Timothy, go to the Grangers and use their phone." He fished a piece of paper out of his trousers. "Here is Beth Ann's number. Call her and tell her to come *now*!"

Timothy grabbed the page and ran out.

With Joshua's arm guiding her, Rebekah went to the bedroom. She reached it as another contraction began. They were coming close together. Why hadn't she had more warning? Then she realized she had. Her aching back could have been mild contractions. She'd ignored them.

After he helped her lie down on the wide bed, he said, "And I thought we'd had enough excitement tonight."

She tried to smile, but another contraction bore down on her, and she couldn't think of anything but riding its crest until it receded. She opened her eyes and saw Joshua's worried face.

"Do you think Beth Ann will get here in time?" he asked.

"I hope so." She clutched his hand. Looking up at him, she said, "I'm glad you're here, Joshua."

"I wouldn't be anywhere else."

There was so much she longed to say, to tell him how she loved him and how sorry she was to have ever believed he would treat her as Lloyd had. Gripping his hand, she focused on the *boppli*, who was coming whether the midwife was there or not.

Chapter 15

The bedroom was quiet. The *kinder* were upstairs, tucked in their beds for the night. Beth Ann had finished up and left along with the doctor. Sadie would be returning in a few hours to help with the new *boppli* and take care of the household until Rebekah could manage on her own again.

Joshua put the dish towel on the rack where it could dry. Taking a deep breath, he yawned as he gazed out the window. The moon had set, and the stars were a glittering tapestry of God's glory. To the east, a thin, gray line announced the coming of a new day.

The day another *kind* had joined their family.

This is the day which the Lord hath made; we will rejoice and be glad in it. His favorite verse echoed in his mind, this time a praise instead of an urging to get through yet another day while weighed down with grief.

Wanting to see the little one again, because it had been

so long since there had been a *boppli* in the house, Joshua tiptoed into the downstairs bedroom to make sure *mamm* and *boppli* were doing well.

Despite his efforts to be quiet as he edged around the bed, Rebekah's eyes blinked open. With her magnificent red hair scattered across the pillows and a joyful smile warming her lips, she was more beautiful than he'd imagined. She held out a hand to him.

Sitting on the very edge of the bed, he asked, "How are you doing?"

"Happy."

"*Ja*, I know." He didn't say any more. There wasn't any need.

The night had begun as a nightmare. One that left his hands shaking whenever he thought of what could have happened when his inexperienced son had driven that powerful car along the twisting, hilly road. It had ended with healing between him and his oldest, as well as the appearance of his youngest.

At that thought, he reached down into the cradle Jeremiah had made and lifted out a swaddled bundle.

"She is sweet," he said. "Debbie is going to be so pleased to have a sister."

"Wanda Almina Stoltzfus," Rebekah murmured. "Welcome to the world."

He handed the *boppli* to her. "*Mamm* will be pleased that you want to name this little one in her honor."

"I was named for my *grossmammi*, and I loved having that connection. Little Wanda will have that same connection with your *mamm* and mine."

"A very special gift for her very first birthday."

"I'm glad you think so." She looked from the beautiful *boppli* to him. "*Danki* for being here, Joshua."

"Where else would I be when our *boppli* was being born?"

"Our *boppli*," she whispered.

"I cannot think of her any other way. I am blessed to have three sons and two daughters." He chuckled. "They make me *ab in kopp* way too often, but I am even crazier in love with you." He became serious. "I told you that earlier tonight how I love you. Do you love me?"

"*Ja.* Looking back, I think I started falling in love with you the day you came with your nervous proposal." She laced her fingers through his much wider ones. "At first I tried to stop myself because I knew you still loved Tildie."

"But—"

"Let me say this, Joshua." When he nodded, she continued. "I knew that you still love Tildie, and I thought there was no place in your heart for me. It took me far too long to realize that our hearts can expand to love many people. Timothy, Levi and Debbie hold a place in my heart as surely as if I had given birth to them. I see you with Sammy and Wanda, and I know you'll be a devoted and loving *daed* for them." She laughed. "Look how far my heart has expanded to welcome your *mamm*, your six brothers, your two sisters and the rest of your family. I'm blessed that there's no limit to the number of people a heart will hold."

"As long as there's always a place for me."

"There always will be."

He gently kissed her lips, knowing she was spent after the night's events. There would be plenty of opportunities in the future to kiss her more deeply, and, as Rebekah Mast Burkholder Stoltzfus's husband, he didn't intend to let a single one pass them by.

* * * * *